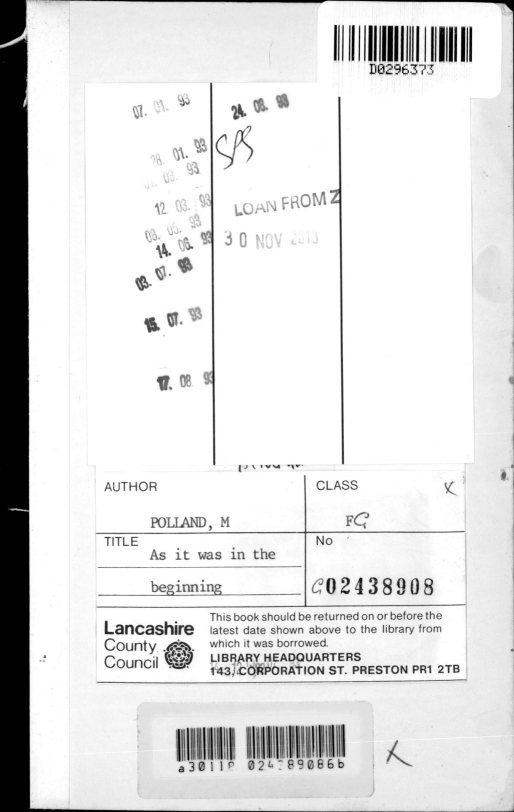

As It Was
in the Beginning

As It Was
in the Beginning

Madeleine Polland

PIATKUS

Copyright © 1987 by Madeleine A. Polland

This edition first published in
Great Britain in 1987 by
Judy Piatkus (Publishers) Ltd of
5 Windmill Street, London W1

British Library Cataloguing in Publication Data

Polland, Madeleine A.
  As it was in the beginning.
  I. Title
823′.914[F]   PR6066.04/

  ISBN 0–86188–608–9

Phototypeset in 11/12pt Linotron Times by
Phoenix Photosetting, Chatham
Printed and bound in Great Britain by
Biddles Ltd, Guildford & King's Lynn

Author's Note

With the Easter Rising of 1916, Ireland broke into a bitter rebellion that ended with the granting of Independence to Southern Ireland, with the Treaty of 1922.

Through these six years, as in any Civil War, both families and lovers were thrown into misery by the tug of conflicting loyalties.

This story, set in these terrible years, is based on a certain degree of truth.

DEDICATION

For my father and my son

Acknowledgement

Thanks to Ralph Macdonald for telling me
exactly what I could and could not do
with gelignite

Chapter 1

'I'd not want him to be a soldier,' the mother said. Carefully she pressed the end of her thread to make a point of it, and threaded her needle against the lamplight, her eyes screwed up in concentration. 'Not a soldier,' she said again, as with a small air of triumph she pulled the black thread through the needle. As long as she could do that she was still way ahead of Mary Plunkett down there on the Tuam Road, looking like an owl in a pair of glasses, round as saucers, that she bought for sixpence in some shop in Galway. And as proud of them as if she could see St. Brendan's Isle from the strand at Salthill.

Her hands fell on the dark heavy serge of her husband's trousers which she patched at the worn knee. Across the lamplight she looked at him with a faint expression of despair, as if she knew that little heed would be given to what she said.

'Not a soldier, James,' she said as firmly as she would say anything to him. 'Not a soldier. Isn't England at war, and not only with Germany but now away off with the Turks as well? God knows what corner of the world he'd get to.'

Or die in, she thought, but did not say it. And he the youngest.

James was unexpectedly amenable, smoothing on the scrubbed table his week old copy of the *Irish Times*. Shadows gathered in the corners of the big whitewashed kitchen. The last glow of the scarlet sunset was clear through the window, far away across the lake and the bog where night was already gathered. The couple sat at the table corner in the pale glow of the globed lamp, soft patterns of ferns and flowers from its etched glass thrown above them on the ceiling. Turf glowed

1

gently in the big open hearth where the kettle sang on a trivet, waiting for the son they discussed.

'I'd not say necessarily a soldier,' the husband said, and she knew that even though he would talk about it with her, some decision had already been made. He turned on her the mild blue eyes that hid his strength and obstinacy.

'I was thinking of the R.I.C.,' he said. 'The Royal Irish Constabulary.'

As though she didn't know what it stood for. But she heard the touch of pride coming into his voice.

'Isn't that the same,' she said. 'Isn't the R.I.C. the British Army too.'

She didn't in her heart want her son in uniform at all, much preferring that he should be a priest like his brother.

'It's not the same, Annie, and you know it. The R.I.C's for the Irish and not for the English, except for the officers. And he'd never leave Ireland if that's what you want. You should be proud if they take the lad. He'd have to go up to Dublin Castle to get an interview, and it's not all of them get through it at all.'

The mother brushed a few black threads from the spotless white apron she put on every evening when the work was done and the men fed. Only a sidestep from the dressing for dinner in the great houses of the Establishment around the country: and, indeed, in all the big Catholic houses still owned and held through all the persecutions, by her own widespread family.

A similar sidestep was the unconscious pattern which they imposed upon their children.

The eldest son was marked down for the land, to work it with his father until the old man died, and by then he should have a wife and sons of his own coming up to follow him. There was no anxiety about this, Patrick the eldest well married to a good girl, and three children already in the cottage on the edge of the land where he would live until the time came for him to take the farm. Should James, God keep him, die first, then the mother would go down to live in the cottage. A strong woman herself, she would ask no girl to share a house with her.

The son would get an inheritance of three hundred acres,

2

proud possession in these landless days, and a position in the county such that no man would dare to try and snatch it from him. As they were with the foreign landlords. Though there was small need for James to call the English foreign. He had no grudge against them, and wasn't he about to give them his youngest son.

The second son, as in all good Catholic households of tradition, was a priest. He had gone years back from Maynooth, straight on to the Foreign Missions, leaving his mother uplifted that she had given a son to God, and comforted by the regular bland letters in a still childlike hand that came under the postmark of Nigeria.

Two daughters after that had gone into the Presentation Convent in Galway, the younger one so anxious to follow her sister that they had conceded her vocation, and produced another generous dowry from the tin cash box hidden in the bottom of the wardrobe in the good bedroom. A sound man like James, and his father before him, would lay little trust in banks.

The last girl – and the father's face would soften at the mention of her name as it did for no one else: his black-haired Rose, his little gypsy fallen from some tinker's cart, he would call her – she was well and safely married to a good lad of a farmer out near Ennis. Two fine children there already and another on the way.

So there was only Ned to settle now, a tall, upright redhead the spit of his grandfather and his mother, born when they felt sure Annie would never have another child.

Apart from Rose, there was no sentiment in the father's review of his children. Children to James and those like him were something God sent to any good Catholic household: the woman's business when they were small, to be fed and clothed and, in this house at least, sent to as good a school as possible. Night and morning they all walked the four Irish miles to Tuam, the girls to the Convent and the boys to the ancient foundation of St. Jarlath's. If there were those who thought James Brannick had ideas above his station, with all this education he was willing to let them think so, and do for his children as he thought fit.

Only for the mother were the sleepless nights, and the

prayers that these her small ones might know some measure of happiness where God had called them. She herself had never sought nor hoped for it, marrying as her parents had told her, finding for her hard James an astonished secret love that laid its serene mark to this day on her ageing face. It was in the softness of her eyes when they rested on him and in her refusal ever to go against him. Only the silent, dogmatic James himself, to whom duty and the proper conduct of life was everything, knew that he needed her as much as she needed him, although he would have faced torture rather than admit it.

From this home came Ned, life a little softer for him because he was the youngest, but still reared to an unshakeable sense of duty and responsibility, and the conviction that life gave no other choices.

His father was still thinking about him and his education at St. Jarlath's. It would help him. There was promotion to think about. He wouldn't want to stay a village constable for ever.

He sucked his pipe in the quiet room which was filled by the heavy ticking of the kitchen clock, and the far sunset faded into darkness beyond Annie's geraniums in the window. He had even shamefacedly given her a patch of land in front of the house for growing the flowers she loved. 'It's for the woman,' he would say with embarrassment to visitors, waving a hand at the tangle of roses and lilies, fuchsias and nasturtiums and snapdragons. His friends would say to each other afterwards that James Brannick was a soft man, sparing a quarter of an acre for his wife to be growing flowers. Further west, they were having to steal that much to grow food.

Both of them were quiet, Annie's workworn hands resting in her lap, the patching for the moment forgotten. Exactly as her husband's, her fading blue eyes were looking backwards on the long line of their children, even the one gone, poor small thing, from diphtheria at the age of two. Time was, the house was too small for them with their jostling and talking, and she hard put to find clothes for them all. The poor lad who was going now came off worst of all, with little more ever than his brother's hand-me-downs. Her thin mouth curved in a slight smile as she remembered the time he got the first new suit of his own. Well, he'd have enough new clothes now, in

4

that fine uniform so dark a green it was almost black, and beautiful cloth no lord would be ashamed to wear, every uniform tailored exactly for the man concerned.

She put away a pang of sorrow that he couldn't be an officer. That was for the gentry and even the English. No farmer's son could be an officer, but no gentry would have looked finer than her tall straight son in the green tunic with the braided frogging all down the front, and the high boots and the helmet with a spike on it that made them all seven feet high.

It was not for Ned. He would look well enough when he came on leave in his short scarlet walking out jacket and the round strap under his chin and the cane under his arm. Like Peggy Quinlan's son from Taraquin, and she thinking herself royalty for it, even though her son was a good two inches shorter than her own Ned who'd outshine the lot.

The last lad, she thought, and knew that James across the table with his unyielding face had the same thoughts. The last lad.

There was a thump in the hall and the rattle of the latch into the kitchen and the last lad was with them, bringing on his clothes the cold damp of the December evening, his muffler round his neck and his cap pulled down, long wrists and hands red with the cold.

His father straightened at the table.

'Well,' was all he said. 'Did you sell them?'

'Well, I haven't,' said the boy, 'any of them under me jacket, so I must have done.'

As he pulled off his cap and threw it on a chair, rubbing his cold hands, his eyes were alight with mischief and the satisfaction that no one could find fault with what he'd done.

'Did you get a good price?' the father asked, and would have no jokes about his farm or his business, his heavy brows down.

'Better than you expected.' The young face was triumphant as he reached into his pocket and pulled out a roll of notes, carefully wrapped in newspaper.

'How much is it?'

'Count it and see.' Ned would not let go easily of his triumph and savoured it happily as his father counted through the grimy notes.

5

James lifted his head at last.

'You did well,' he said, then almost grudgingly, 'B'God, maybe I should keep you here on the farm, and not let you go.'

Ned was not listening.

'Mam, I'm famished – have you anything to eat.'

His mother smiled as she folded up her work.

'I might have an odd crust somewhere,' she said. 'Did you not eat at Lennan's? Your father said you could take the money.'

'I wasn't hungry then,' he said, and felt the empty ache of his stomach calling him a liar. It had not yet been dawn when he had set off for Tuam market with a flock of sheep: only the first pale pewter glimmer of light in the lake as he passed it, and the crunch of the night's frost under his boots in the puddles. The only feeling in his stomach then had been a cramp of nervous terror lest he wouldn't get a proper price for the sheep. It was the only time he had ever come to the market alone. Two days ago, the father had put the tine of a fork through his foot and couldn't get a boot on, and Patrick was too busy with the ploughing.

'Let the lad take them,' the father said, and Ned's brother had grinned his wide, dark-eyed grin.

'I'll leave him to you,' he said, 'if he comes home with a penny for each.' But his slap on the shoulder told Ned he thought he could do it, and do it well.

By four o'clock, and his sale triumphantly over, he was so hungry that it hurt, almost slavering at the smell of frying chops clinging to the air outside the small grimy restaurant where all the farmers ate when they had made money to eat with. But he was too diffident, even if he starved, to shove his way in alone amongst them and shout loudly enough to make Bessie Lennan even turn her head, let alone bring him his dinner. He turned for home, thinking already, desperately, of what his mother would have to give him when he got there, his hand firmly clasped on the money in his pocket, his mind on nothing but food and the sight of his father's face when he saw the money.

Now his mother was blowing the turf to a red hot glow and setting the griddle across it. She looked up at him.

'You're late, Ned, if you didn't stop to eat.'

There was a moment of silence; a glance at the father across the table.

'I met Kate Mary Pearse in the town, and it was getting dark so I walked her home.'

'You gave yerself a long walk,' said his father, and the gleam in his eye brought the blood up into Ned's fair-skinned face.

'Wouldn't you have done the same!' he said, challenging.

'I would indeed,' said his father. 'I would indeed. Your mother ran me over three-quarters of Galway before I caught her.'

Annie smiled, as the girl might have smiled in that long ago chase, and then as she laid long strips of bacon beside the three mutton chops already sizzling on the griddle, her smile faded.

'Poor girl, she said. 'Poor Kate.'

James had gone back to the newspaper of a week ago, spread on the table before him. A joke with his son was one thing, but the sorrows of some young girl were talk for women. Annie straightened from the hearth, her fine face so like her son's flushed from the heat of the glowing turf. She pushed a strand of grey hair away behind her ear.

'I hear she's away to an aunt or a cousin or something.'

Ned sat down at the spotless table, hardly able to contain himself and his hungry young stomach at the delicious smell of mutton and bacon. His mother cut a round potato cake into four triangles.

'You'll eat them all?' she asked him and he grinned, his bony face lighting with sudden charm.

'I'll try,' he said. 'Yes, she's off to Westport, or near it, to an aunt. Her mother's cousin in truth. When the father died, and that not expected for many a long year, there was only the one son.'

'And he a solicitor in Tuam, and no thought of the land.'

Ned didn't notice that she had taken up the story, his face absorbed as he remembered hearing all of it that afternoon, in the grey cattle-filthy street of Tuam, with the smell of the market still thick on the air. Small boys, shrill with authority, herded groups of sheep and cattle along street and pavement

7

alike through the first pale squares of lamplight, while the beasts' new owners, inside the bars, poured dark porter down their throats and argued about what they had to pay.

On a corner, he had walked into Kate Mary, thin and strange in her black clothes, eyes enormous in the sad face under her soft-brimmed hat. But no sorrow could alter the poise of her erect young figure, or its lightness that made him speak at once lest she be gone as fast and sudden as she had appeared, someone's half dozen of filthy sheep milling between them in the falling light from a corner shop.

'Kate,' he said. 'Kate Mary.'

And then did not know how to go on, the easy colour rising to his face. He was as unwilling to speak of womens' sorrows as his father, who had marched as decency ordered in the long column of her father's funeral and then found nothing to say to her afterwards.

'I'm sorry,' Ned managed to blurt out. 'I'm sorry for your trouble.'

His grey eyes said to her that he knew his words were poor and nothing, but not to step around him through the sheep and go away. Not to go away. Please.

Kate Mary had no idea of going away. From she was a growing child she had watched this tall boy with the bony face and the high strong nose so like his mother's, though exchanging no more than the occasional word at a fair or a féis. Never knowing him better because even before her mother died, the two families had never been close, and after that she had always gone to stay with Aunt Margaret in the holidays, her bereft father having small use for a girl child in his lonely house. Above all one that grew every day more like the wife he had lost. But somewhere in the back of Kate's mind, the boy Ned had always held a place. Some part of the future; like growing up itself.

But now her father was gone, most people saying he was never a mite of good from the day his woman died, and it was to be Aunt Margaret's for good. The chance meeting struck in Kate a thread of extra sadness, for what opportunity would she have of seeing the tall, shy boy again? What would bring him so far?

The same thought was troubling him to the point of panic,

8

and he struggled for the determination not to waste this one moment, long mouth compressed with the effort of overcoming his shyness.

A young bewildered heifer tried to push its way between them where the sheep had gone, confused by the shrill orders of a small shaven-headed child with a sally rod and by the misery of finding itself adrift in the darkening street, instead of the rich green pasture it had known since its mother dropped it among the buttercups in the early summer.

Ned gave it a belt on its manure-stained rump, furious to be interrupted when he had just got his courage up, and Kate Mary jumped out of the way, laughing, and suddenly it was easier.

'Get it away out of that, or I'll take the stick to you,' Ned shouted at the child. And then to Kate: 'Did it soil your dress?'

'No, the poor creature, no. It's frightened out of its life.'

Ned could not risk any more distractions.

'M-may I walk you home?' he said.

Kate regarded him in the lamplight, her eyes huge and dark in the shadow of her hat.

'You'll give yourself a long walk,' she said, as his father was to say later, and then could have bitten out her tongue lest she had discouraged him. She added reluctantly, 'And I have my bicycle.'

'It's no matter,' he said quickly. 'I have nothing to do. And I'll push the bike.'

Then she smiled at him and left him speechless, so they threaded their way in silence through the last wanderers of the fair, four-legged or two. The country carts were clattering off one by one into the darkness beyond the little town, and the flat long carts of the Connemara men faced into their longer journey, fine-shawled women with their children perched indifferent among a few precious cattle. They were the only women who came with their men to the fair, tall and civil and quiet spoken as their husbands, and equally without the English tongue. As befitted the royalty they once were.

The cooling night was heavy with the utterly Irish reek of turf smoke and manure that could rend the hearts of exiles half across the world when they got some whiff of something

9

that might bring it to their minds. It clung even as the huddle of the town spread out into more scattered houses, fading only as they reached at last the empty lightless country, following the unmade road by the gleam of a half made moon, coming slow and ghostly over the hills to the west.

Ned had retrieved the bicycle from the yard behind Fitzsimmon's drapers shop, delighted to be doing something for her, and now he pushed it over the stones at her side, full of exhilaration, touched by a sense of the manhood he always felt to be eluding him in the presence of his father and his brother, for all his eighteen years. It was hard to be a man when you were the last child at home.

'Wouldn't you be afraid coming this way alone?' he said. Hoping to feel even stronger. But Kate Mary only shrugged.

'Who would harm me?' she said.

His romantic and excited mind raced to the old legend his mother used to tell them as children: how in the time of Queen Maeve, and she a Moran like her own family, a fair maiden could walk from end to end of Ireland with no more than a sally rod in her hand, and no one would molest her. He had forgotten that before he ever reached the age for school, he had rejected it, asking in his small piercing voice why would the girl walk all Ireland, were there no trains in those days or had her Dada not even a donkey and cart?

All he knew at the moment was a swelling desire to do something brave in protection of this fair maiden who stepped out so briskly at his side.

Womanlike, she was concerned only to get all the information she could before this short hour's walk would end.

'How old are you then, Ned Brannick?' she asked him directly, and he stammered, shaken from his dreams where he was as tall as Cuchulain and as brave as Finn McCool.

'Eighteen,' he said, and added at once, 'and three months.'

'And are you home on the farm?'

It was easier to answer questions when he was yet too shy to ask his own.

'I am,' he said. 'But I'm not staying there. There's not room on the farm for three men of the family, but Dada said there was no harm spending a year learning about it.

'Me brother could always die,' he said, and then could have

bitten out his crude and clumsy tongue. He was glad of the darkness to hide that uncontrollable scarlet mounting to his face.

'I'm sorry,' he muttered. 'I'm an eejit.'

There was a moment of silence, her loss too recent for her to accept it easily.

Then, ''Tis all right, Ned. You meant nothing.'

In the chilly darkness, he could have died for her.

'And you, Kate Mary,' he said hoarsely, to get the talk back to normal, 'would you be seventeen?'

'No,' she said. 'Sixteen. Had me father not died, I'd probably have had another year at school.'

'And where was that?'

A borheen turned off up a slope to the right, and the dim light of a farmhouse lay at the end of it. Hessian's already. The devil take it, the walk was going too fast. From the yard a dog barked at the clink of the bicycle over the stones.

She answered him. 'Kilcolgen. The nuns.'

'Did you like it?'

'Prison,' she said succinctly, dismissing one of the best schools in the west of Ireland. At a time when only the rich and aristocratic of England sent their children to boarding schools, the convents and monasteries of Ireland were full of the families of these middle-class farmers. From families with an ancient tradition of learning, who since the Penal Days had nowhere else to educate their children other than a hedge school; or a broken down ruin where some willing woman, urged on by the Parish priest taught catechism and the three Rs, paying for the occasional book and slate out of her own pocket.

Ned was amused by her vehemence, forgetting his blunder.

'Did you hate it? I have cousins there and they seem all right.'

'Probably they all want to be nuns.'

'Not you?'

'Never. Cold black things with eyes in the back of their heads.'

Ned laughed out loud.

'I have two sisters, nuns in the Presentation in Galway.'

She stopped still, and he could sense the appalled look

11

under the dark shadow of her hat.

'And Aunt Margaret has four. Dear God, what a waste! Think of all the children they'll never have.'

Ned was floundering. This girl was younger than himself, and talking openly of things men never talked about at all. And all going against the atmosphere of holy pride he had grown up with, his mother humbly grateful for the privilege of giving two girls to God, perfectly certain that there could be no better life for them.

'And how many priests have you?' she asked him then.

'Only the one.' He felt he should be apologising even for him. 'My brother Tom. He's in the Foreign Missions.'

She began to giggle, and even though he couldn't see her properly he felt a rush of pleasure to hear her laugh, smiling himself, foolishly, in the darkness: thinking how the laughter must change the pale sad face under the hat. He could see her teeth, small and very white.

'What is it?'

'I had to pay a halfpenny a month at school for a black baby,' she said, 'to bring him to God. We were supposed to have adopted him. I called mine Patrick! Maybe your brother's looking after him for me. You're not going to be a priest, are you?' she added suddenly.

In two days' time she was going away and would probably never see him again, but suddenly could not bear the thought of that other and far more final loss.

'I am not,' he said easily. 'That's not in me.'

The lights of Balliclune over to their left and a dog barked again in the small scattered houses. Another followed it half-heartedly, and when they stopped the silence of the cold night fell absolute until they heard the rattle of a cart behind them on the road. Ned drew the bicycle into the side and they waited for it to pass.

The donkey clattered past, small hooves fiercely busy with the happy task of taking him home. A high-sided cart lurched behind.

'G'night there,' called the man, and they called it back.

'What then,' said Kate, 'if you don't want to be a priest or a farmer?'

'Well, in my family, it's the parents decide.'

12

'And have they decided?'

She knew this was the case in most families, so different from her own: her brother turning his back on the land to go for the law, and never a word of reproach from her father, left alone on the farm.

Ned straightened the bicycle to go on.

'Your dress guard is loose,' he said. 'Mind it doesn't catch in the spokes or you could take a terrible fall.'

'Johnny will do it when I get to Aunt Margaret's.'

'Johnny?'

He felt a stab of jealousy so swift and sharp it surprised him.

'My cousin, more or less. Aunt Margaret was my mother's cousin; God knows where that leaves her son to me.'

He sensed in her a great liveliness as though, were she not subdued by recent death, she might be hopping and skipping along beside him. As it was, he had to make an effort to keep the bicycle up with her.

'They think,' he said, 'that I don't know what's in their minds. The Dada would like me to be a soldier. But the Mam is afraid of me being killed, now the English are at war with the Germans.'

Her face flashed round to him, clearer in the rising moon.

'My cousin Johnny would say it's the English are the enemy, and the Germans our real friends.'

'He's a Fenian?'

'He is. And mad with it.'

A certain stubbornness came into Ned's voice.

'There's nothing like that with us. If it's not the Army then it will be the R.I.C., and I've not any quarrel with that either.' He grinned one of his rare sudden grins at her across the bicycle. 'Would your cousin Johnny mind if I joined the Police?'

Her teeth flashed back at him.

'I have a notion, Ned Brannick,' she said, 'you'd not pay a lot of heed if he did.'

Ned was enchanted with her, the first girl he had ever managed to talk to without being reduced to blistering shyness by the batting of the eyelashes and tossing of the hair and flouncing of skirts. This one was as direct as if she was another boy. Mind you it was dark, and he didn't have to be conscious of how easily he blushed, or his big nose, or the huge hands and feet that had still to be grown into.

'I have,' he said proudly, and forgave himself of any intent to try an impress her. He was legitimately proud. 'I have to go up to Dublin Castle for an interview. The parents think I know nothing about it, but I've found it all out for myself. I wouldn't tell them I have, though,' he added kindly. 'They like to think they're telling me what to do, the creatures.'

She nodded, joined in the conspiracy of all children to protect the innocence of their poor elders.

'Were you ever in Dublin before?' she asked him, stepping carefully over a little rill of water that ran across the road, tangled with flags and sedge where it burbled under the wall. Ned lifted the bicycle after her.

'I was,' he said, and thought he would leave it there to impress her. Honesty and the memory of the occasion took over. 'Once,' he added. 'My father took me up to Croke Park for a hurling final. And my brother Patrick.'

In silence he relived all the wonder of that long past day. He had been very small. It had begun in the black darkness before the dawn, catching the special train in Tuam that would take them in to Galway to catch the morning Mail, graving the names of the journey on his young mind: Ballinasloe, Athlone, and all the small stations beyond the wide gleam of the Shannon, hurtled through in the bright morning. Then Westland Row, Dublin, and the doors clanging all down the train, as clear in his thoughts as if it were yesterday.

'I was in Roscommon often for the same reason,' he said carelessly, to make nothing of Dublin, fearful suddenly lest she think him an ignorant omodaun who had never been anywhere and set too much store by it.

'Oh, and I too,' she said. 'With my brother. Solicitor and all, he's mad about the hurling.'

He wanted to say to her, if he could get the words out, that maybe they could go together someday, and then he remembered that after this one walk there were no days.

'What will you do with yourself at the aunt's?' he said, and grinned. 'Will she go to the hurling?'

'No,' she said, 'but Johnny will. But he surely always has a

14

girl of some sort. They're all wild after him.'

The pang of jealousy hit him again unrecognised. He only knew he felt suddenly angry at the thought of her doing no more than working round the house and feeding the hens and tossing a bit of hay when the time came. And the lad Johnny there beside her all the time.

But that wasn't the plan.

''Tis all arranged for me,' she said. 'Aunt Margaret always wanted me to do this anyway when I left the school. The nuns at the Holy Cross in Westport have built a new Model School there for the town, and all the children sitting up as bold as brass with tables and inkpots and pens and all the things too good for us even at Kilcolgen.'

'At Jarlath's,' he said, 'we had no more than a slate, and the Mam had to buy the chalk.'

But even as he spoke, just to keep her talking, he was thinking how easy the words came to her, and how light and quick, like her walking. When she was herself again and the father's death behind her, that would be the time to know her. And the pang touched him again, deep and sad, that this was not to be. For wild moments, he thought of forgetting all his father's plans and going off to get himself some work in Westport. The father would never speak to him again, not to mention the shame of it, doing it just to be near a girl. He'd be the laughing stock of West Galway: lovesick Ned, and the girl only sixteen at that, and he without a penny to his name.

He shook away his foolishness and companionably they walked with the bicycle between them along the uneven road, speaking of this and that and telling each other small tales of their families and their childhood and of things that had made them sad and happy; the first unformed shape of a relationship, but they would never have given their small talking so grand a name.

They were still in the middle of it all when she pointed out the lights of her home ahead of them: the moon risen now but hazed in mist, its light opaque and vague over the flat, treeless country, low and damp to the very edges of being bogland. From the house the lamplight was pale and bloomy, but where they had stopped at a wide iron gate, he could see the two-storey slate-roofed dwelling, the shadows of barns and

15

buildings clustered round it. On the bohreen that led up to the door were spaced a few wind driven thorns, leaning to the loose stone walls but giving the faint semblance of an avenue.

'And all this?' he asked her when they stopped. 'What happens to all this?'

'Ah, my brother has it all arranged. My father has been ill sometime, you know. Some man from Tuam is taking it. My brother arranges everything. He's the kind of fellow would be a solicitor even if he wasn't one, if you understand me.'

Yes, he understood her, and delighted in her, but he still asked her gravely: 'But do you not mind leaving? Leaving it all?'

He knew that, simple though it was, he was going to mind leaving Clumbane. All the places he had known since he could walk. Like the deep, deep well, forbidden as a child, where you could smell the icy chill of the water before bringing it up, so cold it hurt your throat to drink it. They said it came through from the bog, where it might have lain a thousand years.

There was the lake across the road below the farm, the shore pebbled like a little inland sea, where his brothers had taught him to skim stones and where he liked to walk alone to this day, in the evenings watching the daylight die in the dark water, listening to the curlews sobbing from the bog beyond. But he'd be ready to die himself before anyone should know that these things mattered to him. How deep his feelings ran.

But Kate Mary obviously knew without being told, for she turned to face him, taking the handlebars of the bike from him. The misty moon shone straight into her face and he could see the clear lines of it: the bright alert eyes with the hint of a smile, the mouth curling up good-humouredly at the corners. Black hair, she had, he remembered that, straight as a fall of water.

'It's not like you, Ned,' she said. 'Your family have had your house since Brian Boru. I can understand you'd not want to leave it. But my father was just a city man who fancied a bit of farming and bought it for himself. And it's not been much of a home since my mother died, and that's ten years ago. I'll be happier with Aunt Margaret.'

There was a long uneasy pause and nothing said, both of

16

them too young and shy to handle openly the sorrows they had raised. Ned felt thick and useless, groping for words that should comfort her, and she felt ashamed for having brought up things he could do nothing about. It was on the tip of her tongue to ask him in for a cup of tea, but she knew there could be no question of that. It would be the same as asking him for a promise of marriage. Even as they stood there in their awkward silence, the man from the farm beyond came up behind them, driving four heifers, thrifty purchase at the fair, and no cart to drive them home.

The animals shouldered past in their high smell of fear and caked manure, frightened hooves clattering on the stones, and the man threw a sharp glance at Ned and Kate from under the peak of his cap.

'G'night to ye, Miss Pearse,' he said, and nothing at all to Ned.

Kate Mary gave a small laugh and their difficult moment was over, the farmer and his cattle vanishing into the hazy night.

'Will you open the gate for me, Ned? 'Tis as well I'm going away: my character's now destroyed entirely. Out at night with a fellow, and my poor father not cold in his grave.'

The joke faded a little at the end, and he could hear her voice catch. With blundering unaccustomed tenderness that he had never known before, except perhaps for his mother, he opened the long iron gate and helped her to push the bicycle through.

'Remember the dress guard,' he said hoarsely: all he could think to offer her.

'I will. I will,' she said. 'Then I won't see you again, Ned Brannick.'

'No,' he said. 'No.' Willing to run to Timbuctoo or swim the Pacific Ocean or travel to any name she asked on his school atlas; plunge over waterfalls or climb volcanoes or any of the other far, unreal things that he read about.

To see her again.

'No,' he repeated sadly. 'No.' Fifty miles across country was too far, and that only the beginning: God knew where the R.I.C. would send him.

Too far in their small world.

17

Somewhere in the blanched, misty darkness, a cock crew. He saw the gleam of her teeth.

'That fella has his clock wrong,' she said. 'Goodbye then, Ned Brannick. Will you close the gate?'

She climbed on to the bike, and, lightless and unerring, tacked off up the dark bohreen, bouncing between the stones.

Ned watched her a few moments and then carefully fastened the heavy iron latch. It would him no good with her if he let the cows out. Then he turned towards the empty stretches of moon pale countryside, facing his long walk home and deciding to leave the road and cut over the fields. As he climbed the loose stone wall, he stamped firmly on his foolish sense of loss.

There was everything there had been before he walked into her this evening on the street corner back in Tuam. Above all, he told himself as he leapt a little river thick with sedges and pale with the caught light of the moon, there was his career with the Police. He gave a wry grin. No one had seen fit to mention it yet, and until the father spoke he must carry on the notion that he knew nothing about it.

Nor did they mention it until he was settled at the meal his young stomach clamoured for. None of the bloom had worn off his moonlight walk with Kate Mary, but his last meal had been before the dawn and for the moment she was forgotten.

He could barely wait, watching his mother take three mutton chops off the griddle, and the sweet sizzling slices of bacon, and put them on the white plate, warming on the hob. The mouthwatering smell filled the room. She replaced the meat with three triangles of potato cake, and from under them the hot fat ran down and spat into the scarlet turf.

'For God's sake will you hurry up, Mam,' Ned said, and she turned and smiled at him, the wide rare smile so like his own.

'Take this to be going on with,' she said, and laid down in front of him the plate of chops and bacon. From the dairy out at the back she brought a pitcher of cool, sharp buttermilk and poured it into an earthen mug beside his plate, going next for the potato cakes which she split and laid down, running with hot salted butter of her own making.

A moment then she paused, and touched him gently on the

18

shoulder. Ned looked up over a forkful of food and his eyes were warm on her thin old face.

Only a touch, in this house where the father made it clear that any show of love or sentiment was weakness. Only a touch but in it a lifetime's love for this, her youngest child. Telling him that were the world hers she would give it to him, and not only a plate of bacon and chops: and telling him in painful silence that the time had come for him to go away.

Ned, close to her all his life in spite of their enforced detachment, knew every thought that was passing through her mind. He thought again of Kate Mary then, and felt oppressed by the whole evening, a burden of sorrow that must be got through before he could go out and claim his own place in his own world.

It was her task in the end to put it all into words, it being another tradition of this house that although the man made every decision, it was the woman who had to do the talking. Ned's elder brother always said it was the Father fashioned the bullets, but the Mam who always had to shoot them.

At last when Ned was finished eating, sitting content with a red enamel mug of tea steaming in front of him, there was a jerk of the head from James across the table: signal to his wife to tell the boy of the decision that had been made. Neither of them expected any opposition. In this day in the Irish countryside, save for the occasional renegade who roared off into some different world, children of all ages did as they were bid. Or at least pretended to.

Ned pretended to. He had no objections and it was what he wanted to do anyway, but he did a good showing of the submissive son and was rewarded by the relief and pleasure in his mother's eyes across the lamplight. It only came hard on her if the children tried to cross their father. Instinctively she blessed herself as she thought of the terrible time when Tom had held out against being a priest.

'What's that for, Mam?' Ned said with the gentleness he always felt towards her, bringing his father's eyes on him, suspicious of any hint of softness. 'I'm only going to be a policeman, Mam. No danger of hell fire.' Or of any other kind of fire come to that, he thought to himself, his only fear being that of sticking in some isolated country barracks with never

19

more to deal with than two ladeens claiming ownership of the same sheep.

He would prove, he was determined, right from the beginning, that he was worth more than that.

His mother was flustered, caught in her involuntary gesture, the colour rising up her thin-skinned face as easily as it did his own.

'Ah, it's no harm,' she said, 'no matter what you're doing, to ask God's blessing on it.'

The father folded his paper and smoothed it for tomorrow's reading.

'It's time,' he said, as he said every night, 'that all decent people were in bed.'

And neither Ned nor his mother would dare to stay up even five minutes longer.

At the door, the father turned, glaring at Ned as if he were already in dereliction of both these things. 'Duty,' he said severely, heavy brows drawn down, 'duty and responsibility. That is all you must think of. Duty and responsibility.'

Sunk in the lumpy old feather bed that he now had all to himself, looking up at the black night above the skylight of his attic room, Ned thought of what his father had said. Lightly, because as far as he could see, duty and responsibility were all his life would be. He couldn't see that there would be any other choice. There was an oath to take, of loyalty and duty, and that was that. But he knew, too, that if he were at the end of the earth and failed in either of these things, he would feel his father's hand on his shoulder: dead or alive.

Drowsing asleep, he thought again of Kate Mary, and put her away with all the other secret precious things of his mind: like the memory of going to Croke Park for the hurling, and the solitary evening walks around the lake.

Chapter 2

In Connorstown, seven Irish miles from the town of Westport, the Post Office was a small dim shambles of disorder: one room of a poor house in the village square, smelling airlessly of chalk and old paper, and whatever might be cooking in the kitchen behind it. A wooden counter divided it, kicked paintless by years of anxious feet, the top covered by worn oilcloth, holding pattern only at the far ends against the walls, the centre a high, worn shine. On the floor the same pattern had receded to the corners like a receding tide, and before the counter the high polish had given way to a long narrow hole, worn through to the cement beneath.

Behind the counter, solid as a bastion without even a flap for coming and going, was a chaos of parcels and packages, flung haphazard on the floor. Baby clothes from Switzers in Dublin for the expectations of the wife of the Resident Magistrate, side by side with a scythe rusting in a sack, long waited for by a farmer out somewhere in the back of beyond. But he had tired of asking and no one troubled to tell him it was there.

'An' they want their belongings,' the Postmistress would say tartly, 'can't they come and get them. Hasn't Peter Garrett enough to do to carry the letters.'

If they did come in they were as likely to get someone else's parcel instead of their own, absently handed to them by the Postmistress, absorbed in holding some interesting letter up to the dim light, magically managing with her myopic eyes to read what was inside the thin cheap envelope, for little else came to Connorstown Post Office.

21

As blind as the proverbial bat, her critics said, and barely knowing a stamp from a postal order, but knowing more about the affairs of the little town than the town itself. If any letter defeated her from the outside, it was taken shamelessly into the back kitchen and steamed open by the kettle always ready on the hob. Should anyone miss anything, they would ask without offence had she forgotten it in there in the kitchen? It was one of the things of life, like the grey sad village and the broken streets and the grey rain of winter, that Elsie O'Flyn read the letters before anybody else.

Anyone who wasn't a firm Sinn Feiner, and ready to cry to Hell with England, they might never get anything from her at all.

Behind her was a block of pigeon holes into which she rarely had time to put the letters, and on a bench in the corner, the two mysteries of her calling. What she called the gazebo that only she could handle to send wires, and the tall black telephone which frightened her half out of her life. Should there be nobody to hear, she let it ring until it stopped, asking herself what would she be doing talking to all those strangers from the good God knew where. Furtively she would bless herself when silence fell again, a small smile on her face that she had got away with it.

A small stout woman with pebble glasses, she sat behind her counter like a malevolent frog, receiving all except a few of her cronies with suspicion, and somehow, through the grimy window and the heavy glasses, keeping a sharp and accurate survey on everything in the Square outside.

Nothing moved there in the cool late afternoon of a day at the end of November, 1918. The drab open space was quiet in the last of a gold sun touching the Cross in the centre. Later in the evening, all the young boys would come and sit around the steps of it, and the girls walk round and round, flouncing their skirts and giggling and pretending there wasn't a boy in miles. From behind bleak railings and a drab concrete yard, Father Martin Brennan, the parish priest, watched them hawk-eyed through his lace curtain, alert for the smallest Occasion of Sin.

On the other side of the Square, in his comfortable house between the crumbling church and a small, untidy graveyard

22

rambling with weeds, the Church of Ireland Vicar read peacefully before the first fire of the year. Most of his parishioners were of advancing age, and their poor sins few and far between; their occasions for them even less.

The Mail Cart from Westport had just gone rumbling through the golden afternoon, and in the Post Office Elsie was going through the mail with a practised eye. Beside her on the counter was a large, square parcel labelled 'books', stuck with thick glued paper and tied round and round with twine. She couldn't keep her hands or eyes off it. There was no opening it, and she wouldn't have dared anyway, but she kept laying a hand on it in fascination. The pale eyes were bright behind the pebble glasses and some deep satisfaction clamped the wide mouth. As the door darkened against the sun, she moved away sharply and gave a grunt of displeasure.

That ould Miss Greeley from out of the Lawn. In a world where spinsterhood was as great a stigma as idiocy or illegitimacy, Miss Ellen Greeley was the only other spinster of uncertain age in the small parish, and no use Johnny O'Connor saying with that laugh of his that all the spinsters in Ireland were in the convents, and did they let them all out every man could have three wives apiece. Elsie O'Flynn hated Ellen Greeley for being like herself, just as she hated herself for being as she was.

Ellen Greeley was also the only person in the village who pursued a running, bitter battle to stop the Postmistress from reading her letters. Like an old crow, Elsie thought, with her long face and the smart glasses with no rims perched on her nose and the gold chain hanging down from them. Black clothes from head to foot, that she always indicated sadly, without saying so, were for some long dead lover. The only lover she ever got near, Elsie would think savagely, was between the covers of some penny dreadful Father Brennan would excomunicate her for reading.

She hated her most because she wouldn't play by the rules. The whole village accepted that the mail was left to Elsie until she got the best out of it. How else would anybody know anything?

'Ah, Miss O'Flynn.' The high cracking voice with its careful refinement was as irritating to Elsie as everything else about the woman. 'I see the post has come.'

'It wasn't sorted yet.'

With some instinct of secrecy, she gave a push to the box labelled 'Books'. It resisted her, heavy, and a small smile touched her face.

'Ai have no objection to waiting. Thanks to the prosperity of mai good father, rest his soul, mai taime, thank God, is mai own.'

'Not a pauper behind a counter, like you, Miss O'Flynn,' was what she was saying, and Elsie knew it. But she also knew that wait Miss Greeley would, and it was no defence Elsie beginning to sort the letters into their pigeon holes. Miss Greeley's eyes were sharp and she watched the placing of every letter. Elsie had learned the only thing to do was sift through the lot of them and give the old crow what she had to get and no more.

'Though why she expects letters,' she always said, 'God knows, for she never writes one. If she came in here for a stamp, she'd want it half price.'

Today Miss Greeley was not easily got rid of. While Elsie sorted angrily through the handful of letters, she peered determinedly down at the address on the big square parcel.

'Johnny O'Connor of Caherliss!' The high voice went even higher. 'A box of books?' She gave a shrill whinnying laugh. 'What would that fella be doing with a book, let alone a box of them? Maybe it's reading that he and Bridie Bannion get up to together.'

Like Elsie she gave a small push to the box, meant to be derisory, and it failed to move.

There was a moment of silence, each woman measuring the other, and Elsie knew in that moment that the old crow would never give up until she found what it was all about. When the altar flowers were done, she thought viciously, what else did the woman have to do but pry into other people's affairs? If only she could have put the box down on the floor. But she knew it was beyond her on her own. Even the mail man had protested, and he a big strong fellow. Books, he had said, as one who knew nothing about them, was terrible heavy.

'There's no mail for you, Miss Greeley,' she said firmly.

'Very,' said Miss Greeley, the parting shot as she turned to go, 'heavy reading there for Johnny O'Connor.'

'Nosey-minded old crow,' spat Elsie aloud at the black departing back, then, seeing no humour, settled herself comfortably on her stool to get on with the careful examination of the town's letters. Intrusive curiosity was the lawful right of Elsie O'Flynn only, as if she had been given one of these warrants for it by the King of England.

After a few minutes the pale eyes lifted again and looked speculatively at the parcel. 'Twould be as well for Johnny to come in for it soon before it attracted any more unwelcome attention. It wasn't only the old crow would know Johnny was no reader, and he'd be neither to be held nor bound did it get all round the village. Reluctantly she abandoned her cherished task, and scrabbled on the floor for a few innocuous parcels to pile up against the big one and hide the label and address.

As the shadows lengthened in the Square, people began to move about, life returning after the silent afternoon, as in hotter countries people would come to their doors and yawn and scratch themselves after their siesta. A tiny driven-looking woman darted across the Square and into Elsie's Post Office, a grimy grey apron over her black skirt and a grimy grey baby, chewing a hard crust, in her arms. Her hair hung in ratty tails and bare feet bulged through the sides of her broken shoes.

'Nothing, Rosie,' Elsie said before she could speak, fixing her with a cold magnified eye, relishing the power to make the poor worn face crumple towards tears.

'But,' the thin voice was a hopeless wail, 'but, musha, didn't he *promise* me. There's been time now for a letter. Didn't he promise to send me all he earned, and the street of England running with gold and good positions. Didn't he *promise*.'

As though the promise itself would have brought a letter on some mystical wings of honesty.

Elsie had no such faith in Rosie's wayward husband.

'G'won outa that, Rosie.' She was indifferent. 'Wouldn't he have it spent on drink within the hour of getting it.'

Outside the door there was the clatter of a horse and cart being reined too fast, a clutter of curses for the horse and a

25

shout of greeting for a friend. Poor Rosie, trying vainly and proudly to hide the scalding tears, did her best to dodge round the tall young man who had thrown his reins aside and come in throught the door like the fresh breath of the evening itself. A brown, work-roughened hand caught her firmly on the arm.

'What's on you now, Rose? What's the trouble?'

For a moment the blazing charm of the face above her was stilled to compassion by the sight of her, no one else in his mind. 'What, Rosie?' The tiny woman stopped and gulped, trust implicit under the touch of the young man's hand.

''Tis that Batty of hers,' Elsie said dispassionately. 'Gone to England to earn money, and drinking the lot of it.'

'Ye don't know that,' flashed Rosie, fury proud through her tears. 'Ye, don't know that, and there's no call to give him the bad word. 'Tis possible it's the posts, Mr. O'Connor.' Her voice was a poor shamed whisper now. 'But he did promise to send me the money. He did promise and I've the childer at home, God help me, and not a bite of food in the house.'

Johnny's hand was already in his pocket.

'Ah, you know what letters are, Rosie. They lose the half of them and Elsie here loses the rest. Take that, Rosie, to help out.'

Elsie's face was a pudding of disapproving creases. No more than her place that Johnny O'Connor should make a joke with her, but no call at all to share it with that Rosie Culcannon, with more than half the gypsy to her.

No drowning man grabbed a lifebelt faster than Rosie grabbed the two half crowns, and for a moment Johnny thought she was going to kiss his hand.

''Tis all right, Rosie. 'Tis all right.'

'Ah, Mr. O'Connor, yer a good man. A good man. Better than that one is a woman!'

With a jerk of her head she shot out of the door and across the Square, racing for the grocery, the baby's head jogging up and down over her shoulder like a target on a range.

Johnny O'Connor turned his wide splendid smile on the Postmistress, creating as always the sense that he filled a room without help from anybody else.

'She should tell that to the English,' he said. 'Wouldn't you

26

think so, Elsie, that I'm a good man? And the Polis, too.'

He stopped smiling, intent, excited.

'Has it come?' he asked her.

Over six feet tall, with all the young inbuilt strength of a life of farm work, but with it some special natural grace from the long generations behind him: dark as many westerners were dark, with sparking blue eyes behind lashes thick and straight as a pair of paint brushes. Bright hilarious eyes that could in a moment turn cold and hard as sapphires.

Elsie was already tossing the concealing parcels back on to the floor, completely indifferent to one labelled 'Fragile'. Behind her thick glasses the pale eyes glittered, and the shared excitement made her fingers tremble. It was doubtful if she could have said herself if she was the dedicated die-for-Ireland Sinn Feiner she made out or whether a great deal of her fervour lay in the contact it gave her with this tall, easy-moving man. She would never know if she were willing to die for Ireland or for Johnny, who gave her the same idle attention he would give his dog.

Her lips compressed with triumph that she had got him what he wanted.

'There you are, Johnny. There you are.'

Johnny laid a hand on the parcel with something close to reverence, and like a suitable benediction one of the last rays of the setting sun struck through the dirty window and lit with gold the label that said 'Books'.

'Ah,' said Johnny, and there was fierce contained excitement on his face. 'Good evening to you, Mrs. Mackay.'

He stood with his hand resting on the box, to wait for a fat woman with her hat down over her eyebrows like a pudding bowl clapped over her round pale face. With clucking irritation Elsie scrabbled on the floor for a parcel Mrs. Mackay should have had three days ago.

'Books, is it Johnny?' the fat woman said tartly. 'I'd have said it was far from books your mind was, and your mother such a good saintly woman.'

Johnny held his temper and looked at her blandly.

'We can all change, Mrs. Mackay. We can all change.'

His long mouth was tight as he watched her out. The one thing he could do without was to have it all over the district

27

that Johnny O'Connor had taken to the reading, and a great parcel of books waiting for him at the Post Office. Some fool of a policeman would listen to that for the unlikely tale it was, and start asking questions. The sooner it wasn't a parcel any more, the better.

Elsie saw his face, and didn't mention that Miss Greeley had already had her eye on it.

'I'll take it, Elsie.'

Her sallow face flushed when for one second their hands touched as she helped him move the parcel to the edge of the counter. He was in his working clothes, a striped collarless shirt open at his strong brown throat, homespun trousers above his muddy farm boots, and a bahneen jacket, grey with age, hanging loose above the lot. His father's long before it was his.

He took the parcel, hefting it even with an effort for him, and grinned again at Elsie.

'Jesus, Mary and Joseph,' he said, 'doesn't it take strength to be a reader in Ireland, Elsie.'

She gazed at him as fervently as Miss Greeley ever did at the tabernacle and the gleaming candles on the high altar on a Sunday.

'Strength and then something more, Johnny.' Her voice was hoarse and intense. 'More than strength, Gold help us all.'

But Johnny was out the door, letting down the back of his farm cart and easing the parcel on to it, covering it with an old sack. His dark face was as eager and his blue eyes bright as a child's at Christmas, were it possible for the edges of the child's ecstasy to be touched with determination and hate: its mind on murder and bloodshed.

He turned then to a girl who had arrived while he was inside. She leaned against the side of the cart with an attitude she might have copied from one of the lurid magazines smuggled out of England, and handed round the village girls until it was read to pieces. But Bridie had small need to copy anybody. All her own instincts were so subtly provocative that her body echoed them with no telling. Shameless, the older people called her. Shameless and shamed, too, now by the length of time she'd been going with Johnny O'Connor

28

and no sign yet of a ring. Or even the promise of it.

Her arms were folded in their green woollen sleeves, dragging her jacket tight around her, and her thin ankles crossed one over the other, showing off their fineness and the silk stockings worn by no one else in Connorstown. Weren't they enough in themselves, the old ones said, to show the fast creature she was. Bright red hair was pushed under a tam-o-shanter and her porcelain white and rose complexion was luminous in the cool dusk, her enormous green eyes hungry on Johnny.

'There,' he said, when the parcel was hidden to his satisfaction. 'There now, Bridie. It's come!'

She was nonchalant to his excitement, only the fire of the huge eyes showing a character that, like his own, would stop at nothing.

'You'll be telling them tonight then?' she said and he nodded.

'But that's not enough,' he said, hitting the hidden box with his fist. 'That's only the nalf of it. We have to get the rest now.'

'Who's to stop us?' she said, and then the dark blue eyes sparked into the green ones and the current of his excitement flared between them.

'I'll pick you up tonight,' he said.

'Johnny, Johnny! Wait for me!'

A clear girl's voice called through the evening, and Johnny turned to it, a half smile already on his face, the sharpened look of fanaticism fading.

'Johnny, you should get going.' Bridie could not stop herself. 'Alone. It's safer.'

Johnny turned to her briefly, his face cool, and then looked back to where the other girl was pedalling hard up the street past the Police Barracks, where she lifted an unsteady hand to wave to the elderly Sergeant standing in the doorway. She was thin and energetic, and smiling to see Johnny, her black skirt gathering round her legs.

'And what difference,' said Johnny, 'will Kate Mary make? Doesn't she know everything that goes on in the house.'

He was already moving forward to meet her as she lurched into the Square, catching the handlebars as the bicycle almost fell into his hands, the front brakes catching better than the back with all the effect of a catapult.

'And how do you stop when you haven't me to fall on?' he asked Kate Mary, grinning, and Bridie's face was tight with displeasure. His face was indulgent and he banged the bicycle amiably.

'Every time you come home, I mend this yoke for you,' he said, 'and every time you come back it's no use again.'

'Ah, Johnny, it's like myself. It doesn't care for the travelling. And weren't we both so glad to see you here, thinking we'd have to go on all the way by ourselves. Good evening, Miss Bannion.'

Kate Mary, bright-eyed and flushed from her long ride through the evening cool, was polite but no more, touched by an instinctive antagonism to this green-eyed redhead who set herself up in the town as Johnny's girl, and he too idle and indifferent to do anything about it. Part of her play to catch him was this business of being as rabid a Fenian as himself, one of the Cumn na Bahn, the women who marched in secret with Sinn Fein, finding them safe houses and bringing them food and medical help when they were on the run. They were fierce and dedicated with all the passion for Ireland of the men. This one would have followed Johnny into hell itself, like that poor woman in the Post Office, and called it patriotism.

Kate Mary looked at Bridie with her cool intelligent eyes, and knew her dedicated to nothing but getting Johnny to the altar, and that would be disaster itself.

Bridie turned away and went off irritably across the Square without so much as a goodbye. What did that child have to come pushing herself in there for? Firmly she labelled Kate Mary as still a child, protecting herself from the insanity of jealousy that would swamp her did she ever acknowledge the flowering beauty that was up there at Caherliss in the same house as Johnny.

She passed a bent old woman creeping like a snail towards the Chapel for her Rosary after her drowsy afternoon beside the hearth, the beads of the Sacred Heart dangling from her withered fingers.

'Good evening, Mrs. O'Bourke,' said Bridie sweetly, the hard green eyes as soft as gooseberries. 'Will you say a prayer for my Intention?'

The old woman looked up at her from under her shawl, her milky eyes full of the simplicity of her gentle life. There were many had no good word to say about Bridie Bannion but she found the girl always very civil. Very civil.

'I will, Bridie. I will. May God listen.'

'Thank you, Mrs. O'Rourke.'

May God listen indeed. She went on up the street past the corn merchants, where she had to step into the gutter to avoid the sacks of grain along the narrow pavement. Her sensuous mouth was tight with a cynical smile. No harm ever to keep anyone on her side, no matter who. And there was no need to tell the poor old eejit that the only intention that troubled her was to get Johnny where she wanted him, and that was in her bed, and she didn't think God would listen much to that. Nor was she concerned about marriage first. If she got him that far, then he'd have to marry her: she'd raise enough scandal to see to that.

The old woman struggled with the unwilling gate into the Chapel yard. Removed from most of the village gossip, and living in her own pure world of saints and Virgins and the love of God, she saw Bridie only as a poor lovely girl with some secret sorrow, and what more could it be at that age than the wanting of some good man to take her to the altar.

She resolved to say a decade of the Rosary for her.

The bicycle perched precariously on the sack-covered box, Johnny whipped up the pony and clattered out through the village on to the unmade road leading the last three miles to his mother's farm.

Kate Mary settled herself on the hard front seat of the cart beside him.

'Isn't that great I caught you,' she said happily. 'Every autumn when I start again it seems longer.'

'And how's Mrs. Geary?'

'As if you'd want to know, Johnny. She's a cantankerous old whiner.' She added dispassionately, 'But I give her no cause for complaint. I'm safer there than living with the crows in the Convent.'

The long ride home from Westport had proved too much for Kate Mary in the winter months. Since she flatly refused to stay with the nuns, Aunt Margaret had found her a room with a friend of hers in Westport.

'Wait,' said Johnny, carefully easing the cart around a wandering sheep. 'Get on outa that,' he told it. 'Wait until you start bringing some fellow home. Then the sparks will fly.'

'You have only one thing in your mind, Johnny O'Connor.' Kate Mary gave him her wide, curling smile, but her eyes were sharp. 'That's men for women and women for men.'

Johnny grinned amiably back.

'And what else is there in this world?' he said. 'Where would you and I be without it?' He paused. 'One other thing,' he said then, and she was aware of simmering excitement that had been holding him ever since she climbed on the cart.

They lurched over a pothole and the box thumped in the back.

'Jesus,' said Johnny.

'Johnny,' she couldn't stop herself asking. 'Johnny, you're not getting in with that Bridie woman.'

'Woman?' he said. 'She's the same age you are yourself.'

Kate Mary sighed, knowing this was true. She also knew that Johnny had given no answer.

He was too exalted to keep quiet. Besides, as he had said to Bridie, didn't Kate Mary live in the same house. She'd have to know sooner or later. Driving blindly towards his own purposes, he couldn't believe that anyone might be against them.

He gave a small laugh, a whinny of pure excitement, and glanced at her sideways from blazing blue eyes.

'I got something today will advance the Cause like nothing we've had before.'

Kate Mary was silent. The cart ground and rattled on the rough road and Johnny raised a hand in greeting to a man rebuilding a loose stone wall after he had put a horse in through the gap, into a pasture the size of a handkerchief.

The sky above them was the colour of a thrush's egg, but purple dusk gathered round the distant edges of the green, green land, lambent in the last clear night.

The Cause, Kate Mary thought. The Cause. Freedom for Ireland from the long persecution of history. True for him, true for all of them. But they were all throwing away their lives for a dream. A dream. Did she say to him, Johnny, this is actually Ireland: all this green beautiful land and the lakes and the grey villages, and what is going to happen to it on the way? She had seen for herself the burnt out ruins in Westport, and the people weeping in the streets. Did she say this, Johnny would look around, not understanding, and say what was she on about, wasn't it just a few fields and the Cause was Ireland. Dead martyrs, hanged for the Cause, leaving bereaved and broken families, were more real to him than living people. And how could she blame him? He would die himself, his eyes aglow, for Ireland and miss no one in his going, were he sure it was for the Cause.

'The Cause,' she said aloud. Aunt Margaret's house was in sight, the stone walls climbing up to it on a gentle slope of land. The house where Johnny was born. Would his passion for the Cause allow him to see that flaming into the sky some dark night, Aunt Margaret clutching her poor possessions in the pasture outside, tear-drenched face lit by the scarlet light of fire?

She sighed. Johnny would accept it, and allow the neighbours to take in his mother while he went screaming for revenge across the country: until he managed to get some Police Barracks blazing as his home had done. Death was nothing.

And so it would go on.

Fear touched her, colder than the darkening evening. Johnny's elation could only mean he had got arms. And that, only a little while back, had been made illegal with fearsome penalties. Possession of even so much as a shotgun to keep the crows from the fields was outlawed. As yet, he and his fanatical group of Volunteers had not been able to do much, armed as they were with little more than broom handles and hurling sticks. Drilling out in the bog in the dark night, learning one at a time in the secret places in the hills to fire the rusty old rifles stolen from their fathers.

All they had been able to do was cause trouble wherever they could find it. Starting illegal meetings that vanished into the fields and the bog by the time the Police got there, only to be reported screaming their defiance five miles away an hour later. Never caught, driving the authorities to frenzy: bidding

33

the Police a calm good day as they strolled home in harmless ones or twos from meetings they could swear had never happened.

The Town Band blared Fenian tunes loud enough to be heard all over Connorstown, the furious Police arriving to find the instruments vanished and the members of the Band grinning in the street and offering them the time of day. How could they search the whole town for drums and pipes and bugles whisked in through sympathetic windows and handed on over garden walls into hilarious oblivion?

With arms and ammunition it would be different, and God help them all.

'Johnny,' she cried, 'Johnny!' Desperate, because she loved him dearly and could not think of his death. 'Johnny, why go on with it? Can't you read in every paper that no matter what you do here, the North will never come in with you. Never. And all you'll have is our grandchildren fighting in fifty years' time. One half of Ireland against the other!'

Johnny's whole face lit with a grin.

'*Our* grandchildren. Ah, God, Kate Mary, I never knew you had that notion about me. When will we do it? Do you want a priest or will we have a clutch of little bastards?'

She turned and thumped him. Laughing, he fended her off.

'It's not worth it, Johnny. There must be some other way of doing it!'

His fine handsome face grew serious then, his eyes grave and sad and dark, dark blue.

'There's some of us think it worth it, Kate Mary,' he said. 'Indeed there's many – as you know.

'Worth dying for,' he added. 'And, please God, did anything happen to me, I'd like to have the courage to die for Ireland with a smile on my lips, like all the brave lads after the Rising in 1916.'

Kate Mary felt a rush of uncontrollable anger at the very thought of the fine disarming Johnny coming to the same end as all those poor young men in Dublin.

'I'd believe it's hard, Johnny,' she said tartly and fiercely, and she felt the tears blur her eyes, 'to die with a smile on your lips, for Ireland or for anything else, when a hangman's rope is choking you.'

34

He chucked at the pony and stopped the cart then, looking down at her long and questioningly, as though for the first time ever he had listened to what she said.

'And whose man are you then, Kate Mary?' he asked her at last very gently. 'What side are you on? Are you for England and the soldiers and the Police, and no freedom for your own country?'

For a long time she looked down at her brown woollen gloves, aware she had raised something she hardly knew how to answer, then she lifted her beautiful direct eyes and looked back at him.

'I'm my own man, Johnny. I'm for myself and I want no part of it. I'm on no one's side.'

As he sat there on the cart at the end of the bohreen leading round to the yard of Caherliss, something happened to Johnny O'Connor as abrupt as a bolt of lightning or the burst of a bullet he thought so precious.

Abruptly he saw that here no longer was the young Kate Mary he had taken cheerfully as a little sister through the last four years. Here was a young woman, strong and firm, whose eyes told him she meant what she said and would stick by it. And beautiful, he thought, amazed as though he had never seen her before. Beautiful enough to shame the angels.

He smiled slowly like a man who has walked into sunlight, and Kate Mary smiled back because she found it hard to quarrel with him, but she still saw nothing more than the Johnny she had known since she came to Caherliss four years ago. She loved him, to be honest, far more than she loved her own brother who was a cold ould stick; but no more than that. Nothing different.

Johnny shook the reins and started the cart up the bohreen past a dirty cottage where a few scrawny hens and a pig foraged in the mud around the open door through which gleamed on some shelf the small red lamp of faith in the eternal bounty and goodness of the Sacred Heart. A man piled a meagre heap of turf against the gable end for winter, helped by a small staggering barefoot boy whose brother's trousers fell loose about his calves. One quick glance assessed the poor pile rising on the stained wall and Johnny halted the pony again, watching for a few moments in silence. On his

35

mobile face expressions could pass as swiftly as the cloud shadows on his native hills, driven by his impetuous thoughts, but now it was held by the same quick compassion with which he had looked at the gipsy in the Post Office.

'Is that all you have, Batty?'

'It is, Mr. O'Connor. Can afford no more.'

Johnny nodded and made no comment, clicking to the pony to start.

'He can't dig it himself, and he sick,' he said. 'That won't last the winter. We'll have to find him a bit more somewhere.'

Out of your own generous pocket, thought Kate Mary, but Johnny half turned to her, laying his hand on hers. The gesture surprised her. He took no heed of the pony who could find his way home blindfold.

'You'll not be able to go on being your own man, Kate Mary, alannah,' he said quietly. 'You're sitting on the fence and no man can do that in Ireland now. One of these days you must climb down on one side or the other.'

She didn't answer him, unable to.

Up in the house, Aunt Margaret put a lamp in the window of the kitchen, warm gold light like a beacon of permanence and security, belying everything Johnny said. Why could not life go on as it was?

Over the green country in Clumbane, Ned Brannick had come home for ten days' furlough.

Four years of discipline and drill had brought him to a fine young man, his long bony frame filled out and strong, and a young moustache curving on his upper lip. He was pleased it was darker than his hair, and every day sought carefully for it to be long enough to wax the ends into spikes: the small cube of amber wax doing little more at the moment than smear the sides of his mouth. With the help of God, he'd be a Sergeant soon the way things were going, and it gave a man authority to have a waxed moustache.

The wax was kept in its little silver box in the leather case the R.I.C. provided for him, with the cut-throat razor and the tin box for the Pears unscented soap, clear amber like the wax. Under their own straps were two black hairbrushes and a clothesbrush. As he grew older, Ned had grown fastidious.

36

Even without the training in the Police, something in his own character compelled him to absolute care and cleanliness of every smallest thing he might possess.

His boots shone like glass, and his light red hair lay immaculate, pomaded to a high parting which he daily pounded with the hairbrushes to suppress the small wilful hint of curl that shamed him.

On several days he went into Tuam with his mother to please her, feeling her pride beside him in his short red walking out jacket with the gold braid, his pillbox cap tilted over one eye and the swagger cane underneath his arm.

His mother walked as tall as he did himself, her bony face suffused with pleasure in her fine son, seeing nothing else. Ned himself was well aware, although he pretended not to look, that there were many who would sooner have spat than smile at him; put a bullet through him rather than pass the time of day. He knew he was tolerated only for his mother.

Since 1916, he was used to this, and knew that it was getting worse, although he knew also that the true worst was yet to come. Sin Fein grew stronger and more daring, feeding on their own success, driven by a passionate patriotism that he crushed furiously within himself. Their natural prey were the Police and the soldiers who stood between them and everything they called freedom.

He was as tender to his mother as his father's disapproval would allow, and happiest trying to forget the whole business: back in his old farm clothes, his neck eased from the high tight collar that did much for the erect carriage that was her pride. He helped his father and brother on the farm, and his brother never spoke of what he did and what he was, but Ned knew that Patrick thought him little better than a traitor. In the evenings he would sit with his parents in the lamplight when the table was cleared, telling them all he was allowed of his life, and what he did.

'As soon as I go back,' he said, 'I am to be transferred.'

'Ah.' His mother carefully hung the heavy iron pot on the hook above the glowing turf. A good mutton stew. Ned liked that. At the moment, everything was for Ned, defying the downdrawn brows of the father, who though indulgence soft and not fitting to a young man in Ned's position. 'Where,

Ned? Where will they send you?'

Wouldn't God be good if it were Tuam? she thought, and he be close at hand, leaving to God the chance that it might be to his own home Ned could stagger, drenched with blood and dying, like so many a police man before him. She realised at least that he might be safer somewhere quieter. Tuam was full of hotheads and already there'd been burnings and stealing of arms and, of course, reprisals by the Police.

Ned was careful.

'I don't know,' he said. 'I'll not know till I go back.'

He was not sure himself what he wanted. Two years in the depot at Newtownards followed by the rest of the time in the windswept quiet of Lisdoonvarna had left him bored. But he knew clearly what it would mean to be moved into heat of trouble.

He said as much, doubtfully, more to his mother than his father, yet knowing that she would not understand. For her it was all a dream of the bright uniform and the bullets that would somehow fly wide because it was her Ned.

'Were it a hard area I'd go to,' he said, 'I'd have to learn to kill, I've been told. I've not done that.'

He sat withdrawn, thinking of some of the things he had been told.

From across the table, his father spoke sharply, rattling his paper.

'Whatever you are confronted with,' he said, 'you do your duty. Whatever the conditions when you joined, did you lay down any for yourself? You have to take what comes.'

Ned looked at him, and in his eyes there was no more the old fear and respect for his father: an old man sitting behind his paper and knowing everything.

'What else would I do,' he said, 'except my duty.'

But he was not isolated like his father on this lonely farm, reading his old newspapers. He knew that when he had taken his oath, he had chosen his side in this simmering war. God knew he would do his duty, but he had begun to wonder lately where it might take him.

'There's one thing,' he said, to ease the moment. 'I'll get Sergeant a lot sooner. Since the Rising, there's few lads joining the R.I.C. and a good deal of them have left. 'Tis easier to get up the ladder now. An ill wind.'

'Sergeant,' breathed his mother proudly. 'Sergeant. Wouldn't that be grand.' His father only growled.

'Traitors,' he said. 'And cowards with it. To leave when their duty got hard.'

Ned smiled, more tolerant now of his father's dogmatic views.

'It's not that, Dada, exactly,' he said patiently. 'They feel now they are fighting for England against Ireland, and they can't do that.'

Across the table he met the father's piercing eye.

'And you?' he demanded.

Ned looked back at him.

'I took an oath,' he said patiently.

Nor could he ever break it. Whether he might in time regret it was another matter, and the proud young face was sombre.

Johnny heaved the bicycle and the box off the cart and Kate Mary waited for him while he unharnessed the pony and put her into the stable. The animals were all quiet and the fowl, save for the occasional cackle of some restless hen, quiet with waiting for the coming night. Only one truculent goose followed them with small threatening hisses across the darkening yard as they went together towards the warm glow of the light, Johnny staggering a little with his burden. Aunt Margaret was in the kitchen, her sharp eyes falling at once on what Johnny carried. Without speaking, she made room for it on the kitchen table. Even after an absence this was not a kissing family, and her greeting to the girl was no more than a nod. Kate Mary went on down the long passage to her room.

Caherliss was old, built by people who had no idea but to build one room on to another as their families grew larger, adding to the original two-roomed house until they had a long corridor-like slate-roofed building, totally impracticable since those in the end bedrooms had to go through all the others to get where they belonged.

It was Aunt Margaret's husband, long dead of a consumption that ate him to a skeleton, who had built the passage the whole length of the house at the back of it, roofing it with glass on which the rain drummed like an advancing army, leaking

39

through the joins to run in cold streams down the walls of the original house.

With some idea of warming that end of it, he had built a fireplace where the passage ended, and a chimney. A few old armchairs and a sofa with a couple of aspidistras in Balik pots made it a sort of extra living-room, and from some romantic reading in those days of her youth, Aunt Margaret always referred to it as the vestibule. Kate's room was at the very end beside the fireplace that helped in wet weather to fill the whole place with a fog of damp.

But it was her happy and secret place, for no one else ever bothered to come this far down, and an ancient high-backed chair before the grate made it hers alone. Beside her, a window looked out on to her great pleasure in Caherliss.

Half natural rock, and half built of big stones with rough steps up through them, a rampart at the end of the house held back a small meadow, curiously placed up level with the roof. Like the vestibule it had its own grand name from bygone days: the High Garden. But no garden grew there except for the wild clumps of pink and yellow saxifrage cascading down between the stones, and the daisies and harebells scattering the grass in summer. The goats grazed there, and any lambs or sheep that Johnny wanted close to his eye, among their feet a few adventurous hens that rambled up to look for better pickings than they found in the yard. But they, and Johnny if he had need, came up the long slope from the big meadow, never troubling Kate Mary in her small private kingdom.

She delighted in the cool rough wall immediately outside the window, where she could watch the little coloured finches nesting in the spring. She knew every stone and plant and would climb up on the summer evenings to sit with her back against a rock, surveying the long length of the house and the farmyard below her and Johnny and the Lad in the far meadows loading up the hay. Beyond them the green soft country stretched between its patchwork of stone walls away to where, in the far distance, the blue cone of Croagh Patrick stood black against the fiery sun.

All greens and blues and the brown streaks of the bog, shivering white with cotton in the summer: soft colours and grey rain and tight into the very fabric of her heart. She could not see it as Johnny saw it, oblivious to all the peace and beauty, no more than a political issue to be fought over by its own people. There must be some other way. Who could kill Irish people in the name of Ireland, and forget what might happen to Ireland on the way?

'Kate Mary, the supper is on the table.'

'Coming, Aunt Margaret.'

She left the window and came back along to the kitchen, sniffing gratefully at the smell of bacon and cabbage, watching Aunt Margaret put a good knob of yellow butter on the floury potatoes she had poured into a dish.

'Oh, Aunt Margaret, you know how I love bacon and cabbage.'

Aunt Margaret kept her sharp indifferent expression, but Kate Mary knew it had been cooked because she was coming home. Before she could say anything Aunt Margaret had rounded on Johnny, coming in as Kate Mary had done, sniffing at the smell of his supper.

'Willya get that thing off the table.' Sharply she pointed at the box with her big kitchen knife. 'If we're to have anything to eat at all.'

Johnny grinned and eased the box to the floor.

'And what's in it, will you tell me?' she said.

'Books, mother,' said Johnny with terrible innocence. What else? Doesn't it say so?'

'Books, is it?' There was nervous fear in the way Aunt Margaret slammed the plate of bacon on to the table, but she managed to glare at Johnny.

'Since when,' she said scathingly, 'were you able to read anything beyond the racing news?'

The meal was an awkward one for every one except Johnny. Kate Mary and Aunt Margaret were both acutely aware of the brown parcel on the floor, Aunt Margaret's thin face touched with actual fear. Only Johnny was in the highest spirits, coming back for more and more to eat as though he strengthened himself against something, jollying both the women with foolish tales. No word more was said between them as to what was in the parcel.

In silence Kate Mary and her aunt cleared off the table and washed the vessels in the cold scullery out at the back, lit by

41

the small oil lamp on the window sill that was never allowed to go out, ready to be carried by anyone moving round the dark house in the night.

They settled on each side of the fire, the older woman's worn hands for once quiet in her lap, a small smile on her face as she watched Kate Mary knitting inexpertly at some grey wool, ferociously mumbling the numbers of her stitches. Both of them pretended not to notice Johnny's restlessness, walking the house aimlessly from one end of the vestibule to the other. Aunt Margaret at least knew her son well enough to know he was craving to release his secret, for secret he had. She had never seen Johnny with a book in his life, once they freed him from school.

He dragged a chair screeching across the flagstones and sat with them a while, chatting aimlessly and teasing Kate Mary about her knitting. Then he was off again, rambling in and out and watching the old wag-at-the-wall clock above the mantel. His mother's thin mouth was tight. They were similar enough that she would see him in hell before she would ask him. Books indeed! May the good Lord grant it wasn't what she thought, but even if it was, wasn't she a good Irishwoman and would put no hand out to stop her son doing whatever his mind told him.

'I'll show you me books,' he burst out in the end, as if that was what he had been deciding all along, and a small smile touched his mother's lips below her frightened eyes. The same Johnny since he was a child, and who could hold him even if she wanted to. Johnny's voice was high, touched with an excitement he could hardly contain. Kate Mary laid down her knitting, frankly curious, for she could never see Johnny reading a book and there was something in that parcel had him like a cat on hot bricks. His mother looked into the fire in strained silence, and later Kate Mary realised that for all her little jokes about Johnny and the racing news, she had sat there cold with the certainty of what was in the box. Had known all along her son's dangerous secrets.

Johnny hefted the box again on to the kitchen table and went out for a knife to cut the twine that tied it.

When sorrow had taken all of them and life crumbled into bitterness and death, Kate Mary would look back and feel

42

that the loss of all she held dear dated from that moment when Johnny stood with the patchy light of the oil lamp on his handsome face, sawing away with the knife at the thick twine around the parcel labelled 'Books'. Not smiling now, his long lips compressed with intensity.

The twine was off and he wrenched open the sealing paper, throwing it on the floor, tearing back the flaps of the cardboard box inside, and the layers of newspaper that wrapped whatever it held. His fingers, now he had decided to open it, were clumsy, frenetic. It was full of smaller boxes, and as he looked at them he quieted down, passionately careful, even reverent, and his breathing could be heard through all the silent room. He eased out one small box, his fanatical eyes now on Kate Mary with some message especially for her. When he took off the tight-fitting lid, then he looked down: at the close packed gleaming bullets. His face held something of the excited tender pride he might have felt for a child that had pleased him.

'There,' he said, and Kate Mary recoiled from the expression on his face. 'There. Aren't these good books to give the English. They'll get to the heart of them.'

A sense of fury so great it suffocated her took hold of Kate Mary. She yelled at him, blind with helpless rage.

'For God's sake, Johnny O'Connor, isn't every one of those a dead man. 'Tis lives you have on that table. Lives!'

Johnny smiled and there was evil in it that frightened her.

'You're right, alannah. Every one of them a dead policeman, do we use them properly.'

She fell silent, filled with despair. As well protest the wind howling round the house in winter or the grey teeming of the rain. She knew a sick mad premonition of the end of happiness, grieving already for the new Johnny who stood before her at the table. Johnny she had never known.

All Aunt Margaret asked him coolly was where would he put them, but Kate Mary could hear at the edge of her voice all the fear and sorrow that had gripped herself.

'Under the bed,' he said. 'For the minnit.'

'And if the house be searched, wouldn't I be in Westport Jail beside you. Or before you, were you out of it.'

'They have no reason to search the house,' said Johnny.

43

'Yet. When they do, they'll not find them.'

He grinned suddenly, bringing back even for a moment the familiar Johnny. But a chasm had opened, a darkness fallen, and Kate Mary knew that nothing would ever be the same again. Johnny, who had talked and flirted with rebellion with all the young hotheads of the town, had with the gleaming bullets on his mother's table, declared himself.

Kate Mary felt cold and sad and frightened, but Johnny looked briskly once more at the clock.

'I'm off out now,' he said. 'Don't give them to anyone while I'm gone.'

He closed the big box again and carried it along the vestibule to his room. When he came back he was in his good blue suit, and with his cap pulled down over his eyes and a muffler round his neck against the cold he was off, with a brief goodnight, into the darkness. They could hear him whistling down the pasture to the gate, the proud defiant tune of the *Fenian Boys*.

Between the two women at the fire came a sad wordless agreement that the less said the better: wiser to pretend the whole thing never happened, although in their silence it passed through the minds of both of them to take the box and throw it down the well. Neither gave way to the thought, Aunt Margaret because she believed whatever Johnny did was right. Right or wrong, good or evil, for her Johnny could do only what was best. God help them all while he followed his road, but he must follow it. Kate Mary said nothing because she knew that was exactly how her Aunt would think. Be they for killing herself, she would never help to drag Johnny's bullets to the well.

She sighed. The knitting was now in a hopeless tangle, and awkwardly, with silence and small talk, they passed the time until Kate Mary could claim that she was tired and would like to go to bed.

'Will we say the Rosary now, Aunt Margaret,' she said.

Aunt Margaret nodded and took her beads from the pocket of her apron, kneeling down beside the turf glow that had warmed her through a lifetime of quiet evenings.

Through all the gloom and suffering of the decade of the Sorrowful Mysteries – and God knows, thought Kate Mary, it

44

would have to be the Sorrowful Mysteries tonight, shadowed by grief and death – Kate Mary was not sure who in anguish she prayed for.

For Johnny and where his wild elated patriotism might lead him, or for poor Aunt Margaret who in her careful silence might come to the greatest sorrow of them all.

When he came home in the small hours of the morning, Johnny was whistling even more cheerfully, marching briskly under a dark sky glittering with stars, his fists dug into his pockets against the first sharp touch of frost.

Kate Mary woke and heard him, all the way up the sloping pasture to the house. Something, she thought sadly, had gone well. Probably to do with the ammunition.

Johnny paused to relieve himself contentedly of a fair load of porter, under a rose bush that for this very reason bloomed with perfumed splendour surpassing every other one in his mother's half wild garden. There was no more lavatory in this house than the wide bog beyond it, and on his way home he always stopped at this same bush before the door.

He had reason to be pleased. Everything was boiling up nicely after the years of doing it all by halves. The whole Committee were wild with themselves, and him, about the ammunition. Cart before the horse, maybe, but they'd get the rifles in good time. They'd get them. It was all in his head, and every man Jack of the Committee on his toes to see the real thing started and the end of the hurling sticks and the few old rusty rifles out in the bog.

He sighed with relief and didn't bother to button his flies, sure what was the use, and the trousers coming off him the minnit he was inside anyway. There'd been a wild bit of a toss with Bridie after the meeting behind the handball court. He grinned to remember it, although a small voice of caution told him he'd need to be careful with the girl. She was altogether too willing and could have him up at the altar before you could say a Hail Mary for the one reason he couldn't argue with. And Bridie, some deep part of him knew, was not the girl he wanted at the altar.

Now young Mary Kate, he thought, and halted before the door, surprised. She was one for the altar. Not for her the giggling tussles behind the gravestones in the old Abbey, and b'God he'd murder any fella that tried it with her.

Before he let himself sink into the depths of the ancient feather bed, he leaned over and looked again at the box of ammunition under it, patting it as he might a new and exciting toy. Out in the yard, a disturbed cockerel flew to the roof of the hen coop and spread his wings, raucously announcing the dawn. Johnny yawned.

'Ah, God damn you, you liar,' he said. 'Willya be quiet. There's hours yet. Even for a famer.'

In seconds he was in a contented sleep.

Along the vestibule passage, Kate Mary, disturbed by the whistling and the crowing, and thinking one not unlike the other, lay wide-eyed in her own bed. Thinking about Johnny and about Ireland and about the ammunition. Her heart was cold. You didn't go around buying stuff like that without you planned some use for it.

Chapter 3

When Ned was posted to Connorstown, he learned about Kate Mary long before she knew about him.

The elderly Sergeant was retiring gratefully, and thanking God to be doing it before the whole terrible business got out of hand. He longed to be off to the North of Ireland to the village where he was born, to a world blessedly free of Johnny O'Connor and Sinn Fein and all the things that for the last couple of years had left him in cold fear of his life. Long ago he had sent his wife away, and when he went to Westport for the speeches and the handshakes and the good gold watch they gave him, he thrust to the back of his mind some guilty feeling that had he been younger, Johnny O'Connor would not now be King of Connorstown.

When he stood with Ned before the big map of the district nailed to the wall of the Day Room in the Police Barracks, he was pleased to see the new Sergeant's youth. Along the street, although Ned had been in the town little more than an hour, Elsie O'Flyn was not so pleased, sending out details of him over her own particular wire service.

'Young,' she said disapprovingly, as though realising already that the easy days of the old Sergeant might be over. She nodded with pursed lips at one of her cronies, mother of two of Johnny's Lieutenants in the Volunteers. 'Young. And a big tall fella with a bit of a strong look about him. He could be a nuisance. These young ones do get terrible keen.'

'Ah, musha,' said her friend with contempt. 'Young or old, won't Johnny and the boys have the measure of him.'

Elsie was reassured and together they stood at the Post

Office door and stared down the street at the blank white face of the Barracks, desiring even with their glances to do harm to it. At the door, Constable Daly stood on idle guard duty in the frail December sun and knew their thoughts, thinking his own ugly and unsuitable ones about old women who couldn't mind their own business.

Inside, Ned ran his finger round the parameters of his new kingdom.

Flat land, he reflected, rising to the hills about twelve miles off. Not many roads. Like his own part of the country, indeed. It shouldn't provide too many hiding places. He said as much, and the old Sergeant laughed. His heavy cheeks quivered and his small eyes on Ned were shrewd and a little pitying. He laid a hand on his shoulder.

'Son,' he said, 'and don't be taking me wrong: the lot you have here would hide a machine gun under a blade of grass and laugh in your face while you searched for it.'

'Are they well armed?'

Ned was beginning to have a glimmer that his quiet life was over. The older man's face grew grim.

'They haven't been,' he said. 'They haven't been. But these last few weeks they've been so cock-a-hoop about something that my senses are warning me.'

'You know them all? You have names?'

'Ah, sure to God, every child in the village knows the names.' He concealed his impatience with the young green-horn. In what bit of the bog had he spent his last years? 'They'll dance round you shouting them and defy you to prove it.' He laid a thick finger with a broken nail against a spot on the map ringed in red.

'Caherliss Farm,' he said, heavily. 'There'll be the thorn in your side.'

'Who's there?'

Ned was impatient to be rid of the slow talkative old man and his senses warning him, and all that cod. No one was going to dance in rings round *him*. Once he knew who the rebels were, he'd have them watched and caught the moment they lifted their heads. 'Who's there then?'

'Johnny O'Connor is there. And as slippery a customer and as dangerous a man as you'll meet. And nearly all of the

48

village following him like dogs.'

He stood there, nodding his grey head, hesitating to admit his disappointment at leaving the place without getting Johnny O'Connor.

'I'd have been glad,' he said finally, 'to have had the privilege of getting him hung.'

He didn't notice that Ned had fallen silent, his eyes on the red circle but in his mind as fresh as yesterday the memory of a clear-eyed girl with a broken dress guard on her bicycle. Going to live with an aunt near Westport. Her cousin Johnny, she had said, would mend the bicycle.

'He's the ringleader?' he said carefully.

'Ringleader, is it? Commandant of the Volunteers. He's the kind of Sinn Feiner would strangle the King of England with his own two hands and die laughing for doing it. He's the very devil himself.'

'And who else lives there?'

Ned felt cold and apprehensive as he asked the question. Was part of his job to hunt down Kate Mary and send her to prison or the gallows like any other of them?

'Well,' the old man said, 'the father is long dead, and the mother owns the farm. Johnny farms it. Ah – and there's a niece, Kate Mary Pearse.' Ned could see clearly the softening of his face. 'She teaches at the Convent in Westport and lodges there. Coming and going to Caherliss on the bicycle.'

The light blue eyes swivelled firmly on to Ned's face.

'I've never heard,' the Sergeant said, 'one word that she is involved in any of Johnny's capers. In anything,' he repeated like a warning. Ned swallowed, light with relief. 'She's a good, respectable girl and well liked. Now Johnny's old mother pretends all the time to know nothing about anything, but she'd defend Johnny like a she-cat.'

There was a long pause, Sergeant Crane staring at the map as though it had defeated him.

'O'Connor is the man you have to catch,' he said. On his florid face lay disappointment, and a flicker of compassion for the new young Sergeant. He looked too raw to be any match for Johnny who, God knew, was only young himself but reared in a hard school.

Behind his civilly attentive face, Ned had no intention of

finishing up in Connorstown disappointed. If this O'Connor fellow stepped as much as an inch out of line, he'd nail him. But he had taken a sickening blow a few minutes ago, when he realised that Caherliss was Kate Mary's home and saw her in his mind at Johnny's side in Cumn na Bahn, the women's Sinn Fein organisation, with her own gun in her hand and her oath sworn; quarry like all the rest of them.

He hid his pleasure and relief to learn it was not so, and asked Sergeant Crane for a full list of all those to be watched, thinking he was probably wasting his breath. The old fella didn't look likely to be too well organised. He would carry it all in his head and then write reports of three sentences.

'You have it all here,' the old man said, and turned, disturbing Constable Doyle, who was at the door picking his teeth with a sharpened match and watching Ned, wondering was the fellow going to give them a hard time, and he younger than themselves.

Hastily, under Ned's cold eye, he threw away the match.

Ned signed then for everything in the place, including Constable Doyle himself. He had, he noted, three men. One on guard at the door, one more out on patrol in the village, and one off duty. And every one of them hated as he would be hated, if they attempted to do their duty. Four of them against all Connnorstown, should things go bad. The old Sergeant had been given a half pardon because he had been there so long, but Ned knew there would be no mercy for him.

Sergeant Crane took his cap off a nail on the wall, looking at the black harp and the crown above it, as though he was saying goodbye.

'I'll be off now,' he said, 'but I'll be in Connorstown for a couple of days, did you want to know anything.'

'And where do you go then?' Ned asked out of civility.

'Ah, back to a bit of peace and me pension in Donegal. Grow a few cabbages.' He smiled then, a curiously childlike smile, and shook Ned by the hand. 'Good luck to you, Sergeant' he said. 'I've a notion you may need it. Unless I'm much mistaken, the pot here is just coming to the boil.'

He was gone then, leaving Connorstown to Ned. Also the list of trouble makers, which to Ned's shamefaced surprise proved to be a detailed dossier on every living soul in the town. It filled him with respect for the old man, and the certainty that it would have taken him years to gather such knowledge for himself.

A danger spot, his superiors had said, sending him here. A danger spot. Sergeant Crane's dossier did nothing to deny it.

It did not take him long, the next day, to walk his kingdom: no more than a couple of dozen streets, straggling off into the dirt roads to outlying farms. No one was uncivil, all cautiously bidding him the time of day, but he was conscious at every door and window of being watched, measured and assessed.

The map was printed on his mind, and it was not difficult to find the road that would take him to Caherliss. Standing at a windy crossroads between tumbling stone walls, he looked out over the damp green fields towards Kate Mary's home.

Kate Mary. He had never forgotten her, holding her image always through the inevitable casual encounters through the last four years. He made no move to go out to Caherliss. That house would be touchy as a powder keg if it held the Sinn Fein leader, and his time in uniform had taught him caution. Despite what the Sergeant had said, Kate Mary might be loyal to O'Connor; want to spit on Ned's hated uniform. He would find her in his own good time, when he knew a lot more of Johnny O'Connor and how the wind blew.

In any case, didn't she live most of the time in Westport.

A farmer in his turf cart came rattling by and touched his cap, taking no special notice of the new Sergeant spying out the land towards Caherliss.

'Wasn't it no more than where you'd expect him to be,' he said afterwards to his wife. 'But he'll have to be up early in the morning to catch Johnny O'Connor.'

'Kate Mary,' said Johnny a couple of week-ends later. 'If I drive you to Westport on Monday morning, could I have the loan of your bicycle for the week.'

Kate Mary's strong brows drew down, suspicious immediately of anything that was out of the ordinary at the present time.

'And how do I get out from town next Friday?'

'Ah, there'll always be someone about at that time of day to give you a lift.'

51

'And if there isn't, I'll be the one walking from Westport with you careering the country on my bicycle. What d'you want it for anyway?'

He had the pony and cart, and the trap. What did he want with her bicycle as well? Fear touched her as it so easily did about Johnny. Nameless, shapeless fear because she didn't know what he was about. Now there was this new Sergeant in Connorstown, out to sweep the place clean, they said, like any new broom. And the first thing to be swept away was Johnny. She'd not seen him herself yet since she'd spent the last week-end with her friend in Westport, but Aunt Margaret had told her he was a big determined-looking fellow, a great deal sharper than old Tom Crane. Everyone knew the three constables couldn't catch a fly with its legs in a jampot, but there were rumours that this lad was something else entirely.

She never gave him a thought except as a threat to Johnny, who answered her question easily.

'I have to go and see a man,' he said. 'Out at the back of beyond, and the bohreen up to his house not wide enough for the trap.'

'Couldn't you use the legs God gave you?' she asked him, her voice sharp with her anxiety. And then fell silent, caught by Johnny's too easy smile. She looked through the scullery door to where Aunt Margaret stood at the stone bench, mashing meal for the hens, and saw the same studied disinterest as on the night he had brought home the bullets.

Bleakly, she knew that if she didn't give it to him, he'd take it just the same, and for God knew what purpose.

'Right,' she said, 'but don't break it.' Almost she said, 'I don't want it back with a bullet through the spokes.' But Aunt Margaret's rigid back forbade it.

'Ah, alannah.' He put an arm round her waist, and looked down at her. 'Aren't you the bicycle breaker and me the bicycle mender. But you're a grand girl.'

She knew a sudden suffocating discomfort she had never known before at Johnny's touch: the arm just a little too tight round her waist, hand a little high and fingers pressing, and behind the smile in the blue eyes, a bright intentness that brought the blood to her face.

At the bench, Aunt Margaret moved to take the basin of mash out to the fowl pen.

'I'll take that, Aunt Margaret,' she said quickly, and moved away from Johnny, his familar strength changed suddenly from a reassurance to a vague threat, or at least to an embarrassment. Gratefully she got away out into the clear last light of the evening, the first stars pricking sharp above the darkness of the High Garden, and she got comfort from the ordinary sight of the hens clamouring at their gate, wanting their good warm meal before they scrambled and flapped to their perches for the night.

She scraped the meal-smelling mash into the trough, pushing aside the greedy little heads, and thought about Johnny. It was almost like he was a little drunk. No, not drunk, she decided, but wild with some excitement he couldn't hide. Wild with something about to happen, wild enough to try his hand with her as he had never done before.

It wasn't possible to live in a small isolated place like Connorstown with about four men to every girl, without learning early to fend off the groping hands, the tightening grip in the middle of a dance, or the hoarse, anxious requests to come out for a while behind the ball alley. Always qualified by a rush of respectful whispers that they knew she was a lady and a good girl and everything like that, but wouldn't she think of it just for the once. Always she tried to put them off with a smile and not to crush the poor creatures. But then there was always Johnny to take her home. And he always did, the moment she asked him, even if he turned the trap at the front door and went back to his own business.

Which would, of course, be Bridie Bannion, puffing her cigarette and leading on anyone she could lay hands on, but waiting only for Johnny.

Carefully Kate Mary latched the gate of the hen run, feeling the cold of the coming night on her hands. No great harm if the hens got out, but all the harm in the world if a fox got in.

It wasn't she was a prig or anything like that. Just that all these hot squeezing hands and tussles in the graveyard were not for her. There would be someone soon, she felt sure, with whom it would all be very different.

Though where, she thought ruefully, she was going to find

him, between Connorstown and Mrs. Garvey's at Westport, was another matter. Crossing the yard, she grinned to think of Mrs. Garvey's spinsterish house full of eligible young men, refreshed in herself by her small journey in the sharp cold and the warm fluttering enjoyment of the hens as they got their supper. Weren't they the lucky ones, with not another thing to think about.

Johnny was standing at the far end of the house, shadowy in the light of the lamp in the vestibule, looking at the wall of the High Garden. Lifting the clumps of drying plants, he ran his hands around the rocks hammered in to shore up the wall.

Even an hour ago, she would have gone to him at once, and asked him what he was doing. The too intimate gesture, taking her for granted, the fingers on her breast, had raised some barrier. It had made him, like on the night of the bullets, into a different Johnny that she hardly knew. Better if he had indeed been drunk. Better than launching himself off into some scheme that these days could be his death.

Oh, dear God, help them all.

He turned then and looked at her, lamplight falling clear on his quiet face. At once she felt a fool. Imagining things. She was no better, she told herself, than the church-mad Children of Mary who were supposed to cross the street if they saw a man.

'What are you doing with my wall, Johnny?' she said then, and smiled at him, cursing herself for a fool as he sauntered the length of the house, lovely long handsome thing that he was; as good looking a man as she would ever know, and no more in his eyes when he reached her, than there had ever been.

'I'm looking at it,' he said, and didn't deny that it was her wall. He took the basin from her.

'Your hands are cold,' he said. Come in now to the fire. The day is done.'

'Have you seen the new Sergeant over there in Connorstown?' Aunt Margaret asked from the hearth where she piled fresh turf under the oven.

Quietness left Johnny's face and an expression of bright hilarity took its place.

'I have,' he said. 'Altogether too serious a fellow. Needs a bit of divarsion to get his mind off his business.' He was

54

laughing, pleased with himself, but Kate Mary caught behind his eyes the fanatical determined glitter she had come to fear. What was he up to now?

'Have you seen him yourself, Mother?'

'What would I be doing, flaunting myself round Connorstown were it not for Mass. And he kept himself to himself last Sunday it seems, except to go to the First Mass.'

Kate Mary smiled affectionately at the idea of Aunt Margaret flaunting herself anywhere, and Johnny laughed outright.

'Well, if you're flaunting yourself at Mass tomorrow, Mother, you might get a sight of him.'

Both women looked at him and did not look at each other. What was planned for tomorrow?

Aunt Margaret put on her blank expression.

'Kate Mary and I,' she said, 'are away to Anfield tomorrow to see Ulick. We'll get Mass there in the house. And it would do you no harm to come too,' she added tartly.

'I have something else to do,' Johnny said. 'You'll be all right with Kate Mary. She's a famous driver.'

He still grinned at some secret joke, but there was an air of discomfort at the table.

'What's he like?' she said, to ease the awkwardness. 'The Sergeant?'

Johnny answered disparagingly.

'A big raw-boned fellow. Very keen on his job – and too young for it,' he added on a sour note.

Young enough, thought Kate Mary with sudden insight, to have alarmed you. He'll probably not be so easy codded as old Tom Crane. Big raw-boned fellow. Afterwards she was to marvel that she had never for one moment thought it might be Ned.

'He needs to learn a few things.' Johnny's smile was gone, his face sharpened and his voice cold.

His mother began to bring the meal from the fire to the table and, anxious to get away from the awkwardness, Kate Mary too got up and started to help.

'What time will we be off tomorrow, Aunt Margaret?'

'Arragh, early. About half-past eight.'

*   *   *

55

With her dutiful visiting, Kate Mary missed the first of Johnny's 'divarsions' and with it, Ned.

The following morning, when she was long arrived at the cousin's house in the country, the bell in Connorstown was ringing for the last five minutes before late Mass. Flat and tinny, clanging plain and uncompromising as the grey Chapel itself behind the iron fence. Religion was for the saving of your immortal soul and had no truck with gratification of the senses.

Last Mass. The last chance between them all and the mortal sin of missing it. The Sluggards' Mass.

Ned had gone early at six o'clock with the creeping company of a devout handful of old women who would come back again later, shapeless in their black shawls in the cold dark morning not yet forsaken by the stars. As the late bell clanged for the lazy ones, he was at the table in the Day Room of the Barracks, deep in his methodical study of the village dossier that had been left to him.

Even including Pearse, Kate Mary, Caherliss Farm.

He had passed that one with a lightened heart. Nothing known against her, but even more important, no political affiliations. No political activities that were no more than treason by another name.

Even without her name on it, the list he was making in the neat copperplate beloved of R.I.C. reports, grew longer and longer and more alarming. Simmering, they had told him about Connorstown. Simmering. B'God if this lot ever came up to the boil, he'd have his hands full.

Absorbed, still trying to fit faces to histories, it took him seconds to recognise the sounds from the streets. They came from the direction of the church, confused by the clanging bell. But he had flung down his pen and was round the table and out before Constable Murphy on the outside of it had done more than gape.

Marching feet. Boots thumping hard and disciplined on the stones. Forbidden sound of forbidden trouble. He burst into the street, unable to believe in the sight of the end of a column swinging round the bottom of the Square and up past the Chapel. No uniforms on any of them, but all with the forbidden Sinn Fein armband, the colours of green, white and

56

orange that the French had left to them with their dead and dying when they sailed home defeated after the Rising of '98. Something like rifles across the column's shoulders. . . .

Ned wasted one second gasping at the sheer effrontery of it. O'Connor could hang for less than this. But even as he began to run, pulling his revolver from its holster, he asked himself what his few men could do against so many.

'Telephone Westport!' he bawled back at Constable Murphy, not yet knowing that the ever open line was apt to be closed by Elsie O'Flyn whenever her brothers so ordered her. 'Telephone Westport!' Ned yelled. 'Unlock the rifles!'

It was about two hundred yards from the Barracks down to the Square. Ned took it at record speed, long legs pounding the road, his mind racing with all the possibilities of attack. It wasn't the Barracks. They were marching away from it.

He hurtled into the Square, gun in hand. And crashed to an abrupt halt.

There was no sight or sound of a marching man in the streets.

Only a larger number of Mass goers than usual, most of them men, flocking innocently towards the chapel gates, and Johnny O'Connor lying up against the gates themselves with a grin to his face from ear to ear, and his cap on the back of his head.

'Good, day to you, Sergeant. Were you in a hurry somewhere? Is it Mass. Sure, there's time yet.'

Speechless with fury, Ned knew it useless to go after them. Useless to make Johnny turn his pockets out. There would be no armband there, nor in anybody else's either. He would only make himself a bigger fool than they had already made him.

The column would have dissolved the second they were round the corner from his sight; many of them doubtless now piously in the chapel on their knees, mouthing the prayers before Mass, the armbands passed to the women. It took more courage than Ned had to go searching them.

The rest of them would have whipped into the small houses along the street, waiting with open doors, and would now be laughing their heads off with a bottle of porter before the fire.

Tight-lipped under Johnny's grin, Ned tried the crowd

57

going into Mass. Had they seen anything?

'Men?' A wrinkled ancient peered from under her shawl. 'Ah, musha, Sergeant dear, haven't I enough men at home, with my own man and six sons, and every one of them able to eat a bullock. What would I do coming into the street to look for men? Bad cess to the lot of them.'

'Well, Sergeant, me eyes are not good.' Old eyes as bright as buttons gleamed at him from under a soft cap, alive with glee to see the peeler made a fool of. 'It could have happened, d'you see it like that, and me know nothing about it at all. Nothing at all.'

'Men? And they marching?' This one was plump from childbearing, tightly cased in a black dress too small for her, 'Ah, no, Sergeant, wasn't I in at the house giving a wee sup of milk to the baby, with sugar in it, and she crying with the teeth. Only this very minnit did I give her to my mother and step into the street to go to Mass. I didn't see a thing. Arragh, not a thing.'

'Maybe, Sergeant.' This one was wise and grave as a judge. 'Maybe it was the Russians. Did they have snow on their boots, do you know? I have heard tell they were seen over in England, and they with snow on their boots.'

No one was smiling. They all treated him with fearful courtesy, but there was a collective grin over all the village. A barely concealed derision that brought the blood up to Ned's thin-skinned face. They looked at him with guileless faces he could happily have put his fist through. Carefully he held his temper, and as the bell ended its flat clangour and they streamed into Mass, he turned back to the Barracks, holding his dignity as carefully as his anger, facing the painful business of telling the District Inspector in Westport that it was all a cod, and he had fallen for it.

Johnny O'Connor lounged where he was, and did not go into Mass, but beside him now was a young woman with improperly short skirts and red hair, who met the young Sergeant's eye with a brazen mixture of contempt and the invitation she could withhold from no good-looking man.

Bannion, Bridget, Bridie, the dossier had said.

Cumn na Bahn. Family Sinn Fein. Doubtful character. To be watched.

At that moment, reinforcements arrived in the way of Constable Doyle, pounding perspiring into the Square on his bicycle, eyes popping with terror and determination, having been told at the far end of the village that the Sergeant was being beaten to death in the Square.

Ned grinned then.

'It was decent of you to come, Constable,' he said. 'In the circumstances who could blame you did you go hell for leather the other way.'

Thanks to Elsie O'Flynn, Constable Murphy had failed to get through to Westport, and still sat at the table, round face red with anxiety, winding madly at the telephone; and too bursting with the sense of failed duty to realise as Ned came quietly in that there could be nothing wrong.

When Mass was over, Ned resisted the temptation to go pedalling out to Caherliss, knowing he'd have nothing to say when he got there. Wouldn't the whole population be willing to swear nothing had happened. There was no sense in making a fool of himself, or more than Johnny O'Connor had made of him already: and probably before Kate Mary, too.

First round, he thought grimly, to Johnny.

Kate Mary. He was restless to see her, to see how she had changed. Did she have a man that she was already bound to? The thought lurched unhappily into his mind that it might be Johnny O'Connor himself. It meant nothing to marry your cousin in these parts, no matter what the Church said.

Anger rose in him again as he thought of the young man lounging outside the Chapel there with that redhead, and the pair of them grinning like Cheshire cats. Making a fool of him. No man for Kate Mary.

Caution and his sense of duty calmed him. Did he himself go out courting to Caherliss, there'd be scant welcome for him, and little approval from his superiors either. He was here to do his duty and that was all, no matter who was concerned.

In the dossier, he was as far as O'Flyn. Six of them, and every man Jack from the father down rotten with rebellion. Even, it seemed, that dumpy little frog in the Post Office.

He looked up at the big map on the wall, seeing nothing, thinking of Elsie O'Flyn. Could he shoot a woman he was asking himself, did his duty demand it?

Could he shoot Kate Mary?

It was the week of what Johnny called his 'divarsions.'

Monday night was the night of the fire.

A miserable night, the fine clear weather gone and mist drifting like phantoms round the dripping fields. Ned patrolled the dark streets of the village, buttoned to his neck in his waterproof cape, feeling the damp on his cold face. No more than the odd light gleamed behind drawn blinds, and he paused outside the grocery store, proud, profitable business of Desmond Gorman who emptied the bar at the back of his shop every night with religious self righteousness. On the dot of closing time.

Ned looked at the establishment now: shuttered and dark, innocent as a child's bedroom.

He could do one of two things, and he had thought about it a great deal on these patrols through the seemingly dark town.

He could go round to where the big back kitchen would be curtained against the smallest show of light, silent and innocent as the front. Constable Doyle had taught him the knock. Three slow raps with a penny and then a couple of fast ones.

The young Constable had looked then at his Sergeant's face.

'But you wouldn't go raiding Gorman's, Sergeant.'

As well to say he would set fire to Dublin Castle or the Vatican in Rome. Too shocking a thought to be entertained in Connorstown.

'Afraid I might find you there, Constable?' he said, and the young man flushed furiously, then spoke up bravely.

'You'd catch everybody who was anybody in the town, Sergeant, so I'd be very small fry for you,' he said bluntly. Then his long thing face creased in a grin. 'I'm not sure you wouldn't be preached against from the pulpit. And the old Sergeant'd come back all the way from Donegal to shoot you, and he having kept the same chair warm in there these ten years back.'

Ned had given no answer, but now he stood indecisive in

60

the dark, damp street. He could feel a cold drip on the end of his nose and reluctantly took off a glove to grope for a handkerchief. He knew what he would find inside Gorman's at this time of night, did he make up his mind to go in. The huge kitchen warmly furnished with red curtains and cushioned chairs, and a pile of red hot turf glowing in the range. Brass lamps and pictures and all the worst rebels in the town sitting in there soaking up the rich black porter as fast as Desmond could serve it.

He could go in like a Sergeant. Break the whole thing up and have them all up before the Resident Magistrate in the morning for illegal drinking, if he could get them on nothing more.

If they would go.

Many of the Sinn Fein refused now to accept the authority of the English Courts, and his superiors might not thank him for putting a match to that bit of tinder at the moment.

Duty dictated he should go in, even though it would be a declaration of war on Connorstown and deepen the hostility already thick as the night mist.

He put his handkerchief away and pulled on his glove, hand grown cold even in the few minutes.

On the other hand, he could do as the old man before him and walk in with a good time of night to all of them; ordering his own glass of the black stuff, and settling by the fire. Taking away forever his authority over any of them. Making an unspoken pact that their affairs were their own.

And never a day's respect for himself again.

In the cold darkness, he sighed, and knew he would just keep on back to the Barracks, shelving the decision once again; telling himself, rightly, that it was early days yet for such decisive action. He could scare away the very ones he was after. These were the ones who stayed when the others were gone, joined in darkness and secrecy when the lamps were lowered, to plot against England and against him, and everything they both stood for. Johnny O'Connor and his henchmen. They were the ones he was after.

You can only, he had been told once, catch a tiger by getting its tail. And only that by creeping up on it.

The sudden crash of pounding boots was like a machine gun

in the darkness; pausing; stopping; and then racing on as if the runner looked for someone. One of his men. He began to run himself, towards the noise, annoyed at the sound of his own thumping footsteps. In this battle, his enemy wore old shoes and crept quietly through the nights about their evil business.

At the next corner, he hurtled into Constable Murphy.

'What is it, man?'

'Is it you, Sergeant?'

'Who else? What's on you?'

A gasping and heaving of breath. Ned decided that, apart from anything else, his men were out of training.

'A fire, Sergeant. A big one. And it looking to be in the direction of the Resident Magistrate's house.'

He could bear the shock and outrage in the young man's voice. These things hadn't happened in his two years with the old man.

Ned was thinking rapidly. And what had the R.M. done to get his house burnt down, except to be English? He declined to pound through the streets with Constable Murphy, marching him back rapidly and correctly to the Barracks where he telephoned, miraculously quickly, for re-inforcements from Westport. Even as he climbed on to his high old issue bicycle, some part of his mind was already uneasy, conscious that the village was too quiet. For all the pounding boots and the shouting, not one lamp had been kindled nor a window raised in a village that, like all others, minded other people's business better than it did its own.

There was no doubt about the fire. From the country out beyond the end of the street the red glow pulsed and flickered, pink hazed round the edges with the mist. Ned pedalled furiously along the pitch black country road, the small glimmer of his acetylene lamp doing no more than bounce back from the damp darkness. He longed for the speed and comfort of a motor car like the bigger Barracks. It could be no harder to drive than a horse and cart, easier than heaving this thing along the rutted road that threatened with every bump to throw him into the ditches of dripping sedge. His mind ran endlessly over any reasons for present grievance against the R.M.

Reaching the fire, he heaved himself off, panting. Constable Murphy toiled to a halt behind him, and together they stood, wordless looking at the flames which engulfed an abandoned ruin of a farm, obviously packed with rubbish and brushwood and set alight, blazing merrily into the misty night as though it chuckled at the fiery farce it was.

There was a smell of paraffin, and they saw empty cans in the red light of the flames, but there was not a soul in sight. Nevertheless, in his mind's eye, Ned could see Johnny O'Connor standing there grinning as he had done outside the Chapel the day before.

'Nothing here for us, Constable,' he said grimly, and reluctantly Constable Murphy, who had been glad of the rest, climbed back on to his own machine and followed his Sergeant in no small anxiety along another few miles of road to where the car from Westport sat waiting outside the dark bulk of the R.M.'s house. Mist swirled round its headlamps and there were four policemen with rifles in it, and the District Inspector himself.

'Dear God,' Ned said to himself when he saw him. 'I'm back to Constable.' And Constable Murphy held back into the shadows and hoped not to be seen at all.

The darkness was as thick outside the headlamps as the shades of hell, and the big stone house beyond the lawns as silent as the village. Mr. Bonnington Clay and his lady were sleeping the sleep of the just and self-assured, and no Irish servant in his right mind would come out to ask what the polis were doing outside the house at one o'clock in the morning. Bedclothes would no doubt be drawn over heads, with fervent Hail Marys that it was nothing to do with them or theirs.

'They're playing games with you, Sergeant,' the Inspector said when he reported what he had found, and Ned nodded, furious and ashamed, not noticing something very close to a smile on the other man's long, composed face where the waxed whiskers were as stiff and imposing as Ned hoped to grow his own.

Not that it would matter if he managed to grow them a foot on each side of his face. Two weeks in the place, and he'd tried to alert Westport on two loads of rubbish. A few more of these incidents and they'd have him back growing cabbages for his mother. Or just chasing chicken thieves out in the bog somewhere.

'Don't let them run you too hard.' The smile was gone now. In the hissing flicker of the headlamps, the D.I.'s face was hard. 'They're up to something. Keep your wits about you, and try and catch the moment it's real.'

Ned tried to apologise, rigid to attention.

'They've made fools of better men than you, Sergeant. Take care they haven't robbed the Barracks, with you on a wild goose chase out here.'

Oh, dear God! Ned could hardly wait to salute as the motor chugged off into the night.

The journey back was endless, even with his long legs powered by fury and anxiety and shame, cursing himself for every kind of a fool as they passed the now smouldering fire, poor Constable Murphy panting noisily behind him. Halfway back the wind rose suddenly against him, doubling his effort, and with it came a cold heavy rain, gusting chill and numbing into his tired, angry face.

The Barracks, when at last he reached it, was exactly as he had left it, Constable Daly staggering up sleepily from beside the dying fire. The village, too, lay silent, and as he stood at the door listening for any sign of trouble, he seemed to hear sniggering in the hissing rain and derisive laughter blowing on the wet wind. He could envisage them all sleeping with grins on their faces. Once again the impulse was to go raging out to Caherliss, where without doubt Johnny O'Connor would be deep in innocent sleep, and his old mother ready to swear he had been so all the night.

It was still only 1918. Not yet the days of the Auxiliaries and the Black and Tans, free to drag a man from his bed for no more than suspicion, to shoot him by the roadside within earshot of his screaming family and ask their questions laters.

In the cities it was coming to that, but in the country even a known Sinn Feiner needed to be caught in treason.

And by God, he'd not rest until he had caught Johnny O'Connor.

Turning back into the Barracks, he deliberately calmed himself.

'Put some turf on the fire, Constable,' he said, and make us a cup of tea. Then go to your bed and I'll stand the rest of the night.'

Tuesday night was the night of the bands.

As soon as darkness fell, the blare of rebel songs and the thump of drums, and the raucous ill blown trumpeting came drifting on the wind across the sodden fields. As soon as they thought they had the noise pinpointed, silence fell, and then the torn *Lament for Robert Emmett* or the thump of the *Old Fenian Boys* would come drifting in from somewhere else.

Banned instruments. Forbidden songs.

Ned walked the streets of the town, his normal good-natured expression grown tight, aware that he was watched from every house, all of them waiting to kill themselves laughing when he went racing out into the country as he had the night before. When Constable Daly, rain running from the peak of his cap, saluted him from the shadows, he told him to keep on his patrol and watch did he see anyone actually with band instruments. Not that he would.

Turning from the disappointed face, he went at a slow, controlled pace back to the Barracks where Constable Doyle was waiting anxiously at the door.

'What'll we do, Sergeant?'

His thin pale face was nervous.

Deliberately Ned took off his rain cape and hung it up, turning to warm his hands at the fire.

'We do nothing, Constable,' he said. 'Let them blow and bang until they are tired and wet.'

The policeman looked even more harrassed, longing for the good peaceful days of the old Sergeant.

'And what if the R.M. or the Inspector or somebody like that hears them, and the Inspector displeased with us already?'

Ned smiled then, and his long face with the flush of cold on the high cheekbones lost its harshness.

'I don't think either of those gentlemen,' he said, 'are likely to be out in the edges of the bog on a dank night like this.'

Constable Doyle was ambitious and fearful, ever mindful of future promotion. Ferret Face, the children called him. His narrow mouth was tight.

'Someone could report it,' he said stubbornly.

'In that case, it'll be my business.' Enough chat from a subordinate was enough. 'Now have you details of that land grab out at Knockban for me?'

In due course the music died away and, wet, deflated and a little puzzled, the musicians came back to their homes where there was no sniggering that night as they dried their sodden coats before the fire.

The Committee, sneaking into Gormans when the lamps went down to their secret glow, looked at each other, baffled. Johnny was not dismayed, stretching his long legs out to the fire, the grin on his face recognising his adversary.

'I'd not know what he's up to,' he said, 'but that Sergeant's no fool. We'll not play cat and mouse with him for long. Enough to have him off his balance this week, but I'd say that was the end of it. Now we have other matters to discuss. Instructions for Thursday night. Are you listening Bridie? Willya pull your skirts down and not be distracting all the lads, and pay attention.'

Ned by this time was in the hard iron-framed bed in the small room he had to himself in the Barracks. Cold, and thinking nostalgically of the warm feather bed at home in Clumbane. Thinking with some relish of what he was going to do in the morning; thinking he had been over a fortnight in the village and had not yet set eyes on Kate Mary; thinking what chance did he have anyway, and he a Sergeant of Police that most girls would spit at.

But Kate Mary wasn't most girls.

He fell asleep, the waterfall of black hair gleaming in his mind's eye. And the wide, wise candour of her eyes. And the grace of her walking. Not most girls. Not any other girl. Kate Mary, whom he had never forgotten.

Nor had he forgotten the Town Band.

Next morning he paraded his three Constables, wishing they were ten more. By the time even the three of them were finished in Connorstown today, the grins would be faded and the knives out.

'I have a list here,' he said, 'of the Town Band. And a few more for good measure, that do practise with them.'

He laid down the list and they looked at him as if he was an eejit. Didn't they know every man Jack in the Town Band. What would they want a list for?

'Search their houses,' Ned said tersely. 'I want no one

harmed, but I want their homes turned upside down. If I come past the most of what they own isn't out in the streets, then that's where you could well find yourselves. See they have no easy, task putting it all straight.'

Constable Doyle's narrow eyes glittered, but Constable Murphy had been too long with the old Sergeant. His mouth fell open.

'But Sergeant, Sir,' he said, 'won't it cause terrible trouble in the town.'

Ned eyed him coldly.

'That is exactly what I want, Constable. Terrible trouble in the town, and I'm sending you out to make it. This is a Police Barracks, but you seem here to have forgotten the word duty. Away with you.'

They came back with only a cornet, a small bugle and a battered drum. Ned had expected no more, but when he himself, with cool disinterested face, went out to patrol the streets where people were still gathering the belongings that had been tossed out the windows, he knew that the time of jokes was over. The truce was at an end.

The night was silent, but in the morning they found someone had daubed 'British Scum,' in white paint on the green door of the Barracks:

Constable Murphy was scandalised.

'And me,' he said, 'born and bred in Tralee, and all my family before me!'

'In that case, Constable,' said Ned, 'aren't you the very man to get out the green paint and paint it over.'

For Constable Murphy too, the truce was over.

Thursday night was in total silence.

Only two soldiers on patrol outside Westport reported a drunk in a pony and trap going home from a wedding, making for the direction of Connorstown.

'Too drunk to bite 'is own finger, Sir,' the Corporal reported. 'The 'orse was takin' 'im 'ome. Couldn 'a bin up to nothin' in that state.'

The report was filed away as was every one on people moving in the district after dark.

*   *   *

On Friday, since there was a customer in the Post Office to watch her, Elsie O'Flyn reluctantly answered the jangle of the telephone, admitting with the same reluctance, lest she involve herself in anything, that she was the Connorstown Post Office. Then she listened, an ugly pleasure dawning in her small face.

'G'wan away out of that,' she said to her customer as she hung the receiver back in its rest. 'G'wan away outa that.' The poor man protested that all he wanted was a penny stamp. 'Didn't I tell you to get out of it,' she said. 'You can get yer stamp later. Haven't I a message to go.'

Hustling him out into the street, she locked the Post Office door and scuttled as fast as her thick black-clad legs would carry her, up the road to the chandlers. Her brother Liam lurked in the dark overcrowded shadows, surrounded by sacks of meal and coils of rope and ploughshares and seed potatoes. It smelt dank and earthy as though it were all underground.

Elsie didn't even notice it.

'Liam,' she said urgently. 'Liam! Willya guess who's coming into town this afternoon, and no more than a lady's maid with her!'

She told him, and Liam blinked and put behind his ear the stub of a pencil he had been using for his accounts. He began to unbutton his long brown cotton coat, his freckled face cold.

'She's a fool,' he said. 'And he's a bigger fool to allow her.'

'Well now,' said Elsie reasonably, but her eyes were bright and malicious behind the pebble glasses, 'why wouldn't she come in, the creature. Connorstown never did anyone any harm.'

'That,' said Liam, 'was yesterday.'

Kate Mary got a lift to Connorstown that afternoon with the local doctor who came to the village twice a week, leaving it to God to help those who were foolish enough to fall sick on any other day and to old one-eyed Ellen Doherty to deliver their babies should she be sober enough.

He put Kate Mary down at the edge of the village, where he had a call to make.

'Will that do, Miss Pearse?'

'It'll do me well, Doctor. And thanks. Goodbye now.'

Kate Mary walked the length of a straight grey street, still plastered with the dung of Wednesday's Fair, and thought it strangely empty. Many of the shops close to the Square were standing open without their owners. Puzzled, she went on, and turned into the Square itself.

Most of the villager's were there, gathered strangely silent, and there was no laughter to be heard among them, only an air of unkind satisfaction that made her at once uncomfortable, like seeing a shadow that had not been there before. God help her, was it the shadow of Johnny and his friends?

Over on the other side of the square, she could see him, up above them all on the seat of his cart, and anxiously she pushed her way towards him. He held out a hand to help her over the wheel, and like all the rest of them, his face was inimical: only his lazy eyes gleaming with some unholy pleasure.

'What is it, Johnny? What's happening?'

Before he could answer, she saw first Bridie in the Post Office door, bald pleasure in the grin on her face. Then on the broken pavement she saw a young woman, as tall as herself but fair, dressed beautifully in a fawn dustcoat and a beaver hat. She was standing absolutely straight and still, as if alone in this hostile Square, her dignity defiant and contemptuous. Beside her a little maid in black sobbed noisily and wrung her hands.

At the kerb was a beautiful varnished dog cart, sitting foolishly like a box on the road; the wheels gone and the horse vanished from between the fallen shafts.

'Johnny, for God's sake! It's Mrs. Bonnington Clay!'

'It is indeed.' Johnny was laconic.

'Well, what happened? What in heaven happened?'

Kate Mary was appalled at the slow line of tears following one another down the girl's proud face.

'It seems,' Johnny said with immense innocence, 'she sent her maid to the Medical Hall and went in to Elsie for some parcel from Dublin. Bridie was before her in there and in some trouble with a letter – '

'Bridie!' Kate Mary began to see it all. The poor girl!

'So Mrs. Resident Magistrate was a long time waiting, and

69

didn't some dastardly fellows come along and have the horse loose and the wheels off before you could say hand me my parcel.'

'Ah, Johnny. Would you do that to a woman.'

His attitude was changed. Once he would have regarded this as a jape, laughing his sides sore. Now there was only the same cold unkindness as on all the other faces. Something must have happened in the week she was away.

'And the horse?'

'Oh, he made for home like he should never have left it, and the Sergeant after him with his long legs when he passed the Barracks. The wheels went another way on a tinker's cart. I'd envisage they're in the bog by now. He has a half crown for doing it.'

In silence she accepted that Johnny had planned it all. Successfully.

'But where are the Police?'

'There's one in the country on his day off, and one in there bullying hell out of poor Elsie to know why it all took so long. The good Sergeant left the horse to go home and is no doubt banging and slamming at that yoke of a telephone to get on to Westport or the R.M. while he still has his stripes. Her man'll have to get out that big red motor car of his to come and get her. I think we'll go home now before it happens.'

Bridie came past the cart at that moment, and her small secret smile held triumph and congratulation. The look of pure venom she turned on Kate Mary was like a physical shock.

'What have I done to her?' she asked instinctively, and read the answer in Johnny's silence, knowing nothing of a flaming row during the week when Bridie accused him of paying too much attention to Kate Mary. He had had no answer because he knew; that in his heart he had already left her, even if Kate Mary would as yet, have none of him.

Caught between two women, by damn, like any green fool, and now no satisfaction to be got from either of them.

He shook up the reins to start the pony and Kate Mary looked over to where the girl stood immobile, her maid now screaming abuse in some language that only made the faces round her break into grins of derision. She saw poor silly old

Miss Greeley from the Lawn sidling up to the girl with a fawning smile, as one lady to another. It got her no more than a glance of total indifference, as if she wasn't there, causing in Kate Mary a spurt of irritation. She didn't go along with Johnny but were they so superior, these English, that the young woman couldn't even take a word of kindness when she got one?

She was sick and cold and full of fear. Once Johnny and his friends started tangling with people like the R.M., they'd be hunted like dogs. And Johnny's charmed luck couldn't hold out forever.

Clear of the town through which they had driven in silence, all the people looking at Johnny from the corners of their eyes, Kate Mary spoke again.

'I'd feel sorry for her, Johnny,' she said. 'Alone there and all the people hating her,' she thought again of the shape of the fawn dustcoat. 'And I'd think she's not all that long away from having a baby.'

'Then she should stay at home,' Johnny answered shortly. 'And I mean in England. She has no right in Ireland.'

Kate Mary didn't answer.

'No R.M. has a right in Ireland,' he went on, and there was anger and enmity in his voice she hadn't heard before. 'Isn't he cramming our lads into jail ever time the Court sits in Westport, and the Police there dressed up in their high boots and their spiked helmets to look after him. We want them all out. Every single damned one of them.'

'So that's why you did it.'

'It is.'

'And the Police too, do you want them out as well?'

'The Police, is it?' We do want them out. Turning on their own people.'

Fleetingly she remembered the boy who had walked home with her from Tuam on that night long ago, although it was miles out of his way. What, she wondered briefly, had become of him?

'They're only doing their duty, Johnny. Only doing what they always did. Isn't it the people have turned against them?'

'You talk like the English!'

She looked through the blue and gold evening, the sky to

71

the west draped scarlet with the last banners of a torn sunset, the fields so green behind their stone walls, it would hurt your heart.

'Ah, no, Johnny, I'm Irish.' She was wrenched with sadness that it seemed suddenly so difficult to be what she had always been.

'Then you must make up your mind,' he said as he had said before. But not gently now. Not with laughter.

Then he did start to laugh, suddenly.

'It was well done,' he said. 'Liam and I planned it with Elsie and Bridie, and all since the morning. They won't come back to Connorstown in a hurry.'

'And you think nothing will be done about it, Johnny? The R.M. and the Police? They'll not leave it.'

'Oh, we have the measure of them. They have no idea who to look for.'

For a little while he whistled happily and turned to look at Kate Mary as if it was the first time he had seen her that day. The expression in his eyes, running all over her made her nervous again. It couldn't be that he was admiring her old grey coat and cap.

'Kate Mary, alannah,' he said, 'but you're beautiful.' For a moment he stared at her in silence. 'You're turning into a grand girl. Have you a man over there in Westport? Do you have, I'll need to kill him! Now tomorrow night, you'll come to the Dance with me, won't you? This time, you'll come.'

He squeezed her knee and her temper rose, 'I will not, Johnny. You'll be wanting to talk over with Bridie how well you upset that poor woman. It's no place for me.'

Johnny grew angry too.

'Get along with you. You're a prig, Kate Mary.'

His voice was harsh and his handsome face fallen into the sullen lines of a thwarted child. All his life, Johnny had had his own sublime way. He could not accept now that anyone, from the Police to Kate Mary, could halt his gallop.

But Kate Mary was looking up at the long line of the white house of Caherliss, and thinking of reprisals. The Police didn't wait for much proof these days before they came with the paraffin cans and burnt out the ones that gave them trouble. Trouble had only just begun in Connorstown. How long for Caherliss?

Sombre, she turned her wide sad eyes on his furious face with an insulted expression.

'I'm not a prig, Johnny. But I'm afraid.'

Johnny went out that night after the meal as he so often did, and after a bit of sewing by the fire, and the quiet murmuring of the Rosary, kneeling at their chairs, Kate Mary and Aunt Margaret went to bed.

It was into total darkness that Kate Mary woke from a deep sleep. Even the fire was dead at the end of the vestibule; no smallest glow coming from the door which was always left open to warm her room.

Tensely she listening for the sound that had awakened her, thinking again of the fox in the hen run. There was no attempt now to disguise noises. There was the ring of pick on stone, a wheelbarrow rattling across the yard, restless stirrings from the pony in a moment of silence, the soft protesting clucks of the disturbed hens. She lay stiff, her eyes wide, not frightened yet for she could find nothing to be frightened of. She was so intense on her listening that the darkness broke into bright circles before her staring eyes.

She waited for uproar: for Johnny to come racing, shouting, from his room; for Aunt Margaret to come calling after him what was it in the name of God? In a country district in Ireland, there were no robbers. What a man did not have, to till his land, the neighbours lent him. There was no cause to steal.

Slowly she realised that there would be no uproar. The noises outside went on, and with them the occasional murmur of men's voices but the house itself remained as silent as the grave her terrified imagination could see being dug outside. Whose grave? Whatever was going on, Johnny was involved in it, and Aunt Margaret keeping prudently in her bed and deliberately knowing nothing at all.

He tongue was dry against her mouth. Whatever was being done was being done at dead of night because it couldn't be done by light of day, when anyone might see it, including her.

In a surge of obstinacy, she threw back the quilts and slipped out of bed, her feet cramping against the icy cold of the stone floor which seeped through the worn carpet. Shivering, she wrapped herself in the old black shawl she kept for the house at night, and went out into the vestibule in thick darkness. It was a little warmer from the last embers of the fire, but she shook still, from apprehension, glancing at Aunt Margaret's door and Johnny's, both firmly closed. Then she turned to the faint glow out in the yard.

Not too close to the window, she thought cautiously, lest even the small lantern show the pale blur of her face. For the first time, she felt frightened for herself, overlaying her constant fear for Johnny. He might not be pleased at her probing his secrets, although God knew, with all the noise they were making, he couldn't expect her not to hear.

The lantern hung on a nail at the end of the house, and in its frail light they had removed the big stones from the banking of the High Garden. The stones gone, piled at the side, they were making a sort of cave in the earth behind them, trundling the loose, telltale stuff away somewhere in a wheelbarrow. As Kate Mary crept to the window, they were completing their cave, shoring it up with lengths of timber clearly cut beforehand to the right length. Forgetting, she put her face up against the window to see better.

For God's sake, what were they up to?

There were Johnny and Paddy and Liam O'Flyn, Elsie's brothers, and Pierce Caffery from the mill, but although they spoke now and then, she could hear nothing: only catch the intentness of conspiracy.

A hiding place? For what? And a secret one, or why else make it at the dead of night with no one there to see – except her. And fear touched her again.

They were building back the stones now, even stuffing in the plants where they had pulled them out, and she was just about to turn and go, to hide in her bed like Aunt Margaret and know nothing, when Johnny saw her.

For a shattered moment, he paused, caught by the shock of seeing what seemed to be Kate Mary's disembodied face, floating inside the window. The small light of the lantern fell full on his face, and she didn't understand his stunned and wide-eyed look, not thinking of the picture she made with her black hair falling loose around her face and the black shawl wrapped to her chin, only her face white and luminous in the light.

74

The she moved and the banshee vision vanished and became Kate Mary, and at the fear in her face Johnny gave a small enigmatic smile, calm and triumphant. He didn't give a damn what she had seen. Indeed, he was pleased. She was in it now like the rest of them, whether she would or not.

He turned to pick up another rock, and she ran, shaking, back to her bed, even the heavy shawl cold against her skin, and the bitter chill of the floor reaching up along her shin bones. None of it was colder than her fear for Johnny. If he ever came to grief it would be because of this devil-may-care attitude that would never stoop to care or secrecy.

Huddled under the bedclothes, she couldn't stop thinking about the expression she had seen in his eyes. As well as the message of indifference, there was a private one in those few quick seconds that reminded her of the quick caress in the kitchen, and the way he had squeezed her knee coming home in the cart.

'All I am doing, Kate Mary,' his eyes seemed to say, 'you are involved in. And involved with me, too.'

'I am not,' she thought stubbornly. 'I am not.'

For the first time since she had come to Caherliss she lay awake, aware of the quietening of the sounds outside, and the settling of the disturbed livestock. Aware, as never before, of her open door, and Johnny's room along the vestibule where he must come when he was finished, knowing she was awake. Her cold skin crawled with uneasy and unhappy nerves. Not with any fear that she could not cope with Johnny, but with the sad knowledge that she had never before had to think of it. The passing of the dark cold night saw for Kate Mary the end of more securities than one.

She heard them in the kitchen then: the bang of the kettle on the teapot and a lot of fierce low-toned talk. The others went, and there was the slam of the kitchen door. Johnny's step came along the passage, and she realised she was lying rigid, listening. He came along the vestibule and turned at once into his own room, closing the door.

Feeling a little foolish, she snuggled down then and slowly the warmth of the feather bed crept in to soothe away both cold and anxiety. But there was no sleep until after the first raucous blaring of the cock, after the first touch of pale winter light had made a square of the vestibule window, leaving the wall above the high garden still in shadow.

Even as she drifted at last into sleep, there crept like a snake through her tired mind the certainty of what it was that Johnny and the others were hiding behind the rocks and flowers of the High Garden.

It might all have been a dream when she looked out in the morning. The wall seemed untouched. She went into the kitchen where the fire glowed scarlet, and said good morning to her aunt, who stood expressionless at the kitchen table, laying strips of bacon in the big black pan.

'Did you sleep well?' she could not help asking her.

Aunt Margaret didn't look up, intent on what she did, as though to lay a strip of bacon straight took all the concentration in the world.

'I did,' she said. 'Thank God. Why wouldn't I?'

With a sense that everything was sliding away from under her feet, leaving a great hole full of fear, Kate Mary noticed that her aunt showed no surprise at the question, although such small courtesies were not the normal tenor of Caherliss.

'I'll let the hens out,' she said.

To get into the yard and have a better look.

The clumps of saxifrage had been carefully rearranged between the stones, and who would notice if a couple of them died in the winter? They often did. In the clear morning light there was a sparkle between the paving stones where water lay after their washing down of the yard, and a bright pool lay around the pump. Otherwise there was no smallest trace of what had been done. Where was the tell tale earth? The hiding place was perfect. For what? For the means and starting point of violence and death.

The beautiful chilly morning was dark with her fear and foreboding for Johnny. Death or imprisonment or having to race by night for the first boat to America. They weren't safe even in England nowadays.

Oh, Johnny. And Aunt Margaret knew.

As she stood there weighed with this feeling of heaviness, as though she had suddenly grown old, he came into the yard, whistling cheerfully. He was up from the milk pen with a bucket of milk for his mother. The Lad would bring the rest up to the icy dairy after breakfast. No traces of the night lay on Johnny, his face fresh with the air of the morning, and his long body calm with his own private satisfaction.

His eyes gleamed when he saw her there by the back door, staring at the wall, and for a moment she almost stepped at once back into the house. Then she steadied herself, shocked. This was still Johnny.

'Didn't we make a good job of it,' he said with pride, as though she had known about it all along.

'It depends,' she answered cautiously, 'what the job was for. There are some jobs are never good.'

Johnny set down the bucket of milk, splashing white on the damp stones, and bringing the yard cat racing, followed by a couple of thwarted hens. As though he realised her impulse to run from him, he put a long arm out, hand against the wall, to bar her way. Only a week ago she would have given him a push, tussled cheerfully to get past. Now she stood quiet, uncomfortable, the tabby lapping round her feet. It was clear from Johnny's face that he was going to say something unwelcome, something that would cause trouble. She hoped to God, sensing what it would be, that it wouldn't all be too difficult. Why could things never stay the same?

His eyes were very blue and clear, intent on her face.

'Kate Mary,' he said, 'it's Saturday. The Dance, in the village. Will you come with me as my partner?'

Come with him? Many years she had come with him, since she was first old enough to be let go at all, but always to dance with anyone who asked her from the long line of boys on the other side of the cold hall. And Johnny there to keep an eye on her, and on them, and take her home whenever she wanted to go.

'A child's life, Kate Mary Pearse,' she told herself sharply now. 'How could you hope it would go on forever?'

Actually going with him was something different, a declaration to the whole village. His request was almost a proposal of marriage.

'And what,' she asked him bluntly, being Kate Mary and not apt for deviousness, 'of Bridie Bannion?'

He had been making this declaration publicly with Bridie

77

for as long as she could remember and hadn't honoured it. Shaming her, as much as Bridie would accept shame, before everyone.

Johnny's long mouth compressed to a hard line.

'That's none of your business. I ask who I like.'

'It is my business, and I'll not play second fiddle to Bridie Bannion, and all Connorstown watching and red hot with gossip about what's going on. And she fit to murder me into the bargain. I have more respect for myself, Johnny.'

She couldn't add that the Johnny of the bullets and the wall – and dear God was she right about what they had put in there? – was a different Johnny, a new person that she didn't know and wouldn't commit herself to, just like that. She looked at him now, her face so close to his, with caution and concern.

'No, Johnny.'

'Kate Mary – '

'No.' She shook her head. She wouldn't even go with him as she had always done. It wouldn't be the same. Ever again. Nothing would ever be the same. Something good had passed and the future was uncertain and cold.

She sighed.

'Ah, Johnny,' she said. 'I'm sorry.'

And meant for everything. For all the change and the lost bright easy happiness that she knew would never be recovered.

Without saying more, he moved his arm and let her into the kitchen to the things that still remained the same. The smell of bacon in the pan, and the hot fresh bread Aunt Margaret would have been up to bake at cockcrow. The Lad, who always had his breakfast with them, was there already, apple-cheeked and respectful, sitting at the end of the table, where he would eat his meal in silence, covered in confusion if anyone should speak to him. Then he would vanish, touching his thin forelock, back to his long day's work.

A gangling man of over thirty, Aunt Margaret had had him since he really was a lad, and thought him worth three of any other men, plying him with Johnny's old clothes and baskets of food for the small cottage where he lived alone with his devoted dog.

Even he, behind his blank retiring face, was aware that the Aunt was fussy and restless, as though her night's sleep had not been good. And some sullen thundercloud lay on Johnny's handsome face across the table.

Gratefully, as soon as he swallowed the last bite, the Lad grabbed his cap and slid out the door to another day of his steady, single-minded work.

Chapter 4

Kate Mary had heard of the theft of some gelignite before she came home the previous day, but had heeded it no more than all the other tales of death and violence edging their lives with fear. It was as bad as any other, with the implied threat of more trouble to come, but no close concern of hers.

Mrs. Garvey had arrived back from early Mass in a high state of alarm and indignation. As she began to unwind her black shawl and ladle out the thick stirabout she had made the night before, she was full of her drama.

The limestone quarry out on the road to Leenane had been raided by a gang of the rebel villains; Mrs. Garvey herself had been staunchly for King and Country, as meaning England, ever since the day when she was a young woman and the present King was the Prince of Wales. She had gone to see him on his state visit to Ireland with the late and little lamented Tom Garvey. When the inlet got too narrow the destroyer bringing the Prince had been forced to moor below Leenane, but the good loyal people had put ropes on a boat and dragged him all the rest of the way, until he ate his dinner like any decent man there in McKeown's Hotel.

The incident had left a lasting impression of his ordinary pleasantness and she had felt it all to be no more than he deserved, and he such a fine figure of a man. With that day forever in her mind, she felt every rebel to be the direct enemy of the English Crown.

Furious loyalty drove her to relate all the details of the robbery.

Only God would know, it seemed, how many devils there

were, with the quarry criss-crossed like a cat's cradle with bicycle tracks. On bicycles, if you please! The store for the dynamite was broken open, and the poor old night watchman tied up with a cloth put in his mouth so he could hardly draw his breath.

'What, will you tell me,' she cried, slapping down the stirabout in front of Kate Mary, 'are the villains going to blow up with that lot? We'll never be safe in our beds, not to be exploded there.'

'Ah, Mrs. Garvey, I doubt they'd want to blow us up. Sure, what would be doing to annoy them?'

Kate Mary made a careful hole in the middle of her stirabout, relishing the mealy, wintry smell of it, and filled it with milk, then reached for the sugar. She barely ever listened to Mrs. Garvey's sagas.

'We could,' said her landlady darkly, 'be passing or something.'

Her thin little face was alive with the sensation and Kate Mary didn't trouble to sort out how they could have been passing by some explosion in their beds.

'Did they take much?' she asked with little interest, handing back her empty bowl and getting in exchange two rashers and a big golden egg, fresh from the pan on the range. Mrs. Garvey was an old crab, but her food was grand. Warm inside you on a cold morning. Kate Mary found it hard to believe in these local lads blowing up buildings; killing people. Would they go so far? Surely these things only happened in Dublin, and the other cities.

'Take much?' Mrs. Garvey slammed the black heavy pan back on the range and looked up at the gaudy picture of the Sacred Heart above the fire, blessing herself with an air of desperation. 'They'd have taken all they needed, the rogues, for whatever dastardly act is planned.'

They'd have to hide it somewhere.' Kate Mary knew nothing about gelignite, and why would she? Was it big or small or what, or something like gunpowder? She thought of Johnny and the bullets. Nothing to do with him, thank God, away over there.

'They'd hide it,' said Mrs. Garvey grimly. 'Isn't that their business. And don't they do it well.'

Even then, Kate Mary was touched by no more than a general apprehension of something that would not come close to her.

She finished her breakfast, and the old wag-at-the-wall clock told her it was time to leave the warm kitchen and go reluctantly into the ice cold world of the Convent School, where all the newfangled amenities did not include heating of any kind. The children sat with little pinched and red-nosed faces, huddled in all the clothes their poor mothers could provide, and like herself scratched their chilblains in misery all the winter.

There was something special about the cold of a Convent. Not even in the softest summer did this place get warm, and she had long concluded that as nuns never changed their clothes anyway, they never knew one weather from the other. Or cared. It would come between them and God. Sometimes, more deeply and more muddled, she wondered whether the lack of all earthly affection could lay its chill even on bricks and stone.

In the endless battle against the chilblains, she pulled on a pair of woollen mittens.

'I'll be away to Caherliss straight after school, Mrs. Garvey,' she said at the door. 'I have to look for a lift. Johnny has my bicycle for the week.'

And still she didn't think.

No thread of warning touched her about the bicycle. When she did reach Connorstown it was all put out of her head by the dreadful trick they played on poor Mrs. Bonnington Clay which was much more real and upsetting than some vague fear of being blown from her bed in Mrs. Garvey's back bedroom.

As Kate Mary sat down to her breakfast, Aunt Margaret asked her to go into Connorstown for some shopping.

'Is my bicycle here, Johnny?' she asked.

'It is. Why wouldn't it be?'

The blue eyes were cold. He was still not pleased with her.

'And not broken?'

She tried to tease him.

'Ah, Kate Mary. Give it over.'

82

It wasn't broken when she went out into the grey morning to get it from the open barn where it was stored between the plough and the harrow and the winter's hay.

But it was covered with white dust.

She looked at it for a long time, feeling faint and sick, as though even to touch it would implicate her.

What a fool she was. A fool, a fool, a fool! It should have slammed into her head the moment Mrs. Garvey had said the raid was done on bicycles. Then she cursed Johnny for an even bigger fool then she was, that he hadn't cleaned it. Other people wouldn't be as slow in putting two and two together.

'Ah, God, Johnny!' she thought, and grief and fear closed her throat. 'Ah, Johnny, you eejit. You *eejit* that you cannot leave it all alone.

Hastily, her hands trembling she pushed the bicycle over to the pump and filled a bucket, not even noticing the anguish of the cold water against her swollen chilblains. Most of the dust was on one side, embedded in the pedals and thick round the rims of the wheel and on the dress guard, as though it had been thrown down where the stuff was thick. What kind of a fool was Johnny to have left it like that?

Carefully and thoroughly she washed it, her mouth dry with fear, getting the old scrubbing brush from the yard to clean the pedal. She could hear Aunt Margaret along in the bedroom, Johnny long gone to the fields. Well for him, she thought bitterly, to be out of it if anything happened. He could run for it from down there.

It happened just as she was finishing, wringing the cloth with numbed fingers. She crouched defensively, to be pretending still cleaning the wheel to distract herself from the meaning of the hammering on the front door; men's shouting voices and Aunt Margaret answering them in shrill anger.

'Oh, God,' she whispered, as though he were there. 'Oh, God, Johnny, run for it.'

Rubbing stupidly at what was already clean.

She heard the heavy boots clattering on the floors, thumping down the vestibule, the doors flung open. They were beginning to search the house, Aunt Margaret screaming abuse behind them.

From the open door of the scullery, Ned burst into the yard.

She found it impossible even to get up, crouched there beside the bicycle in the puddled water with cold red hands, nor could he move another step. Both of them were immobile in the moment they had imagined for years but never foreseen like this. It was destroyed by the manner of their meeting.

Ned recovered first, duty over-riding everything. In the raging journey out, hell bent on this time catching his man, he had actually forgotten Kate Mary and was now as stunned as she was by the confrontation.

But duty was duty.

'Why are you cleaning that bicycle?' he demanded, ferocity hopelessly undermined by the shattering pleasure of watching her stand up slowly to her full graceful height. She'd grown, by God, to perfection. She stood facing him with her head in the air and not a trace of fear on her.

'Because it's dirty, Ned Brannick,' she said. 'Don't I clean it every Saturday.

Far from feeling no trace of fear, she was sick with it. But as she stood up the warm irresistible pleasure of seeing him again took over. He looked a lot older, a lot, and harder, and at the moment he was raging, two blazes of colour high on the thin skin of his cheekbones. Still he was very smart, with the two little spikes of his moustache.

Aunt Margaret came to the scullery door, white with fright and anger.

'Willya tell these two savages of yours,' she yelled at Ned, 'to leave my house alone.'

Kate Mary could see one of them through the vestibule window, dragging the drawers from the chest and flinging all there was in them on to the floor.

'We've nothing for you here.'

Aunt Margaret's voice was beginning to waver and Kate Mary went over quickly and put an arm round her.

'They're only doing their duty, ma'am,' Ned said. 'And I must do mine.'

He raced over and began tearing apart the hay stacked in the open barn while Kate Mary watched him, her mouth compressed and her tongue dry, forcing herself not to look over at the wall. She had noticed nothing unusual about it this morning; the dry plants of winter hanging down apparently undisturbed.

'What in the name of God are they looking for? What would Johnny have here?'

Kate Mary realised that Aunt Margaret really didn't know. Maybe Johnny had never hidden anything at home before. The bullets had seemed to vanish.

How big was dynamite? Would it go in the hole in the wall?

Ned had worked his destructive way along the barn, heaving out everything he could lay hands on, and then from the shed beside it. Now the hens fled squawking through the chaos as he ploughed into the hen house.

'Ah, the fool,' yelled Aunt Margaret, recovering her spirit. 'Look at the size of him. Won't he knock it down?'

He didn't, but when he came out awkwardly, backwards, his cap had been knocked off and there were feathers in his hair and on his dark tunic. Furiously he brushed at them, shamed to look ridiculous before Kate Mary. She tried to keep a smile from her mouth.

Angry and defeated he glared round him, everywhere but at her; saw the steps to the High Garden.

'What's up there?'

'None of your business.'

The search was finding nothing and Aunt Margaret beginning to flame back.

Ned strode across the yard and up the wall, and Kate Mary felt her face set tight with fear, goose pimples running along her arms. She took her arm away from Aunt Margaret lest she feel the trembling. What if his big boots shook loose the stones?

As he was prowling on the grass of the High Garden, Johnny came charging up from the fields where someone had raced to warn him. Although he stormed into the yard with every appearance of anger, Kate Mary could see the alarm leap to his eyes when he saw where the Sergeant was, a tall black figure up above them against the clear blue winter sky.

She knew Johnny waited as she did, dry-mouthed, for Ned's weight to cave in the roof of the hole or bring down the stones. Neither happened, and when Ned saw Johnny he came down.

Johnny made a careful pretence of calm, his hands in his pockets and a long straw picked from the ground trailing from his mouth, but in his eyes blazed the excitement of the danger he loved.

Ned was baffled, furious, having to look at the man he wanted lounging idly in front of him, staring him up and down with mocking eyes.

'What are you doing here, O'Connor? Shouldn't you be running for your life?'

Johnny took the straw slowly from his mouth.

'What would I be running from, Sergeant?' he said easily, 'Would it be from your two boyos making a pig's nest of my mother's house, because they have nothing better to do? Get them on away, and see if you can't catch a child stealing an egg or something.'

Kate Mary could see the rigidity of Ned's tall body. She realised he was longing to put a fist through Johnny's teeth.

All he said was, with careful formality, 'Where were you on Thursday night?'

Johnny turned innocent eyes on his mother.

'Where was I on Thursday night, Mama?'

'Weren't you here asleep in your bed. Where else would he be?' she spat at Ned.

'Were you in Westport?'

'Did anybody see me there?'

'They might have done.'

Ned knew he was on ground so thin that it was no ground at all. Dragged back to be questioned again on their report, the two soldiers who had met the drunk in the pony and trap couldn't even agree on the size of the man they had seen; protesting it was black as the 'obs of 'ell, and he had the peak of his cap down over his face.

They were also unwilling to help too much to identify him as, when found, he could well reveal that while out on patrol they had both gladly had a swig of his whisky bottle.

Johnny had seen to it that they would never know him again, warm with laughter as he trotted off into the night, the whole pile of gelignite in the well of the trap. All the others had gone in on bicycles, and brought it to him where he waited in a bohreen a mile away. They had all gone their separate ways home along the back roads, and he alone along the main one.

Now there it all was, safely behind the wall, and the big lad of a Sergeant looking like a bull that had just been penned. God, but it was a great life for Ireland. Everything was going grand.

'Did you want me for anything else, Sergeant?' he said reasonably, and Kate Mary thought Ned would burst. 'I'll need to help my mother tidy her house.'

There was silence inside, and Constable Doyle came out of the scullery door. He saluted Ned.

'Well?'

'Nothing, Sergeant. Not a gun nor a bullet nor a thing.'

He sounded defeated and amazed, and Johnny looked at him with contempt. What sort of an eejit did they think he was?

'I could always kill someone, Constable,' he said caustically, 'with the knife me mother keeps for the meat. Did you think of that?'

Ned stood irresolute and fuming. He couldn't arrest Johnny O'Connor because a couple of soldiers had seen a drunk they would never recognise again. He had looked at the trap, not a trace of dust, and he would never know about the bicycle. He bit like a bullet on the thought that Kate Mary could be implicated.

Into the silence Kate Mary spoke suddenly, and as soon as she had done so, was ashamed of her forwardness. She thought her racing heart would betray her.

'I'll be going,' she said to Aunt Margaret, 'down to the town for the messages before Gorman's closes. I'll help you clear all this up afterwards.'

She dare not look at Ned as she went into the house to get her purse, but heard him dismissing the two Constables, who climbed on their bicycles and rode stony-faced through the small jeering crowd that had gathered at the farm gate.

Ned came through the house to follow them, and Aunt Margaret, white-faced, sat down suddenly in a chair in the middle of her kitchen.

Ned turned at the door.

'You're away with it again, O'Connor,' he said. 'But value

87

your time. I'll have you in the end.'

'You and what army?' said Johnny with contempt.

'The British,' Ned answered levelly. 'If I need them, the British. Goodbye now, Kate Mary. And be careful. You're keeping bad company.'

'Kate Mary. Kate Mary!' Johnny's blue eyes flamed as he watched Ned take his bicycle from beyond the window. 'Thick-headed eejit! Who in hell is he to call you Kate Mary?'

'An old friend,' Kate Mary said, and she too watched as the tall dark-uniformed back went away across the pasture lane. 'And you be the one to be careful, Johnny. He's not thick-headed.'

'He's that and more.'

Johnny stormed off out to clear up the yard.

'I'll go now, Aunt Margaret.'

She looked at the white shocked face of the older woman, but Aunt Margaret's mouth was set in a hard line of anger and Kate Mary knew she was in no danger of collapsing.

Out in the yard she took her clean bicycle, and trembled to think that her action might have saved Johnny's life. The fool! She ignored him where he was slamming things furiously back into the barn, and bumped off down the stones of the back bohreen. She would with the help of God be just about right. A small smile that she could not keep from her face despite all that had happened faded with the thought that she might have misjudged the whole business and would find herself doing no more than going into Connorstown to the store. Ah, no. That would be terrible.

Ned had looked very stern, and it could be that he had no more on his mind than the raid. For the moment she banished all thought of Johnny running headlong into danger, unable to do anything but wonder had she been right about Ned and the unspoken message that had passed between them?

She was right.

She found him exactly as she thought she would, in a lonely stretch of road about half a mile beyond the end of the bohreen, fiddling busily with his bicycle at the side of the wall, his uniform still dusty from the barn.

Trembling, and furious with herself for doing so, she dragged her own machine to a halt, and there were a few moments while they both pretended it was chance that had brought them together again, groping for words to bridge both time and all that had happened up at the house. Then Kate Mary broke into a wide smile, useless at subterfuge.

'You can leave it alone now, Ned,' she said. 'Sure, there's nothing the matter with it.'

Ned clung to his dignity and wouldn't give in so easily.

'My chain,' he said. ''Twas loose.'

There was oil on his fingers, and under Kate Mary's grin his face was sheepish as he wiped them on the grass.

'I'm sorry about the house,' he said, and all the time they were looking at each other; secretly marvelling at the pleasure of meeting again; suddenly without constraint as Ned smiled back at her. Exactly as if they were just going on with that long dark walk out from Tuam.

''Tis hard on my aunt,' Kate Mary said, 'and nothing there.'

'We had reason to think there was.'

His face hardened and the moment of happiness was gone. Scattered like the straw in the barn.

'And whatever it was,' Kate Mary snapped at him, 'did you think you'd find it in the little drawer where she keeps her rosaries and her bottle of holy water? Or in the middle of all my stockings?'

How big, she wondered again in her anger, was this gelignite? Or dynamite or whatever they called it. Small enough to go into the wall anyway.

She saw the tightening of his face; the flare of anger in his eyes.

'Is he your man, or something, that Johnny one?' he demanded, and was cut by the very thought.

'He's my cousin,' she snapped back, and it told him nothing that he wanted to know. Was she still free, as he was himself? With no one else ever in his mind.

'Do you know about what he's up to?'

Her head went up.

'And if I did, I wouldn't tell you. I'm no informer Ned Brannick. And no Sinn Feiner either, if that's any satisfaction to you.'

Hostility, ever close to the surface in their sad land, flared between them. But as they glared at each other, they both became aware again of a face never forgotten; of something beyond politics and the miserable strife tearing apart their world.

'Don't be against me, Kate Mary,' Ned said more gently. He sighed. 'We have hard times with us, and it's hard to believe anyone is on no side at all.'

'I am,' she said stubbornly, and he knew that proud tilt of her head would always make putty of him. 'I want none of it.'

Poor girl, he thought. Poor girl. She'd find it hard to live in the same house as Johnny O'Connor and want none of it. Wasn't her home all over the yard this morning, as she said, and all for Johnny and the side he took.

In the silence, Kate Mary was in all honesty admitting the same thing to herself. Remembering the same conversation with Johnny, and all that she had learnt since. For a long sad moment, she and Ned looked at each other, knowing the uselessness of anything they could say; foreseeing all the difficulties ahead of them.

Ned thought swiftly. He couldn't have her vanishing again. There'd be no time nor place for the formalities. No long peaceful courtship in Connorstown, taking evening walks out round the graveyard road and back across the Lawn like all the other lovers of the town, a declaration of intent as clear and formal as taking a girl to the dance on a Saturday night.

None of that for them; with what he was, and she from the home of Johnny O'Connor, no matter what she claimed for her allegiances.

He knew, too, that it was neither wise nor suitable for him to pursue her, that duty indeed forbade it. But for the first time in his life, duty's demands clamoured against deaf ears.

'Kate Mary,' he said, all his anger gone, 'could I see more of you? Could we meet?'

Touched with instant hopelessness, aware of all that could lie ahead of this one splendid moment of their meeting, she looked away from him, off down the road as though she was already gone, scraping the bright toe of her boot as she kicked a stone.

'There'd be no peace in it for either of us, Ned.'

He grasped at the fact that she hadn't said no.

'Not in Connorstown,' he said urgently. 'That'd be disastrous. But I have to go to Westport every week to report to the D.I. Then it's my day off. Couldn't we meet there?'

Kate Mary knew then that she was looking utterly relieved; delighted. That she was making it all too easy, and most people would say she was being shameless. But it was not in her to dissemble, and she knew deep in her heart that she had waited all these years in the hope of seeing Ned again. Why be coy now?

'I'd be glad,' she said simply, and lifted her face and smiled at him. Ned nearly sat down in the ditch from the pleasure of it. He touched her cold hand, and his own austere face was blurred with his relief. Her hand found its way into his big warm one, and even as they stood there Kate Mary became intensely aware of the long wet grass in the ditch at their feet, and of the seagulls shrieking and clamouring behind a plough two fields away, far inland, driven by storm from the wild hungry seas. It all seemed to mark the moment, and she would treasure it against the future sorrow they could scarcely avoid.

Even then, a bit of her mind was anxious, wondering if the farmer could see them. Ned spoke her thoughts for her.

'Get on now then, Kate Mary,' he said gently and unwillingly. ''Tis not good for either one of us to be seen talking here.'

She sighed and for a moment did not move. This Trouble lay like a black hand over everything.

'What day would it be?'

'Tuesday. Can you do that?'

She nodded.

'I'll be at the gates of the Big House at four o'clock. We mustn't let Mrs. Garvey see us.'

'Mrs. Garvey.'

'My landlady. For her, all men are made in hell for the downfall of young women.'

'But she must have had a man of her own. *Mrs*. Garvey?'

'God rest his poor suffering soul,' Kate Mary said piously, and they both laughed, knowing their first light, forgetful moment, looking into each other's eyes. It was harder then than ever to part.

'Go on,' he urged her. 'Before we're seen.'

He held the saddle for her to get up.

'Is it the same bicycle?' he asked her.

'It is.'

As she wobbled off, it gave him a small mean pleasure to see the dress guard was still trailing. Johnny O'Connor wasn't so perfect after all.

She went on wings to Gorman's, her happiness dimmed only by the realisation that if she saw Ned in the town she mustn't speak to him, never show that they were friendly. She knew what they did to women they believed were informers; nor would they ever wait to be sure they were right.

As she rattled round the corner of the Square, Bridie Bannion glared at her from where she talked with Elsie O'Flyn outside the Post Office. Kate Mary thought ruefully how recently she was telling Johnny that Bridie was no girl to get involved with. Did she have the chance now, she'd shove him into her arms. The argument about the Dance tonight wasn't over yet.

If only she could go there openly with Ned. One or other of the three Constables always used to be there, but it was harder for them now with all Connorstown against them.

She propped her bicycle against the overcrowded window, and in the dark shop Desmond Gorman served her himself. He had flat fair hair and oddly smooth skin that looked an utter stranger to a razor. Across the butter and the bacon he regarded her with caution, his smile never reaching his expressionless eyes. Things were getting serious now and she could be dangerous in Johnny's house. No one knew exactly where she stood. Johnny would never even hear her spoken ill of, sweet on her himself maybe, and that would cause all damnation. 'Twould please Bridie Bannion, too! If it ever came to anything, there'd be hell to pay there.

For all his thoughts, his soft voice was calm and deferential.

'There now, Miss Pearse. Let me put them in the bicycle for you.'

Sugar. Tea. Mustard that Johnny was so fond of with his meat. Robin Starch for his shirt collars, and the extravagance of some shop soap and bacon. They would be killing a pig for Christmas next week, and the smoked sides hanging from the ceiling were near to finished. Thank God she'd be away when they did it, or she'd have to run fields away where she couldn't hear the poor thing screaming.

Aunt Margaret was derisive, calling her a city miss.

'You'll not object to a good bit of roasted pork, or a crubeen to your cabbage, when somebody else has done it.'

'I will,' was Kate Mary's answer, 'if I hear it, or think about it too much.'

Aunt Margaret didn't understand her.

Did she want to be a farmer's wife, she had said, she'd have to get used to these things.

Kate Mary gaped at her. Was Aunt Margaret also determined to marry her off to Johnny? Well, of course. How comfortable, to have it all under one roof. And how simple and silly she had been not to have realised it. She kept silent, glad of the warning, and frightened by the dangers of her own innocence.

As she went back through the Square from Gorman's, Elsie O'Flyn and Bridie broke off their conversation to stare at her, and Kate Mary was certain they had been talking about her.

She hugged to herself the warm knowledge of Ned. That would give them something for their wagging tongues! Let them talk. Not the devil himself could make her nervous today.

When she rode back into the yard at Caherliss, Johnny had the barn tidied, but there was hay still scattered everywhere in wisps and he was busy sweeping up spilt grain and shovelling it back into a sack.

'I had to put the bloody hens in,' he said, 'or they'd have burst themselves. Did you get me cigarettes?'

'I did.'

She fished in the basket for the blue packet of Woodbines. He straightened from the work to take them, and she felt the clutch of fear and sorrow that was becoming familiar. Hard to believe that no time at all ago he was bright as the morning, singing in his cart along the stony roads; ready to do anything for anyone, blue eyes alight.

'Johnny,' she thought sadly, in the words of the song, 'Johnny, we hardly knew you. There was this other man there all the time.'

93

It was the other man who stood up to take the Woodbines; fine face dark with anger and the lines of a stubborn fury beginning to settle around his mouth. His remarkable eyes were as cold and hard as flints. She sighed and would have walked away.

He caught the saddle of her bicycle.

'You haven't answered me about the Dance.'

'I have, Johnny.'

'You haven't said yes.'

'Nor am I going to,' she flared at him. Grieved for him she might be, but she didn't have to go running the moment he crooked his finger. Now above all. 'Go with Bridie,' she said tartly. 'She's down there in the Square with all the look of waiting for you.'

The storm that had brought the seagulls was reaching the farm, and hay and grain whipped round the yard in the first sudden gust of wind.

'Bad cess to that fool of a policeman,' roared Johnny, and then his eyes came back to her.

'What is he to you?' he demanded again. 'Kate Mary this, and Kate Mary that . . . 'Tis Miss Pearse you are to any savage of a peeler.'

'He's an old friend of my family. When I had one,' she said steadily, even though fear cramped her at the thought of how Johnny would behave when he found out the truth.

'Family? Family?' said Johnny. 'Amn't I your family now?'

The blue eyes blazed at her as though he knew the truth already.

'I'd not be pleased,' he said coldly, and she had trouble standing her ground against the expression on his face, 'I'd not be too pleased with any cousin of mine being friendly with a policeman.' Then his face changed, and sorrow touched her again for him. 'You'll not come to the Dance with me?'

'I won't.'

But her tone was gentler, and she reached out to touch his arm, striving for peace between them.

'Ah, Johnny,' she said, 'I – '

But he turned away, swiping viciously with the brush at the grain, the wind tearing it away even as he swept it.

Slowly she went into the barn to leave her bicycle, and to

take the messages in to Aunt Margaret in the house where she was stoically washing potatoes for the dinner in the scullery, the chaos only half settled in the kitchen beyond her and her worn face as expressionless over this as over anything else that concerned her son.

Bridie Bannion got ready for the Dance that night in her parents' house just off the Square, pushing irritably at the litter in the crowded room she shared with her three sisters. They were all younger than herself and as dirty in her eyes as the pigs down in the yard below the window. It would be the gift of God to leave this house and set up somewhere on her own, like the forward girls she read of in her English magazines. But that would be too much altogether for Connorstown. They'd drum her out forever. There was some of them would like to do that anyway.

She knelt down and felt under the bed for the old toffee tin where she kept her precious pots of cream and rouge, and the stuff she got in Dublin to darken her pale eyelashes. She kept her hairbrush there too. Did she leave it out it would be filthy in two days, if not vanished altogether.

There was almost nothing in the room but the two big double brass-knobbed beds, pushed so close together that to get into the second one, you had to climb over the first. Seniority and determination gave her the best place on the outside of the first one, and even then her face was no more than inches from the gaudy wallpaper of faded yellow roses. There was no rug on the narrow patch of icy brown linoleum when she stepped out. A battered dressing table, fought over like any battlefield of the war just gone, took most of the light from the one window looking down on to the yard and the pigs, and when she objected to them her father asked her unkindly did she not relish her bit of fresh bacon as well as any of them. A crack running diagonally across the old mirror lent ugly distortions even to the most beautiful face, and the flyblows pocked it with spots.

Beside it along the wall was a marble-topped washstand with one broken leg propped up on a brick and a basin and a ewer with the spout cracked off, so that water came out from it in uncontrollable gushes. And every drop of it had to be carried up from the tap in the yard. 'Twas as well she was the only one bothered much with washing.

It was plain her sisters didn't much care for it. The rank smell of them hung in the room but it was more wrestling than she could be bothered with to get the uneven window behind the dressing table open, and to prop it with something before it came crashing down on her fingers.

Pushing back the chamber pot she had moved to get her tin, she rummaged for a pair of good silk stockings in the one drawer that was hers alone, under pain of terrible reprisals against her two sisters. Not that it always worked. It wouldn't be past that Maureen to have them on her legs at this very minnit.

For a moment she stood and looked hopelessly at her image in the blurred mirror no light ever reached.

She hated it passionately, every shabby stick and stone of her home; her whining mother and self-satisfied porter-sodden mountain of a father who'd have taken every penny she had were it not for the fact that she was himself all over again: a match for him. He got nothing out of her except the bare cost of her food.

Most of all she loathed this bedroom where her beauty had to struggle for survival against the awfulness of the sagging beds and the flyblown mirror. Her surroundings seemed to quench her like the wick of a candle, from gold light to a small charred stick.

She had money. She could go away to Dublin. Driven by the ruthlessness that had dried into mulish stubborness in her father, and helped by her startling beauty, she had got herself a job with the one solicitor in Connorstown, a sub office to the one he had in Westport. Often she was in sole charge of it. A cut above the rest, Bridie felt herself, and she was disliked in the village for her hardness and her sharp tongue; watched and talked about and disapproved of for her fast clothes and her painted face, and her shameless carry on with Johnny O'Connor.

Johnny O'Connor. She paused with her rabbit's foot in the box of Poudre Takalon, and looked at herself critically between the brown patches of the mirror.

Johnny. That was the reason she didn't go off to Dublin

with the money she had secretly hidden away in this fearful room where you could scarcely hide your blushes, did you have any.

But for him, she'd be gone in the morning. Long ago. And lately she'd begun to wonder, almost in a sick panic, if she'd been wasting her time. Too much attention was going to that high-nosed frozen stick of a cousin of his. The very thinking of Johnny made her body soft with longing, her eyes in their mirror image wide and hazy with desire. She bit her lips to keep her tongue between them, feeling his wide mouth pressed down on them. His hands . . .

God save us, but she was mad for him. It had been days now. Or nights. And some excuse every time. This or that. Always the Cause or something to plan for it, keeping him away. Wasn't she involved too? Why should the Cause keep him away? It was that brought them closer together. Were it only the Cause, she would forgive him, for that would all end when the English were driven out and he could turn to her.

But she wasn't so sure it was only the Cause.

Kate Mary came into her mind like a threat, shivering all she had ever planned for her happiness, even if she never got a bedroom much different to the one she had how; never the pink drapes and the flounced beds of the magazines.

But the room would be clean, and the brass bedstead out in Caherliss would have Johnny sprawling in the feather tick, and that was all she wanted.

Her face lost the blurred look of desire, hardening to hatred, the huge green eyes blazing back at her unevenly from the mirror.

She would never let him go to Kate Mary Pearse.

Never.

She'd see him dead first.

As she was just finishing the last twist of the thick red rope of hair on the back of her neck, her younger sister crashed in, seizing from the litter on the bed an ancient gansey with holes in the elbows; dragging it over a tangle of curls the colour of Bridie's own.

'God bless the work,' she hooted, as her freckled face emerged and she eyed all Bridie's careful get up. 'God bless

97

the work, and they tell me you'll need all of it, and he not as keen on you as he used to be.'

'Get on outa that,' Bridie hissed at her, and would have thrown the hairbrush but that Corrinne danced grinning out of the door and along the passage, laced boots clattering on the oilcloth.

'Lost him,' she jeered. 'Lost him! Lost him!'

And away down the stairs.

Bridie's hands were shaking as she put her jars and bottles back in the toffee tin and pushed it under the bed, her sister's taunting words laying open the wound she hadn't yet acknowledged to herself. It wasn't true. Not true. He just had a lot on his mind for the Cause. Be damned to Corrinne!

By the time she went downstairs, she had recovered the image the village knew: head in air, red hair burnished, and the lace collar miraculously white against her black dress, long silk-stockinged legs – and God help Corrinne if she dared touch the other pair hidden in her pillow. An old shawl of her grandmother's was thrown stylishly around her shoulders, as her grandmother would never have thought to wear it.

Out in the kitchen at the back her mother was clattering vessels in the stone sink, and her father sprawled in an old carpet-covered armchair beside the fire of stubbornly smoking turf. His waistcoat was open over his soiled shirt and his boots unlaced; the day's stubble a dark smear on his florid face.

He belched, slopping the glass of porter in his hand, eyeing her with a sort of jealous contempt.

'Ah, so you're away,' he said to her as she crossed to the street door. 'And where would the Duchess be going tonight? Would it be the Vice Regal Lodge, or maybe even the King's Palace in London itself? Sure they'll every one of them be waiting for you, dropping their curtseys and waving their ta-ra-ras. Have you not a ta-ra-ra yourself, yer Grace?'

His guffaws at his own wit followed her as she slammed the door, and fury kept her head in the air and the colour in her cheeks as she made her way across the Square and round to the Church Hall beside the Barracks.

Fury, shame and disgust. All the things that had her desperate before God to get out of that house and the smell of dirt and porter and neglected chamber pots. To Caherliss where it was all clean, and the mother even put a pot of water at the hob for Johnny to have a hot wash in the evenings after work so that he smelt in her arms only of soap and his own excited flesh and the faint, loved, ever-present smell of his farm. She could refuse him nothing. Nothing. From her eager body to her willingness to go flaming off to die for Ireland at his command.

And Kate Mary Pearse had it all to share with him, living in the same house and his mother making it known all over the village that she wanted her to be his wife.

Thinking that, she was cold in the soft night by the time she reached the Hall, shivering a little and hollow with excitement and anticipation as always. Shivering tonight with added uneasy, unfamiliar nerves.

Johnny wasn't there.

No tall figure stood in the lamplight streaming from the hall, passing the time of evening and a joke with all the people going in; teasing the girls and flattering the women, white teeth gleaming in the light. A meaning glance and a whispered word for many of the men.

Years now, every Saturday it had been like that. Tonight there was nothing but the humiliation of standing alone, pale with her rising anger; trying to pretend under all the curious glances that that was how they had arranged it for this evening.

Some of them even asked.

'Has he left you, Bridie?'

'Are you stood up, Bridie? Did the peelers get him?'

Grinning slyly, quite pleased if she was. They didn't like her, and she knew it. No girl was her friend. She was too good for them, she told herself furiously. Too good for them, the ignorant women in their shawls and thick stockings; the lads in from the country in their ancient, crumpled suits, plastered with stinking macassar oil above their white foreheads where the sun never reached them in the fields.

Johnny wasn't like that. He never wore a cap in the fields and his clear skin was sunburnt right up to his hair.

Johnny this, Johnny that, and everyone that went in compared to him. The crowd thinning and her cold fingers shaking

99

under the shawl. Anger and sick misery trembling at the corners of her mouth.

The music starting up inside, two fiddles and Peter Moynihan with his accordion, belting out the first chords to get them all up for the *Walls of Limerick*. Laughter and the hum of talk and the clink of bottles from the lads who never went further than the inside of the door.

The doors closed, and she was in the dark. Cold, sick, the brazen Bridie Bannion hollow with disappointment like any other forlorn poor girl whose lad had walked out on her. Ned walked by and she turned her face from him.

She couldn't go home and face the jeers and taunts of her father and Corrinne, so she was still standing there, between tears and fury, when he came swinging round the corner from O'Flyn's where he always left the horse and trap in the yard.

Fury took over.

'What's on you, Johnny O'Connor, leaving me standing in the street like this? Would you think I'm some street girl?'

There was darkness now with the doors closed, light streaming out only on to two alleyways, one each side of the Hall; favourite patrols fo the parish priest at night, searching to prevent sin and the hopeful occasions of it.

She couldn't see Johnny's face but sensed his irritability matching her own.

'Haven't I had to help my mother to put the whole house straight after those eejits this morning? Haven't I things on my mind other than dancing?'

'The girl is there,' she flared at him, raw at the very thought of it, 'to help your mother clean the house.'

'That's none of your business.'

He hated her at that moment because she wasn't Kate Mary; her ripe beauty suddenly repugnant, the smell of her Dublin perfume sickening. His mind and body longed for a cool girl whose grey eyes gave him no encouragement. A girl he'd be proud to bring in there on his arm, who had refused him yet again in the early evening when he'd pressed her to come with him. Some new light was in her eyes that baffled him and made her all the more desirable, driving him to quarrel with her on the only grounds he could find.

'If that policeman comes here again I'll want you not speaking to him. You can go to your own room.'

Kate Mary had flamed.

'If that policeman comes here again, it'll be you that brings him! And who am I to agree to that?'

He had flung off, making a great performance about taking his pot of water from the hob and washing himself for the evening; yelling to his mother for a clean shirt and putting on his good suit. Then sitting sullen on the edge of the bed for a long time, smoking thin cigarette after cigarette before he could bring himself to go out and put the pony in the trap to drive into the town.

'Well,' Bridie said, 'will we go in or not?'

She did her best to keep the note of pleading from her voice, tried to make it sound as though she had a thousand other things to do, sick with fright lest he turn and walk away.

'We will not,' said Johnny. 'We'll go to Westport.'

He was unable to stand even one more evening with her flaunting herself in there at his side possessively, leading the whole village to think she had him on a string.

'To Westport?'

'Indeed. We'll have a drink at the hotel.'

He was already off towards O'Flyn's yard, leaving her to follow at his heels. A drink in the hotel should have been a grand thing. Special. A step up in her certainty of Johnny.

But it only brought a sinking miserable heart; the panicky feeling that she was losing him. That even as his tall figure disappeared round the corner, she had already lost him.

To Kate Mary Pearse.

He drove the pony at a spanking pace through the cold damp night, and she shivered in her shawl beside him and did not dare even lie up against him for warmth as she would usually do, the pony managing with one of his hands while with the other held her close.

It was rare that they went to the hotel in Westport. A couple of times before Johnny had taken her there. She had been proud as punch of her fine smiling man; basking provocatively in getting the eye from all the other men in the bar, with Johnny finally threatening to kill the lot of them for daring to look at her like that.

It had seemed to her a grand exciting place, offering her a

high quality of life from which she could preen herself and look down on the poor ignorant peasants of Connorstown.

Tonight, in Johnny's glum silence, she could see it for what it was. It was he had given her the rose-coloured glasses, and without them it was a sad shabby place with red wallpaper fading down to orange on the walls and the paint along the bar kicked to smithereens by customers' boots. She saw now a few seedy commercial travellers, no more, and a couple of farmers who would have been wiser had they gone home long ago to their wives in the country.

Nothing more. It had been her passion for Johnny that made it a place of elegance and splendour for her. It was nothing now that he sat in sullen silence across from her, pouring too many whiskies down his throat, and looking at her as though he couldn't stand the sight of her.

Not for a moment did she blame him, wanting him as passionately as ever; beginning to wonder in hollow fear was she going to have to live without him? Was she getting the push? And if she was, dear merciful Mother of God, how could she stand it? It was only Johnny that made life possible. The slatternly house and the coarse father; the huddled bedroom and the girls on top of her all the time and nothing to say to any of them. The sly disapproving grins of the village people because she dared to be different.

Because they knew she wanted Johnny O'Connor and hadn't got him yet.

It had all been bearable because he was there, pleasure in his eyes to see her, and up until now, no other girl. So there was always hope. Plotting and planning all the time on how to lay hands on him for good; listening patiently to all the other plotting and planning that went on in the back kitchen of Gorman's. She was there only because, as Kate Mary had suspected, it kept her close to Johnny, brought to their relationship a high excitement and fevour that put an edge to love. If he only knew it, she'd see Ireland and all the Cause and the fighting at the bottom of the sea if she could only have Johnny and his ring on her finger. England could have Ireland, or anybody else that wanted it.

Now he put his glass down abruptly as though he could bear something no longer.

102

'C'mon,' he said shortly. 'We'll go home now.'

'No pleasure it's been to me,' she blazed at him suddenly. 'With you there all evening and not a word from you.'

He said nothing, swinging out through the dark panelled hall and down the steps, but fury and mad frustration drove Bridie on. She knew she shouldn't say it, it would only make matters worse, but she couldn't stop herself.

'Is it Kate Mary Pearse is on your mind?'

He gave her one look then in the lamplight of the hotel yard and she could have wept for her mistake. You'd think Kate Mark Pearse was the Virgin Mary or something, that she must never be mentioned.

In dead angry silence he urged the pony through the streets of Westport, and she could find nothing more to say. She had said too much already. But halfway home in the lightless country, he turned the trap suddenly into a field and there, on the damp cold grass, still without a word, made such savage love to her as left her bruised and gasping.

And hopeful. Wildly hopeful and exultant, even as she pulled her clothes around herself against the cold wind, her hands still shaking. Whatever drove him – and it was out of him now, lying face down and silent in the grass, ruining his good suit – whatever drove him, it had driven him too far this time. With God's help, from this night's work she could have a baby, she could have a baby and Johnny to the altar, and that would be the end of Kate Mary.

He was kinder to her on the way home, his arm about her to stop her shivering, but he put her down at her door without a kiss.

'I'm sorry, Bridie,' was all he said, and clattered off into the night, leaving her to take her sore body up through the dark house, past the little lamp that burned on the landing before the statue of the Sacred Heart, and into the lumpy bed beside Corrinne.

She smelt of sweat.

And I, thought Bridie, still smell of Johnny.

In the darkness, she put her hand across her stomach where a child could swell, and prayed as she had never prayed before, an irresistible hopeful smile on her bruised lips.

*　　　*　　　*

103

Christmas passed in quietness as though there was a truce between both sides in Connorstown, as there had been that strange first Christmas of the war when the Germans laid down their arms and came singing from the trenches for a day of peace.

They killed the pig at Caherliss while Kate Mary was away, but she was home for the plucking of the goose, the whole scullery adrift with the soft white down that would go into their beds and pillows, and Aunt Margaret benign with the gentleness of the season. She stoned the raisins for the Christmas barm brack, and cycled into Connorstown for a bottle of stout for the plum pudding, relieved and happy that Johnny seemed to have recovered his good humour and some of the old air of content lay over Caherliss.

Her own happiness she hugged in secret to herself. Just the one afternoon they had had in Westport, but it seemed they had been together all their lives. And she knew this would be, God willing, in the future.

She saw him at Midnight Mass, across the aisle and in front of her, so she was able to look at his red hair, head and shoulders above the rest of them; admire the straight set of his back and the endearing vigour with which he sang the *Adeste Fidelas*.

This loved hymn of Christmas, warming her with the certainty that it was the happiest one she would ever know. Ned, her Christmas gift.

He spoke of her afterwards in the crowd going out.

'A happy Christmas, Miss Pearse.'

'And to you too, Sergeant.'

He wasn't in the mob of people in Gorman's for hot punch before going home, but she was not upset. There was no hurry about Ned. They had a lifetime for everything. She wasn't even irritated by Bridie Bannion, who kept at a civil distance with Aunt Margaret there and looked somewhat pale and uncertain.

There was a brief forgetfulness of death and danger, vanished in the soft hopes of Christmas. Johnny sang in the trap going home, filling the cold night with his fine voice, and in the moonlight Kate Mary could see the small smile of content on Aunt Margaret's face.

For her, too, for a brief while, the world had steadied.

And next Tuesday, thought Kate Mary, leaning amiably against Johnny and singing with him, she would see Ned again.

Chapter 5

Tuesday.

Soon she began to feel that even the sound of the day was different; touched with light, marked out from all the other days when there was nothing to do but wait, and dream dreams where hope and happiness were dimmed always by anxiety.

That very first Tuesday before Christmas, he had been late. Patiently she stood outside the iron gates of Westport House in her good coat and shoes, feeling the thin cool sunlight of the declining year on her face, and watching the breeze ripple the long water of Clew Bay. Carrigahowly Castle was reflected dark in the centre of it against the low sun. Around the top of Croagh Patrick on her left lay the white crown of cloud that never left it. As the time passed, she fought away sick disappointment. He would come. Of course he would come. She concentrated carefully on the quiet sea and on the gardens of the beautiful red brick mansion behind her. Even so, by the time she saw him striding round the corner of the hedge, she realised her hands were clenched around her purse, and the bones of her jaws ached from tension.

She let out a long breath and allowed it all to fall away.

Ned. She was too relieved even to think of being cross.

'Ah, Kate Mary, I was mortal afraid you'd have gone away. I wouldn't have blamed you.'

He stood looking down at her, obviously as relieved as she was herself, but frowning, furious.

Gone away? She'd have stayed there till night drove her home, even if he was in a rage at something.

''Tis that – Inspector.' He caught back a word. 'Your pardon, Kate Mary, but he had a great deal to say.'

He was still smarting from the clear accusations of failure. The D.I. was as sure as he was that the gelignite was out in Connorstown. It had been Ned's given job to find it, and to arrest Johnny O'Connor. He had managed neither.

'I'll do a raid on Gorman's,' he had said at the end of the meeting. 'They're all there at nights. It could be the stuff is there too.'

He didn't believe it, but he had had to say something.

The D.I. had tapped with his pencil on the table, his fine eyes hard. Gone was the attitude of amiable warning from the night of the fire. Ned was aware of a long-nosed Sergeant at a table the other side of the office looking at him with a degree of pity and contempt as he listened, pretending to be writing in the day book. An older man who would never get further, and quite pleased to see this jumped up young fellow taken down a peg or two. They were making Sergeants from the very cradle these days, and little good they were. Ned read his expression and carefully kept his temper down. Superior look or not, he was not the one dealing with Johnny O'Connor, slippery and clever as a bag of eels.

'I don't know,' said the D.I. coldly, 'why it hasn't been done long ago. I have the R.M. breathing hellfire down my neck since they made a fool of his wife, and not a finger lifted to stop them.'

Ned sat silent. No good telling the D.I. that the devils were so quick and clever it was all done before you could say policeman. And they standing around then, grinning and waiting for him to make a fool of himself.

As the D.I. clearly thought he was. And the R.M. He'd be losing his stripes before they even had time to get dirty.

He had held back from raiding Gorman's because his growing experience of Johnny O'Connor told him he was not likely to walk in there and catch them all making bottle bombs and the women rolling bandages. Or doing anything else either that they shouldn't be doing, except drinking. All he'd get would be all Connorstown laughing round his head again, and Johnny nailed for no more than a fine of a few shillings for drinking after hours.

The gelignite, he could have told the D.I., would not be there.

All his instincts told him it was out at Caherliss.

Kate Mary looked at him, at his angry eyes and the red patches on his high cheekbones which always betrayed him, however he held to his temper.

How could she say to him, 'Well, amn't I sorry you didn't catch Johnny?' But she knew that were Johnny behind bars in the jail this fine afternoon, Ned would be proud and happy. Never mind about her.

She could say nothing and felt her own temper rising, furious with the both of them that they should spoil this precious afternoon. When she had first begun to fear for Johnny, it was only for his own danger. Now it seemed he could destroy all she so wanted for herself. Poor Ned could only do his duty. It could all end before it had even begun.

In turn, Ned looked at her, and for a few moments all he could think was that his disgrace was because of that rebel cousin of hers. That did he only have his hands on him, all would be well. He knew, too, it would be no help to him in his troubles to be seen out with her. Then he realised who he was with, after all these years. Kate Mary was actually beside him, her fine grey eyes as troubled as his own, no happiness in her face.

The first strain. The day already dimmed.

He pressed down his irritability, and his face altered.

'Ah, Kate Mary, alannah. You're a sight for sore eyes. Will we talk of something else? Anything else? Make the best of it before I'm posted to some village in the bogs with my stripes gone.'

He grinned down at her with confidence he didn't feel. How could he ever protect her from the sorrow that bastard was bound to bring her? Would she stay with him, if it was he caused the sorrow, caused the end of Johnny?

'Will we walk along the shore?' he asked her gently.

He looked at her really for the first time and felt the familiar grip like a fist round his heart. So neat always, but it was more than neatness. That special style she had so you could never imagine her being careless or untidy. Her beautiful face, framed by a small dark hat, was troubled and sad.

God damn Johnny O'Connor! He could kill him for taking the smile from Kate Mary's face, never mind what else he did.

'Will we walk along the shore?'

The loneliest place. The place they were least likely to be seen. The necessity for it increased his irritation, but they both calmed as they walked away from the town, out the long arm of the Bay, looking over at the green cone of Croagh Patrick. Making small talk of this and that, wanting only to be together. Suddenly a little shy.

A small curve in the shore hid them from the town, and with a long sigh he looked all around him in the silence and took his cap off. Kate Mary longed to ease with her finger the cruel red circle left by its weight.

Ned felt the anxiety slipping from him.

'Grand,' he said, and really smiled for the first time since they had met. 'Not a soul but ourselves, and the swans and the seagulls.'

Kate Mary looked over at the Holy Mountain, the shrine on top of it lost in the crown of cloud. Like Ned she groped for easy conversation, knowing that while they walked with such danger, nothing could ever be easy between them.

'Did you ever climb it?' she asked him.

'I did not. But my poor mother did, God help her, and on her hands and knees, the creature. I don't know what sins she thought she had committed to deserve that, the poor good soul. Maybe she was doing it for me.'

He grinned then, the wide easy grin that transformed his austere face and turned Kate Mary's heart.

Maybe, she thought, usually a little impatient with shrines and holy wells and all the other folklore of the Irish faith; maybe, if she went up there and asked the Saint, he would help her. Help her to get through it all and have Ned for always.

They rambled on out towards the old castle, their feet scrunching on the pebbled beach where the wild Atlantic seas of winter had worn every stone to the smoothness of an egg, from the small ones at the sea's edge to the boulders above them as large as little houses. Kate Mary could have told Ned that on a wild night you could hear the roar and rattle of them right up within the town.

He was looking at the square bulk of Carrigahowly on Clare Island in the middle of the bay, darkening against the lemon sky of evening.

'You know,' he said to Kate Mary, 'I'd think she might have been a bit like you.'

'Like me?'

Kate Mary felt a tremble of pleasure; the first personal remark he had made, and the teasing in his eyes told her it was a compliment. But she wasn't going to let him get away with it easily.

'Who was like me?'

'Ah, come on, Kate Mary. You're from this part of the world and don't know about Queen Grainne there on Clare Island with her fleet, persecuting all the galleons of Elizabeth of England?'

'And she called the Queen Elizabeth "sister" when she met her to make a truce.' Kate Mary laughed. 'Ah, I know all about Granuaille. But like me? Wasn't she a fighting harridan with a sword in her belt like a man, and all her fleet of boats tied at night to her big toe so no one could take her by surprise?'

''Twas she who took the galleons of England by surprise,' Ned said. 'No, I can see you doing it, and that nose of yours in the air, and all your men about you.'

'Thank you for that, Ned Brannick. Wasn't she as ugly as sin and all her teeth black and a tangle of red hair to her waist? And Ned – '

Her eyes were bright, challenging, but behind their teasing lay sheer excitement that they were together and beginning to enjoy it. Let the world say what it would.

'Ned.'

'Yes?'

She had taken her hat off and the soft late sun was in the sheen of her black hair, the wind flicking tendrils round her animated face.

'Ned, she was fighting for Ireland! Even then. Against the English. Isn't it what I say, it'll never end. They'll never stop it. It'll be our grandchildren too.'

Quick as a flash Ned rounded on her.

'Didn't it finish then? Because Grainne had the sense to

110

give in for the sake of Ireland. It could finish now in the same way, if the people had their wits.'

In a few words their golden afternoon was gone. Even the dying sun had lost its warmth and the blue waters of Clew Bay turned to grey and cold as Ned's own eyes.

Johnny O'Connor stood between them again, palpable as if he were there in the flesh, and Kate Mary could have choked herself for bringing him there. Johnny and all he stood for, and Ned's gnawing doubts as to whether Kate Mary stood with him.

'You have nothing on him,' Kate Mary said stubbornly, as though his name had been mentioned, and crammed her hat back on to her head as if to end the day.

'Isn't that what the D.I. was telling me!' Ned answered bitterly. 'I *know* he took that gelignite. For God's sake, Kate Mary, what is he going to do with it?'

Her anger died at the trouble in his face. She sat down on one of the big round stones and stared miserably at the sea.

She looked up at him.

'I don't know, Ned. I honestly don't *know*. And, look, isn't it better that way? Then no one can blame me for not telling.'

'But you wouldn't tell even if you did know.'

He was a stubborn as she.

'Ah, Ned. Can't you leave things as they are?'

She was on the edge of tears, their very first hours together ruined in seconds by the Trouble. Was it going to ruin their whole lives, if they ever got that far?'

Ned, who had sworn to himself to speak no word of politics or of Johnny, was sick with fury at his clumsiness. Dropping down beside her on the rock, he took her two cold hands in his and looked into her unhappy eyes.

'Kate Mary, I'm sorry. Amn't I the eejit, to upset you. I swore to myself that not one word of it would pass my lips, and here I am spoiling everything. Amn't I every kind of fool.'

Sheer fright was gripping him that with his clumsiness he could drive her into the very arms of O'Connor. But all Kate Mary could think of now was the warmth and strength of his hands round hers; his nearness; his bigness; and she crushed her own shabby fears that he only wanted her so that he could get information about Johnny.

The remorse and concern in his eyes were deep and real, and her heart lifted like a butterfly.

''Tis all right, Ned,' she said gently. ''Tis all right. All I want is to be left in peace about it all.'

Ned's eyes clouded, and with a gesture of protection he folded her two hands together inside his own.

'I'll try, Kate Mary, alannah. I'll try.'

She knew she could refuse him nothing. On the chilling shore, eyes locked together, with the tide beginning to rumble in the stones below them, they wordlessly promised each other the future, if they had one, fully aware of all the anguish and sorrow that could go with it.

'Come on now, asthore,' he said gently and got up, pulling her to her feet. 'You'll be getting cold. And,' he added wryly, 'I've ruined my best trousers.'

'And I'd better not stay out much longer either.' Kate Mary grinned. 'Or Mrs. Garvey'll have the Police out looking for me.'

Ned was not quite ready to laugh yet.

'Well, thank God the Police have found you. Or one of them.'

But they were lighthearted on the way back, teasing each other, already looking forward to next Tuesday. They skimmed stones on the swelling tide. When Kate Mary turned to look back from the end of the Bay, the swans were rocking restlessly on the rising water and Carrigahowly Castle was a black threatening mass against the sky; even Croagh Patrick was sunk in shadow, the last sun rosy on its crown of cloud. But away to the west over the Atlantic, the far sky was scarlet with the promise of another perfect day.

Like an omen, she thought hopefully. Like an omen. A promise.

'Where's your bicycle, Ned?'

'At the barracks.'

'Ah, I'll be going the other way.'

'Can I not see you home?'

She wouldn't let it blight her happiness.

'No, Ned. You know it wouldn't be wise. Did Mrs. Garvey see us, she'd be on her bicycle and roaring out to Aunt

Margaret with her tongue hanging out with it all. Not because you're a policeman, but because you're a *man*.'

'The forbidden article.'

'Indeed.'

'Well, I'll walk as far as the station with you. Man or policeman or both, no one much should see us on that road.'

They had not yet reached the stage where every fresh parting was heartbreak, bouyed still by the excitement of meeting, and they were light-hearted along the lonely road with nothing on it but a few tumbledown cottages.

When they came into the town and towards Station Square, Ned grew cautious.

'I'll leave you here, Kate Mary,' he said. 'Mrs. Garvey might be coming off the train.'

Kate Mary smiled, but absently, staring over at the station.

'It's certainly not her that's going on to it,' she said. 'Look who's going away.'

Outside the station a large red motor car was parked, a chauffeur piling heaps of costly looking luggage out of the *tonneau*, fussed over by a small self-important man in a hard hat.

A tall young woman waited by the entrance to the station, her maid in black beside her.

'Ned! That's . . .'

'I know,' said Ned dourly. 'It looks as though the next accusation against me will be that I've allowed the Resident Magistrate's wife to be driven out of Ireland.'

'Id expect,' Kate Mary said soothingly, 'that she's only going home to her mother to have her baby. Wouldn't that be normal? But the poor creature'll have to go through Dublin to get the boat, and by all accounts it's terrible up there. And she alone with her maid.'

'She'll be looked after,' Ned said shortly. 'Better than I did it. There'll be a couple of plain clothes police all the way with her. But you're right about Dublin. We know nothing of the Troubles in Connorstown.'

Kate Mary looked over at the tall girl, her coat bulging gently with her baby, whom she had last seen outside the Post Office in Connorstown with her dismantled dog cart beside her. Would she herself one day, she wondered with sad premonition, have to stand like this at some station, waiting to leave everything she loved?

'God, Kate Mary,' Ned said at her side, 'I hope you'll be good at rearing hens and cabbages out in the back of beyond, because that's where I'll finish up. I'd have done better to be a priest like me brother.'

'Goodbye now,' he said abruptly. 'And thanks for the afternoon.'

Formal words that hid his churning alarm for her. It was no joke about his being sent away. The D.I. had coldly hinted at it this very morning, did he not do better in Connorstown. Then some character might come there with a faster hand than his and less regard for the letter of the law. The girl's house could be in flames above her head, and she herself in prison for the company she was found in.

He thought of the dossier on Johnny in the Barracks back in Connorstown, and knew a prick of fear he would never feel for himself. It could only be a matter of time . . .

Desperately, he caught her hands. 'Could you not,' he said a little hoarsely, 'stay all the time in Westport at the present time? I'd come in to see you.'

She saw the fearful anxiety in his eyes.

'And not go to Connorstown at all?'

'Not at present.'

'Not,' she thought sadly, 'until you catch Johnny.'

Firmly, she disengaged her hands. The evening train for Galway belched and clattered from the station, and a few moments later the small pompous Mr. Bonnington Clay, somehow deflated, emerged from the doors and climbed into his red motor car, seen off by the bowing Station Master, his tall hat in his hands.

As he went back in, and the big red car chugged off around the corner, Kate Mary looked at the deserted pavement and thought of the young woman off on her long lonely journey to England, leaving her husband.

Her chin tilted in the proud gesture he loved, but that at the moment brought him to despair. Coolly she looked him in the eyes.

'I'm not one, Ned Brannick,' she said, 'for running away.'

'Well, I wish you were, my darling. I wish you were. There's times that it's wise.'

His heart was in his voice, and the endearment took them both by surprise.

'I'm sorry, Kate Mary,' he muttered, the easy scarlet flooding to his cheeks. 'I had no wish to be foreward.'

Kate Mary's eyes were soft.

'No matter, Ned. But goodbye now, or the widow Garvey will be looking out for me.'

'Perhaps we could marry her off to the D.I. and make the both of them happy. Keep his mind off me,' he said bitterly.

Was there ever a man so caught? His superiors giving him hell for not getting Johnny O'Connor for the hangman, and Kate Mary here fit to break her heart if he did. And herself at risk by the very fact of living in his house.

'You'll be here next Tuesday?'

'I will.'

He let her go reluctantly, and when she looked back he stood still on the grey street corner, dark and erect in his uniform as though he were standing guard. She was captured by the trained economy of his every movement. And it was not just because he was a policeman. It was something upright and incorruptible in the man himself. It made her love him, and it made her fear him. He would do his duty, whatever the cost.

On the way back through the drab streets of the town, she saw nothing, neither police nor soldiers, nor gave one thought to Ned's fears for her. Her thoughts were softer, occupied in remembering every word he had said to her, every turn of his head, his long strong hands. And next Tuesday.

Mrs. Garvey surveyed her as she came in, giving her a long stare, aware of something different.

'It's yourself is looking in good health this evening,' she said dourly. There was something here she should disapprove of, she knew, but she was unable to see anything but the glowing, bright-eyed face of the girl before her.

Kate Mary couldn't dislike even Mrs. Garvey at the moment.

'I took a turn along the shore.'

How she longed to tell someone who she took it with; of his

115

good looks and what a fine man he was, and the amazing way they had met again, and all he said and did and he a Sergeant already and so young.

The glow faded as she realised she could tell no one. No one. Not even her friend in the Convent, Aileen Murphy, to whom she told everything.

No one. Who could know in this terrible world who was a friend and who was an enemy.

'Your tea is on the table,' said Mrs. Garvey. Kate Mary blessed herself and sat down in silence.

1920.

Through the weeks of the early year, when the wind turned soft and primroses and violets jostled in the shooting grass along the ditches, there was a strange and baffling absence of activity.

Ned didn't like it, filled with a watchful certainty that it was only the lull before some storm.

Johnny was cool but equable, and like Ned, Kate Mary watched him as one might watch a wild animal confronted, trying to estimate which way it might leap.

He sat before the fire in Caherliss, reading a week-old paper someone had given him. Newspapers never came to Connorstown, unless someone brought one in from Westport, and they relied for the news on people's letters, and the garbled information pouring in on the telephone in Elsie O'Flyn's Post Office.

Johnny alone seemed always darkly full of information he would impart to no one. Only, with a blue glare at Kate Mary, inveighing against the violence and viciousness of police and soldiers.

Somehow they all knew, from reluctant travellers and the occasional paper, that the situation in Dublin was fearful. All the familiar streets were laced with barbed wire and sandbags, and after the murder of a policeman on February 20th, blackened and emptied by curfew from midnight until five a.m.

This empty darkness was shattered night after night by the thunder of armoured cars and the shouting of soldiers; the hopeless screaming of women and children as the man of their family was dragged off into the night and crammed into the armoured car, probably never to be seen again.

Prisons were full to bursting, and in Mountjoy the hunger strikes had begun. Hundreds of ordinary men, many of them little more than boys, terrified of what they were about to do, starved themselves even to death to support their demand that they were not criminals. Not criminals but patriots, with a right to fight for Ireland.

Political prisoners.

Their strength and fanatical determination seeped down through the country districts, reinforcing the blazing dreams of such as Johnny, that life was only of value if it were laid down for Ireland, no death more glorious than if it came fighting for the freedom of their country.

Johnny was away a lot. He had business in Castlebar, he said, and Kate Mary understood it was there that he went to see his masters. Baiting Ned Brannick and the Constables, was something he could do hilariously on his own, with the help of his local Committee, but by 1920, the battle to free Ireland had become organised, planned by its officers and generals like any other campaign.

Kate Mary knew too from his sodden boots and trousers that he was often in the bog at night, drilling his Volunteers in the secret open spaces for some action yet to come.

Over all Connorstown lay an air of false calm that left Ned pacing the streets, restless and suspicious, needled by the bland stares of Johnny's friends; biting his nails and sitting hour after hour at night trying to reason out where the next attack might be coming from; seeing nothing and finding nothing in a village that went about its business as innocent as if Sinn Fein had never been heard of.

There was the gelignite yet neither found nor used, and nothing could shake his certainty that O'Connor had it. For what? If he could get in first with that one, it could stop the D.I. glaring at him as if he was the worst thing that had happened to the District in all his time.

He was torn, too, about Kate Mary. All the instincts of duty told him he should be having nothing to do with her unless he was prepared to use her. Here, to his hand, could be all the answers about Johnny O'Connor.

But he didn't think so. Looking into her candid eyes, he couldn't think so.

Sometimes he could not help trying to question her, his anxiety too great for him to manage the ordinary trivial talk of a young man in love.

'I'm told he goes a lot to Castlebar,' he said to her suddenly one day, oblivious of the blue spring light over the sea, Croagh Patrick's lower slopes as green as emeralds; oblivious to Kate Mary as herself, only as the nearest he could get to Johnny.

'Do you know where he goes?'

Kate Mary stared at him, astonished at the blunt question. Usually he was so careful to pretend when they were together that Johnny didn't exist.

'No,' she said flatly, and was glad she didn't. She could never bring herself to tell lies to Ned, but she could never tell him the truth either. Even about the Johnny who was no longer Johnny; the hard light of fanaticism glittering in his eyes, his body taut with restlessness, unable to sit quiet in a chair.

Waiting for something to happen.

Waiting for what?

Ned answered her. 'They'll be waiting for the fine weather,' he said broodily, staring over at the green cone of the mountain.

'Why?' Kate Mary couldn't be annoyed at his preoccupation, concerned for her own reasons about Johnny, fearful for him, and yet wondering often would he ever stop being there between her and Ned, as real as across the dinner table in Caherliss. Turning, horrified, from the thought as she acknowledged that it would only happen if he were dead.

Or if Ned were. Dear God, it had come to this. And so soon.

Try as she might, she found it hard to agonise over the whole terrible conflict between England and Ireland; the deaths, the sorrow, the grief; the young ones marching to the firing squad or the hangman's noose, head high, with shining eyes, and the name of Ireland on their lips.

For her that conflict had narrowed down to two men and she knew sickeningly that only the death of one would clear it.

From Johnny there was undisguised hatred. Even though they did their best to keep their meetings secret, she felt sure he knew about her and Ned.

He never asked her now to go out with him, but she would catch his eyes on her across the table, dark and broody, as though like Connorstown he waited through these soft spring days for something that had not yet come.

Johnny would kill Ned for love of her, and tell himself it was for Ireland. Would he expect her, if it were done, to go rushing griefless to his arms, glad for Ireland's sake?

And Ned? Into his voice at the very mention of Johnny's name came a hardness and ugliness that closed her soul against him.

Ned would kill Johnny and call it duty, but as she lay wakeful in the dark house, listening to the wind about the roof, she tried hard to believe he wouldn't be glad to do it.

Her love for both of them was full of anguish, bitter sweet with the awakening knowledge through these gentle lengthening days of spring that there could be nothing but death between them.

Nor could it be long coming.

But it was Ned's arms she was in as they sat together on a green bank above the shore among the first small flowers in the short grass; the sweet spring day around them made for impossible happiness and love.

'Why, Ned?' she said again. 'Why waiting for the fine weather?'

Let him talk it out. Hopeless to get him to speak of anything else, and indeed what else was there to speak of? The first fine pleasure of just being together was gone; they had no present they dare admit to, no future they could plan. Let him talk of what filled his mind.

'Because,' said Ned, 'and it's no secret, we've warning that with the fine weather they'll be taking to the hills in a guerilla campaign around here.'

'They' to Johnny, were Ned and his policemen.

'They' to Ned, were Johnny and his Sinn Fein Volunteers.

'Guerilla? What's that? That's monkeys!'

Ned wouldn't smile, too anxious, too desperate.

''Tis a form of warfare begun by their leader, Michael

Collins – they take to the hills they know, only emerging for attacks on barracks and the like, and then vanish again. And for people not knowing the country so well, 'tis very hard to find them. They can't do it in the winter, of course. In the summer they live rough and on what food the women can bring out to them.'

Both separately thought of Bridie Bannion. Ned, that she must be watched as she'd be the leader in all that, and Kate Mary wondering would the girl would get a better grip on Johnny if he owed his life to her.

She stared ahead, her face bleak. The young summer that should have brought them content promised no more than rising violence, and the grey face of sorrow.

Watching her, Ned immediately wondered whether he should have spoken at all. Would it be a warning taken to O'Connor? At once he felt ashamed for doubting her.

'Ah, Kate Mary,' he said. 'My love, 'tis no time for us.'

He tightened his arms about her, and they sat clinging together, her head buried in his shoulder, too lost in their troubles for her even to raise her face for his kiss.

Unwillingly, as the sky darkened, they silently rose to go. As always their day had settled nothing; left them only with the same desperate need for patience; for waiting for God knew what.

Ned was preoccupied as they walked back the high narrow road above the sea. It nagged him night and day that he was missing something; some dereliction of duty that would bring them all out again, laughing, into the streets.

One thing he could not see the answer to. If they were going in for this guerilla warfare, then he was baffled as to what they were going to conduct it with. You couldn't run a summer's campaign on a few pounds of gelignite, and he'd not got a sniff of a rifle or a bullet in the whole damned town. But they must have weapons . . .

The raid on Gorman's had been a failure.

Only the fact that the D.I. had put in three extra men who found as little as Ned did himself kept the stripes on his arm, and his uneasy position safe in Connorstown.

Ned was warned of the meeting by a desperate little ferret

of a man he used for such purposes. He would have sold his own mother's life for the price of a pint of porter, and selling the Sinn Fein was nothing. He'd sell the Police as easily the next week, with the same crawling smile on his small face.

As Ned had been instructed, he sent Constable Doyle at once on his bicycle to Westport. This was no conversation to have that frog-faced Cumn na Bahn in the Post Office hanging on to.

They sent the supercilious older Sergeant who listened to him with such contempt most weeks when he went to Westport with his baffled reports, but the plans were well-laid. He came secretly after dark the night before the raid with two extra Constables, walking in from a motor car parked outside the town; sliding one by one to the Barracks, unseen by anyone in the damp street. Even a report of one extra policeman in the village would have alerted Johnny sky high, and every Sinn Feiner in the district would have stayed at home beside the fire.

They paraded in the bleak Day Room of the Barracks, the faces of Ned's own three Constables alive with responsibility and determination. It was the first time they had ever done anything on this scale and they were all out to show the lads from Westport that there was no need for them to be there at all. Connorstown could look after its own, and no need for help.

Facing them, Ned outlined his plan, seething under the cold stare of the older Sergeant who had been instructed not to interfere; not to give any orders. But if things went wrong, he was there to say why.

Nothing, thought Ned bitterly, looking at his impassive face, but a common spy.

In thick misty darkness, he placed his men early, Constable Doyle sidling carefully into a broken down house across the road from Gorman's bright official front door, and Constable Daly easing his four square body into the thick wet bushes close beside the ever open door at the back of Gorman's yard. The late illicit drinkers came this way, quietly at night, to give their special knock on the back door with a penny. Later, when even these had gone, came the ones Ned wanted.

He wouldn't trust poor Constable Murphy to creep in

121

secretly to anywhere, holding him back until the point where noise and clumsiness no longer mattered, and he could kick tin cans and stumble over dogs to his heart's content, without doing harm.

In the back room of the Barracks, he waited with the other Sergeant and the two extra Constables, his long face hard and cool and his eyes on the clock. Constable Murphy was out in front to present an innocent aspect in the Day Room; dealing with any righteous citizen of Connorstown who might come in with his cow stolen or his head laid open by a bottle. Or even with old Peter Foley who came when he had a dram or two and nowhere to go, to tear apart for the thousandth time the legal perfidy of John Galway who cheated him of an acre of land ten years ago, and no atom of justice since for a decent man.

But even Constable Murphy had a dull time, self-important as the keeper of the Tower of London himself. Preoccupied as he was, Ned's ears stuck out like jug handles in the back room lest Murphy become bored and in his excitement tell any passing comer what was happening.

There were no passing comers. The slow hands of the clock ticked by in heavy silence and Ned was damned if he would talk to this interloper sent here to spy on him. In his turn, the Sergeant from Westport refused to acknowledge a young upstart ten years his junior and with the same stripes as himself. Instead he occupied himself by staring critically at the bare whitewashed walls and the padlocked rack of six rifles across from him, their barrels gleaming dully in the lamplight.

Looking, no doubt, thought Ned bitterly, before they even set out to find some imperfection he could go running back to Westport to report.

The two Constables could not talk when their superiors didn't, and sat fiddling with their caps and listening miserably to the comfortable sound of Constable Murphy putting more coal on the fire in the Day Room. The spring night had cooled, and the back room that had originally been a kitchen was unheated, cold and bleak.

The hands of the clock crept tediously round to one, its flat ticking the loudest sound in the Barracks. By this time, the pattern of Gorman's should have taken shape; even the latest drinkers gone, and those left having no good reason to be there. Open to be arrested now, under the new law forbidding secret gatherings of any kind.

The waiting over the dull hours was past. Although he stayed quiet and controlled, excitement raced through Ned. Only Kate Mary would have known his feelings from the warm flush high on his bony cheekbones.

Was this the night, by God, he wondered, that he was going to put paid to Johnny O'Connor and all his capers? If only he could have done it for himself without this po-faced fellow from Westport.

He took his cap from the table, controlling his breathing, calming himself.

'I'll go now and check with my men,' he said, and the other Sergeant nodded reluctantly. Not everyone in Connorstown went to bed like good Christians when they should, and he could not risk being seen too early. The news of a strange Sergeant would go flying through an apparently sleeping town like chaff before the wind.

'Now, Constable,' Ned said to Constable Murphy on the way out, 'you understand, if I am not back in seven minutes, you lead the Sergeant and his men to Gorman's front door. The front door. You understand?'

Constable Murphy stood rigid to attention, quivering with importance, his eyeballs rolling.

'I do, Sir. I do. Front door. Seven minnits. Front door.'

'Ah, well,' thought Ned resignedly. 'If he comes to the back it makes little difference.'

'And lock the Barracks when you leave, Constable.'

'Sergeant, Sir!'

All was well. The Constables at front and back told of all who had gone in and all who had come out.

The ones still inside were the ones they wanted. All the stars, by God, of the old Sergeant's dossier; men and women. All the Sinn Fein fanatics of Connorstown. And Johnny O'Connor.

It seemed an hour before Constable Murphy arrived, breathing heavily, triumphantly in the right place at exactly at the right time.

123

Gorman's was in pitch darkness, as was to be expected; a respectable village saloon, closed for the night, without sight or sound of occupation.

'Are you sure they're there?' whispered the man from Westport, ready from the first moment to doubt.

'I am. On the count of my men, there are eleven of them, including Gorman himself.'

Four constables at the back where the conspirators might be expected to make a run for it. Constable Murphy at the front where, if he could do no more, he could at least recognise them. The two Sergeants to go in.

Ned took a deep breath and hammered on the dark front door of the saloon, conscious of the noise in the still damp night, and hammered again, cursing the need.

Not a sound or a light in Gorman's but windows going up all along the street and voices yelling in God's name, what was going on at all, and couldn't decent people get their sleep? Some heads popped in again like Punch and Judy the moment they set eyes on the dark shapes of the Police.

A few doors opened and men rushed out into the darkness dragging on their clothes. Were there going to be a fight of any kind, they wanted into it.

Ned hammered again.

'Break it down,' said the man from Westport. 'You're letting them get away.'

'There's nowhere they can go,' said Ned tersely.

But he was about to throw his weight on the door when they heard the sound of footsteps, firm and unhurried, across the oilcloth floor of the bar; the slow careful pulling back of the big bolts a righteous man had need of to protect his property.

The round dubious face of Desmond Gorman glimmered like a full moon above a candle.

'Sergeant – ?'

They left him to his pleasantries, crashing past him to the back kitchen where all their guilty ones should be, had they not already rushed into the arms of the Police waiting outside, armed and ready.

The big kitchen was empty, save for the ample Mrs. Gorman sitting comfortably on a velvet sofa up against the wall, her skirts, spread about her. The fire burned merrily, shining in the grate, and the drawn red curtains were warm against the chilly night beyond the windows.

Mrs. Gorman didn't get up.

'Were you wanting a drink, Sergeant?' she said amiably. 'You'd need to be desperate. 'Tis after the hour, you understand.'

Ned glared at her and charged to the back door, flinging it open.

'Did anyone come out?' he bellowed.

'They did not. Not a one,' four voices answered him.

Every press on the wall was crashed open; then, clattering up the oilcloth stairs, the same in all the bedrooms. Every press, every wardrobe, under all the beds of the big house, hurtling through the obviously empty drawing-room where a parrot shrieked curses from a cage beside the fire.

All Ned's intelligence told him he was wasting his time. Eleven people could not be in any of these places.

Rage and a small flare of panic was rising within him as, furious, he wheeled back towards the stairs.

'The cellar,' he shouted. 'The cellar!'

It had to be.

Desmond had by that time followed them down the hall, round face still carefully imperturbable.

'I don't know what you'd be looking for, Sergeant Brannick,' he said helpfully, 'but if you want to go down the cellar, let me get you a light. You'll need a candle.'

Ned could not look at the man from Westport, aware by now that something had gone badly wrong. In God's name what? There was only the two doors, and did they go over the roof they'd have been seen.

Doggedly he had searched the house from top to bottom and found nothing that he wouldn't have found in his mother's. Mrs. Gorman sat blandly all the time on her velvet sofa as if such raids at one in the morning were no more than could happen to anyone, and must be taken in her stride.

Ned glared at her, waiting impatiently while Desmond took all the time in the world to light the candle. At the back of Ned's mind, he knew there was something wrong with Mrs. Gorman's behaviour. Wouldn't a woman in the circumstances be creating fit to be heard from here to Bantry Bay? Didn't they all? Before he could think further, Desmond lifted the candle as proudly as though he had invented electricity itself.

'Ye can come down now, Sergeant.'

He also was too placid, too unconcerned.

Mother of Christ, had he missed again?

'Will ye mind yereselves on the cellar steps,' Mrs. Gorman said kindly when they go that far. ''Tis very steep.'

In his fury Ned almost fell down them, and only at the bottom did he pause. No people upstairs but you could hide anything in this jumble of casks and sacks and boxes. He looked at the other Sergeant, and Desmond Gorman read their thoughts in the soft light.

'Go on with it,' he said, and the bright white smile never left his face. 'You can open anything you chose. 'Tis only what it says it is. Every bit of it.'

In baffled rage they opened everything, spreading the floor with bacon and jelly babies, raisins and black treacle, slit sacks of flour and yellow meal, sugar and oats and a whole new chest of tea. They could do nothing about the casks, so they opened the bungs, streams of black porter joining the shambles on the floor. If there was liquid in them, then there wouldn't be guns or ammunition.

Bottles could hold nothing but what they said.

The light of the candle guttered and flickered over the low dirty ceiling, and made the shambles on the floor look like a sort of dreadful devil's Christmas. Ned stopped and stared at it and knew he deserved nothing more than the ridicule that flickered in Desmond Gorman's eyes.

Ashamed, baffled and raging, he charged up again, brought to a halt by the sight of Mrs. Gorman still sitting there on the crimson sofa, beside a tall statue of the Sacred Heart on a mahogany pedestal; a votive lamp glowing in front of it, and a red damask curtain from floor to ceiling, hanging at its back.

Ned stopped, now more ashamed even than he was angry, brought entirely to a helpless blank. There was no one here. He had failed again.

'I'm sorry for your trouble, ma'am,' he said to her, hoarsely and dutifully.

Mrs. Gorman inclined her head.

126

''Twas your duty, Sergeant,' she said kindly. ''Twas no more and no less.'

He made no apologies to Desmond Gorman, brushing past him with the maddened certainty that he had been tricked by this smooth-faced smiling rogue. Although before God, he could not see how.

They pushed their way through the tittering, half-dressed crowd that was gathered now in the dark street, gleefully aware that once again the peelers had been made fools of, even the old lad of a Sergeant they said came from Westport, and he old enough to have his wits about him.

They shivered and never noticed it in the cold damp mist that was almost rain, hugging their victory, for there wasn't a man Jack of them didn't know where the meeting had melted to. And sure they'd all be in tomorrow to help Desmond clear up.

Ned blew his whistle to summon all his small defeated force, trying not to see the villagers' grinning faces. He was almost humble with the other Sergeant.

'I'm at my wit's end,' he said. 'At my wit's end.'

The other man was magnanimous, exhilarated by the noisy pleasure of smashing up Gorman's cellar. He had got something out of the night after all.

'You did all you could,' he said. 'Unless your men were counting ghosts.'

'No,' Ned said soberly. 'There's something else to it than that.'

The four men arrived from the back of the house, swearing that not a soul had left. Ned told them to be quiet with half the village listening, and formed them up to march back to the Barracks.

As their heavy boots thumped down the street into the Square, laughter and catcalls broke out behind them, and a shower of stones clattered on their caps and shoulders.

'Don't break,' Ned ordered them ferociously. 'Don't break. Get on where you are going.'

He wouldn't give them the pleasure of a pitched battle in their nightshirts, and all the complaints going in afterwards about being attacked in the middle of the night by the Police.

At the Barracks, they found that Constable Murphy in his

excitement had forgotten to lock the door, and old Peter Foley was fast asleep in the chair before the fire, six rifles racked along the wall behind him.

Desmond Gorman closed his door against the crowd, and came back into the back kitchen to his wife.

'Did they make a great mess, Desmond?' she asked.

He set down the candle and blew it out.

'They did, the bastards, but they got nothing for it.'

'Wasn't it well,' she said, 'it wasn't next week.'

It was. For a moment, his white smile reached his eyes. 'And didn't you,' he said, 'look like the Queen herself, sitting there spreading your skirts over a few hundred rounds of ammunition.'

'Ah,' she said, 'I didn't want to get up lest the creatures feel the lumps in the cushions. Will you just, Desmond,' she added, 'see the door is well closed. It could blow the curtain.'

Eugene went over to the red hanging behind the Sacred Heart and pulled it to one side, testing to see that the door into the next house was properly shut.

'Ah, thank you, pet. We'll go to bed now and clear up in the morning.'

On the damp ground behind the ball alley, Johnny O'Connor tumbled joyfully with Bridie Bannion, whom he hadn't touched in weeks, and laughed so much that he was almost sick, crowing with triumph and content.

So lost was he in his hilarity that Bridie didn't find it difficult to lead him on past the point of common sense.

Hoping again, desperately after last month's disappointment, that this time he had gone too far.

After the raid, even Aunt Margaret spoke out.

'Wasn't that a desperate bad thing they did to poor Desmond Gorman. Not a thing in his cellar left fit to sell in the shop, the man. And every drop of drink spilt. 'Twas like stirabout down in the cellar they tell me. And the man's living there in it all.'

She shot a sharp look at Kate Mary across the fire, more directly accusing than she had ever been, and the girl felt a tremor of apprehension. Although she was sure that she and Ned had never been seen, it had come into the village too, this air of people watching her; of suspicion and hostility; all friendship gone. As though it were she who had raided Gorman's and made a pudding of his stock.

Aunt Margaret had gone into the cold gloom of the dairy behind the kitchen to churn the butter, and Kate Mary sat beside the kitchen table, sewing a lace collar to a dress. It was pretty, dug out of an old box of bits and pieces belonging to Aunt Margaret, some of which Kate Mary recognised as priceless although much of it came by the half mile from the diligently made lace pillows of the four crows in the Convent in Galway.

She smoothed the collar on the scrubbed table with appreciative fingers, hoping Ned would like it.

Aunt Margaret was a little darting woman, driven always by her thoughts. She'd lay down anything if a thought should strike her to follow it at once, spending half her days going back to finish tasks she had left in the middle as something struck her.

Now she shot in from the dairy as though she knew Kate Mary's thoughts as well as her own, fluttering to rest like a butterfly on the chair opposite. Fiercely she glared at the girl through her round, steel-rimmed glasses.

'Is it true,' she said, taking the bull by the horns, eyes wide with the importance of her question, 'that you're going with a policeman, over there in Westport?'

Kate Mary went on sewing, but she felt tight and cold deep in her stomach. She didn't look up.

'How do you know?'

'Don't you lodge with a friend of mine?'

So old gossip Garvey had found out. This angered Kate Mary so much she no longer felt frightened. She snapped her thread with her teeth and glared back at Aunt Margaret. Why couldn't people mind their own business?

'Haven't I known him since I was a child,' she said, 'from my own part of the country. Is there anything wrong with that?'

Aunt Margaret's small mouth went tight.

'Isn't he a policeman? What would Johnny say about that?'

Kate Mary's eyes took on a sudden coldness that hinted at the strength behind her serene face.

'And what of Johnny?' she said clearly. 'And what he thinks? Is he God? Is there a law to say I have to think as Johnny O'Connor does? Is there?'

Poor Aunt Margaret gaped at her. No one before had ever challenged her certainty that her fine handsome son might not be God but did not rank very far behind. And that what he thought, she should think, and everybody else too.

'You're not Sinn Fein, you mean,' she said unbelievingly. Her face had crumpled like a shocked child's.

'Did I ever say I was?' the girl asked more gently. 'Did I ever say I was?'

Aunt Margaret shook her head. Surely, as Johnny thought, everybody in the house must think also. Weren't the very nuns in the Convent rolling bandages for their brother and all the other brave lads?

'Then what are you, Kate Mary?' she demanded, a small flicker of her usual spirit returning. 'What are you?'

Kate Mary laid down the lace and answered her as she had answered Johnny on that day that seemed a hundred happy years ago. The day of the bullets.

'I'm myself, Aunt Margaret,' she said quietly. No more.

Through their silence, the bright sun of spring struck though the votive lamp burning always on the window sill, beside a picture of the Sacred Heart. Sunlight fell in a pool on the table between them, over Kate Mary's face. It was red, like blood.

In the dead dark of the nights, happily encouraged by the failure of the raid on Gorman's, Elsie O'Flyn was passing bulky parcels out of the side door of the Post Office to her brother and his friends. Confidently they slipped with them through deserted streets, guarded by lookouts, to stash them in their hiding places; grinning still that the fools had found nothing and nobody in Gorman's with fat Molly sitting cool as a cucumber on all that ammunition while they searched.

Johnny was pleased. By the time the weather warmed, they'd be well ready.

Chapter 6

Through all these weeks Johnny was still meeting Kate Mary on a Friday afternoon, when she came back from Wesport; heaving her bicycle into the back of the cart and driving her home to Caherliss.

She had become nervous of these journeys. It was the only time he was alone with her, and she was afraid he would try and press his desire. But even that would have been better, she thought as the weeks went on, than the cold bitter silence that now chilled even the brightest of spring days. His blue eyes were like flints, and his only words given to the people he passed on the roads.

He would never have come out for me at all, she thought bitterly, did not Aunt Margaret make him.

Or did she? Kate Mary was certain now that Johnny knew about Ned. Aunt Margaret would never have kept it to herself. And God knew how long the widow Garvey would have stopped in Connorstown on her tale-bearing expedition out to Caherliss; just gossiping in all probability, for she would never have stopped to think of the implications of Johnny O'Connor's cousin going out with a policeman.

Mrs. Garvey's concern would only have been that Ned was a man. Wouldn't Kate Mary, who had been a good respectable girl until now, be far better off going into the Convent where she would be safe from what her landlady felt to be a fate a thousand times worse than death.

Not for the first time Kate Mary wondered, and had often laughed with Ned about it, what exactly the poor late Mr. Garvey had done. In the sepia photograph in the parlour, he looked the most inoffensive of men; gazing out on what had been his home with mild protruberant eyes that could have threatened no one.

But Mrs. Garvey could, with her gossip, have confirmed all the suspicions of Connorstown, pleasing no one but Bridie Bannion, who would cling to any straw. Probably, thought Kate Mary wearily, they all believed now that she herself was passing information to the Police, and was the enemy of them all. They probably thought she had informed about the meeting that had brought the raid on Gorman's.

The Saturday after that Johnny had forbidden her to go into the town for Aunt Margaret's messages, and she had her first indication that she might be in actual danger.

'Give me that list,' Johnny said curtly. 'I'll go and get what you want. You stay here in the house.'

'Well, there's some things – Aunt Margaret wants thread and buttons. It'd be hard for you to get them.'

She almost smiled at the idea of Johnny going into the dark drapers for thread and buttons, but he was in no mood to smile back.

'I'll take her down in the week in the pony and trap. Tell me what you want now, Mam.'

Kate Mary stood in the small walled flower garden and watched him go out of the yard and off across the pasture to the gate. He had a bicycle himself now, although she couldn't understand why he needed it, having the cart and trap.

For one moment as he turned into the road he looked back at her as though knowing she watched him, and in that moment she understood.

Johnny was protecting her against his friends. She understood with sudden poignant clarity that the hard-eyed, cold-voiced Johnny was only the echo of his own sorrow. Ned and all, Johnny still loved her and would not see her harmed, above all on his behalf.

Never had she loved him more as she stood watching his dark figure on the high bicycle, growing distant against the pattern of grey stone walls. She felt tender and ashamed, crushing down the feeling that it would all have been easier had he hated her.

She could do no more than say a prayer for him as she knelt

down with the dibber at Aunt Margaret's flowerbeds, rooting away at the weeds outgrowing the flowers in the wild damp richness of the Irish spring.

'Please God, keep him safe,' she whispered, and even as she said it knew it impossible for even God to hold safety for both of them. Each was at risk from the other.

And she had chosen. Hopeless guilt drove her hands to the vicious destruction of the dockens and the long rank grass among the shooting flowers, as though taking it out on God himself because he couldn't help her.

On the following Friday, Johnny was late. She trundled into the Square, the old dressguard still trailing, trying not to look in the direction of the Barracks; hoping desperately that something would have Ned in the streets, so she could just see him although they couldn't speak properly.

But even 'Good afternoon, Sergeant' and 'Good day to you, Miss Pearse', and the quick secret message of his eyes below the bright peak of his cap, was like a drink of water in the desert.

Ned was not there to speak to her, and nor was anybody else. There were a few people here and there. That poor Mrs. Culcannon with her last baby in her arms was cadging a penny from anyone who would give. It seemed the useless husband came home from England only to add another child to her burdens, and then went off again.

Kate Mary fished in her pocket for a few coppers, and noticed fat Elsie O'Flyn at the Post Office door, glaring at her through her thick glasses.

Not a smile or a nod from one of them as she stood irresolute beside her bicycle. Kate Mary had the cold and frightening feeling that they all drew away from her, unified in their silent hostility. Even Mrs. Culcannon, as Kate Mary gave her the pennies, looked at her guiltily and then over her shoulder at Elsie O'Flyn, as though asking permission to take them.

Then a woman passing by spat at her. A decent, quiet woman Kate Mary had known through all her years in Caherliss; never known anything to come from her but the civil time of day. The spittle missed, but Kate Mary could not have been

133

more wounded had a thrown rock hit her on the skull. She looked down at the small obscene pool beside her shoe in sick disbelief, the old familiar grey square of Connorstown suddenly a place she wanted to run away from, never to see again.

'Ned,' she thought. 'Ned.' Only just there down the road, and this could happen to her. She stood stiff with fear, not for the one small act but for all that might come after it. Fear this time for herself as well as for Johnny and Ned.

Spittle this time, a bullet the next if they thought she had gone too far.

As she raised her eyes to watch Mrs. McNulty walk away, past Elsie O'Flyn's delighted grin, she remembered the woman would have had two sons that night in Gorman's. They thought her responsible for that!

She almost raced down the road and into the Barracks, to fling herself into Ned's arms and weep and cry that it wasn't fair. It had nothing to do with her. Nothing to deserve this degrading hatred that hung, palpable as mist, in the golden sunshine of the Square.

Carefully, she calmed herself, bending to fiddle with the trailing dressguard so that she needn't look at any of them. Dear God, of course it wasn't fair. And by the time this whole tragedy was over, there would be more, right up to death, that wasn't fair.

By the time Johnny eventually came, the worst of the shock had passed and she was even surprised at the mad clatter of hooves along the Archway Road, and the speed at which his cart came hurtling into the Square, scattering a few squawking geese that had chosen to cross at that moment.

He stared at her anxiously, the poor horse blowing and sweating at the sides, outraged at having been driven from Caherliss like the chariot of Ben Hur.

'Are you all right?' Johnny demanded. 'I'm late. Are you all right?'

Before she could answer, his eyes swept the grey Square from which everyone had miraculously disappeared, even Elsie O'Flyn returning to the darkness of her kingdom.

'Did anything happen?'

It was in that moment that she really understood his feel-

134

ings for her. Even though she had rejected him, and that not kindly; even hating Ned enough to kill him for himself, let alone for Ireland, Johnny still wanted to protect her.

Touched and shamed again, she smiled up at him as she had not smiled for months, and his eyes grew very still.

'Of course not, Johnny. What could happen to me here?'

She moved away from the drying spittle as he jumped down to take the bicycle.

'Thanks for coming,' she said softly.

Johnny flashed her a sideways look.

'Do I not always?'

'Yes. But thanks for today.'

There was a strange brittle light over the countryside, the grey walls like painted strips criss-crossed on the aching brilliance of the green fields, geese and cottages unnaturally white, and even the old brown horse strongly delineated in front of them against the muddy road.

Johnny's mood, which had been sombre for so long, was as brittle as the light, swinging between some secret wild hilarity and sudden poignant regrets as if he waited on some splendid excitement but could not hold away the cold touch of sorrow.

'Ah, Kate Mary,' he said suddenly, as they rumbled and sloshed along the mud, and the cart lurched through newly washed out potholes. 'Ah, Kate Mary, darling, if you had only loved me.'

His eyes were tender and regretful, soft as they used to be, and the cold thought struck her that such sad resignation belonged usually only to people facing death.

The living battled on for what they wanted.

She didn't know what to say.

'Haven't I always loved you, Johnny?'

'Ah, not in the way I wanted.' His voice was sad but without reproach.

All in the past. Everything he said was in the past. She remembered numbly what Ned had told her about them going into the hills for the summer. Johnny spoke as though he had small chance of coming back.

'You talk as if you're going off somewhere, Johnny.'

She tried to speak lightly, carefully, not to give away anything, but her lips were stiff.

135

'I could be. I could be that.'

'Will it be good?' What else could she say?

''Twill be good for Ireland. For me's another matter. But if it comes to the worst, won't I die happy.'

'For Ireland?'

'For Ireland, God save her.'

His tone was final and content, in it a calm acceptance that chilled her heart. Empty, helpless words were all she could find to say.

'I'd rather you lived for me, Johnny.'

'Ah, but you don't want me, Kate Mary. That'll make it easier to die, does it happen.'

She sat up straight, shocked almost to tears.

'Don't say that, Johnny! Don't say that!' she cried.

Guilt, too, to be added to all the difficulties of loving Ned? Guilt because she couldn't love Johnny as he wanted. They said a soldier would be killed quicker in any battle if he already wanted to die.

'It's not fair, Johnny, to say that. I can't turn the love on like a tap. It's not fair.'

'But you could give the tap a small turn, alannah, and see if it works.'

'Oh, it works,' she thought heavily. 'It works. But my poor Johnny, not for you.'

She was close to weeping. There was something doomed in his brittle light-heartedness. A great darkness lying behind it.

Like any soldier going off to war, he was trailing the shadow of his own death.

She laid her head against his shoulder, and he put an arm round her, and they rattled on up the bohreen apparently in the same content they had once known; separated now by the pain of their different loves.

Then he began to sing 'She is far from the land where her young hero sleeps,' the sad, sad song by Thomas More of the death of the young patriot Robert Emmett.

Quickly she put a hand to his lips.

'Not that Johnny, please. Not that.' Dear God, not now.

'Take no heed of me, Kate Mary, love,' he said at once, 'take no heed of me. I'm neither here nor there. Would *Phil the Fluter's Ball* be better?'

136

They were both singing, the tears still bright on Kate Mary's lashes, as they clattered into the yard. Aunt Margaret looked up from the pump and didn't know what to make of their bright faces, calling a cheerful greeting to her.

Had Kate Mary given up with the peeler, she thought with sudden hope, and turned to Johnny after all? Maybe all her desperate decades of the Rosary hadn't been for nothing.

As was her way, she asked them no questions but turned into the kitchen with her bucket of water and a severe comment about the mud on the cart. At least, she thought, the house might be a mite more cheerful for whatever future there was.

'Come on in, Kate Mary,' Johnny said as he unharnessed the horse, ignoring his mother. 'Come on in, and I'll beat the hide off you at a game of draughts.'

Such a little thing, but so long since they had done it. So long since she had done anything in simple pleasure with him.

She didn't know whether to be happy, or sick with the cold premonition of grief soon to come.

'Have you heard,' said Johnny, as he set out the board on the kitchen table, 'the news from Dublin? The poor peelers are losing Ireland. They can't keep it on their own. There's some load of lads come over from England to help them now, the poor creatures. The Black and Tans, they call them, the scrapings of the English prisons by all accounts. Well, they can send the King himself, but 'twill be no help. Ireland is winning. Come on, Kate Mary, will you be black or white? I'll have the beating of you, whatever you choose, like we have the beating of England.'

Kate Mary went back to Westport as usual on the Monday morning. On the Tuesday evening, just before six o'clock, old Miss Greeley of the Lawn came mincing into the Post Office, leading the way with her long nose, sniffing for anything she could find to complain about.

'Would you have any letters for me, Miss O'Flyn?'

Elsie didn't move, glaring belligerently across the heavy counter.

'I haven't them sorted.'

'Then I'll wait. Ai'm in no hurry.'

There had only been six letters for the whole of Connorstown that day, none of them for Miss Greeley and Elsie knew it. But she wasn't going to let the old crow away that easy. Let her cool her ould heels for a while.

'And Ai'm expecting a parcel,' cried Miss Greeley. 'You can look for that too!'

At that moment, the telephone rang. Muttering obstinately, Elsie turned to answer it. When she heard the voice at the other end she gave an anxious glance at Miss Greeley and turned her back, putting her squat bulk between the old lady and the instrument. God help them all if that old gossip heard one word!

Immediately Miss Greeley leaned over the counter and began to finger the parcels leaning behind it. There were several long ones tall enough to reach, and her cunning fingers probed them rapidly. Then she stopped and felt one of them again more carefully, unbelievingly, her old jaw dropping, eyes glittering with sudden shock and excitement behind the rimless glasses.

When Elsie hung up the telephone and turned back, Miss Greeley had put down her ancient purse and was using both hands to try and drag the long parcel to her, over the counter.

'Willya leave that,' Elsie shrieked, sick with fright, and made a dive to drag the parcel back. She grabbed. Miss Greeley heaved and pulled at the other end, thin old hands full of the strength of her excitement. The longed for defeat of Elsie O'Flyn was in her grasp; years of antagonism tightened her fingers.

'I know what you have in them,' she panted. 'Didn't I feel it. And there's more than one! I see them!'

''Tis not your business,' hissed Elsie. 'Give it here!'

''Tis my business. I'll take it to the Barracks.'

Miss Greeley was old, and at the disadvantage of leaning over the counter. By the end of the fierce silent battle, her grip was slipping. Desperately she clawed at the paper itself and a piece of it tore in her hands.

With a triumphant crow, she grabbed a fistful of the packing underneath, and tore it out. There between them, in the moment of unbelieving silence that unnerved both of them, clear through the hole in the torn parcel was the dull blue glint of a rifle barrel.

138

Her thin black bosom heaving with over exertion and self-righteousness, Miss Greeley glared at the Postmistress from her side of the counter, and on the other Elsie stood appalled, shaking already from sick fear of what would happen to her. What would happen to them all. Johnny and her brother would have the head off her. The bigger terrors had not yet touched her. There would be someone, her cringing mind told her, to save her from things like an English prison or the gallows.

At that moment the Angelus rang, flat and tinny from the grey church across the Square. Automatically, still heaving and panting, they abandoned their argument and blessed themselves, eyes still locked in the combat that the sweet habit of their childhood had forced them to abandon.

'The Angel of the Lord declared unto Mary – '

Muttering the prayer, they stood in the middle of Miss Greeley's triumph, although the poor old creature had little inkling of the extent of it. She cared only for the heady pleasure of catching Elsie O'Flyn doing something she shouldn't. Beyond that she saw nothing.

Outside, the silence of the Angelus, the age old prayer that halted war and work and pleasure twice a day, held the whole town. In the second that they blessed themselves at the end of it, their heads came up at once, eyes blazing. Somehow, Miss Greeley's hat had fallen to one side, increasing Elsie's feeling that she had nothing but an old fool to deal with. The boys would know what to do with her.

'I'll tell the Sergeant,' hissed Miss Greeley. 'I'll tell him now. I'll go now. This minnit.'

Her accent slipped a little under stress.

'You'll not. It's his day in Westport,' snapped Elsie.

Their only hope. If the old eejit waited until tomorrow, they could surely get everything clear tonight. But, dear God, where to? It was all so close, the whole village was stuffed like an arsenal. They had thought the Post Office safe.

'I'll see him first thing in the morning. You'll not be away with this, Elsie O'Flyn. I'll put a halt to your gallop.'

In her excitement and triumph, Miss Greeley had now completely lost her refined accent and spoke in the broad tones of the village. Elsie could hardly speak at all, desperate

139

for the old hen to go so that she could race up and tell Liam. She was shaking with fright as to what he would say to her when she did. And as for Johnny! She was almost weeping, desperate to go and yet terrified of what would happen.

'Gwan out of here,' she said hoarsely. 'You're nothing but a meddling old fool.'

'We'll see what the Sergeant says,' hooted Miss Greeley, and made her triumphant exit into the grey rain, her hat on the side of her head. In between the Post Office and the Barracks she put up her umbrella, green with age but with the ivory handle carefully cleaned with Fuller's Earth. Outside the Barracks she stood under it a long moment, irresolute. Would she go in at once and tell one of the Constables? She could see the long thin one inside the door.

From the safe shadows of the Day Room, Constable Doyle looked out at her. Getting to be only sixpence in the shilling, the old soul, he thought, and looking worse than ever today with her hat on one side as if she'd been brawling with someone.

He grinned at the idea, and moved further back out of sight lest she accost him for some reason.

Miss Greeley walked on. It was not suitable for Euphemia Greeley to talk to a common Constable. In any case it was always a pleasure to have the opportunity of speaking with that nice handsome young Sergeant. Such good manners. He knew how to treat a lady with respect. Umbrella erect, she made for home, relishing the treat in store tomorrow.

There would be trouble for that rude O'Flyn woman, and a nice chat with the Sergeant. She would be able to tell him her begonias were just shooting. He had always seemed so interested in gardening. A smile of anticipation on her thin lips, she picked her way delicately between the puddles, careful of her good boots.

Behind her, Elsie locked the door, trembling, and raced up to her brother's shop. Her teeth were chattering. Prison and even death yawned before her now that she had begun to think. Liam and Johnny must do something! She could always say of course, that she never knew what was in the parcels, but then there was the Mail Man from Westport. He knew what

140

was in them, but to save his own skin could well say that none of them had ever seen a Post Office until they reached Connorstown.

By the time she got to Liam, the rain had drenched her.

He looked up amazed from the bill he was writing for a burly farmer whose only raincoat was an old sack about his shoulders.

'What's on you, Elsie?' he said, and in that second caught a hint of her anxiety. 'What made you come out like that? You're soaked to the skin!'

She couldn't speak. It was blurt it all out or nothing. Dumbly she nodded at the farmer, and collapsed on to a bag of meal in the shadows to wait, wiping the rain from her glasses on the end of her scarlet petticoat with shaking fingers.

Even in the dark shop she could see that Liam's face went ash grey when she told him, but he wasted no words or time on reproaches.

'They'll have you before the Committee, girl,' was all he said, already taking off his long grey overall.

'I did nothing, Liam, nothing. Th' old crow leaned over and started pulling at the parcels. Hasn't she been a thorn in my side as long as I've been there?'

'You must have turned your back on her.'

He was pulling on an ancient mackintosh of faded gaberdine that had clearly belonged to his taller and bigger father. Putting a foot up on a sack, he folded the ends of his trousers rapidly into his bicycle clips.

Elsie put her desperate face down to his, beginning to weep now with fright.

'Wasn't it Ennis on the telephone, checking it had all arrived? If I hadn't turned my head, she'd have heard me. She has the ears of a bat, that one.'

Even as he pulled his cloth cap well down on his head, Liam felt coldly certain what must be done. But he couldn't give the order on his own.

'Where are you going?' quavered Elsie.

'Caherliss. Where else?'

He was thinking frantically. It was the worst danger that had ever confronted them. All the peelers ramping round Desmond's had been no more than a joke. They would never hide arms where people might be discovered, then the one could always deny the other. The ammunition in the sofa should never have been there at all; and as for the people, the poor peelers never saw hair nor hide of them.

This was another matter.

Even if they cleared the Post Office this very night – and that would be a nuisance, for where better to hide parcels than among a lot of other parcels? – it would never be safe again. They'd be opening every parcel that came to it, and watching it night and day.

And Peter Garrett from Westport who brought it all in the Mail Cart. Did they put pressure on him, he could give away Ennis and then the whole organisation for the area was blown to smithereens. He began to sweat slightly, not acknowledging any fear for himself but for all they had all built up over the years that was only now, at last, coming to be used.

He gave no thought to his sister. She faced the same risks as them all, and did she die at the hands of the enemy then it would be for Ireland, and what more glorious death for any of them?

Elsie, whimpering on the meal sack, appeared to have forgotten all about the glory of death for Ireland.

'What about me?'

He looked at her white terrified face.

'You pull yourself together and get back to where you belong as if nothing had happened.'

'Supposing she comes back and tells them, before you see Johnny?'

'You said she went straight home.'

'She did. She stopped a minnit in front of the Barracks as is she would go in, there and then, and then she went on towards the Lawn.'

'She'll not come back in this weather.' He tossed her an empty sack. 'Here, put this over your shoulders and get going.'

He wheeled his bicycle in from the back room and locked the shop behind them both, looking carefully up and down the grey abandoned street before he did so. It was just enough out of the ordinary for himself and Elsie to be where they were to attract the attention of some patrolling policeman.

142

Not even a hen rambled from the yard, looking for the fallen pickings outside the shop.

'Get going,' he said to his sister.

Elsie scuttled off back to the Post Office where Rosie Culcannon with two bedraggled babies was hanging round the door, still hoping for the money from England.

'Where were you?' she demanded as if she were the best customer the Post Office ever had. 'Where were you, keeping people waiting in the rain?'

Elsie was still shattered, ashen, her fingers shaking too much to find the key.

'Get on outa me way,' she hissed at the poor woman, and at her cross voice a baby began to howl. 'Get on outa me way. There's nothing for you and never will be.'

Roughly she pushed Rosie and the babies aside, knocking the older one on to the wet street, never dreaming that in her moment of frantic unkindness she had helped to set a seal on her long future years in an English prison.

She left Rosie unheeded outside the door, yelling abuse at her, both babies screaming, and crawled under her counter flap. Among the incriminating parcels, she stood and tried to steady the mad thudding of her heart and the fear that was sickness in her stomach.

She needed to go to the chamber.

It would be all right, she told herself. It would be all right, Johnny and Liam would settle it.

Ned came towards the Barracks from the opposite direction, the rain streaming from his cape and the peak of his cap. He looked along the street at the small draggled figure of Rosie Culcannon, going dejectedly away from the Post Office with the two crying babies.

Poor girl, he thought, for she was no more. Poor girl. No money again. Many a day he gave her a shilling.

Liam put his head down and pushed as hard as he could for Caherliss, through the grey relentless downpour. 'Twould be no weather for the hills anyway.

He caught Johnny down in the low field, walking behind the old hand plough, turning stubble into the dark, peaty soil

143

to lie for a few weeks and then be turned again, and harrowed for the new sowing.

The anxiety in Liam's pinched face as he peered over the stone wall made Johnny stop at once and call the old horse to stand. He had no need to be told there was something wrong. Liam was breaking one of the strict rules of the Committee even to be seen here, looking for him in daylight. Two men leaving their work to talk would be enough to make any policeman think.

It must be something desperate to have him here like this. Johnny reached him at the wall, and the awful pallor and anxious eyes of the small man did nothing to reassure him.

'What's on you?'

Liam told him.

'Sacred mother in Heaven,' said Johnny. 'Was your sister out of her mind?'

'I'd think so,' said Liam flatly. No concern for Elsie entered either of their faces, only the dreadful fear of all their carefully laid plans.

'Who knows?' Johnny asked sharply.

'Not a soul but meself and me sister. And the ould woman, of course.'

'Where is she?'

'She went on home to the Lawn, me sister said, on account of the Sergeant being in Westport. She's coming back to report it in the morning.'

'She mustn't.'

Between the blue angry eyes and the pale myopic ones of Elsie's brother lay a cold certainty.

'She must be stopped.'

Johnny was calmer now, acknowledging their unspoken decisions and aware that the small man was waiting for him to take the lead. For a few moments he felt total contempt for him. Wasn't it his sister had made the mess, and now all he could do was stand there with the rain on those bottle glasses and wait to have it all put right for him.

'There's only one way to stop her,' he said coldly, and in dumb agreement Liam nodded.

''Tis Elsie should do it,' Johnny said, and the pale O'Flyn eyes widened.

144

'Sure, Johnny, she couldn't do a thing like that.'

'Could you?'

Liam blinked, considering the question as though it were nothing to do with him, and Johnny's eyes were cold as flints. Like all of them, Liam had a lot to learn. They were all ready still to do anything at a distance. Fire a rifle from behind a wall or fling a torch into a Barracks and off like the wind. The real thing had never touched them. No blood yet, the creatures, on their own two hands.

Their day would come, and was coming fast.

'I'd – I'd think not,' said Liam.

'And you me Lieutenant,' said Johnny scathingly. 'I'll do it meself,' he said. It had begun to rain again and he brushed the plastered hair up off his forehead. 'She'll go to no Barracks in the morning. Now go on back before the whole place is looking for you.'

Slowly Liam climbed back on his bicycle, and pedalled off through the rain, finding excuses for himself.

Wasn't Sinn Fein supposed to be for men fighting each other? Wasn't that what he had joined for? Not things like this.

And in any case, wasn't it right that the Commandant should do the hard jobs?

Johnny came in from the fields with a calm face, peeling the sodden sack from his shoulders and ate an excellent dinner of his mother's mutton stew.

'That was grand, Mama,' he said. 'Grand.'

He went off then into his bedroom, and carefully closed the door. He was too well prepared a soldier for his revolver to need oiling, but he'd check it just the same.

It was the little girl who cleaned the house who found Miss Greeley the next morning.

She was puzzled to find the front door open. Miss Greeley thought the habit of the ever open door was only for the lower classes. Anyone who came to see her must ring her doorbell in a civilised fashion, and wait to be let in.

Even though it was open, Annie didn't dare go through it. Her place was at the back door into the scullery, and round there she went. Again she was puzzled. This door, usually opened for her, was locked.

Always afraid of doing something wrong in the eyes of her demanding employer, her knock was timid.

'Miss Greeley,' she called. 'Miss Greeley.'

There was nothing. Not even the cat, who had always came rubbing at her legs.

Ah, the poor woman, she thought. She must have taken sick. She'll be in there in her bed not able to get up.

Should she, she wondered, go back for her mother? But it mightn't please Miss Greeley, if she was in a bit of a weakness or something. She hated being seen by anyone, if she and the house were not tidy enough for the Pope himself to come into it.

Carefully, Annie pushed through the front door into the polished hall.

'Miss Greeley, ma'am.'

Silence. No Miss Greeley. And no cat.

Annie went into the kitchen which was spotless from the blue oilcloth floor to the geraniums in the window between the white lace curtains. The Sacred Heart was on one wall and Our Blessed Lady on the other, a row of glittering tins on the mantelpiece.

There were no signs of breakfast. No vessels to be washed up in the stone sink in the scullery. Carefully she put out a finger and touched the range. It was cold. Usually Miss Greeley was up before seven, fresh turf on the range and her breakfast eaten before Annie ever got there. God help her, the poor woman must be sick.

The bedroom door across the hall was slightly ajar, and when she got no answer to her knock, she bravely opened it a little further and peered in round it at the bed.

Miss Greeley was there but she was long past sickness. Everything on the high brass bedstead was snow white, even the heavy crochet quilt she had made herself in the long solitary hours of which she had had so many; all the whiteness an instinctive demonstration of the virginity she had worn like a badge.

So that although there was not a great deal of blood, it showed up dark and terrifying against the white. Miss Greeley's own composed face was as ashen as the lace-edged pillows.

146

She had been shot through the heart as she slept, unknowing, her hands still clasped, darkened with blood, around the red Rosary of the Sacred Heart as her mother had taught her, lest God take her in the night.

As indeed He had, by someone else's hand.

Annie could not walk one step into the room, her eyes widening and becoming fixed. She was unaware of the cat that had jumped from its cushion on the chair and was rubbing eagerly against her legs, asking why he hadn't had his breakfast when it was long past time.

She never felt him as she turned and blundered in dead silence from the house, out into a glittering morning clear as glass after all the rain; across the wet green spaces of the Lawn spangled with cobwebs and through the gate in the wall; up the narrow cobbled alley where a surprised old terrier chased her, barking and snapping at her heels. She never even noticed him, and he gave up when she burst on to the road, racing for the Barracks as fast as her thin legs could pound it. Glassy-eyed, her hair flying, she was totally indifferent to the few early passers by, who would tell for years to come the story of how weren't they the ones actually saw young Annie Lennane tearing for the Barracks with the news, like the devil himself was after her.

Inside the Barracks she crashed to a halt in front of Ned at the table, her thin chest heaving, fixing him with these unfocussed eyes, dark with shock and horror.

Then and only then, she started screaming.

It took them minutes to quieten her and get it out of her.

'Give her a cup of tea, Constable Murphy,' Ned said quietly, 'and send for her mother.'

The plump and kindly Constable already had the shaking child in a chair, his arm around her.

'Isn't her mother me cousin,' he said, as though that solved everything. 'I'll care for her.'

'Constable Doyle,' said Ned, 'you come with me.'

He was already on his way out through the door to the yard to get his bicycle.

'I don't know, Sir,' he said despairingly to his frosty-faced D.I. later in the day. 'I just don't know. Whoever it was came

147

round by the yard and got in the scullery window. Not a foot-
print nor a thing. It was early in the night, the doctor says. Still
raining. Presumably they left by the front door, since that was
open.'

'Apart from what you *know*, Sergeant, what do you *think*?'

Ned looked him straight in the face, shaken by the strange
senseless killing of the old woman. The act was so violent and
she so peaceful, as though she had lain there unmoving and
accepted the Will of God with not even her eyes opened.
Whoever did it had no wish to frighten her; only to be rid of
her.

'I think, Sir,' he said, 'what we all think of every violent
death in Ireland at the present time – that it's the work of Sinn
Fein. Here that means O'Connor and his henchmen, but I can
see no reason for their killing old Miss Greeley. No reason at
all. It's me natural instinct to race out and arrest O'Connor,
but all my reason tells me that'd be useless. He'll be as
innocent as a baby with every alibi the angels themselves
could dream up. I'll need some harder evidence than just the
corpse, Sir.'

'Would she be a spy of any kind?'

'Well, she'd have to be ours, Sir,' said Ned reasonably, 'for
them to kill her. And I don't think we're desperate enough to
be using an old woman of over seventy.'

He paused, his eyes reflective, stroking one of the now long
points of his moustache.

'There's only one thing, Sir.'

'Yes?' The D.I. was more tolerant now, realising at last
that Ned was not a fool but faced here in Connorstown with a
measure of intelligence and cunning it was going to be difficult
to break. 'Yes?'

'I think possibly she may have learned something, Sir. By
accident. And they had to see she didn't talk.'

'A bit extreme. Couldn't they just have frightened her?'

Ned thought of the erect and determined old lady, chatting
with such careful refinement about her garden. Why in God's
name had she always thought he cared about gardens? But
she took some getting away from.

'I'd not think she'd frighten easy, Sir. She'd be a great one
for her duty.'

148

'As,' he thought sadly and bleakly, 'I will have to be. Johnny O'Connor has brought murder to the village, and now no one can be taken easy. No one.'

The D.I. stood up.

'Keep in touch, Sergeant.'

Ned stood up too, and to attention.

He was thinking with anguish that that included Kate Mary.

Johnny was waiting for her when she rode into the Square on Friday, full of horrified questions about the murder. News of it had reached Westport, and Mrs. Garvey had been bubbling over when she came home from early Mass that morning, hardly having the patience to hang up her shawl.

'It'll be the Sinn Feiners,' she said, attacking the stirabout with a wooden spoons as though it were Michael Collins himself. 'Heed what I say – it'll be the Sinn Feiners.'

'But why an old woman like that? What harm could she be to them? She could do nothing.'

'They'll have had their reasons,' said Mrs. Garvey darkly. 'They'll have had their reasons, the villains.'

Her habit of saying everything twice failed this time to irritate Kate Mary, sitting silent at the kitchen table, suddenly not wanting to eat her breakfast. Fear filled her that Mrs. Garvey could be right, choking her against the warm milky stirabout, and the delicious smell of eggs and bacon sizzling on the range. Surely Johnny, not even Johnny who thought nothing of death, could do that. Or send someone else to do it.

She pushed her plate away, as she pushed down the thought.

'Are you sick?' demanded Mrs. Garvey.

No one was allowed to refuse her food. To avoid a barrage of questions and resentment all the rest of the day, Kate Mary drew back her plate and forced herself to eat.

It reassured her somewhat to see Johnny sitting calm-faced in the cart, and she saw Bridie Bannion going off up towards Gorman's as though she had just been talking to him. She realised she had more than half expected to find the lot of them in jail, and sighed with relief to see it was not so. The

149

murder could be nothing at all to do with Johnny. It must have been someone who thought the old lady had something to steal. Connorstown was full of rumours that she was rotten rich.

She listened too much to Mrs. Garvey, she decided, as she dragged the old bicycle to a stop.

'Hallo there, Johnny,' she said, but before she could say more, or he could answer, Constable Doyle came round from the other side of the cart. He saluted her formally, which startled her.

'Good day, Miss Pearse. The Sergeant says will you please step into the Barracks for a moment.'

She stared at him, her mouth open.

'The Sergeant?'

'Sergeant Brannick, Miss Pearse.'

'I know his name,' Kate Mary snapped, feeling the whole business was going from her control and that she didn't know how to handle it. What could Ned want to talk to her about, and sending this ferret-faced policeman to get her?

She looked at Johnny, temper already blazing in her eyes, accusing him wordlessly of having got her into it.

'You have to go, Kate Mary,' he said, and his expression held unkind pleasure. 'He wants to ask you where you were when old Miss Greeley was killed on Tuesday last.'

'But I was – ' Kate Mary protested, and then stopped.

'We all know that,' said Johnny unpleasantly. 'And who should know better than the Sergeant where you were on a Tuesday.'

She felt she had been hit in the stomach, winded. But how could you hope to keep anything a secret in Ireland, where the very stones had tongues.

Johnny's mother had known, so why shouldn't he? But he had never mentioned it before, and, foolishly, she had thought her secret safe. No doubt all Connorstown knew, fool that she was.

From the corners of her eyes, for she wouldn't gratify them by turning her head, she could see the people who had sprung from nowhere around the edges of the Square. They had been drawn, no doubt, by the comedy of Kate Mary Pearse, who was going with the Sergeant, being called in for questioning by him.

150

She felt her cheeks go scarlet as Ned's own when he was under stress.

'Will you please come, Miss Pearse. The Sergeant is heart scalded trying to get the rights of this, and he not here at all on the Tuesday.'

She glanced at the policeman sharply.

'Nor was I.'

'Indeed, Miss Pearse. But will you tell the Sergeant that, and he can write it down.'

Was he too making a fool of her? she wondered as she leaned the bicycle against the cart. Would she feel now that everything said to her in the village would have a double meaning; all part of the hostility she had felt lately, chilling her. Making her an outsider like the police themselves. Did they all think that if she did have anything to do with the murder, then the Sergeant would let her off, she being his girl?

Her hands were shaking and she clenched them close together as she walked down the street with Constable Doyle, aware of Elsie O'Flyn peering from the Post Office; of other watching eyes she wouldn't meet.

In the Barracks, Ned was still carefully playing the game, regarding her sombrely from his chair behind the Day Room table, a list of every man, woman and child who lived in Connorstown in front of him. He looked composed and completely in control, and she couldn't know that his heart was racing like a mail train under his tunic, and his hands were below the table so he could surreptitiously wipe the sweat away from them on the knees of his trousers.

'Good evening, Miss Pearse.'

'Good evening, Sergeant.'

They tried not to look at each other. He above all since the low sun through the barred window was catching the tendrils of hair pulled loose from her cap on the bicycle ride, making him long to take them and curl them round his fingers, kissing her while he did so. As on happier days.

'I'm investigating a murder, Miss Pearse, and I have to ask you, like everyone else in the village, to account for your movements on Tuesday of last week.'

Now she looked at him and lost all patience with the

charade, sick and tired that she couldn't have her love in the open like any other girl. She was infuriated by the hint of a smirk on Constable Doyle's face as he sat down to record her every word in the careful copperplate of the R.I.C.

Her head went up and her hands stopped shaking. She looked at Ned, and he could see the blazing anger in her eyes. He felt helpless. Who could blame her for it, and who could be surprised if in the end the whole business cost their love?

'Go easy, Kate Mary darling,' he wanted to say to her. 'Go easy. I love you. This means nothing.'

Kate Mary had no intention of going easy, her head in the air and her temper up.

'D'you mind telling me, Miss Pearse?'

'I do not, Sergeant Brannick.' Her voice was cool and cut him to the heart. 'I do not. I was in the school, in the Convent in Westport until four o'clock, and then I went out to meet – ' she paused – 'a friend. I met him at the gates of Westport House and we went for a walk along the road to Mulranny. We sat for some time on some old steps out above the sea, and then walked back. My friend – ' again the small pointed pause – 'left me near the railway station and I was back in my lodgings for the supper at seven. My landlady, Mrs. Garvey, can tell you I didn't go out again.'

She never took her eyes off him, and all Ned's training and self-discipline couldn't prevent the tide of scarlet rising to his face as she spoke. Fortunately, Constable Doyle was too concerned with his slow writing to lift his head, but Ned felt about the size of a leprechaun and could not help himself by raising an anger to match hers.

He could only feel a sick, trapped sorrow. He could lose her over this. She could go riding off with her blue-eyed Johnny, and he never see her again, except in the distance.

'Ah, Kate Mary, I love you. Don't be angry.' He almost said it aloud.

Constable Doyle was slow, having difficulty spelling Mulranny, dipping and dipping his pen in the china inkpot, as though more ink would help him.

There was time in the cold fading sunlight of the impersonal room for her temper to cool down but no moment for her to say she was sorry, sitting there in silence with Ned who could

152

not look directly at her, and Constable Doyle a barrier between them, scratching away at his piece of paper.

Her throat was thickening, and she could feel the tears hot under her eyelids.

'Can I go now?' she managed to say.

'You have to sign this.' Ned's own voice was rough, and he couldn't manage a word too many.

They sat there in helpless silence that seemed to last hours, waiting for Constable Doyle to scratch patiently to the end of what she had said. Her eyes went involuntarily towards the wall of the Day Room beyond which there was hammering and banging. Ned tried to ease the moment, grasping at something to say.

'We've taken the house next door,' he told her. 'I'm to have three more constables.'

Now she looked at him, shaken, thinking of only Johnny. They'd get him in the end, simply by force of numbers. The others were not important. It was Johnny they wanted, the very second they could pin him with anything.

Her eyes were full of tears and dark with sorrow, loving Ned with all her heart yet knowing him the enemy. If this piece of paper she was about to sign could hang Johnny, then Ned would use it and love her none the less. But where could forgiveness lie?

Johnny couldn't have killed Miss Greeley. There was no reason. The poor old creature, what threat could she be to Sinn Fein? Over this, at least, there could be nothing to fear.

'I'm ready, Sir,' Constable Doyle said with an air of triumph, breathing a little heavily and laying down his pen.

Ned read it to her, his voice carefully expressionless as if it were the meaningless tale of strangers; the stone steps above the sea on the way to Mulranny a place he had never heard of.

'Will you sign that?'

'I will.'

'I'm afraid the nib is little good.' He tried to smile.

What difference could it make to anyone, she thought, she wasn't even in the town.

She signed. Both of them were composed now, playing their parts for the Constable, and then she got up to go with nothing more said; no questions asked nor answered.

Miss Greeley's death was no concern of hers or Johnny's. Please God, let it be no concern of Johnny's.

Ned, his heart full of pain, could not let her go like that.

'Miss Pearse,' he said to her as she reached the door.

'Yes?' She turned, and had he been looking even Constable Doyle could not have missed all that was reflected in their eyes.

'If I need to know any more, I'll be in Westport on Tuesday. Will you be there?'

At the usual place, my love? he was asking her desperately. At the usual place, alannah. Will you be there? For God's sake, be there.

'Yes, Sergeant,' she said. 'I'll be there.'

It was all so foolish, she thought as she went down the street, that she wanted to laugh. So ridiculous. But the tears came suddenly instead, and she had to bend down in the street and pretend to tie her bootlace before she could go on to face Johnny, who sat watching her from the cart, his own face inimical, knowing well what she was doing.

He leaned down and gave her a hand up the wheel on to the cart, and without another word chucked the reins and set the pony going, out of the unnaturally quiet Square, and off along the road to Caherliss; silent, without any of last week's exuberance. There would, thought Kate Mary sadly, be no game of draughts this evening.

Behind her in the Barracks, Constable Doyle laid her statement in the old-fashioned box file on top of all the others. His long face was rebellious.

'And why,' he asked 'go upsetting a good girl like Kate Mary Pearse? Doesn't all Connorstown know she wouldn't be in the place on a Tuesday?'

Ned looked at him sharply but he seemed to have meant no more than just what he had said, shuffling all the statements into tidiness, many of them signed with no more than a cross.

'Duty, Constable,' he said firmly. 'Duty does not pick and choose.'

'The day,' said Constable Doyle equally firmly, and meeting his eye, 'might well be coming when it does.'

He turned to fit the file into its space on the shelf, and Ned, touched by some sense of alarm, let the comment

154

pass, resolving nevertheless to keep an eye on Constable Doyle.

Rumbling along between the green fields, softened by the lambent blue of an Irish evening, Kate Mary could not hold back her weeping. The severe beauty of the spring country-side against the turmoil of her own feelings was too great a contrast for her to bear.

She sat bolt upright on the seat beside Johnny, hoping that if she didn't move he wouldn't notice the tears following each other ever more rapidly down her cheeks, so that she had to lick them fiercely from the corners of her mouth.

He didn't even turn his head, but he had noticed.

'I never knew you were fond of her,' he said.

'Fond of who?'

She had to give in, groping in her coat pocket for a hand-kerchief.

'Old Euphemia Greeley. Isn't that who you're crying for?'

Angrily she blew her nose.

'Of course not!'

'Well, who could it be then?'

He turned the cart into the back bohreen, and although the man in the cottage on the corner waved and called 'Good day!' standing by the shrinking turf stack Johnny had pro-vided, he never answered or turned his head.

'Who would you be crying for?' he repeated.

Stung, she wheeled on him, her face still wet.

'You, I suppose,' she snapped at him. 'You. Me. All of us with the sorrow round us.'

'And why cry for me, Kate Mary? I've no need for your tears. It's your love I'm asking for, not your weeping.'

'But I do love you, Johnny, that's why I cry.'

'You do not, or you'd have proved it by now.'

'Oh, Johnny.' She felt desperate for him to understand, be gentle and affectionate again while she was oppressed by this terrible fear that time for everything was running short. 'Johnny, there's more than one kind of love.'

'I only know one kind, and you'll have none of that.'

He turned the pony sharply into the yard as if that closed the conversation.

155

Kate Mary's head went up. Galled by the unfairness, she rounded on him as the cart stopped.

'And did you never love Bridie Bannion?'

His eyes were pale and cold as ice, merciless.

'I did not,' he said calmly, 'never a day of it.'

'Then why – ?'

'A man takes his pleasures as he finds them,' he said. 'Until he finds the right woman, and that's another thing altogether.'

Kate Mary sat limp, making no move to leave the cart. She no longer thought of Johnny, only of poor Bridie who, no matter what they said of her, was no more than a girl like herself, loving a man.

She knew she herself loved Ned so much that if anything went wrong about it, she'd not want to live at all.

'God help her,' she said then slowly. 'The poor creature, God help her.'

Then another thought struck her. Something in the twist of Bridie's lip. A chill behind the softness of the great green eyes. She would not go easily without what she wanted.

'Take care, Johnny,' she said suddenly. 'Take care. Don't be taking her too far. She could be a bad enemy.'

Then he laughed out aloud, and his eyes were blue again.

'Is it me be afraid of Bridie Bannion? Get on down out of that, Kate Mary, and let me put the horse away before he falls asleep in the yard.'

She got down, and left him to put the bicycle away, going in through the scullery past the broody hen Aunt Margaret had there, sitting round and white on a clutch of eggs like a china hen on someone's mantelpiece. In the dusky kitchen where the lamps were not yet lit the turf glowed scarlet around the bastable oven with its delicious smell of roasting beef. In the quietness Aunt Margaret was just laying the last of the table, and on the window sill the small red lamp of the Sacred Heart gave eternal promise of peace and safety to them all.

Kate Mary paused in the door way.

Dear God, she thought, if it could only be no more than this. Always. Always. But she knew the peace and safety promised by the little red lamp was an illusion. And the Sacred Heart was there to guard them through death as well as life.

156

Fiercely she shook off her mood of sadness and premonition and smiled at her aunt.

'Hallo, Aunt Margaret.'

'You're late.'

'I was asked to go down to the Barracks to make a
statement to Sergeant Brannick about where I was when Miss
Greeley was killed.'

At the very mention of Ned's name, peace fled the comfortable kitchen and the chill of hostility took its place.

Aunt Margaret didn't answer, taking a spill of paper from
the tin on the mantelpiece and bending down to kindle it in
the fire that she might busy herself lighting the lamps.

They buried Miss Greeley the next Wednesday in the cold
grey chapel that had changed little since, as a small protected
child, devout and filled with faith, she had said her prayers
and warbled her favourite hymns; walked self-conscious in
her white dress and wreath on Corpus Christi, scattering the
flowers of innocence before the monstrance in the procession of the Sacred Heart.

Her relatives had arrived in Westport from Dublin the
evening before, coming down the dim gaslit station platform
in a drift of black crêpe and hard hats. The women were
already weeping suitably, more from the shame of having a
murder in the family than from grief because none of them
had set eyes on Aunt Euphemia these last twenty years.

Having settled them in the hotel, where they wanted only
the best in view of their expectations, the men went off to the
Police Barracks, sombre in their black suits and high white
collars, all of them anxious to get it over and done with.

Murdered or not, wasn't old Euphemia dead and the three
of them, sons of her only sister, were the ones left to expect
something. The formalities were little but a nuisance to them.

By all accounts Aunt Euphemia was a very warm woman,
left everything by her doting father when he died and not a
penny to their mother.

A warm woman she must be, and now it was all theirs by
rights. Carefully, as they approached the grey block of the
Barracks, they composed their faces, two red and one pale
and waxy as a candle, into suitable expressions of appalled

grief; patient only for the all important moment tomorrow, when the Solicitor they had been in touch with would read them the Will in his branch office in Connorstown, Aunt Euphemia safely in her grave.

Confident that they would get it all back, they had spared no expense in the funeral arrangements with the undertaker in Westport.

The day was still and fair with warmth in the spring sun shining down on the bare heads of all the people of Connorstown who filled the Square. They stared and whispered and nudged each other at the splendour of the four black horses with their nodding plumes, and the fine glass-sided hearse with engraved pictures like in the mahogany doors of Gorman's Bar. And the whole thing garnished, would you ever believe it, with knobs and curlicues of real silver. The whole lot of it, with the coffin inside, had arrived the evening before, to be locked in a stable out on the Westport edge of the village, attracting as much attention and excitement from the children as the annual arrival of Duffy's Circus.

Apart from the six members of the family, who came in a hired carriage from Westport, crêpe veils drifting in the soft wind, and Ned who was there from duty, the church was empty.

For every other funeral ever held in Connorstown, the church had been full; packed by all the men of the town, there to pay their respects in their best dark suits, their cloth caps in their hands. The women stood outside in the Square to comfort the bereaved, and to bless themselves and gabble a prayer as the coffin left the church.

Usually it was in the back of a farm cart. The men would follow it on the long slow uphill walk to the graveyard away out on the Dublin road. The grey rocks of the land pushing up between the graves, and the big Celtic cross that reared against the sky, usually served as gravestones. With Miss Greeley it would be different. Marble, the brothers planned, and maybe even a weeping angel.

For this funeral, no man set foot in the church lest his very presence should show some complicity in the murder; and the old lady, with all her superior notions had had no friends.

O'Connor was nowhere to be seen.

Ned and Ned alone stood at the back of the chapel by the ugly stone font, looking up at the coffin with its solitary wreath before the altar. The dusty catalfalque was touched by a ray of sunshine falling through the unfortunate pale yellow glass of the windows. It could do nothing to warm or comfort the cold grey building with all the rows of empty pews.

He could hear the sniffing and sobbing of the women from where he stood, and see the clutching of large white handkerchiefs. He wondered unkindly again why, if there was so much grief for Miss Greeley now, they had never set foot in Connorstown before.

In trying to solve the strange and senseless murder, he had achieved nothing. Connorstown had closed its ranks, as only that maddening grey clump of a village could. No one knew anything; had heard anything; had seen anything. No one would say anything.

Johnny O'Connor had even been in Castlebar, for God's sake, and taken care to be seen there by the police. Ned tried to curb his feeling that everything bad that happened in Connorstown had Johnny at the back of it. He could see nothing political in the killing of this old woman. It made no sense.

But what else could he see? What did make sense? Nothing, nothing at all. And the D.I. breathing down his neck from Westport, convinced that it was all tied in somewhere with Sinn Fein. He had said so the evening before, when the relatives had come to the Barracks in Westport.

Miss Greeley's nephew had laughed out loud when Ned had suggested this, forgetting his grief and then hastily rearranging his features.

His poor old aunt, he said sadly, wouldn't have known politics from the kitchen cat. At this point, too, Ned had wondered how they knew so much about her, admitting to only one letter a year at Christmas.

In any case, said the nephew, as if he answering him, wasn't she too old to be any use to anybody? Politics indeed! If he let that one run, they might hold up the funeral. Sweat stood on his fleshy forehead.

With that Ned had had to agree, not satisfied but at the moment defeated.

159

The priest pronounced the last blessing over the lonely coffin and the three nephews stood up with the undertaker to carry it out the door for there no one in the village would put a shoulder to it.

As though, thought Ned, it was cursed. All for an old woman. But knowing Connorstown, he felt sure that in that costly dark oak with its one wreath there was some clue to everything that was evading him. Something that had all the village, man and woman, waiting silent in the sun outside the church; evading his eye as he came out. Waiting for the moment, he thought, when their secret would be safely buried. Touched by the shifty movements of a collective guilt.

He gritted his teeth.

Their secret would never be buried until he found out what it was, no matter where Miss Greeley was.

No one spoke to him as he stood in the crowd and saw the coffin loaded into the ornate hearse; watched the black plumes nodding as the horses drew it off out of the Square and down towards the Mill, followed by the one overcrowded carriage of black-clad mourners.

No one from the village moved to walk behind it, and Ned felt a pang of pity for the old woman who had been an old snob and a nuisance, God knew, but had surely done nothing to deserve this.

He moved to go back to the Barracks and found himself held up by two women in the crowded street, unaware of him under the hooded shadow of their shawls.

One blessed herself and sighed.

'God ha' mercy on her,' she said, with a compassion the village had not shown. 'Did you see the grandeur? And the feathers on the horses, and you and me with not even a hat, let alone a feather on it.'

The other nodded.

'I did. I saw it all. There's money there to be lining someone's pocket.'

'There is,' said the first one, and spoke reverently as though she had touched the money itself. 'To think I saw the poor woman, and away home to her death. I must be one of the last ever set eyes on her.'

'Arrah, go on. You were not. And where was she?'

'Didn't she come out of the Post Office, and put up her umbrella. 'Twas just past the Angelus. And outside the Barracks the creature stopped just as I was passing. "Good evening, Miss Greeley," I said to her, in manners, but divil the answer she gave me; staring over at the Barracks as if she had something on her mind. Then off she goes towards the Lawn and whatever happened to her, the poor soul. And it raining,' she added, as though even murder could be made worse by rain.

Ned had heard all he needed. By damn, the Post Office! He had seen that day the poor Rosie Culcannon being hurled into the street by that sneering little frog, sister to the O'Flyn's. Something had been wrong there. What had the poor old woman seen? His first impulse was to crash through the thinning crowd, but he realised he'd have half of them in on top of him in two minutes, and no chance of finding anything. And the other half of them away to warn anybody they might think concerned.

Quietly, his steady face hiding a hopefully churning mind, he made his way over through the last of the people to where Constable Daly stood rock solid on the corner on the other side of the Square, watching as he had been told for anything unusual. As if, thought Ned, the whole thing wasn't as unusual as a turkey laying a bantam's egg. Disciplined, he stood a moment or two beside the policeman before he spoke.

'All quiet, Constable?'

'All quiet, Sir.'

'Well, then, quietly ourselves, I want you to stroll over with me to the Post Office. I'll go in, and do you stay outside and see no one comes in after me. No one. Do you understand? And stand on the corner so you can see both doors.'

'I do, Sergeant.' He looked at Ned's face, the two patches of high colour alone betraying his superior's excitement. 'What is it, Sir? Have we got something?'

'You'll know soon enough. Come on now.'

By the time they reached the Post Office the Square was empty, the priest closing the gate in the railings of the church.

Miss Greeley might never have existed.

161

Chapter 7

Ned didn't rush at her, even when he was inside the door.

He simply stood and unbuttoned the flap of his revolver, and could see from the pure terror in the face across the counter that he was in the right place.

She backed away, her tongue suddenly clinging to the roof of her mouth, her stomach balled into a knot. Death in glory for Ireland was, all in a moment, strictly for other people. She tried not to wet herself, and struggled for defiance. The boys had said every single parcel had been taken so she had nothing to fear. Nothing, she told herself. Nothing.

Only that they'd killed the woman. Did they have to go that far? That was none of her business anyway.

'What d'you want in here with that, Sergeant?' she managed through her dry lips, but she knew her voice was thin and silly. 'Put the gun away.'

'Open the flap, Elsie,' said Ned flatly. 'And don't try to bolt through the kitchen door. I have a man outside.'

Nothing there, she told herself again. Nothing to find. Panic was running through her brain like ants as he came through under the counter. He went over to the kitchen door, locked it and dropped the key in his pocket.

'Sit there.'

He pointed to a chair by the telephone, and numbly Elsie sat, looking at the rectangle of sun beyond the door; craving to see Johnny or her brother coming racing in to put this peeler in his place. All she could see was the dark back of Constable Daly.

Ned, revolver beside him on the counter, had begun to go

through the parcels, reading the addresses, feeling the shapes; thinking it no wonder the woman needed glasses as thick as lemonade bottles if she had to work in the half dark like this all day. It'd be something if she cleaned the window, and let a bit of light in.

He was deliberately calming himself, being coolly methodical, arming himself against yet another failure, afraid he had reached it again as he discarded all but the last few parcels. He shrank from the creeping touch of disappointment.

Watching him, confidence was beginning to flood back into the small fat figure on the chair beside the telephone, and the sneer was back on her fat lips. The boys, good luck to them, had the peeler on a wild goose chase after all.

It was the third to last parcel.

It was square and heavy, and as he lifted it on to the counter he heard a gasp of indrawn breath from Elsie. He turned and looked at her, and saw by her expression of terror and fury that he was right.

Mr. Seamus Taggart.

The address was just Connorstown, no more. It would be in most cases except . . .

He wheeled on Elsie. 'There's no one called Seamus Taggart in the town!'

Her eyes stared at him in the shadow, magnified like those of a trapped animal, and she couldn't speak to deny it.

Now Ned was no longer cool but hot with excitement, ripping at the wrappings of the parcel; grabbing for Elsie's scissors to do it faster, breathing, and he knew it, like a steam engine. He paused only for one splendid moment of satisfaction as he came to the small boxes in the middle of all the wrappings. On instinct, he went back to the wrapping paper and realised that it had no stamp. The parcel had never come through the mail at all.

The man from Westport who drove the Mail Car! And above him, who? All the chain of them. Mother of God, they had them all.

Whipping round on Elsie, he stuck his revolver in her neck and she gave a thin scream, gibbering now with fright.

''Twas the boys. The boys. I knew nothing.'

'Get me the Barracks at Westport on that telephone. And

163

quickly, or me finger could slip with impatience.'

Deliberately he calmed himself, listening to the telephone whirring and clacking at Elsie's ear. The one thing they had to do was hold their element of surprise, but a chilly knowledge of Connorstown told him it was unlikely they would accept that the Constable was just taking the air on the corner out there.

He was lucky. The D.I. was in the Barracks. Quickly and succinctly, trying to keep the triumph from his voice, Ned suggested what they should do.

'Good man,' said the D.I. after a few brisk questions. Darkness still came early, but there would be time for everything to be in place. 'Good man. We have them, Ned, we have them this time.'

Ned grinned at the use of his name from the stiff disciplinarian. The D.I. must be as elated as he was himself. But it all still remained to be done, and racing yelling into the streets would get them nowhere.

'Move an inch and I'll blow your brains out,' he said to Elsie, but there was no danger. In the first place she believed him. In the second she was too paralysed with fright to twitch a finger, her appalled mind full of nothing but fearful visions of the rope and the firing squad for all of them.

Dimly, shivering, she realised she was probably safer now with the man Brannick than with her own furious friends who would have little use for her. As the glow of sun began to die outside the dirty window, she watched him go over to the door and speak to the Constable outside, keeping himself well back into the shadows.

'Do you gather all that now, Constable?' he said softly, urgently. The Square outside seemed deserted, save for two old men sitting at the base of the Cross. For a moment, he frowned at that. It wasn't normal. At this time of evening there should be more people, the Square coming to life as it always did after the long quiet of the afternoon. But, ah sure, he told himself, what was normal nowadays?

'Are you right, Constable, about it all?'

'I am, Sir.'

In the soft falling light, his eyes were very bright and he looked like a dog straining at the leash.

164

'Quietly now,' Ned reminded him. 'Quietly. We don't want all the village alerted by you belting over there like the man who brought the good news from Ghent to Aix.'

Poised to run, Constable Daly looked at him. Had the excitement turned the Sergeant's head?

'Walk, man, walk. That's all I mean. Quietly.'

There was nothing to do now but wait. As he closed the door the Angelus banged out from the chapel and he saw the two old men get slowly up from the foot of the Cross, cloth caps held to their thin chests and white heads bowed. He turned the key in the lock, for one second envying them their innocence out there in the last sun, but he had more on his mind at the moment than the reverent contemplation of the Virgin Birth.

There was almost total darkness now in the Post Office, Elsie muttered the Angelus automatically through slack, shaking lips. As the key clanged in the lock, she followed it frantically with a torrent of other prayers, her chest constricted with terror, convinced the Sergeant was coming to kill her on the spot. He'd sent the other man away so there wouldn't be any witnesses.

'Hail Mary, full of grace – '

She blundered into the *De Profundis*, certain she was praying for her own soul, never thinking the time would come that she would feel it to have been the goodness of God if Ned Brannick had shot her that day in the Post Office.

'Out of the depths I have cried to thee, oh Lord – '

She could feel the rancid sweat breaking out all over her body.

Ned came back towards the counter and the weakness of sheer terror took her, bringing her slithering unconscious to the floor in the mess of torn paper and broken parcels, her bloomers wet. Ned left her. She was as well off there as anywhere else, and she might only have tried to talk to him, which he couldn't have allowed. But, b'God, the smell of her was terrible.

Hitching himself up on the counter, he let his long legs dangle and gave way to enjoying the fine edge of his plans and expectations. Surely he had them this time? Would it be promotion? He was young to be a Sergeant, let alone a Head Constable. But these days it was hard for them to get anyone into the Police and the ones at the top were going up fast.

Head Constable. He pulled happily at the little spikes of his moustache. He liked the sound of that.

Unbidden, in the darkness and the silence, no sound but the noisy breathing of the unconscious woman, the thought of Kate Mary crept into his mind.

Oh, Christ Almighty, what of her? If the night's work went as he hoped and expected, what of her?

His long mouth tightened. Duty was duty. No matter what happened, she must expect that.

The streets had not been as empty as Ned thought after the funeral. Word soon went hissing anxiously from house to house about the peeler gone into the Post Office this hour back, and the other one standing there on the corner like an old woman taking the air for her lungs. And no sight or sound of Elsie O'Flynn.

There was no serious alarm yet, but careful scouts were sent out, children who played hopscotch on the opposite side of the square in the blue luminous dusk until the Father came out and chased them away, taking his own long curious scrutiny of the Constable, standing unmoving on the far corner. He might well, he thought, be losing some of his parishioners. He kept his carefully inscrutable face and went back in to the whisky and water he enjoyed at this time every evening before the fire, winter and summer, for the Presbytery was as cold as the grave he was forever holding before the minds of his congregation. They'd call him if they wanted him. If they got the time.

Old women were sent out, their shawled heads bent, their rosaries dangling from their fingers as they made their way across to the Chapel for an evening visit. Their bright ancient eyes carefully assessed a situation that could in the end cost them their sons and grandsons.

Old men pottered together over the broken stones of the Square to sit a while at the foot of the Cross in the centre, sharing a small pinch of tobacco, puffing their pipes into the soft air.

Only when the Constable went back to the Barracks, as gentle as an evening stroll, leaving the Sergeant shut in there with Elsie, did the Committee, gathered quickly and secretly in Gorman's, decide that there was danger.

'I cannot see it,' said Liam O'Flyn. 'Haven't we stripped every parcel in that place, and the kitchen with it? There's nothing the man can find.'

But his face was doubtful, as though with some sixth sense of the one parcel overlooked by his sister's myopic eyes. His long drooping moustache seemed to sink even further down on to his mouth. Sharply he looked all round the gathering of young men in the darkening kitchen, their faces tense, eyes luminous in the firelight, waiting patiently these past years back to strike their blow for Ireland.

All as ready as he was himself, if the time had come. He decided that it had, feeling his own heart jump like a salmon in his chest.

He cleared his throat but even so his voice came out a little hoarse, not with the clear ring of command he would have wished.

'Send out the word,' he said.

'And Elsie?' asked someone, a certain rebuke in the voice implying he should have asked the question himself. 'What about Elsie in there with the peeler?'

Liam O'Flyn's voice and eyes were steady now. Until they reached Johnny he was in command.

'What does Sinn Fein mean?' he asked the speaker.

'Isn't it, Ourselves Alone?'

'Ourselves Alone. One for all and all for one,' he said levelly. 'Would you think my sister would be wanting to jeopardise the lot of us at this stage? Isn't she better value than that?'

His cool confident face showed nothing of the cold fear that had dictated his decision they all should leave at once: fear that even now the Sergeant could be bullying out of Elsie everything he needed to know. His poor slob of a sister was no soldier.

'Get on with you,' said Liam O'Flyn. 'Get going.'

By unspoken arrangement, no lamps were lit, no open shop doorways flooded the streets with warm light, and Ned, by his determination to hold everything to the surprise of darkness, made no attempt to molest the shadowy figures that slipped out of so many of the houses. He realised that they would go. Time for them later.

Several of them carried dismantled rifles in bundles ready wrapped, cartridge belts around their waists; their eyes a little wild and their trigger fingers twitching.

Mostly they took nothing off into the night but hasty packages of food, and rosaries and crucifixes pressed into their hands by wet-eyed women who held their tears and sent them gladly out for Ireland.

Like Liam O'Flyn, they felt they had nothing to fear from the Post Office, and Johnny himself had not planned to move anything for another couple of weeks. They could come back for it all, they told themselves, gathering silently like shadows in the first darkness between the stone walls of the crossroads outside the town, ready to make their separate ways when they were all there to the rendezvous already set and ready, in the hills.

The youngest O'Flyn, an undersized and shaven-headed child too small to be thought suspicious, had been dispatched at the trot to Caherliss to tell Johnny to come cross-country to meet them.

A soldier of Ireland, he saw himself already, thumping in his brother's old boots along the broken road in the luminous purple dusk that had at last brought open war to Connorstown. His thoughts were belied by the quiet peace of the fields; the animals moving restlessly before they slept; the last of the last peaceful day still green and scarlet away behind him over Croagh Patrick.

His scrawny chest heaved and big eyes blazed in his thin face, every muscle of his little body straining. Wouldn't he be the one to save the life of Johnny O'Connor, and there was little to choose between that and talking about God. No one had seemed to be in a hurry, but he was driven by a desperate feat that he could be too late, and the life of his hero on his head forever.

A soldier for Ireland, he was now, with this on his charge. And wasn't he as good for it, and for dying for Ireland, as any of them.

Johnny told him as much when he arrived at the farm almost too spent to speak, looking like a fledgling bird fallen from the nest, with his great anxious eyes and shaven head; his small chest going in and out.

'You're a hero, Seamus,' he said. 'A hero to all of us. You're a great man.'

He reached into his pocket and gave him a few coppers.

'Give him a bit of bread and tea, Mam,' he said. 'He's a good soldier.' Kate Mary would once have been tenderly familiar with the soft look on his face, the child more in his mind than his own danger.

The boy looked at him urgently, having expected him to go rushing from the house the second he gave him the news.

'Wisha, Mr. O'Connor,' he said, alarmed, 'don't let the peelers catch you. Didn't they say you had to get going.'

Johnny laid a hand on the bristly thatch of the boy's head, and his eyes held the bright blue light of the challenge he loved.

'It'll take more than them, Seamus,' he said, 'to catch Johnny O'Connor. Mam, can you give me a bit of bread and bacon in a bag. The boy is right. I must be off.'

Aunt Margaret's face grew very still but she said nothing, only moving stiffly towards the pantry and the cold shelves where she kept the food.

Johnny was whistling cheerfully along the vestibule as he collected what he wanted, and the eyes of the child at the table grew round as glass marbles as he came back out with his rifle fully assembled and slung nonchalantly across his shoulders.

Johnny rested his eyes on him a moment, then paused.

'Get him safely out of here before anyone can come,' he said to his mother, and she nodded.

She put the cloth bag of food into his hands. Nothing more was said between them, but he bent his dark head and gave her an unaccustomed kiss.

'Be good to yourself now,' he said, calm as if he were only going off to Dublin. 'Keep Kate Mary here, should you be lonely. Tell her not to forget me until I come back.'

'God speed you, son,' was all his mother said, and reached up to make the traditional sign of the Cross on his forehead

169

with her thumb. The good night of all his childhood.

Before he turned away into the hills, Johnny went through the yard gate and across the back pasture.

He walked slowly and steadily down the gentle slope in the darkness, his feet firm on the cool fresh ground, having no need to see where he had walked as long as he could remember walking.

He thought about the grass, thick and fine after all the rain. It should get good milk from his fistful of cows, huddled as usual up against the far wall. The Lad would look after them.

At the small house, candlelight soft in the one window, Patch set up a furious barking behind the door at Johnny's knock, but fell quiet at once when the Lad opened it cautiously, candle in one hand and the dog's collar in the other.

'Ah, 'tis you, Mr. O'Connor,' he said. Behind him the fire glowed on the hearth of his defenceless single room, the candle his only light, in his tone the vast relief of one to whom a knock on the door at night can mean only sickness or disaster. His doubts caught him again.

'Is there anything wrong?'

He let Patch go and shielded the candle flame against the breeze, throwing light on the big calm face that would accept anything for the sake of the family he served, without questions.

Johnny gave him no explanations now. 'Will you go up,' he said, 'and be with my mother tonight?' He held down a hand to Patch who licked it eagerly, white plume of a tail waving. 'Take the dog,' he added.

The Lad peered out, and in the small light of his candle caught the dull gleam from the rifle. He drew a deep breath. He was himself only a man of the land who asked no more than the chance to work for the few shillings that put the boots on his feet and a bit of bread and bacon on the table. He cared not a whit who sat up there in Dublin laying claim to Ireland, or who fought who. But his loyalty to the O'Connors was absolute.

'I will, sir,' he said at once. 'I'll do that.'

Johnny nodded, and with his gun and his calico bag stepped out of the pale ring of the candle, vanishing into the darkness. The Lad leaned out and watched him, following the line of the

170

wall until he could see him no more.

Soberly he blessed himself, his face heavy in the pale light, and beside him the dog whined restlessly until he closed the door.

He sat down and reached for his boots.

'Don't waste your time getting settled,' he said to the dog, who cocked his head and tried to understand. This wasn't the time of the day for boots.

'The Ma'am wants us,' said the Lad, and that was enough for both of them.

Johnny thought about his mother. Thanks be to God, she had always been well able to look after herself. But Kate Mary would give a hand to her, until he came back.

He allowed himself to think about Kate Mary and the sense of loss was as bitter as death. Did he manage to kill the peeler, then he knew his Kate Mary. She'd never forgive him as long as she lived.

Only Ireland, then, to think about on this soft night with the wind on his face and God knew what ahead. Only Ireland and freedom, and that worth dying for.

And until he met Kate Mary, it was all in the world he had ever thought of.

On Wednesday evenings Kate Mary always went to Benediction, normally finding great peace in the simple service: the blaze of candles among the flowers on the altar; the glittering monstrance already out on top of the tabernacle; the slow familiar Latin hymns, dragged out to the wheezy old harmonium at the back of the chapel. Blue dusk or darkness beyond the high narrow windows.

Tranquil pattern of childhood. Pattern of safety and love, like the sign of the Cross on Johnny's forehead.

This evening there was uproar as she passed the big Barracks with its barred windows and sandbags round the door, bleaker and more forbidding even than usual in the falling dusk, that last tender blue becoming in the town as drab and grey as the streets themselves.

But light flowed from the windows of the Barracks and from the door open behind the sandbags, Police and soldiers

171

streamed out, armed with rifles, piling into two big horse drawn vans waiting in the street. The D.I. watched it all, marching up and down, tense and erect, tapping his leg ceaselessly with his swagger stick and throwing quick curt orders to his Sergeants.

There is always someone on an Irish street to tell you everything before you even ask, and as Kate Mary came round the corner, an old woman seized her by the arm.

''Tis Connorstown, God help them,' she said excitedly to Kate Mary as she paused. Her toothless mouth champed with relish underneath her shawl. God knew there was nothing like a bit of disaster for putting a spice to life. Sure half these fellows might never come back. They said the Sinn Feiners out in Connorstown were devils.

'They say,' she said, 'they have half Sinn Fein taken, out there in Connorstown, the creatures. Willya look at all the soldiers. Who could live against them?'

Kate Mary stood for a long moment, staring from the Police running like ants to the old woman.

'Connorstown,' she whispered. 'Are you sure?' One van was already grinding off heavily along the street, rifles bristling along the back between the pale formless faces of men who might even now be going out to kill Johnny.

The old women was charmed to have made such an impression, but had no more time for Kate Mary, hitching up her shawl with a dirty claw and looking for someone else to shock.

'Is it true?' she threw over her shoulder. 'Is it true? Doesn't everybody know it?'

Her eyes glittered, looking around for someone else to grab, but a Constable came across the street and told all the gawping people to move on, helping the old crone on her way with a push.

Numbly, but quietly, Kate Mary moved on towards the Chapel, unwilling to get involved with the Police, and not able to think of anywhere else to go, instinctively searching for some sanctuary and comfort. When whe was a child she used to half close her eyes and merge all the candles of Benediction into one pleasing golden blur.

Hopeless tears blurred them now, as she knelt down. Tears she tried to check for their very uselessness. As useless as the

172

prayers that came surging to her dry lips.

Who did she pray for?

To pray for victory for one meant praying for the almost certain death of the other. Pray for them both? It would be asking God to choose for her.

She realised her fingers were knotted tight around her rosary and tried deliberately to untwine them and get what she could of comfort from the gentle service.

The priest was young, candlelight gleaming in his flat fair hair, his voice sure and strong in his faith as he helped the old harmonium and the choir into the *Tantum Ergo*, apparently oblivious of the mustering of death in the street outside.

Sure in his faith, thought Kate Mary. The answer for him to everything. She was no longer sure of anything except her passionate love of Ned, and not God himself at the moment could help her know where that was leading.

When the two van loads of police and soldiers rumbled noisily into Connorstown in the first thick darkness of the moonlight night, the village was silent.

Inside the closed houses the old men and the women looked at one another without speaking. If they come, the young men had said as they left, be quiet. Don't quarrel with them. Everything is as well hidden as it can be. Be quiet, and let them go away. They'll find nothing.

They didn't go away.

They took the village street by street, putting a soldier at each end to pick up anyone who tried to leave, and systematically stripped the houses.

They found hand grenades up chimneys; rifles sewn in mattresses and petrol bombs in dirty hen houses; revolvers in drawers of womens' clothing and ammunition in pantries and sculleries and under floorboards. In the O'Flyn's they ripped up the grain sacks and the bags of fertilisers, and heaved the drums of sheep dip out into the street to roll down the gentle slope and crash like a reproach into the front of the Post Office, where Elsie now sat damply, all control gone, in the company of a police matron sent out from Westport with the men.

Ned had handcuffed her to a chair, and lit the lamp.

173

'She's as well off there,' he said to the woman, 'until we see if we have more of them. We don't want the Barracks full of them.'

He let himself gratefully out into the fresh night air, and breathed it deeply for a few moments, glad to be away from the stinking bundle of fear and urine that was Elsie. It was no job for a man. Why couldn't the woman keep out of it?

'We'll keep them out of it,' the D.I. said briskly when Ned went down to the Barracks for his orders. 'I've an idea you'll find no one in the village but the women and the old men, and a fistful of loyalists. Leave the women alone.'

'But, Sir, there's Cumn na Bahn here. They'll have been making petrol bombs for months. They're as bad as the men.'

The D.I. looked at him, and spoke clearly to the assembled men.

'Leave them alone,' he said. 'The men will be gone to the hills. Leave the women alone, and in the end they'll lead us to them. Leave them where they are.'

So when Bridie's home was searched, against the cursing and roaring of her father, the weeping of her mother and the uproar of the disturbed pigs and hens out in the yard, she sat unmoving beside the fire, filing her nails and looking with contempt at the searching soldiers. Behind her beautiful unmoved face, she seethed with as much sick anxiety for Johnny as Kate Mary, kneeling in peace before the Blessed Sacrament over in Westport.

He'd be gone, she kept telling herself, watching her parents' few shabby clothes being torn from the press. He'd be gone. They'd sent the child in time.

Johnny would make rings round these eejits, and she knew where he would go, too, when he had all his men settled and disposed as he wanted them.

The biggest man hunt of all would be for him, and they couldn't risk him just on the run in the hills.

She kept her careful face and drew her long legs aside distastefully when one of the soldiers pulled up the hearthrug to search for anything buried underneath.

'Jew see that one?' the soldier said to his mate when they got outside. 'Jew see that one wir' the red 'air? Don't speak to them, the D.I. said. Blimey, I wouldn't 'arf mind speaking to

174

that one. I'd give her rebellion.'

Wistfully he looked back at the house. A veteran of campaigns against the girls of France for four long years, he knew a good'un when he saw her. French girls had always protested so much at first. He'd bet there'd be no protesting from that one. Sadly, he shrugged and followed his mates to the next house.

There'd be one consolation for Bridie when it all died down: she could get out into the hills to see him, taking food and fresh ammunition, though God knew where they were going to get that. Bad cess to Elsie, who was always a fool anyway.

But that Kate Mary one, she thought with satisfaction, would never set eyes on him again, now that he was on the run.

The banging and shouting stopped out in the yard, and two more soldiers blundered past her howling mother and through the kitchen.

She lifted green contemptuous eyes.

'Did you find nothing?' she said. 'Did you not kill the pig? He could have swallowed a bomb or two.'

One of them made a threatening gesture towards her, but the Corporal put out a hand to hold him back.

'We're just away,' he said coolly, in the harsh clacking accent of Northern Ireland, 'to get permission to strip the women.'

The other one cackled with pleasure and they crashed out of the open door into the noise and shouting in the street.

'Did he meant it, Bridie?' quavered her mother. 'Did he mean it, the blackguard?'

Bridie didn't look at her.

'In the name of God, Mother,' she said. 'The likes of him has nothing better to do then frightening women. Pay no heed.'

The D.I. himself drove in his motor car with a Constable and two soldiers out to Caherliss, urging his driver on with the confidence that there would lie the biggest haul of all, in spite of Ned telling him not to waste his time.

'There'll be nothing there, Sir,' he said. 'Nothing. Johnny

O'Connor'll be far too smart for that. He'll not be there himself, either,' he added.

Nor Kate Mary, he thought thankfully.

'He could be,' the D.I. said firmly, not pleased to be questioned. 'He could be. And others with him, run out from the town.'

In the lamplight dayroom, the D.I.'s handsome face was alive and eager, and Ned looked at him with sudden doubt. It was he had flushed the whole thing out. Was the D.I. now going to take all the credit? Well, let him go off out to Caherliss on his wild goose chase. It'd take him out of the way while Ned got on with the real job in hand.

A thought struck him. He didn't know as much as old Sergeant Crane, but he had learnt a lot in his time in Connorstown. Fast and under pressure.

'Sir,' he said, 'I declare to you you'll not find Johnny O'Connor. But his mother might have the farm lad with her, a big fellow with a dog. He has no harm in him against anyone. Leave him alone, do you find him there. You can forget him. He's nothing, and he'll know nothing.'

He thought he had gone too far. Sweat broke out on him at the D.I.'s cold stare across the lamp. Did he know about Kate Mary, and feel protection was being offered to Caherliss? Had he put his big foot in it up to the neck? Made things worse for them?

'You know a lot, Sergeant,' his superior said, eyeing him narrowly. 'About Caherliss.'

Stolidly Ned looked back.

'I make it my business, Sir.'

He himself went into Gorman's.

'Take it to pieces,' he said to the men with him. He took no part in it, staying in the kitchen with Mrs. Gorman whose whole plump frame shook with fear and anger.

'Don't we only just have it right after the last time,' she screamed at him. 'Can't you get away and leave good people in peace.'

'Where's your husband?' asked Ned.

A pause while she fumbled for an answer. The whole thing was too recent and too sudden for her to have one ready.

176

'He's away to Dublin.'

'When?'

'This very morning on the early train.'

'Well, he was in the town for the funeral. Get on out of my way woman, before I put you in the cell with Elsie O'Flyn.'

'Is it me?' she screamed at him, and her plump bosom heaved with temper. 'It'd take more than you to put me in a cell Ned Brannick. Yer no more than an eejit, and all the decent lads of the town making rings round you. No more than an eejit.'

The colour was high on Ned's cheeks, but he kept his patience. He could hear the men beginning to clatter up the cellar steps and it was no thing for discipline to have them listen to her abusing him.

'Sit down there and be quiet,' he told her sharply, giving her a small push towards the sofa. Taken by surprise she staggered against the statue of the Sacred Heart. To Ned's amazement the whole thing moved easily along the wall, catching the curtain behind it, and pulling it aside. Behind it lay a brown door in the wall.

'Jesus,' he yelled, and sent the statue flying on its casters to break in a thousand pieces against the table in the middle of the floor.

'Bring the light,' he yelled at the soldier coming from the cellar. 'Bring the light, and follow me.'

The door opened easily, but they got no further. The lantern held by the soldier caught the gleam of the brass bedstead up against it on the other side, blocking it as though it had been there unmoved forever.

In the yellow light two snow white heads lifted from the pillow, old eyes creased in toothless faces. Man and woman in grimy underwear that was as close as they ever went to night clothes; and on each ancient face a sly triumphant grin.

'Did you want something, Sergeant?' quavered the old man. 'Weren't we both asleep like good Godfearing – '

Savagly Ned heaved the bed, and again it flew across the room on well oiled casters, crashing into the wall across from it, jumping the two old people like marionettes.

He could hear Mrs. Gorman cackling with laughter in the kitchen. Well, she might laugh, and the whole lot of them with her, but God help him, the time would come when he would have them weeping.

'Where's your grandson?' he demanded of the old people, peering through the rails of the bedstead as though he already had them jailed.

Ned knew a spasm of wild irritation. Why did the whole blasted business have to be so beleaguered by farce? Was it the same for every policeman or was it Connorstown alone was full of lunatics?

Behind him the Heffernans were crouching in the bed like two old animals in the litter of their burrow, and about as clean, Ned thought. Their eyes, heads close together, gleamed with malice in the small light.

It was the old woman who answered.

'Ah, Sergeant, the young ones,' she said sadly. 'How would we know where they are at any time? Musha, divil the word they ever tell us, about anything.'

The grandson's room was empty, and so was the house next door. They found their way in there quite easily from a cupboard on the landing with a door in the back of it. Not even locked.

Ned stood a long moment looking at it. Gorman's would have been full of them that night he raided it. Full of them. Every single one that he had wanted. Johnny O'Connor and all.

The old Sergeant could have told him, or any old person in the village, the Gorman's house was only the corner piece of a big house from the better days of Connorstown. Never even a lock put on the doors when it was divided into three. Chosen because of this for all the secret meetings of Sinn Fein, and hadn't it worked like a miracle of God himself the night the lad of a Sergeant came and thought he had them trapped.

Ned ground his teeth in anger and frustration and would have liked to slap the smirk off Mrs. Gorman's face; to remind her that Elsie O'Flyn wasn't smirking any longer.

Well, they had flushed them out this night, and they would hunt them now in the hills like the dogs they were until they got them, every man Jack of them.

Kate Mary was forgotten, and all the complications of her

178

love for Johnny. He and his tribe of ruffians had made a fool of Ned Brannick once too often. Kate Mary herself would not have known his cold and grim-lipped face at that moment.

Down in the kitchen two houses away, he could hear Mrs. Gorman and Pierce Heffernan's grandparents jabbering and shouting.

'Get out,' he said to the two soldiers. 'Get on out. There's nothing for you here.' He wasn't out to catch women and doddering ancients.

He was out for Johnny O'Connor. And to take the smile from the face of the town that carried his name. Tonight might not have done it. But the time would come.

It was late into the night, a pale moon risen, before the two police vans rattled their way back into Westport laden, as the D.I. said, with enough arms to lay siege to Dublin Castle without having to spend a penny.

A gibbering Elsie had been removed earlier in a pony and trap, and half a dozen sullen and tight-lipped men were crammed into the two tiny cells of the Connorstown Barracks.

Ned looked them over grimly in the light of his lantern when he came in, and in proud silence they looked back at him, damned if they would ask anything of any peeler.

He went back in to the Day Room to the D.I.

'They have nothing to do with anything,' he said shaking his head. 'It's their sons and daughters. The sons are gone.'

'Hostages,' said the D.I. succinctly. 'We'll draw the others out of the hills to rescue them.'

Ned frowned and shook his head again.

'You little know them, Sir,' he said. 'They'd die before they'd let them come.'

The D.I. growled, and suddenly all Ned's savage rage deserted him. He felt his mouth go dry.

'Did you find anything out at Caherliss?' he asked carefully.

'We did not. Not a thing.'

'Take any hostages?'

A closed expression came over the D.I.'s face and he turned away.

'No one,' he said. 'No one.'

179

There Ned had to leave it, not daring to show too great an interest. Thank God Kate Mary had been safe in Westport.

He didn't know about the mother. Would Johnny come down from the hills to rescue her?

Lights burned all night in the Barracks at Westport, and the telephone jangled incessantly from Ennis where the mail man had been sent for what they called interrogation.

Dawn was creeping rose and primrose over the water of Clew Bay, the crown of Croagh Patrick touched with gold, when the D.I. finally put the receiver down, his red rimmed eyes blazing with satisfaction. Happily he rubbed at the stubble of his chin.

'The fellow talked,' he said. 'He talked. Sure they all do. We have the whole cell on the run. B'God, that Sergeant in Connorstown will be well thought of up there at the Castle. He'll be having my job here before I know where I am.'

Lights also burned late in one window of the hotel where Miss Greeley's family were gathered in a consternation that had begun in noisy outrage, and gradually subsided through the long hours into defeated silence, with the whisky bottle empty in the middle of the table and the handkerchiefs out again for tears far more copious and real than any that had been shed above the corpse.

All the women were snivelling, pausing only to take gulps of whisky down throats long thickened with weeping.

The men were in their braces and shirtsleeves, collar studs undone, the plump ones crimson in the face and the pale one shaken as colourless as his old aunt when they put her in the coffin. They couldn't look at each other, confronting financial disaster their wives had no inkling of, concerned with no more than the loss of a fur coat and a fine house and a grand life out in Kingstown. Each man was waiting on nerve endings for the women to be gone so that he could tell the others that it was their fault entirely they had signed to buy the bookie's business, before they were sure of the old woman's money.

'How could she?' moaned one of the women. 'How could she?'

'She could and she did,' said her husband bluntly. 'What

180

was it to her, to see us all in the workhouse for the horses and the hearse, and all we did for her. And go easy on the hard stuff. 'Tis likely the last of it you'll ever see.

'And the train to the funeral and the carriage,' said the other men.

'And the price of the hotel. And we living like kings.'

They fell again into appalled silence, brooding over the terrible behaviour of their Aunt Ellen Euphemia who had left to some child the monstrous sum of fifty pounds for the care of her cat, and all the rest, without exception, to the Parish Church.

'Fifty pounds to a cat,' said one through her whisky hoarsely. 'Couldn't you wring its neck'.

They looked at her in sudden hope, but it quietly died. They'd only give the money to the child.

Miss Greeley in her death had brought havoc to a whole cell of Sinn Fein, fury and disaster to her family. The blazing lights of Westport on that April evening were her only memorial. She never had another. The marble angel went to oblivion with all her family's hopes, and the parish priest thought it no duty of his legacy to raise a tombstone, nor would it have occurred to him to have engraved on it, her proper epitaph: Ellen Euphemia Greeley. Spinster. Bringer of death.

By the grey cool light of dawn all the extra policemen were gone, and the prisoners with them in a commandeered cart. The sullen village gathered its belongings back from the streets where they had been thrown out of windows, and tried to sort the chaos of their homes as the sun came up, splendid and indifferent as on any other day, making tawdry with its clear gold light all the heaps of cherished belongings in the gutters.

There was only one comfort as they went with tight mouths and hard eyes about their task. Not one of the real lads had been taken: every one of them safely away. The few they had grabbed because of some ould revolver of their father's, or a shotgun for the rabbits, could tell them nothing about anything.

Ned, standing grimly at the door of the Barracks, glad of the cool freshness on his tired face, his men writing their reports behind him in the Day Room, could only think the same thing.

He must soon write his own report and in his own disappointed mind the raid had been a failure. Granted, thanks to the fat fool in the Post Office, they had smashed the cell right through to Ennis, and driven every Sinn Feiner in the area on to the run. The D.I. was full of praise and commendation for it. But for Ned there was no personal satisfaction. Johnny O'Connor was still free.

Capless, the young sun catching lights from the smooth head of hair Kate Mary loved so much, he walked out and paced the empty street, his hands behind his back.

He tried to fathom his own feelings. Why was such a moment of success as sour as failure in his mouth? Was it because he knew that as long as O'Connor was alive he would regroup and reorganise and start again, that nothing here would be finished until the man was dead?

Or was it because of Kate Mary and his fear that part of her heart was never wholly his. That even now, the blue-eyed charm of O'Connor could carry her away from him. Especially if there was reason to pity him, driven from his home into the hills. Nothing could begin for himself and Kate Mary until the man was dead.

He was going soft, Ned told himself. Soft. And shamed by it. There was nothing ever to be thought of but his duty. Always his duty. And that was to fight rebels to the death, wherever he might find them, whoever they were.

Squaring his shoulders he marched back into the Barracks and proceeded to make hay with the Constables' reports, leaving them glaring at him after the long bitter night; one of them at least wanting nothing but to forget what he had done. Duty or not, and even though he hadn't been there, Ned was trying to kill his hollow fear that Kate Mary would turn against him, when she found out what had happened at Caherliss.

Kate Mary didn't wait for Friday to go out to Connorstown, driven frantic by Mrs. Garvey's tales of half the population of the village being driven to the hills and all the others dead or bleeding in the wreckage of their homes, the very children shot down where they stood, and the whole place stocked with guns and bombs that could have blasted everyone in Westport in their beds.

In Mrs. Garvey's stories, thought a small corner of Kate Mary's frightened mind, everything happened to people in their beds.

But how much of it, dear God, was true this time?

Mrs. Garvey was rattling on, eyes bright with excitement, also too full of her drama to talk coherently.

Elsie O'Flyn, and that Peter Garrett who did the rounds of the country in the Mail Van! Weren't they already over in Roscommon Jail and likely to be hanged in the morning.

Hanged? Kate Mary didn't believe it. That fat, ugly little woman in the Post Office who looked like a frog. How could she be hanged? A strange frightening world crowded in on Kate Mary. Terrifying in its unfamiliarity, coming on top of a sleepless night when violence and death and the elusive faces of Ned and Johnny had haunted her few dozing hours while she waited for the first pale light and the crash of the front door as Mrs. Garvey raced off to Mass.

'What did they do?' she whispered.

'What did they do?' Mrs Garvey's voice rose shrilly. 'Wasn't he bringing her great parcels of guns and bullets and she handing them on to the rebels? Wasn't that what they were doing? Don't they deserve to hang?'

Kate Mary felt sick, the bright clean kitchen darkening around her. Tightly she held to the edges of her chair, afraid for a moment she might fall.

Against the suffocating dark, she could see the smiling bright-eyed Johnny coming swinging from the Post Office, a big parcel under his arm labelled 'Books'. Carefully she stood up, holding on to the chair.

'I must go home, Mrs. Garvey,' she said, quite surprised that she could find her voice; feeling so hollow that she couldn't imagine where it came from. 'At once. To see if my Aunt is all right. Will you go and tell Reverend Mother for me, please?'

Mrs. Garvey wheeled from the range, outraged, her round bland face scarlet from the heat and excitement and the final insult of Kate Mary not wanting to eat the breakfast.

'You'll not go without your breakfast!'

Death or sorrow or disaster, no one left Mrs. Garvey's house unless they had eaten what she cooked.

'*Please*, Mrs. Garvey.'

Even the single-minded woman was halted by the ashen anxiety in her face, and paused, spoon in hand, to look at the girl.

'Ah, well – ' she began. Behind her the acrid smell crept from the range.

'Ah, musha,' she shrieked. 'Haven't I burnt the stirabout!'

While she peered, appalled, at a disaster far greater to her than all Connorstown lying dead, or Elsie O'Flyn dangling at the end of an English rope, Kate Mary slipped out and took her coat and cap from the peg in the hall.

No thought touched her then that it was the end of Mrs. Garvey and her stirabout. That she would never come back other than to gather up her clothes. That it would be the first of many endings before, in the far future, there might be hope of a beginning.

She pushed her way out the long miles to Connorstown, with legs that seemed to belong to someone else, her mind flickering like a moth around the whole situation. Taut with dread as to what she might find.

It took an effort of will to make herself understand there would be no Johnny to meet her in the Square.

There couldn't be. Mrs. Garvey's stories were no doubt wild and sketchy, but Kate Mary knew enough to realise that after a raid like that, there wouldn't be one Volunteer left in the village. It was like the Virgins and their lamps. The wise ones would be in the hills, or hiding in some safe house, and the foolish ones would be behind bars.

Even though she expected nothing, she couldn't help but stop a moment, cold and unhappy with the certainty that it would never be the same again. The days of Johnny grinning down from the cart seat, passing remarks about her bicycle, were gone for ever. Past, lost happiness.

Her sense of desolation was made worse by the emptiness of the Square, the shadows of the bright day sharp on the deserted pavings. The door of the Post Office was closed, a notice pinned to it. No one moved, as though death had taken the whole town, but she felt the unhappy certainty that she was being watched from the houses on the corners. The shadow of a curious face; the quick twitch of a curtain.

It oppressed her and worked up all her carefully controlled fears as to what had happened at Caherliss.

There was no reason to be sure. They could even have got Johnny, although she *was* sure he would have been one of the wise ones.

Her foot was on the pedal to race off.

'Miss Pearse.'

She whipped round, her foot catching in the trailing dress guard, and the bicycle falling away from her. Almost she let it fall, wanting to fling herself into his arms.

'Ned. Oh, Ned!' Tears were suddenly close.

How had all her fear been for Johnny? Ned's heart or head could take a bullet like the rest of them. He had no charmed life either.

'Careful now,' he said. 'There'll be ten pairs of eyes at every window. Try and look like I'm any ould policeman.'

His face was studiously official, but his eyes poured out on her all the love and reassurance she could want and his voice was gentle. He took the bicycle from her and stood it up.

'Sure any ould policeman would do that for a lady,' he said. 'Don't smile now, darling. There's nothing here to smile about.'

'Caherliss,' she said. She licked lips suddenly gone dry, and anger took him that he had to stand here feet away from her and leave her comfortless.

'Your cousin is gone,' he said, and would not use his name. 'Your aunt is all right, but the man she has up there took a bullet in the arm.'

'The Lad?' Her eyes blazed in a quick rush of anger. 'Sure he wouldn't know a Sinn Feiner from the Viceroy of Ireland. Who would shoot him?'

'I believe it was an accident. Look, alannah,' his voice was urgent, 'get on that bicycle and get away from me. I'm no company for you at the moment.'

Tears born of fear and anxiety came hot again to her eyes, blurring his loved face.

185

'You're all the company I'd want,' she said thickly, and for a moment Ned was silent.

'Not here, my darling. Not here. Now go.'

He stepped back and saluted her as he would any stranger, and through a haze of tears she wound the trailing dress guard round the saddle and wobbled off along the road, oblivious to the tall spikes of yellow ragwort and the marguerites in the rank grass along the ditches; the blue of irises and the yellow carpet of kingcups where the road ran low and marshy; the young lambs gambolling in the higher fields.

All these things had belonged to happiness. Lost now as though a cloud had come across them, in dark fear for those she loved.

On both sides.

Aunt Margaret met her unemotionally at Caherliss, but Kate Mary caught behind the round glasses the flicker of gratitude and relief that she had come.

'They let you away from the school?'

'I didn't ask. I sent Mrs. Garvey to tell them.'

She looked round at the disorder, barely touched. Anything Ned and his Constables had done on their last raid had been no more than a gesture. Where they had rummaged, this lot had emptied every mortal possession all over the floors. What they couldn't open they had smashed, and the sliding doors of the old wall bed were splintered on the floor. Since the new rooms along the vestibule had been built, Aunt Margaret had used it as a store and Kate Mary's feet slipped on candles and grew sticky in the jam made from the old damson tree beyond the yard, puddled together with paraffin and sugar.

Appalled, she looked round her and along the vestibule where even every reel of thread and bobbin from their sewing table had been scattered, the machine upended in the middle of it all.

Johnny's door was open, but as yet Kate Mary couldn't bring herself to ask anything.

'They were very thorough,' said her Aunt drily, and then answered the question the girl could not ask.

'Weren't we honoured,' she said. 'They sent the D.I.

186

himself, and a couple of soldiers with him, and a Constable. Strangers, the lot of them. They'd be afraid the local lads might be good to us. Weren't the soldiers even English and I couldn't understand a word they said.'

Her voice was bitter, but Kate Mary was concerned only with her own relief that left her for a moment light-headed, trembling.

Ned had had nothing to do with it.

'And did they find anything?' she asked automatically. Of course they hadn't, or even her poor shattered little aunt would not be here now, presenting her proud and steady face in the ruins of her home.

But Kate Mary saw the controlled face begin to crumple, the tight mouth shaking, tears rising behind the round glasses.

'What, Aunt Margaret, what?'

She dare not race along the littered vestibule to look at the wall of the High Garden.

'What? What happened?'

''Twas something they took.'

'Took?'

'They killed the Lad's dog.'

She sat down as though at last giving way to the fear and dreadfulness of the night, and Kate Mary followed her glance to where a heap of spilled flour on the floor was stained with dry, dark blood.

'Ah, no!'

Kate Mary was sickened sad. The Lad and his dog were like God and the Holy Ghost: indissoluble.

She opened her mouth to say that Ned had told her the Lad was hurt, and then closed it again. It would only anger Aunt Margaret. Best leave Ned out of it.

'What happened? How?'

'One of the soldiers threatened the Lad and the dog went for him. The Lad put out his hand to stop it and took a bullet in the arm. I have him in there in Johnny's bed. There was terrible bleeding. I put him in the trap and took him the back way in to the doctor at Westport. He was very good, the man, and it the middle of the night.'

She was chattering now, weak with the reaction of having Kate Mary there to share it all.

'I buried the dog. I wouldn't want the Lad to see it.'

187

For a long moment the girl stared at her, humbled and amazed at her courage. In the dark of the night, with no one to help her, she had harnessed the pony into the trap and somehow bundled into it the Lad twice the size of herself and no doubt helpless from his wound; bleeding all over her. Then, lightless, she had driven the long rough journey over the narrow back road to Westport.

No wonder the doctor had been good to her. He must have been as staggered as Kate Mary herself.

Then the indomitable little woman had come back and taken a shovel and buried the poor dog, lest it upset the Lad.

No wonder Johnny was the leader of the pack, if this was the mettle he was made from.

Kate Mary took off her coat, knowing she only understood the half of that night of terror and distress.

She glanced at the grey ashes in the hearth that had probably not been without fire since the day Aunt Margaret had come there as a bride. That must be upsetting her but the ashes would still be warm. It shouldn't take long.

'Do you sit there and rest,' she said to her aunt, 'and I'll get the fire lit and the kettle boiling and make you a good teapot full of tea in no time at all.'

'And the Lad. He's asleep, the creature.'

'And the Lad.'

Kate Mary went out into the wild disorder of the yard, where the already bloated hens were gorging on the scattered grain. They were too full even to move when she shouted at them, staggering a few yards and then subsiding. Many, she knew, would die where they fell down. Beyond the open yard gate, down the bohreen, she could see both the horse and the pony, gorging themselves in the long grass along the bottom of the walls. They'd be in the same state as the hens, did she not catch them soon.

Even the kindling she had come for had all been scattered, and it was only as she straightened from gathering a bundle of it that she looked down the yard to the stone wall, where the hanging plants were growing green and fresh, starred with little pink and yellow flowers.

'Thank God,' she thought. 'Thank God. At least they did not find that.'

188

When she came back into the kitchen, reaching down the matches from the mantlepiece, Aunt Margaret was dozing. As Kate Mary knelt before the hearth, she opened her eyes.

'Johnny's away,' she said.

Kate Mary looked up at her, her hands full of wood.

'I know,' she said. 'Mrs. Garvey knew that.'

She looked away again quickly, her fingers shaking as she fiddled with the fire. In Aunt Margaret's eyes there had been a cold hint of hostility, as though she held Kate Mary in some way to blame for it all.

By late afternoon they had got some semblance of order into the house, penned what remained of the chickens and got the horses back into the stable.

The Lad still slept, weak from loss of blood, oblivious to it all.

'The doctor said it'll be a long time before he can use the arm,' Aunt Margaret said suddenly, in each hand the two separate pieces of a broken chair.

'Oh, yes. Months probably.'

Kate Mary wasn't really thinking about what she said as she pushed the hair back from her tired face with hands caked with flour and butter, trying desperately to save all she could from the wreckage on the floor.

Her aunt looked down at her, her face expressionless.

'There's no one would come and work here now,' she said abruptly. 'With Johnny on the run no one would be wanting to be involved. Batty down there at the end of the bohreen might help. Johnny did enough for him. But, sure, he's a sick man.'

She paused, and Kate Mary, down on the floor, felt suddenly cold and helpless, knowing what was coming.

'You'll have to stay, Kate Mary, and help me with the farm.'

She raised her despairing face.

'I know nothing about farming,' she cried. All she could think of to say.

'You'll easy learn,' said Aunt Margaret.

Of course she would easy learn! Wasn't she reared on a farm? And didn't she owe Aunt Margaret?

But if she stayed out here on Caherliss, how in God's name

189

would she ever get to see Ned again?

That was the thought that shrivelled her to misery where she knelt, absently picking the pieces of a broken jam jar from the floor. She looked up at her aunt, and something in the remorseless set of the jaw told her she had also the same idea.

Tuesdays, she thought numbly. Tuesdays. It would all depend on whether Aunt Margaret knew that it was Tuesdays.

Chapter 8

In the small isolation of Connorstown, and even more of Caherliss, they knew little of the whole violent picture of the struggle for freedom in Ireland, taking only their own small part of the battle as it came; grateful now, as Kate Mary was, for the fine weather that allowed them to get their belongings in off the streets, and put together again their shattered homes, before too much harm was done.

Kate Mary had been better off in Westport where she could read a local newspaper and even sometimes the Dublin newspapers, a couple of days late. She was aware of the mounting pressure all over the country against the Police and the British Army; of their slowly losing battle despite these Auxiliaries they had brought in. The Black and Tans, the people called them, from their bright tan jackets and black breeches, high boots stamping their threat along the city streets. Brutal devils apparently, straight from hell itself, with the gun ready first and questions afterwards, when it was too late to give back life.

She thought of all this in the sweet bright weather as she buried the poor bloated hens, digging deep and patient with the idea that they must not be shallow that the dog could dig them up – only to remember with one of the many heartaches of the day that there was no longer any dog.

She rebuilt as best she could the shattered hen house, and patiently sitting in the ground in the yard, sieved the grain she had so wearily swept up. A peck of dust would do none of them any harm at all but a stone could kill a hen.

Johnny and his Republican Army, the handful of good-class, well-disciplined young men who in all Ireland didn't number many over a thousand, were winning. Ned had told her that the Police were getting weary of their job of fighting for a cause that many of them no longer believed in; struggling to keep Ireland from the Irish in a war which no longer made sense to them. In increasing numbers they were laying down their guns and resigning with no stomach any longer for fighting against their own.

Whereas the bands like Johnny and his men in the towns and the villages, and in their secret safe houses in the hills, still had the blazing, selfless dream of freedom to sustain them, tinged now with the hope and fierce excitement of success.

She had read of the obstinate politics of Lloyd George in England, scornfully rejecting the first vague overtures for peace in a conflict that could bring no more than heartbreak and a whole new world to build.

Like so many people caught up in wars, she could care little for all this except to wonder why in God's name someone didn't have the sense to put an end to it before the whole country was destroyed. There were some places the Police had even forbidden the local markets as public meetings. So the people starved in their prosperous fields with nowhere they could sell their goods. She was concerned only with the painful, stupid results of their own local battle: dead hens and broken sheds and scattered grain, and the poor Lad in there the colour of a ghost but still capable of going scarlet with embarrassment at having to be looked after and waited on by Aunt Margaret. Now there was Johnny off on the run. Johnny at risk of being shot on sight in some dugout in the hills. And supposing it was Ned who saw him. Was he meant to press the trigger?

Ned.

Worst of all, and coming before all the troubles of Ireland, she couldn't see how she was going to see him now without being in Westport. How could she do it before all the hating eyes of Connorstown?

'G'won in out of that.'

Irritably she flapped at the last scuttering hen, getting in the sadly small flock safely for the night.

She had done a days work for a man and she was tired,

every muscle in her body aching, oppressed by the fact that at least for a few weeks she and her Aunt were going to have to do the work of two men. Weary and irritable, only halfway through clearing the ravaged yard, and mortally afraid the hen house was going to fall down again on top of the rest of the hens, she could have seen all men and their wars in Jericho. Bad cess to Johnny and all like him. Wouldn't he be better staying at home to care for his land, instead of off playing the hero until there was no land to come back to.

She was almost ready to say she didn't care who won, as long as life could go back to the content they once knew, and her love for Ned have a chance.

At least they could be out of it all a bit now, with Johnny gone. They couldn't hope to find him here.

She raised her eyes to the little trailing flowers hanging down the wall. The rough edges of the gass in the High Garden were green over the top of it, fresh with spring, and she felt cold and despairing.

As long as that was there, they were not out of it. Johnny, or somebody, would have to come back to get it, for whatever dreadful purpose.

Sighing, she felt all her difficulties dated from the day of the bullets, when she had told Johnny she was on no side in this business. He had said she was sitting on the fence, and must one day climb down on one side or the other. Well, she was still up on the fence, and it had become unbearable, watching in anguish a loved man on either side; knowing that one or other of them must fall in the end.

Aunt Margaret came to the kitchen door, her own small face drawn and tired, in the falling dusk.

'Come on in child,' she said. 'I have tea made and a few scones. You'll have the hands raw on you.'

It was Aunt Margaret who went into Connorstown on the following morning to get the weekly shopping and to try and replace some of the stores they hadn't been able to save. All their sweeping and scrubbing had been to take their good food off the floors, to toil with it in a skip down the bohreen and heave it over the wall into the bed of nettles where none of the stock could get at it.

Kate Mary knew her aunt was shamed and angry to be having to go in and buy all these things she had always made for herself, and her mother before her. Some of the candles that heavy bullying boots had ground into the floor had been dipped and moulded by her grandmother when she was a child.

'Can I not come with you?' she asked, feeling her presence might be some comfort even though the small, indomitable woman would accept no word of pity.

''Tis the Will of God, she had said resignedly, and Kate Mary was furious, but silent.

It had nothing to do with God; indeed it was hard to see how any of it had. This was to do only with the will of Johnny and that handsome iron hard D.I. from Westport.

She said nothing, and went out to put the pony in the trap. They had had to bring him back from three farms away.

'I'd not want to leave the Lad alone,' she said when she came out, and Kate Mary nodded. He was feverish now with his wound, chattering away to himself in his delirium, barely knowing who they were when they came into the room.

'I hope he'll be all right,' Kate Mary said. His death would be another impossible burden on this strong woman who already carried so much hurt behind her unwavering face.

'He will. 'Tis only a flesh wound. He'll heal.'

Kate Mary stood and watched as the pony ambled off down the bohreen, her Aunt erect in the trap, her good black velour hat with the amber buckle worn like a banner of defiance. If only it were possible to show her some affection and support, but Aunt Margaret wanted none of it.

She sighed and went back into the quiet house where the only sound was the Lad, chattering in the high thin voice of fever to his long dead mother.

'Oh, God,' Kate Mary said furiously. 'Oh, Jesus wept.'

And slammed out into the scullery to get a bucket and go on with the scrubbing of the floor.

Aunt Margaret had her own reasons for wanting to go into Connorstown alone that morning, and when she came back her thin mouth was set in a hard tight line and the heels of her buttoned boots slammed the floor.

Kate Mary went out to help her bring in what she had

bought, and to put the pony away. A soft teasing wind from the far away sea had got up, searching out grain from corners Kate Mary had never reached, and the yard was full of whirling husks.

'Ah God,' she thought, 'I'll have to get the damned hens in again, or we'll lose more.'

She had been up at six to milk Johnny's precious cows, and felt she had already done a long full day of work. Get used to it, she told herself. It's only begun. And it can only get worse.

When the pony halted in the yard, Aunt Margaret had sat there at the reins as though she too found the day too long.

'Did you get what you wanted?' Kate Mary asked her, and went round to open the back door of the trap.

'I got nothing.' Her aunt glared at her as if it had been her fault.

'Nothing?'

'Isn't Gorman as devastated as ourselves? Devastated! And O'Flyn's isn't even open. Reeking of paraffin. Did anyone put a match near it, they'd burn all Connorstown.'

Kate Mary bleakly took the few packages there were, and selfish hope flared like a turned up lamp.

'I have to go into Westport for my clothes on Tuesday,' she said, desperate to make it sound unimportant, while her heart hammered and her tongue stuck to the roof of her mouth. 'I can get it all there.'

'Tuesday? Do we have to wait till Tuesday? I've no more than a pound of flour in the house.'

Kate Mary lied like a trooper, and realised she had not even the grace to blush, fighting desperately for the one thing she had left.

'Mrs. Garvey is away to her brother at Leenane until Monday evening. You know she often does that. I arranged Tuesday with her.'

She moved away towards the kitchen door with the few bags, trying to evade question or argument.

Nothing had been arranged as she fled the house in Westport in fear and panic. She supposed, though, she must go also and see the nuns. Tell them she wasn't coming back. Even when the Lad was better, Aunt Margaret would still need her now there was no Johnny.

Aunt Margaret was eyeing her sharply as she took the long hat pin from the good hat and laid it on the table, and for a moment Kate Mary trembled. She could say she'd go to Westport and do it all, and see her friend, Mrs. Garvey, who would tell her she hadn't set foot out of Westport in the last month. What then?

Aunt Margaret looked pale and strange, but she wasn't thinking of Westport or Mrs. Garvey, pushing a little absently at the small parcels Kate Mary had put down.

'You'd be as well,' she said then abruptly, 'not to go into Connorstown.'

She spoke as if it was something she had to say, her voice tight and difficult, but Kate Mary didn't heed, seeing it only as another blow. In Connorstown she would have been able to see him in the streets; maybe exchange a few careful words as they had this morning. See that he was well. See that he was there.

'Why not, Aunt Margaret?' she said, bleak as winter, dropped into a fresh pit of loneliness and disappointment.

Aunt Margaret carefully took off her long black coat with the old-fashioned jet buttons and folded it over her arm. A cloud moved across the sun and suddenly the kitchen seemed cold and grey. She looked directly at Kate Mary.

'Because,' she said steadily, 'they think in Connorstown that you informed the Police about what went on in the Post Office.'

Kate Mary gaped. Sheer petrified shock made her knees weak and she leaned speechless on the back of a chair.

'But I – me?' she stammered. 'I – why would I do that?' she managed to get out.

Inform on Johnny? *She* inform on Johnny?

The old woman eyed her coolly.

'Aren't you going with that policeman?' she said, unmoved by Kate Mary's stricken face. 'Weren't you seen talking to him on your way here?'

All the curtains in the Square, she thought. She had felt the eyes behind them, the very windows watching.

'I was seen in that Square a great many years talking to Johnny,' she said sharply, anger taking over. 'And no one thought ill of that.'

196

'You were never in love with Johnny,' his mother said flatly and, watching her, Kate Mary knew that was the nub of it. 'People do queer things when love is on them,' her Aunt added.

Kate Mary looked at her. The sun had come again and the light struck her aunt's glasses so that the girl couldn't see her eyes.

'And you,' she said, 'you, Aunt Margaret, do you believe it?'

There was a long silence, more damning than any words.

'Well,' said Aunt Margaret at last, as if she searched for something to say, 'that Sergeant found out somehow. Didn't he?'

Kate Mary's voice was cold, but not as cold and sick as her heart. She felt hollow. Not from any rush of fear but from the dreadful brunt of this ugliness that she had done nothing to deserve. 'He might have found out for himself. He's not stupid.'

Her aunt said no more, picking up her hat and coat and going out into the vestibule to hang them up. Kate Mary sat down where she was, beside the table, and looked numbly at her hands in her lap, all anger spent.

She had been branded an informer, and clearly Aunt Margaret believed it to be true. The vilest form of life in any Civil War, the informer was the curse of Sinn Fein; there was always some little weasel in the villages, ready to run to the Police with information, for a bit of ready money or to have his small crimes overlooked.

If they caught an informer, Sinn Fein shot him in the kneecaps, a crippled life being far worse than any quick and easy death.

And a woman who informed . . . Instinctively, she put up her hand to her smooth cap of long black hair. Then she shook herself. What matter the evil gossip of the village? Johnny would never believe it and that was all that counted.

'You mean I can't go to Mass tomorrow?' she said, when her aunt came back. Not even a glimpse of Ned.

'Not in Connorstown. When the Lad is fit to be left, we'll drive out to Anfield and get it in the house there. I'll go tomorrow and do you stay with the Lad.'

Anfield. It was like another nail in her Cross, however small. Even if she could have said no word to Ned, she might have seen him striding trim as the morning across the Square, or the sun on his bent head as she tried to keep her mind on the Mass, promising the Blessed Lord all kinds of penances because she couldn't.

But she hated Anfield quite apart from the fact that it was four Irish miles in the wrong direction from Ned. It was an unwarmed and ancient house inhabited by an old cousin of Aunt Margaret's who lived alone with a sour housekeeper and cared for nothing but the welfare of his immortal soul.

He was obsessed with the history of the way his house had remained loyal to the Church through all the Penal days by the use of priest's holes and some secret passage to the ruined chapel on the hill. Mass was said in the house every Sunday by a creepy priest who expected one day to inherit all the old man's money, and a bad meal of tough mutton or an old hen was served after it. It was always more like another celebration of the Eucharist than a cheerful meal.

Sadly, Kate Mary sighed. There was nothing she could do.

That night she surfaced abruptly from her sleep in the middle of the deepest dark, not knowing what had disturbed her; aware she was afraid of something but for the moment not able to remember what, her mind blank with shapeless terror.

The gelignite.

They had come for the gelignite – or the Police had, and that would surely be laid at her door too. Grabbing her shawl, she slid out of bed, her heart banging like a steam hammer. The curtains were drawn over the window beside the fireplace, which now held only a fan of fast fading crimson paper.

There was nothing to be heard. Not a sound, inside or out. Carefully she drew back the curtain and looked out into the yard where frost white moonlight lit the wall as bright as day. All the little flowers held up their heads to it, undisturbed, as they might hold them to the sun.

Her panic ebbed, and she stood a moment waiting for her heart to quiet, her forehead against the cool glass, seeing with half her mind the harrow and the broken staff still lying where they had pulled it from the barn. How, would someone tell her, was she to get that mended?

She didn't feel foolish. Maybe it had not been tonight, but it would be another night. He couldn't let it go unused, but he would be laying his life in danger to come and get it for Caherliss would surely be watched.

Oh, Johnny. And they thought she had informed against him. Oh, Johnny. Pain and anguish as great as over Ned, but different. Let no one ask which was worse. Let no one ask her ever to choose.

Turning from the window at another sound, she saw Aunt Margaret coming through from the kitchen, fully dressed; a candle in one hand throwing shadows on her white tired face, a jug in the other.

'Is there anything wrong, Aunt Margaret? Is it the Lad?'

'He's well enough now,' she said. 'The fever broke and he's asleep. Go back to your bed.'

'Can I do anything?'

The poor old creature looked exhausted, but she answered flatly, as though she wanted Kate mary involved in nothing.

'You can not. Away to your bed.'

The next evening Kate Mary wandered out and down the bohreen for a walk, her rosary in her hands to say a few decades for not going to Mass that morning. Her mind couldn't steady itself enough to pray, the beads idle between her fingers.

Severed, it would seem, from Ned. Severed even from the small pleasure of mixing with the people of Connorstown. Closed up for how long with Aunt Margaret who was carefully normal towards her but made it clear that the girl was now considered the enemy. Johnny's enemy.

Oh, Ned. Even to talk to him about it all would make it easier. Not that he could change anything, but it would help. And the terrible injustice of being called an informer was that even when they did talk together now, he'd be so careful to ask her nothing that might compromise her, and she equally careful to tell him nothing that she knew. What about the gelignite – wouldn't they burn down Caherliss for that, did she even open her mouth.

Informer! Ah, what did it matter. When they were alone, it was themselves she wanted to talk about, not Johnny or Sinn

Fein or Connorstown – although she realised they must hate Ned there now, like the devil himself.

The loved acres of Caherliss had become suddenly a prison, a green rich prison round her, touched with the grape blue light of an evening so still she could hear the Angelus ringing faint across the quiet field from Connorstown.

Automatically she blessed herself and began the small prayer, but her eye was caught by a movement behind the stone wall over to her right. A policeman with a pair of field glasses had acted as automatically as she, taking them down from his eyes to bless himself.

Watching Caherliss, exactly as she had thought. Oh Johnny, be careful. Be careful.

She let the policeman finish his small prayer.

'God bless the work, Constable,' she said then coldly.

He was a stranger, and young enough, startled, to blush scarlet all the way up to his freckled face, crouching foolishly behind the wall.

'I'm no more than doing my duty, Miss,' he said then stubbornly.

'You're on private property!'

'Well then,' he answered, and clearly thought himself fine and smart, 'do you go and call the Police.'

She turned back, all peace destroyed, the still beauty of the blue evening violated. Not even here, in her own home, could she be alone, unwatched. The fact that it was one of Ned's men that was watching her made it even worse.

Bad cess to all of them, she fumed. To all of them, Fenians and Police and every single one of them. There was nothing wrong with life or Ireland before they all started at each other.

Her ill temper dissolved as it had come. Johnny would have her shot, she thought, never mind any of the others, if he could hear her.

Nothing wrong! he'd say. And he ready to lay down his life and all his friends with him, to put it right. She could only hope and pray, she thought sadly, that Johnny's Ireland would be happier when it came. She doubted it.

Were it that united, surely there would hardly be need to fight. But it was not united, and she watched it all with the sad premonition that what she had once said to Johnny was true.

Their grandchildren would be fighting the same battle; men still flying the night with guns, and stubborn policemen hiding behind walls to try and catch them.

She sighed and went in and told Aunt Margaret, hoping that in some way she could get the news to Johnny that he should keep away from Caherliss.

Aunt Margaret didn't even look up from where she bent in the last light over the tear made by the bullet in the sleeve of the Lad's shirt. Mending it carefully, even though after soaking it with salt swept off the floor, the pale stain of blood still showed through the stripes.

'I won't be home early,' Kate Mary said firmly on Tuesday morning as she harnessed the pony into the trap. The yard was almost brought back to normal, except for the fact that all their stocks were down to half.

Already she was concerned as to who would cut the hay. She had never used a scythe in her life, watching with admiration as Johnny and the Lad, brown arms swinging strong in the sunlight, had apparently without effort levelled the three fields, pausing only to smile at her with white teeth in sunburnt faces when she came to them through the heat at dinnertime with jugs of cold tea and a slab of bread and bacon.

Like the old pictures in the Bible, she and Aunt Margaret would move up and down the cut swathes. The neat stacks, like tall beehives, were raised on poles against the damp and between them they gathered the gleanings, as women had done since man first began to plant for fodder.

Kate Mary would stop to rest her aching back, standing in the precious sunshine so vital to their small harvest, aware of her Aunt's reproachful glance.

She would look away over the flat green treeless country, warm with the golden sun, to where Croagh Patrick raised its cone away there by the edges of the sea, soft mountain blue, crowned with its coronet of white, never dreaming then that most of her small experience of love would lie within its shadow.

She knew she had known then absolute content, little more

than that of a child, enjoying the effort of her young body and the feeling of the sun taking her face under the old hat; secure in the love of her Aunt and her fine handsome cousin with the sparkling blue eyes and the splendid smile, who seemed to her as she grew up to be king of all he knew.

Now the hay was growing knee high, and she knew that if she tried to use the scythe, wrapped there in sacking at the back of the stable, she would probably cut her foot off.

It was only one of many things piling against her strength, tired already by even three mornings of staggering down to the milking pen still thick with sleep in the grey light after dawn, herding in the waiting cows who were far more willing than she was herself. She would sit there with her drowsy face sinking against their coarse-haired sides, struggling for the smooth even flow of milk that never seemed to come for her, from the full udders.

Already she hated milk; and worried about the hay; and the turnips didn't seem to be doing as well as they should. She couldn't wait to get away and tell Ned all about it. Even the hens were laying badly, either disturbed by being hounded all over the yard in the middle of the night, or by cropfuls of spoilt grain that would have downed a turkey.

'I may not be early home,' she said, and tried to hide her eagerness to get away. It was as hard on Aunt Margaret with the Lad there like a ghost, and God only knew if he would ever come back from it.

She tried to speak more gently, looking down on her aunt's small figure.

'I'll have to pack all my things,' she said, 'and go and see the nuns and tell them I'll not be back. And then I'll go and see my friend Aileen. I can't just leave without goodbye to her.'

It was a blatant lie. She would see Aileen when she saw the nuns, but so desperate was she to get to Ned that she didn't even pause in the telling of it. Nor blush.

But there must have been something in her manner.

'Where does she live?' Aunt Margaret asked, and the girl tried not to hear the mistrust in her voice. If she knew she was meeting that policeman, then she knew she was meeting him in Westport.

Only half a lie this time, but firm and determined. There

was no knowing what would happen after today, and today she must have.

'She lives in Westport. On the way out to Leenane. But I'll hardly be done with everything before school is over. I'll take tea with her.'

Aunt Margaret was silent a moment and then seemed to conclude there was nothing else she could say.

'Have you the money safe?' she asked.

Kate Mary nodded.

The loss of their food stocks had been so great that Aunt Margaret had been forced to go to the tin box underneath the bed that had mercifully been missed in the ransacking of the house; giving Kate Mary reluctantly a pale gold sovereign.

'You have the list?'

Kate Mary clucked irritably at the pony. Aunt Margaret knew she had everything. What was the carry on about?

It was only when she was into the bohreen, glaring at the offending hay that would not cut itself, that something made her look back.

Her aunt still stood, unmoving, by the yard gate, looking after her, and guilt and compassion welled up, washing away all thoughts of the hay and the cows and the lie about Ned and the determination to stay out as long as she could.

She almost backed up to ask if Aunt Margaret would like to come with her, realising that she, too, had her life in ruins about her. Her home was wrecked and half the belongings of her lifetime destroyed. She, too, must be fretting about the hay and the turnips, and the Lad laid up. Above all she must be fretting about her fine son, driven out from his home to live in the hills, on the run. And with no real certainty that it wasn't Kate Mary who had caused it.

Two of them, two women left alone together, and neither of them quite able to trust the other.

As patiently as she could manage, Kate Mary lived through the earlier part of the day, packing all her clothes and the belongings she had accumulated first into her portmanteau, and then into a big torn cardboard box labelled Dooley's Dip that Mrs. Garvey went over to the corn merchant to get for her.

Firmly she resisted the woman's curiosity. For the first time it drove her to the edge of anger. She didn't, she told her, know *what* had happened. Wasn't she here in Westport and only got there when it was all long over. Yes, there had been a big raid, with police and soldiers, through all Connorstown and the country round it. Yes, it was all to do with what they had found in the Post Office, and no, she wasn't in Connorstown since and didn't know who had been taken.

There was only that out at Caherliss, Johnny was gone and the Lad wounded, and she must go back and stay there to help her aunt.

'Ah, the villains!' cried Mrs. Garvey, eyes bulging with excitement. 'The villains!'

Kate Mary had no idea which she meant.

There was going to be only one real part to this endless day, and that was when she would bring the pony to a halt outside the iron gates of the Big House, and Ned – oh, please God, let Ned be there.

In order to give some semblance of truth to what she had told Aunt Margaret, she threaded her way through sullen streets patrolled by Police and soldiers. These new men, Johnny had said, were the scrapings of the English jails. Rough, aggressive-looking characters, with Lee Enfield rifles slung across their shoulders, swaggering in the uniforms that had at once labelled them the Black and Tans.

Mrs. Garvey had been full of tales of their violence and atrocities that left the Police and the soldiers, she said, like a charrybang outing of the Children of Mary. Even them would have to be the ones that were halfway to heaven already.

She was made welcome as always to the dinner in her friend's house, boiled mutton and a good white sauce which she loved; but even here she was aware of some sense of withdrawal. Only the younger children clamoured round her as they had always done, searching for sweets they knew they would find in her pockets. Around the big table with its white cloth and the pink glass épergae at the middle of it, a few tired marigolds in the small baskets, she had the feeling that the parents, and even Aileen herself, were watching her uneasily from the corners of their eyes, trying to pretend that everything in the long friendship was the same as always.

A sense of their sad distrust stuck the good mutton in her

throat and took the flavour from the smooth sauce. Nor, she noticed, was she pressed warmly to a second helping, as she would once have been.

There was a clear air of relief when she refused an apple, and said that she must go. There was all the shopping to do for Aunt Margaret, she said.

Unlike Mrs. Garvey they had asked no questions, as though they already knew everything, and when she stood up to leave, the father never lifted his eyes to her, sitting in his striped shirt over the remnants of his mutton, leaving the peeling of his own apple to pick his teeth below the soft moustache. He was so absorbed he had not thought, apparently, for goodbyes.

The thin tired mother was effusive but she shushed the children into silence, and Kate Mary had the feeling that she couldn't wait for her to go.

Beside the stag's head in the hall where coats hung on the antlers and the brown glass eyes peered through the ends of a woollen muffler, her friend looked at her, embarrassed and awkward.

'Thank you for the dinner,' said Kate Mary.

'You'll not be coming back now, I suppose,' said Aileen uncomfortably. Kate Mary knew it was what she had been told to say in a whispered conversation with her mother in the kitchen.

She looked at her friend and compassion overrode her anger. Aileen's older brother had been months now on the run in the high bare, cloud-shadowed hills above Leenane, where even the sheep only took a poor living from the thin chalky grass. Something must have been said.

'Aileen,' she said gently, 'I didn't tell anybody anything. I was here in Westport.'

Aileen looked at her, her face crumpled. Kate Mary had been her bosom friend for years, shared all the soft secrets of their growing up; leaders together in the Sodality of the Sacred Heart; putting each other's hair up for the first giggling excited time. There were years of love and trust between them.

But now 'they' were saying things about Kate Mary. People who had been in to Connorstown came back with the story.

Only that the Marm and the Father had been taken by surprise today or she would never have been let inside the door. She looked at Kate Mary with anguish and disbelief, her blue eyes clouded with tears, part for the taste of treachery, and part for the sad unwilling acceptance of lost happiness.

'They're saying,' she whispered hoarsely, 'that you told them all about the Post Office; and Peter Garrett over there now in jail on Roscommon and likely to hang, and his mother a widow, like to go out of her mind.'

Kate Mary felt cold as winter. Here too?

'Aileen, why me?' she said. 'Why me? Why should I tell anybody anything?'

Her friend looked at her and now the round blue eyes had grown condemning, hostile, a hint of jealousy in their depths.

'Aren't you going with that policeman?' she asked.

Exactly as Aunt Margaret had asked.

It was damaging as a physical blow to Kate Mary, winding her. They had been so careful, going always out the lonely shore, separating before the real town; deluding themselves, obviously, that there were not eyes everywhere, exactly as in Connorstown.

'You knew!' she said bleakly.

'Doesn't all Westport know,' said her friend. 'Of course,' she added honestly and fiercely, 'there's many of them here wouldn't mind. Our boys can die for nothing, for all they care.'

She glared at her friend, her eyes full of anger and blind sorrow, and there was nothing more to be said.

Kate Mary went in silence, and as the door closed behind her the face of the house was blank where once Aileen and the children would have waved from the living-room window. One more sad, crippling symbol of happiness she would never know again.

'Ned,' she whispered, 'oh, Ned,' and took her watch from her waistband to count the lonely hours and minutes before she would see him. Might see him. She was sure of nothing now. Nothing except sorrow.

The hard-headed citizens of Westport at least put business before politics, and maybe the ruin of Connorstown had frightened them. She got all she wanted for Aunt Margaret, the springs of the trap squeaking under the load. No comment was made about all she bought, everything weighed and packaged in careful silence, as though even to mention the size of her purchases, and the reason for them, would be an involvement nobody wanted.

They were nervous in Westport, and they had their families to keep.

Nervous herself, her stomach taut with tension and insecurity, she at last turned the pony for the seashore, feeling now that every eye in the town was on her; every passer by in the streets knew where she was going. What matter who saw her, she thought desperately, still unable to believe that she, Kate Mary Pearse, who had done harm to nobody, should be driving like this through Westport, and the only thing lacking to her was a leper's bell.

So what matter! All she wanted was to reach Ned, to know the reassurance of his presence.

Tears of sheer relief started to her eyes when she actually saw him, out of uniform in the grey suit he always wore, and the peak of his old tweed cap pulled down across his eyes. But nothing, she thought, could disguise the erect young set of his shoulders; the air of authority. No one could mistake him for anything other than what he was, standing with his back to the fuchsia hedge of the Big House; able to see both ways without so much as moving his head, his hands behind his back as he would stand on patrol.

Fit target, she thought with a spasm of terror, dry-mouthed, for any passing bullet, and they able to pretend they hadn't known him for what he was.

But he smiled as she drew up beside him, the small spikes of his moustache lifting, sensing her distress at once and easing it with no more than the way he looked at her.

'Are we off in state today then,' he said as he climbed up beside her, and only her own stretched nerves made her aware of his glance, flickering all around them.

He gave her a gentle kiss and would not hurry her for any danger.

'Will we go out by Mallaranny,' he said, his look moving tenderly over her tense face, willing the big anxious eyes to soften into a sense of safety. He clicked at the pony but didn't offer to take the reins, leaving her the small responsibility to steady her.

With exaggerated amazement he kicked at the meal bags and packages in the well of the trap.

'God, me darling,' he said, 'I never realised we were running away together. We have food here for a month. Had you told me, I'd have put me best suit on. Where are we away to? And do we got married to make it dacent?'

Now she laughed, and with a careful tender finger he wiped the last slow tears from her cheeks.

'That's better,' he said. 'Is it food for your aunt?'

She nodded.

'There's not a bit left in Connorstown.'

''Tisn't only your aunt knows that. I had to send Murphy in on the bicycle to get a bit of bread and bacon for ourselves.'

'You were lucky they'd sell it to you.'

He reached over a hand and eased the pony to a halt, never answering her.

'Give me the reins,' he said, and spoke only when they were trotting gently along the road around the Bay, St. Patrick's mountain green, gold and majestic across the blue sunlit water. No time for talk of love or happiness, only the need to know so that they might keep even their occasional meetings possible.

'What happened, my poor love?' he said then. He had received only the formal report that Caherliss had been searched for arms and rebels, and neither of them found. It was not his own men that had done it.

'They hardly left stone upon stone in the house, and Johnny gone, and the Lad still lying there as if death is waiting by the door.'

'Hush, alannah, hush. I know all that. But, Kate Mary, my heart, do you not understand that if your cousin Johnny had moved first, he'd have done the same to us.'

She thought of the bullets and the gelignite still stored behind the wall, and could find no answer.

'He'll do it yet, Kate Mary, love,' he said, and she knew it to be true.

'It's war,' he added. 'War.'

''Tis not,' she cried at him. ''Tis family against family, and brother against brother, and there's no end to that! I told Johnny once our grandchildren would be fighting the same battle! True for me!'

She realised she said this often, but it seemed to her to express, more than anything, the futility of it all.

He took one of her gesticulating hands and kissed it, and his eyes were tender.

'*Our* grandchildren, alannah,' he said. Wearily she laid her head against his shoulder. He put an arm round her, holding her close, leaving the pony to his own ambling way; trying, although he knew he had nothing really to say, to allay all her helpless fears. What could he say, when his own fears were the same?

'Oh, Ned. If only I could see the road to that; clear to anything. But it all gets worse, not better. Horrible! I can't stand it. It's not fair. Not fair!'

'What happened?' he asked her. 'What new has happened?'

'They're saying I told you about the guns in the Post Office. That it's me who has Peter Garrett in the Jail and Elsie O'Flyn. They're saying I'm an informer.'

Ned could hardly trust himself to speak, his arm tightening convulsively about her shoulder. Because of him; because of the proud uniform he wore; because of the loyal oath he had sworn the day they gave it to him. Because of the duty he had sworn to fulfil. Because of all those, the girl he loved more than life itself was weeping at his side in the soft gold sunshine surely meant for hope and happiness; branded as the filthiest thing in all the bitter war: an informer, sneaking off for money or just for senseless treachery or private malice, to plot with the other side for the destruction of her friends.

'Ah, Kate Mary.'

Sorrow so intense he could find no words. His love, his clear-eyed beautiful girl, with all the candour and honesty of a child.

Anger was piling in him like a sickness. The bastards! It was beyond the line of duty now, or oaths of loyalty or proud uniforms. He'd get Johnny O'Connor now for what his friends had said about this girl. He'd see him dancing on a rope in Mountjoy or Kilmainham, or die himself in trying to do it.

209

He looked at down at the girl weeping on his shoulder and hopelessly let his anger ebb. He knew that Johnny's death would do no more than add insupportably to her sorrow, and might lose her to him did she ever suspect there was anything other than his bare duty in his attitude to the man.

She was right. It was a war no one of them could win. Nothing in it to bring anybody comfort.

He cradled her head against his shoulder and let her cry, looking down from the rising road at the swans immobile on the quiet water, Carrigahowly a cardboard castle against the open sea. It was like a far, strange land that had never heard of war. Here was peace and utter silence except for the shrilling of the larks up from the heather, even the seagulls quiet on the shore, not so much as the far rattle of a rifle from the town behind them. The very air was gold with the sun.

'Will we stop, my heart,' he said, after a while, 'here where it's quiet, and try and talk of other things. Like you and me.'

He didn't want to say to her yet that with matters as they were it might not be wise for them to meet again. That things like you and me would have to wait until it was all over, one way or the other. He didn't know how he would stand the pain of that himself, let alone ask it of his love, his girl.

He pulled the pony into the side of the road where it could lean down and graze on the short dry sandy grass, where sea pinks and little yellow scabious raised their faces to the sun.

'Come on now, Kate Mary. There's a rug here in the trap and, God knows, we're in danger of getting hungry.'

She managed a smile for him as he spread the rug a little below the road in shelter from the wind bending the heather flat on the hill above them. A few gulls squabbled now in sudden argument away below them where the great seas in winter rolled in boulders big as houses and round and smooth as marbles.

One of the larks shrilled and trembled in the clear sky immediately above them as though for their special pleasure, and the wind was heavy with the smell of thyme.

None of it was new to Kate Mary, who came out here often from the town, but as she sat down on the rug and pulled off her hat, she closed her eyes against the pain of its unchanging beauty; knowing it to be one of those heightened moments that mark life, never to be forgotten, like great happiness or great grief, or the first cold onset of despair. Everything was already losing colour towards the blue of Irish evening. The blue of sadness, she thought, because she knew no happiness could come from this day.

They were far enough out to see the pointed Achill mountains rising from the sea; the green flanks of Croagh Patrick fading to the blue of grapes; away behind the darkening heights of the Twelve Pins, the rounded uplands of Connemara.

Unbearable. Beauty and happiness should go together. This was like a reproach to misery.

'Come now, alannah.'

Ned took her face in his hand, cupping her chin, looking into the drowned eyes that opened reluctantly on his. What had they done to her, his bright courageous girl? He could kill the lot of them and need no other cause, duty a high crusade for the sorrow of his love, like the days when wars could be over little more than that.

He too took off his cap and his hair seemed to hold life and colour of its own, a bright point in a fading world. She reached up and touched it, smoothing down the few curls that he hated.

'Ned, what can we do?'

What could they do? Each one of them a danger to the other.

'It's not,' she said thickly, 'as though I was ever one of them. How can you betray a cause you've never held to?'

Tightly he held her hands.

'They think now that you're holding to mine.'

She flung her arms around his neck, and he could feel desperation tensing every nerve in her body.

'It's you I'm holding to. You, Ned, only you. I don't give a tinker's damn for any old causes. All I want is you.'

''Tis the same for me. My God help me, but 'tis the same for me.'

Gently he stroked her hair, over and over, until he felt the tension in her begin to subside. Then, taking her chin in his hands, he slowly turned her face to look at him, strong fingers tracing her jaw, caressing the straight line of bone, tenderness

211

and desire clouding his eyes as he looked at her.

Infinitely slowly he started to kiss her, puckering her face in his hands that he might kiss the very inside of her lips, kissing her so softly, so gently but with such firm pressure that gradually all else ceased to exist save the insistence of his kisses and the need to respond to them. Hopelessness forgotten; nothing there but the unshakable certainty of their love. Both worlds lost. Both causes forgotten.

'Kate Mary,' he murmured between the kisses. 'Kate Mary, my Kate Mary, my beautiful Kate Mary.'

'God bless the work,' cried a voice. 'You're doing well.'

Ned broke away with a curse and Kate Mary scrabbled, scarlet-faced, at her disordered clothes, but after a moment they both had to smile at the tall rangy man, brown as the stems of the heather, who stood before them. He regarded them with benign interest as though all the wisdom of the world were his, and all the secrets of human passion calmly known to him. The brim of a battered old trilby waved around his face, and a stained bahneen coat fell in folds on his thin body, made in some bygone time for a larger man.

At his heels a mangy terrier ran around, and a few scrawny goats, half-fed by the wind driven heather, and the sparse grass. He continued to stare at them, a great benign smile like a split potato across his brown face. Slowly it faded and his creased blue eyes grew dark.

'There's sorrow about you,' he said slowly then. They could do no more than listen to him, amazed; Kate Mary even forgetting to pull at her skirt, her hand reaching out to Ned as though what was being said was something they should hear as one.

'Sorrow between you,' he paused. 'But joy in the end. Life won't oblige you with what you want, but in the end it will come. In the end. In life's time.'

The great smile broke out again, like the sun coming over the rim of the morning sea.

'She's a fine girl you have, sir,' he said. 'A fine girl with breeding. Willya look at th'ankles. In a horse or a woman it's th'ankles show the breeding.'

Scarlet flooded Kate Mary's face again and she tried to pull down her skirt, but the warm amicable eyes were as impersonal as if it was the horse he looked at and not the woman.

'Good day now to you both.'

He touched the brim of the faded hat and whistled to the dog.

Ned gathered himself together to say good day but a few paces on the man stopped again, and turned and the smile was gone.

''Twould do you no harm,' he said soberly, 'to go down the hill to the rath and ask the fairies for a bit of luck. 'Tis always as well to have them on your side. Here – '

Fishing in his torn pocket, he stopped back and handed the astonished Ned a piece of coal.

'Take that with you now, and they'll know you're a friend. It'll protect you.'

In silence not for one second touched by laughter, they watched him cross the road, giving the pony a pat as he passed. He plodded off up the hill, lifting his feet in the tall heather, followed by his dog and his goats, until his long figure reached the sky. The pony looked after him as if he knew him, and might even follow him, trap and all.

'The fairies,' Ned said then, looking at the piece of coal in his hand, smooth as a jewel from being rubbed in the man's pocket. Still he didn't laugh. and Kate Mary looked almost touched with a chill of fear.

In this blue desolate world raked by the eerie winds, there were few who laughed if any man believed in fairies.

Ned smiled then and let the moment go, giving Kate Mary a last gentle kiss, and the piece of coal.

'He probably realised,' he said, that we needed all the help we could get. Keep that now, it could bring us luck. Fairies or not.'

From the white convent, away to their right below the village of Mallaranny, the Angelus struck, poignant in the silent evening as their own sorrow.

Automatically Kate Mary bent her head and blessed herself for the small prayer, and Ned looked at her with tenderness, her cap in his hands. In one moment, God bless her, she could move from the fairies to Our Blessed Lady, and her clear lovely eyes not clouded by doubt in either of them.

'Ned, I must go. I have to get out to Caherliss yet, and it's getting late.'

213

He didn't try to hold her. Both of them well knew that country roads after dark were no place for a girl alone. Nor indeed for anybody.

In silence, they got the pony going with his heavy load and it was no more than a few hundred yards before they were coming to where the rath rose above a green meadow by the sea, crowned, as all fairy forts since time began, with one single wind riven thorn.

Planted, so the wise men said, by the followers of Joseph of Aramathea to remember the thorns that crowned their Lord.

Raised, said the country folk who lived with them, by the fairies to live in.

'Did you know,' said Ned suddenly, 'that no farmer will level a rath because if he does the fairies will curse his fields?'

In the blue unearthly evening, hung between sun and dark, left to utter silence save for the wind in the heather and the far wild crying of the seagulls, it was possible to believe anything. And to feel the farmer wise.

Kate Mary didn't answer, looking down at the green rath and fingering the coal in her pocket.

He'd think me a fool, she thought, even to mention it. Aren't we both educated people, and know better than that carry on? What could it do for us? Better to say a Rosary.

Beside her Ned, too, looked down the hill, but out of the corner of his eyes so that he could pretend he wasn't doing it; reminding himself that he was a Sergeant of Police and a hard man, and didn't he leave all that nonsense behind him at his mother's skirts.

'It wouldn't do any actual *harm*,' Kate Mary said suddenly, as though they had both spoken their thoughts aloud, and at once, too honest to pretend the wish was all hers, Ned stopped the pony and threw the reins over a fence post at the roadside.

Hand in hand, saying nothing more, they walked together down the green slope towards the sea, through air clear as glass and smelling of the wild thyme beneath their feet, sharpened with salt from the incoming tide, smashing on to the shore below them.

The shadow of the rath lay long in the setting sun, the thorn bush stretched at its crown.

214

Neither said to the other what they wished for. In a few moments they returned as one towards the trap, their faces still touched with the last glimmering of the sun. Their fear and sorrow for their lives was so great they had turned back like pagans to the oldest legends of their land and could not smile at themselves, taking from what they did some strange comfort old as their own sorrow, that of all unhappy lovers.

The evening was full suddenly of the rush of wings. A flock of starlings flew home to roost, and away out to sea the clouds turned rose above the darkening moutains of Achill.

Kate Mary knew she would remember it, the moment graved on her heart and mind for as long as she might live.

'It will be all right, my heart,' said Ned. 'It will be all right.'

Aunt Margaret made no comment when Kate Mary came into the yard in the first edges of darkness, but in the lamplit kitchen her eyes were evasive and she made small talk about the land and the poor yield of eggs and whether the girl had got all she went for.

That at least brought a small relief to her taut face. Kate Mary turned sadly back out, to unload the trap.

Well, she thought bitterly, her aunt had no reason to worry anymore. For the time being, God only knew when she would see Ned again.

Quietness and painful unexpressed anxiety took over the house.

It was some blank and lonely fortnight later that Kate Mary came out the scullery door, the milk pails in her hands shaking the sleep away in a heavy dawn thick with the soft grey mist that made the grass grow fast enough to see.

Beyond the door she stopped and put down the pails abruptly beside her. Her face was careful, still, but frightened.

She had heard nothing in the night, not a sound, but all the rocks from the wall of the High Garden were scattered in the yard, the earth between them turned to mud by the night of rain. The cave in the wall yawned dark, as they had dug it on that pitch black night so many months ago; the wet cascades of flowers thrust aside, or thrown down in the yard, washed with mud.

No need now to be careful. The gelignite was gone.

As she stood, trying fearfully to understand what it might mean, Aunt Margaret came out behind her with a bucket of steaming mash for the hens.

'Aren't you down yet with the – ' she began irritably, and then stopped as Kate Mary had stopped, and put down her own bucket. Surveying, Kate Mary realised, without any surprise, all the stones and mud about the yard, and the dark square hole in the wall.

'We'll need,' she said expressionlessly, to put all this back.' As though no more had happened than some wall on the land collapsing on its own, allowing stock to roam. A danger a nuisance, no more than that.

Her small mouth was tight with some anger, but Kate Mary felt with amazement that it was more at Johnny for doing an untidy job and messing up the yard than from any concern about what had been taken away, or what was going to be done with it.

She would never know, she realised, and never be told, just how much Aunt Margaret knew. Or what she thought about it.

It was not easy. The stones were big and heavy and slippery with the rain. They could only manage it at all by bringing out a chair from the kitchen, and heaving them first on to that and then on to the wall. Close morning sweat was soon mixing with the rain on their faces, and every stone was heavier than the last. Twelve of them, Kate Mary counted. Would they ever do it before the day was really awake and some nosey body, or even a policeman, might come into the yard?

Not one word was said of Johnny.

The Lad came out then, hearing them. Pale-faced from his bed, in his trousers with braces hanging, and the wet at once beading silver on his old woollen underwear.

'Get on away with you,' Aunt Margaret said sharply. 'You're not fit yet for this.'

He blinked for a moment, his hair short above the snow white forehead that was the mark of any farmer, the rest of his features rust red from the sun in the fields. It was clear there was a battle behind his long steady face, between being given an order by his employer and doing what he thought right.

Then he moved forward, respectfully ignoring her, and even his one-armed strength made it easier. Panting, they heaved in the last of the stones and scraped the soft mud from the ground to pack around them, replacing at last the green lush cascades of the flowers.

Once again the wall looked as it had always looked.

Not even to the Lad was one word said until they were done, and then Aunt Margaret took heed of him, his face the colour of the morning ashes and fresh blood seeping scarlet from his arm as he shook slightly where he stood.

Her tight face softened.

'You did well,' she said. 'Well. Go in now and sit by the fire and I'll be there in no time to get you tea.'

This time he didn't disobey her, and she picked up her bucket for the hens.

Kate Mary flared in sudden anger. Her face was streaked with rain and sweat and mud, and her back ached as though she would never stand up straight again, and her hands bled from the stones.

'And me,' she shouted at her aunt. 'And me? Didn't I do well? Hiding my cousin Johnny's crimes!'

Aunt Margaret gave her one bleak glance through spectacles hazed with wet.

'Wasn't it your duty?' she said. 'Just as it was mine?'

Duty, Kate Mary thought, flaming. Duty. In God's name was there anything, any crime on either side in this stupid struggle, that wasn't excused by the name of duty?

Duty! Even the reason for her lost and grieving love. Couldn't he throw down his belt and his gun like so many others, and go back to the land!

Forget his oath of loyalty and his fine uniform and think for once of her. Bitterness ebbed, and she even smiled a little.

Did he do that, then he would not be Ned.

Aunt Margaret turned and looked back at her from the rickety gate of the hen run, through rain coming down now heavily, the grey sky little higher than the slope of the High Garden.

'Don't be forgetting the cows,' she said.

217

Chapter 9

Kate Mary was now virtually a prisoner at Caherliss, feeling cold hostility even from people on the roads in her evening walks. People she had known as long as she had lived in Caherliss, with nothing before now but a smile and a good word.

'I'm *me*,' she wanted to shout at them. 'I'm Kate Mary. The same person as always!' But the shadow of Ned stood between them. She was friendly with a policeman and therefore dangerous. They passed her by with averted eyes, and left her in a world of her own, alone with Aunt Margaret and the still helpless Lad.

Aunt Margaret was absolutely scrupulous in keeping everything as it had always been, doing her duty by the girl she had adopted. She knew Johnny would baste her did she do otherwise, but failed to keep the cool distrustful look from her own eyes.

She would never go so far herself as to say Kate Mary had informed on Johnny, but her whole loyal being was filled with amazement and resentment that the girl would go off with some stick of a policeman, and Johnny there in the house as fine and handsome a man as any girl could want. Ready to marry her and make Caherliss her home forever, and it was well-known there was more than one girl over in Connorstown would give her eye teeth to be in that position. Johnny, a patriot too, on the run now for Ireland! Enough to fill any girl with pride. Yet Kate Mary wanted none of him.

A policeman!

Aunt Margaret simply couldn't understand it, but every

time she looked at Kate Mary's cool sad face, her resentment swelled, and her doubts. Even if the girl had told nothing deliberately, who knew what could have come out by accident, talking to that policeman. There was no doubt he'd be the clever one at getting things out of her.

At least she didn't seem to be seeing him now. And if she was, her Aunt Margaret thought grimly, there was little she could tell, not knowing where Johnny was any more than anybody else.

Kate Mary in turn looked at her aunt's tight ungiving expression, and wanted to shout at her that she wasn't tied to Johnny. There had never been a promise given; in fact, all the time she had been trying to hold him off. She had a right to fall in love with whom she wished. And even if it were a policeman, before God, Aunt Margaret should have enough sense to know she would never breathe one word against Johnny.

That was the one thing caused friction between her and Ned; that she wouldn't discuss Johnny. And it was brutally unfair to have Aunt Margaret in her every word and look accusing her of putting him on the run.

She wanted to shout at her that she didn't need to come back to Caherliss. She had a job and a place to live in Westport, and didn't need to come back to the wreckage and the wounded Lad, and the milking and the pigs, and the hay growing over the tops of the walls, and never seeing Ned!

She had felt it was her duty to Aunt Margaret who had given her a home.

Duty. It was Ned who always spoke of it, but she was just as bound by it. In coolness and lack of love she and her aunt did their duty to each other, struggling to keep Caherliss going for the one they both, in their own ways, loved; not looking at each other much, keeping their minds on all that needed to be done.

'What'll we do about the hay, Aunt Margaret? If it rains now, we've lost it all.'

They both knew it was too long uncut already.

Fortunately for those in the hills, the summer was hot and dry, but in the last few days the soft clouds had been piling up; the wind chasing their shadows blue over the green land.

'We'll have to get someone in from Connorstown.' Aunt Margaret spoke reluctantly.

'Couldn't Batty do it?'

The poor man at the end of the bohreen was always glad of a bit of work, but too delicate to do much.

'Ah, he's only half a man, the creature. He'd never manage a square yard of it.'

Kate Mary's mouth was tight. She knew why her Aunt was reluctant to get someone in from Connorstown. With Kate Mary at Caherliss, there could be unpleasantness. There was an unspoken agreement that she would be left alone if she was kept at a distance, but Connorstown had suffered, and the people were bitter.

Kate Mary was bitter herself.

'Don't be anxious, Aunt Margaret,' she said. 'If you get someone in, I'll hide under the bed until they go away. You can tell them I've gone to England with the policeman.'

The conversation fell into one of those silences that through the hot quiet days so often occupied the house. Kate Mary began to thank God for the turnips to hoe, and the pigs to feed, and the need to rebuild the hen house, since it kept her out and alone and allowed her to think of Ned – in a panic, sometimes, that if it all went on too long, they would forget each other. There were moments in the hazy sunshine she would find that she couldn't conjure up his face.

'Ned!' She would cry out then aloud to the turnips or the indifferent hens. 'Ned!' As though to shout his name would bring him back to her.

They had given him a car now, and sometimes she would see him on the country roads, erect and severe beside the driver, his moustache bristling, the black open vehicle packed with Constables, their rifles up beside them. Always she pulled back to the roadside wall to see them go by, ankle deep in grass and flowers, her face composed, pretending she watched only as any peasant might, open-mouthed at the thin-wheeled, noisy motor.

Only Ned's eyes dare flash a message, pain in it in the few seconds of passing, and a beseeching for patience; a promise that all was still well. All this in the time it took the motor to lurch past her on the rough road, and if any of the local Constables were there, curiosity was scrawled across their faces, looking from her to their Sergeant to get a clue was there anything in all the village talk. Or any truth in what was whispered in the Barracks, between the sniggers, that the Sergeant in his new motor car patrolled the Caherliss road more than any other. And it was nothing at all, at all, to do with Johnny O'Connor.

Even at night, looking out of the window, Kate Mary would see the round headlamps blurring in the pale mist; the light bouncing on the rough road.

The car would be full, she knew, of police with hand lamps and rifles, hunting Johnny as they would a rat, hoping that under cover of darkness he might be foolish enough to come to his home. Some instinct still to protect Aunt Margaret made her draw the curtains, closing out the summer nights and even the small pleasure of knowing Ned to be there.

Occasionally there would be the far rattle of rifle fire, and in the lamplit room their glances would flicker from what they were doing and they would bless themselves; the Lad awkwardly with his left hand, Aunt Margaret firmly as though she dared God to ignore her.

No mention was ever made of Johnny, no word said among them. But the night he did come, the police were missing.

Smiling to herself afterwards, for who could not admire the audacity, Kate Mary realised they had probably been decoyed away by some caper in the other direction.

The night had been beautiful enough to drag her heart with loneliness for it was a night surely made for love, but all she had was the empty longing of the present and a future without promise. She went out before going to bed, as she had got into the habit of doing. Johnny used to do it always to check that the stock was safely closed in for the night, and that all was well in his small kingdom.

From the yard gate the meadows and the young corn stretched to the edges of the farm, and away beyond it the quiet country was touched with the first silver fingers of light from a full rising moon, coming up like a great lamp beyond the pasture elms. Another hour, she knew, and the whole sweet stretch of land would be bleached with white, stone walls criss-crossing it like the dark unsteady rambling of a child's drawing. No sound in all the blanched night except the far barking of a disturbed dog, probably as far away as Connorstown, so still the air. Unearthly silence, feared by many of the old country people who would close themselves inside their houses, hiding from the full white moon that was the time of spells and lunatics and the coming of the Little People.

For her, it meant only the haunting longing to go walking hand in hand with Ned through the silver splendour; touching with pure magic all the thoughts and plans of their ordinary, earthbound love.

She sighed deep. It would not be tonight. But there would, she told herself staunchly, there would be other nights and other moons. God could not allow it otherwise.

Slowly and reluctantly she went back to the house and bolted the door of the scullery passage, pausing as she passed the first vestibule window to wonder for a moment what had the pony stirring restlessly in the stable. Probably she herself had disturbed him, she decided, and went to bed.

In the morning the hay was cut.

She came out first, Aunt Margaret only stirring in her room. The dawn trailed long streamers of pink and yellow behind the hills and the far out fields were still dark like dusk, heavy with the night's dew. It was no hardship to be up for the milking on a morning like this, and she lifted her face to it and its cool pleasure, giving a pat to the pony who stuck out his head with a sudden urgency as though he had something to say.

Smiling a little, she reached the yard gate and found it open. Anger hit her immediately that someone had been creeping round and spying on them in the night. No dog to warn them now, not that that would matter. They shot the last one, would probably shoot any other, too, and herself and Aunt Margaret and the Lad if they lifted their heads.

'Well, he's not here, you eejits!' she shouted furiously into the empty morning. 'You're wasting your time. He's not here!'

Then she saw the meadows. Not laid in quite the exquisite curving swathes that Johnny and the Lad would usually leave. But cut. All the hay that was costing them so much anxiety laid flat. Cut by the light of God's given moon.

She leaned on the stone wall and laughed and laughed aloud.

222

'Ah Johnny, ah Johnny love, more power to your elbow.'

The Lad came running awkwardly from the house at the shouting, thinking something was wrong, and behind him Aunt Margaret, dragging her husband's old shotgun that she had no idea how to fire.

They looked at Kate Mary standing there in the grass, grinning all over her face, and then they looked at the meadows. Kate Mary watched the tears come slow and unashamed to Aunt Margaret's eyes before she laid the shotgun against the wall and wiped them away with the end of her apron. But the Lad blessed himself fearfully, his face awed, his blue eyes like saucers.

''Tis the Little People,' he whispered. 'The Little People. 'Twas a full moon.'

Kate Mary laughed again, and knew a rush of warm-hearted pleasure for Aunt Margaret that her son had cared enough to risk his life to help her.

'If it's the Little People,' she said to the Lad, 'then one of them's over the six foot mark.' Aunt Margaret smiled even as she dabbed the tears but she was her brisk self again, the moment of sentimental weakness past.

'Get on now with the milking,' she said to Kate Mary. 'We must get it all stooked before the weather goes.'

Kate Mary couldn't help being delighted.

Oh, the audacity of it. The cheek of you, Johnny. The very cheek of you!

Mentally she apologised to Ned, but he'd have to hand this one to Johnny. Oh, well done, Johnny! Well done!

Forgetting that the white blaze of moonlight might have been used as well for other things.

Batty came up from his cottage to see could he do anything during the morning, and went back breathless with the news, racing out to tell anyone who happened to pass along the road. He was halfway in his thinking between Kate Mary and the Lad; well believing Johnny O'Connor could have had the nerve to do it, but leaning, like all his country kind, towards the legends of the Little People.

It didn't take the news long to get in to Connorstown, and well before the dinner two Constables arrived, panting on their bicycles, sweat around their cap brims, and stood staring

223

at the meadows as though the hay could tell them something.

Constable Murphy wrote solemnly in his notebook and then turned to Kate Mary and her Aunt who had come out to them. Kate Mary's face was brimming with laughter, and even her aunt had an unaccustomed smirk on her thin mouth. The Constable's round, flushed face was as grave as he could make it.

'He was here then,' he said portentously.

'Who was here?' Kate Mary asked him, enjoying herself immensely. It would take more than fat Constable Murphy to trap Johnny.

'Your cousin, and his friends'.

'We know nothing,' Aunt Margaret said firmly, 'about who was here at all. We were in our beds asleep like decent people, and in the morning the hay was cut.'

The Lad thrust in his long awed face, nodding like a toy.

''Twas the Little People,' he said.

Constable Murphy tried to give him a crushing glance, but there was doubt in it. The smart uniform was only a very thin covering on the country boy.

'I can't put that in me book,' he said.

Aunt Margaret took over briskly.

'Nor can you put anything else,' she said, for no one here knows anything. Now go on about your business like a good lad, and leave us alone. Get yourself away out of my way.'

She had known Constable Murphy since he was a small fat boy, and carried almost as much authority over him as Ned himself.

Reluctantly he closed his notebook, and put it back into his tunic pocket.

'We'll have you under observation,' he said heavily, trying to keep his position, unable to think of anything else to say.

''tis no more than your job,' Aunt Margaret answered equably.

At the yard gate the other Constable turned. A stranger, and well junior to Constable Murphy, he hadn't spoken so far.

Hard narrow eyes moved over the three of them and his young mouth was like a rat trap. There was something about his revolver and his night stick, that made them seem ready for instant use.

'It would be well,' he said coldly, 'to be quite sure where

224

you were last night, and all those belonging to you. The Constable didn't tell you: there was a stretch of railway line blown up last night, nine miles to the south of Westport. A train went into it and there was a lot of people hurt.'

Aunt Margaret never even blinked.

'And what would that be to concern us,' she said. 'A couple of women and a wounded man – and the police that wounded him. What could we do with blowing up trains, or anything else either, with all we have to do with our one man driven off the farm.'

But Kate Mary's hand flew to her mouth and her eyes widened and the gesture did not escape the young policeman. The gelignite!

Could she in any way have put a stop to it? She felt as guilty as if she herself had stolen the stuff, and in the black night dug the hole for it under the High Garden.

'Good day to you now,' said the Constable, but it was Kate Mary's shattered face he looked at.

He turned for the door, and a red-faced Constable Murphy followed him, searching for breath all the way back to Connorstown to give him a furious lecture on seniority.

Kate Mary walked slowly down and stood looking at the meadow. The brightness was gone from the day, and the pleasure and the joke from the cut hay. All she could think of was a broken train, piled like a great toy in that silver moonlight. People hurt and screaming, who had never done Johnny O'Connor a day's harm.

The Lad was standing sheepish by the kitchen door when she went back in.

'And was it the Little People,' she asked him scathingly, 'wrecked the train as well?'

She was immediately sorry, laying an apologetic hand on his arm. It was nothing to do with the Lad.

Most of the young men were living in dugouts in the hills, carefully excavated and established over long months back, hidden in the lonely places with all the care they had given to replanting the flowers in the wall of the High Garden when they had dug their small cave there; always tucked away in some small curve of the land, below a summit from where a lookout could be kept.

Some were in safe houses. Small isolated cottages of known sympathisers where some old man could sit smoking his clay pipe and enjoying the idle days of his life; in fact scouring the view below him with bright intent eyes for the least movement, the back door always open to the pathless land.

Food had been stacked when the dugouts were built, and more was brought carefully from Connorstown, in stages from house to house out the roads, and never the same way twice, lest some sharp-eyed policeman notice steady traffic.

They were looked after by the girls, the Cumn na Bahn, fully committed now, on the run themselves and open to be shot on sight like any of the men.

It was they who collected the food on the last stages: cooked it for them in the little safe houses where no extra smoke would call attention; bound the occasional wound they couldn't avoid from their skirmishing and kept watch in their turn from the high places of the land.

Bridie was in charge of them. In her element now, splendidly suited by the black dress with the leather belt, a revolver on it in a holster so that she could buy her life dearly if it came to it, and please God take some peeler with her. Her hair blazed under the black tam-o-shanter, and her green eyes blazed also with a mixture of fevour and excitement, but most of all the exquisite pleasure of having got Johnny where that Kate Mary Pearse could never reach him.

Not that she saw a great deal of him. Johnny was in a safe house of his own, where his lieutenants went to meet in secrecy for all the planning. Only when the women were directly concerned did she go, and missed half of what was said with the hungry longing that tore her body; unable to get any closer than to watch his long relaxed figure lounging in the grass, propped against the old stones of the place they met. His blue eyes were alive as never before, tinged with derision for the poor police and soldiers they were outwitting so easily; knowing that all over the country other bands like his were on the attack. They were quick-witted and intelligent, this type of hit and run warfare a gift to their bright minds.

'The cream of Irish youth,' one senior British officer had said sadly. 'The best. If only we had them on our side.'

If it were all successful, it could be the beginning of the end.

Excitement and triumph lit his face as he talked, and Bridie thought she had never seen him so handsome. She was so sick with wanting him, she could hardly answer when he spoke and would see irritability with her cloud his looks.

It was all hopeless now. His thoughts were far from women and she knew always a creeping anger that he had failed to give her a child and settle it all for good. Then she wouldn't need to be up here, risking her neck to be near him.

When the meetings were over, she had to get up and go with all the others, watching him vanish into his own hiding place where, thank God, no peeler would ever find him. There was always afterwards to be thought of, when it was all over and he would be able to remember that all through it, she had been up there at his side. Which was more than could be said about Kate Mary Pearse, creeping around with that peeler. A smile would curve Bridie's soft mouth. It wasn't by chance that word had got around that Kate Mary had told about Elsie O'Flyn.

Afterwards, even in the tiny cottage room with a window like a handkerchief that she shared with two other girls, she washed herself scrupulously and carefully brushed her hair a hundred times, touching her cheeks with the rabbit's foot of rouge, pulling on the tam-o-shanter at a careful angle.

He came unexpectedly around the houses and dugouts, and he must never find her anything but beautiful.

There was an almost wild atmosphere up there in the hills that long dry summer. They were all young, lit with belief and fervour that was almost incandescent, life only a trivial thing to be laid down at any moment, as a privilege for Ireland.

They asked no more of their families than that they should never grieve. Did it come they would wear death as a badge of honour, gladly taken, and expect the same of those that loved them.

Through these months, they lived only at night, coming down from the hills like phantoms to blow railway lines and cut telegraph wires, set fire to isolated barracks and trench the roads where police patrols were likely to come whirling angrily round corners in pursuit of them. A half wild mania was about them, their young faces growing thin, their eyes burning with the delirium of success.

227

If they were aware that the families they had left down on the flat land were beginning to lack food, they didn't care. Was it not for Ireland, like the ready sacrifice of their own young lives? They themselves would starve and never notice it.

Wives and young children and old people, who had listened all their lives to the long tale of hope for Ireland's freedom, were going hungry. The markets and the fairs were closed as places where people could gather in illegal numbers, and there was nowhere they could trade their produce or their stock except in searchround back yards, or by bartering with their neighbours for what they lacked.

With no markets there was no money, and out in the country the hunger began to show in gaunt faces and skeleton children, and the old ones whispered with their memories of the Great Hunger.

A poor land at best, it needed constant care to yield, and as in Caherliss, there was no one to save the turning harvest, and the green crops rotting in the fields, and there was nowhere they could be sold. Frightened and beleaguered families, haunted by the fear of the police, could only eat what they could and leave the rest decaying in the sun. When they got too hungry, they ate their meagre stock, knowing when that was gone, there would be nothing.

Rumbling high-wheeled vans began to go about the country, a white cross painted on their canvas sides, relieving the worst of hunger with food brought with charitable dollars from America.

The visitors could only tell the gaunt and frightened people that they may be hungry, but they were still better off than in the terror of the cities, where the police and the Army and the Black and Tans held a reign of furious violence. Nights and days were hideous with the roar of armoured cars and the rattle of machine guns; the rush and hiss of paraffin fed flames.

The Auxiliaries were frightened themselves now, because these fervent lads out in the hills, strong and disciplined for all their blazing ardour, were beginning to take the country. The police were retreating to the big towns, sandbagged into positions like the trenches of the war, unable to hold their country barracks against these attackers that came like shadows from the hills; their bullets and explosives and their flaming torches crashing home reality before they vanished again, leaving dead policemen and soldiers and burning barracks as the trade mark of their passing.

They drilled and practised up in the hills in the warm days, with the larks shrilling above them and the smell of thyme heavy in the drying grass; the corncrakes grating through the silence in the fields far below, hoping for a harvest that might never come.

They were lighthearted, that splendid summer, speaking little of their wives or families, content that they were willing for any sacrifice, as they were themselves. Only their eyes gave them away; dark with fanaticism and burning with exhilaration. Slowly, slowly they were beginning to reclaim Ireland from the centuries of possession. For the Irish. Ireland for the Irish!

In their determined passion, if they knew that the Irish of the North would not share their dreams, then they set it all on one side, No Irishman could resist the victory when it came. The North would fall in with all the rest, they would themselves. Who would want to leave half Ireland to the English?

They drilled and rested, and the lieutenants had their planning meetings with Johnny. They took their turns to guard on the high shoulders of the hills, seeing the Police combing the country fruitlessly far below them; sending everyone flying for cover if they set their feet upon the slopes. Waiting for the nights, when they would sweep like phantoms on their targets.

For Ned, struggling against them, the area was too big. Even with his extra Constables, the men he had were too few to cover it and help from Westport was reluctantly given unless something was already happening. Then usually it was too late. Smoke dying on a gutted house, or the telegraph wires drooping over the fields from sawn off posts; an ambushed car with flattened tyres and blood across its seats.

Johnny was a genius at planting his activities when all Ned's careful watch was somewhere else.

He had, of course, had his successes, but dead men were no use to him unless one of them was Johnny O'Connor. And even then, he acknowledged to himself, he would feel cheated.

The dead men were no use to any one else either, he thought grimly, as he watched the proud, dry-eyed funerals passing to the Church in Connorstown; the forbidden tricolour covering the coffin.

Nor did he ever tell them to remove it.

Aunt Margaret spoke not one word of all this when she had been visiting Connorstown. Kate Mary got all her news from Batty down at the corner, too simple-minded to be aware of any atmospheres, or that he shouldn't tell all heard. The Lad, too, was able now to drive into town with the eggs and butter which he sold quietly to Gorman's. Kate Mary watched him go each week, ridiculously sick with envy that even that small world was denied to her.

His news was always whispered behind the trap as he took out the pony, or in the yard in the evening when Aunt Margaret was cooking for the meal.

With a tight mouth, she ignored it all. If she could pretend it wasn't happening, she could ignore the terrible schism of her son out hunted in the hills and her niece in love with a policeman, one of the hunters.

The atmosphere in the house was awkward; the poor Lad, who had never gone back to his own cottage, a painful buffer between the two women, who tended to speak only to him and not each other. Both of them were glad to have him as it was only his long lugubrious presence that made life possible at all.

Aunt Margaret was not going to be one of the ones to starve. Long back-breaking days for all of them in the hot fields between the walls harvested the root crops; hard sore hours in the yard chopped the green tops from turnips, carrots and parsnips; and she gave the cabbages to the Lad to sell secretly with the eggs and butter, to Gorman's in the town.

They were still eating last year's bacon, hung in smoky sides from the roof beams of the kitchen, and the hens, recovered from their ordeal, were laying well.

Caherliss had no need of the White Cross vans, and when they came Aunt Margaret, as grim-faced as if she disapproved of them, would pile in all the spare food they had, waving away offers of payment from the ladies who had turned their fine hands to driving the heavy vehicles round the country roads.

Out in the hills the fine heart-catching excitement of success went on, fighting with all they had for what they so passionately believed. In the countryside, left to the children and the old and the ones who did not care, there was little to live on but tales told by their hot-eyed sons, about a dream. They were not to know that when it came true it would make small difference, one way or the other, to their poor few acres.

For the moment, with desperate prayers and candles burning before Our Lady and the Sacred Heart, they could do no more than endure; denying all knowledge of their sons when the Police came. And if death came first, try to tell themselves that it was for the sake of Ireland, and worth it that there would be no one to see them through their sad old age. No one to inherit the meagre land they had toiled on all their lives.

Ned came to Caherliss.

In the name of God, thought Kate Mary, racing to the window at the sound of the motor, he must be desperate to do this. Yet her body trembled with the pleasure of just seeing him, marching grimly up from where they had left the car at the gate. To her understanding eye, there was distaste for his task in every fine tall line of him.

Constable Daly was with him, the both of them with rifles slung across their shoulders, the driver left behind them in the car with another man at his side, their own rifles ready as though all the rebels in Ireland might come rushing across the quiet fields of Caherliss.

Aunt Margaret told the Lad to open the door.

'Do you not,' she said tartly, 'they're likely to break it down, the savages that they are'.

Kate Mary opened her mouth to protest, wanting to cry to her did she not realise that this was Ned! He would never break her door down.

Then she fell silent, realising like a blow to her heart that this wasn't Ned. This was Sergeant Brannick, out hunting the rebel leader, Johnny O'Connor, and he could do anything. Break her door down. Fire the house. Anything. He had the right.

Her mouth was dry as she stood beside her aunt and waited for him to come in. He had, as Johnny did, to duck a little for the low lintel of the hall. Constable Daly, following him, looked angry, and with even less taste for his task than Ned himself. Kate Mary had a sudden foolish recollection of how, when she first came to Caherliss, John Daly used to take her fishing at the ruined bridge before setting off on his ten mile walk home from school. A pleasant, good-tempered boy, who knew everything about the country.

Aunt Margaret attacked at once, her out thrust chin coming to about the second button of Ned's tunic.

'What do you want, Sergeant? Haven't you torn my house to the ground twice? Isn't that enough for you?'

Ned answered levelly. Only Kate Mary could hear the discomfort in his voice, and he never looked at her at all.

'I want your son, Mrs. O'Connor,' he said.

'He isn't here, and well you know it.'

'D'you know where he is?'

'I do not. Isn't he a grown man, comes and goes where he pleases. Why would he tell his mother?'

'Mrs. O'Connor,' Ned's voice was patient, 'there's a price on your son's head. You know where he is. Don't you send him food!'

Startled, Kate Mary glanced first at Ned and then at her aunt. Ned's eyes flickered, but still he wouldn't look at her.

Aunt Margaret's answer was a shrill contemptuous cackle.

'Food, is it? 'Tis little enough you left us for ourselves!'

Through the bravado, Kate Mary could feel the little woman trembling at her side, and saw her shove her hands into her apron pockets to hide their tremor. She moved closer, and put a hand on her shoulder.

'Sergeant,' she said, and could have wept to call him so. Her Ned, Sergeant. 'Before God, I swear to you we do not know where my cousin is. Go back and tell that to whoever sent you, but please leave my aunt alone. Her life is hard enough.'

He looked at her then, his eyes dark with misery in his unmoving face; begging for forgiveness, telling her mutely, beseechingly, that he was still Ned. Her Ned. Doing no more than was his duty, and indeed, far less.

This he made clear, turning back, after one long sad exchange of glances with all Kate Mary's heart in her own desolate eyes, to Aunt Margaret.

'Mrs. O'Connor. There is nothing against you yourself . . .'

'Isn't that decent of you!'

Two scarlet spots blazed in Aunt Margaret's face, and her temper was up. Kate Mary saw the echoing patches of red on Ned's cheekbones, but he went on in his determinedly level voice.

'But we have to find your son, and we are going easy on you at the moment. It would be better for him did you tell us now, and not leave us to hunt him down.'

He paused.

'Because we will. It could be better for you did you help us.'

'Help you!' Aunt Margaret was beside herself. 'And better for me? Does that mean you'll bring the soldiers and the filth of the English jails, like they have in the cities? Coming with big guns and thirty of them to take one old woman? Or those great tank things they used to fight the war in France? I'm told they have them now against hard cases like me!'

She struggled for breath.

'Or burn my house,' she screeched. 'Why not do that? Above my head, and Kate Mary's head with me!'

Constable Daly turned abruptly and stood in the doorway, looking out to the green quiet land. Ned didn't move to reproach him; unable to bring himself either to tell Aunt Margaret that in most districts, that's what the Police would have done long ago.

Kate Mary felt the tears of despair scalding her eyes. Her love. Not to have seen her love so long, and then to have to face him like this; aware of the anguish in her own eyes; aware of how he would be torn by what he was doing.

But it was his duty, and he was Ned.

Lord have mercy on them, but he probably would burn down the house if it was necessary.

He turned then as abruptly as the Constable had done, and pushed his way out the door. Going down the sloping track to the gate, he and Daly walked apart, disordered, as though there was no satisfaction in what had been done.

There was silence in the car jolting back to the Barracks, Constable Daly even more erect and stony-faced than Ned, sitting well into his corner of the back seat as though he wanted no contact.

They stopped in the strangely quiet street at Connorstown, where the Post Office still stood blank and shuttered. But the Barracks was now twice the size, having taken in the house next door, the old couple who owned it left to go where they would. With proper respect, expressionless, Constable Daly allowed Ned to get out first and followed him through the green door of the Barracks, now reinforced by a steel gate.

Ned took off his cap and ran his hand round the damp edges of his hair, still stricken by the meeting at Caherliss. He thought he had been ready for it, but nothing had prepared him for the tragic eyes of his girl, looking as though she had lost all hope, lost all . . .

To his amazement he realised Constable Daly had not only taken off his cap but his belt also, and his revolver and bayonet, and laid them on the table.

There was a long silence, and the other Constables all looked at Ned out of the sides of their eyes, pretending to carry on with what they were doing.

'Are you not still on duty, Constable?' he said coldly.

'I was.' There was a red mark, sweat beaded, around Constable Daly's forehead, and below it the young man's long face was determined; only the small nervous flicker of his eyes showing the effort he was making. He poked the gun belt with a long distasteful finger.

'Ye can keep these,' he said, and under the stress, the country came back into his voice. 'Ye can keep these, for I have no more use for them; fighting against my own, and women into the bargain. I have better things to do for my own respect than frightening women.'

'You mean you're resigning from the Force?'

Ned was carefully cool.

'I am.'

234

He was braver now, firmer once the decision was taken.

Ned looked at him, and could feel nothing but bitter envy. If only he could lay it all down and marry Kate Mary, with a small bit of a house somewhere and children to rear. The Police were doing it all over Ireland, sick, as Daly said, of fighting against their own.

Oh, Kate Mary love, if I could only do it!

But he knew he never could. An oath sworn was to him an oath sworn. A duty accepted to be followed through as long as that existed. Even to the grave.

Bleakly he looked at Constable Daly, who seemed surprised that it was all going so quietly. Ned's eyes were pale and lightless.

'You'll put that in writing to the D.I. and Westport.'

'I will. It'll be no trouble to me.'

Stout now; excitement creeping in that he had actually done it. Proud of himself after weeks of brooding on it.

'You'll have it in by the day after tomorrow, or you'll be arrested as a deserter. You're suspended from duty until then. Get out now.'

Bouyantly, ex-Constable Daly flashed a look around his friends, who dare not flicker an eyelid with the Sergeant watching.

It was only as he stepped out down the street, happily undoing all the black buttons down his tunic, that he realised he had nowhere to go. His parents had sold up the farm a year ago and gone to live with his sister in Sligo, afraid of being alone in the country. Afraid of the Police, with their second son marching with the Volunteers.

His face up to the sun, he started out on the six-mile walk to Caherliss. To Mrs. O'Connor and Kate Mary. To ask them how to get to Johnny.

'The Lad is well and able now to look after the place by himself for a day,' Aunt Margaret said the following Saturday. 'We'll take ourselves to Anfield for Mass.'

Kate Mary's feelings were mixed. She hated the place – dark and doom-laden, haunted – the sort of place that if terrible things had not happened there, then their day would surely come.

She smiled at herself. What terrible things could happen to old Uncle Ulick and his unfriendly housekeeper? The woman was old as himself and as dour, as though life had shrivelled for both of them long ago; no longer holding any interest except as a last chance to prepare for a good death. Not, she thought, that anyone could imagine either of them even getting up to anything.

Unmarried. Closed up as long as anyone could remember in that gloomy house, the flaccid look of the Convent and the Monastery on the faces of the pair of them.

But it was weeks since she had been out of Caherliss and she welcomed the chance to drive through the summer country. To go anywhere. Welcomed the chance, too, to go to Mass again; lending some hint of officialdom to prayers that seemed to be reaching no one from where she said them with desperate pleading each night beside her bed.

Johnny and Ned were both still alive to be sure, but for how much longer? And who would be the one with the blood of the other on his hands? It was probably asking a bit much of God to stop the war, but surely He could do something; have one of them wounded so he was out of it, and then they would both be safe. Shouldn't that be easy enough for God?

'Did you hear me?' Aunt Margaret said sharply 'We'll go to Anfield tomorrow.'

'Yes. Yes, I'd like that.'

What foolishness she was thinking. Nothing but death itself would stop either of those two. This she knew with terrible, cold certainty, as though the banshee that country people swore went wailing over a house before a death had come to roost above her own head. Waiting, like herself, to know who it should cry for.

That evening, her aunt proceeded to make great quantities of potato cakes, pounding and thumping them into circles on the floured table. While they browned on the griddle, she cut down one of the last sides of bacon from the roof beams, and sent the Lad out to the barn for a sackful of vegetables, and another of the potatoes he still turned from the field with difficulty.

Kate Mary stared.

'Are we feeding an army at Anfield?' she asked, and then

236

went cold. Was that exactly what they were doing? Would it all be taken from Anfield to the hills? Potato cakes. Johnny's favourite, the yellow butter running down his chin.

'Don't forget the butter,' she whispered automatically.

'Butter?' Aunt Margaret was sharp. 'Aren't they fortunate enough to get this? They can well manage without butter.'

'Who is it for then?'

'The people around Anfield. I'm told they're near to starving out there.'

Not in Anfield itself, with a fine farm lying over the brow of the hill above the house, and all the workers old as their master and in no danger of picking up a rifle and going on the run with it.

'Will you bring me a bit of parsley,' Aunt Margaret said, 'on your way in from feeding the hens?'

Another way of saying, Stop the conversation and get on with your work.

Thoughtfully, she went out to the grain bins in the scullery and took a scoop of corn. The hens fed, she went as she often did to lean on the yard gate and look out at the blue evening country, away across to the cone of Croagh Patrick. It was some kind of a tie with Ned, that they could both see it. Like the moon that rose and died for both of them.

In the distance down the road, two policemen were cycling one behind the other, no more than black shapes against the limpid sky and only the top of them in view. Like the ducks and things you'd see in a shooting gallery at one of the big Fairs.

'Bang, bang,' said Kate Mary. 'Bang, bang.'

And then thought: Supposing one of them was Ned, and it was no longer a joke. She had laid her head down suddenly on the top rail of the gate and cried.

The next morning when they set out it was grey and damp, not raining yet but it would before the day was out and Aunt Margaret told Kate Mary to put into the trap the two big black umbrellas they could need on the way home.

Kate Mary remembered and smiled to think of the times that she and Johnny had driven together, huddled under one; singing often in the rain. Then she frowned, wondering why

237

Johnny was so much in her mind this morning, as if at any moment he would come striding down the vestibule, demanding was everybody ready. He hated Anfield as much as she did, but was always amiable and easy about pleasing his mother. She felt sorrow suddenly, and a sense of loss.

'For God's sake,' she told herself fiercely as she took the two umbrellas from the tall green pottery stand, 'you cried last night for Ned. Are you going to cry for Johnny this morning?'

She just needed to get out of the house, cooped up too long with her fears. Even Anfield would be a relief.

She helped the Lad put the bacon and potatoes and the vegetables into the trap, and the big grease-stained cardboard box that held all the potato cakes. By the time her aunt came out in her long black coat, her straw hat with the pleated ribbons on the side of it crammed down over her eyebrows, she had set aside all her stupid fears and was able to smile at her.

'Soft day, Aunt Margaret.'

Aunt Margaret was dour.

'We'll be wet on the way back.'

Because she and Kate Mary were both dressed in their best, and it was an outing and not just a journey to buy food, they both went out the front door. The Lad led the pony out the farm gate and along the track round the house, past the well and the ancient elms that had been there longer than any memory, round to the pretty iron gate in the garden wall beside the fading roses.

When they were settled in the trap, he went on ahead of them, down over the sloping meadow where a few sheep grazed, to open the farm gate itself. Standing there respectfully and touching the brim of his old hat as the owner formally left Caherliss.

Kate Mary was exhilarated to be out, taking pleasure in the damp cool day that brought green like a new spring to the steadily rising land between them and Anfield.

Here and there people waved from the bleak yards of lonely cottages, but mostly it was a deserted land, the small farms in the end giving way to the dark stretches of bogland; the bog cotton still on it like snow in the windless day; one

238

solitary man bent over his slane, already cutting turf against the winter; light flashing like a knife from the water beyond him.

In the silence a single curlew called plaintively from the far stretches of brown bog, and beyond it the land rose to hills of scrubby whin and pale dry heather.

Would that, she wondered, be where Johnny was and all his friends? A commander's position if ever there was one, the narrow range of hills looking down on the flat land on either side. Nothing could come, she thought, and nobody, that they couldn't see.

She looked at Aunt Margaret and for a moment thought of saying this, but her aunt stared expressionlessly out between the pony's ears, as though they might be crossing the Andes themselves in South America and it would be all the same to her. So Kate Mary kept silent and her thoughts to herself, enjoying the fresh dank smell of the bogland, the sharp beautiful blue of the flags that grew along its edges, and the tangle of small flowers in the roadside grass, gratefully lifting freshened faces to the damp sky.

She thought about Ned then, since her aunt didn't want to talk, playing a game that he was going to be there waiting when they get to Anfield. But not as a policeman, just as Ned. She had to wipe a foolish smile off her face at her imaginings, suddenly aware that Aunt Margaret might see it and think her gone soft in the head.

Her thoughts were jolted away by a sharp turn the pony took badly, shaking the laden trap over the stones, leaving the bog behind and starting the slope up to Anfield House. It was a narrow road bordered with rough stone walls sprouting with bracken, rowan trees still green along the sides of it.

Aunt Margaret stopped the trap and made Kate Mary get out and walk where the hill became steeper, saying the pony had to much to pull. Once again, plodding up the rutted lane, she wondered about the sacks of potatoes and turnips that had put her out.

The trap waited at the gates of the desmesne, tall between ancient pillars covered with moss and ivy; the gates themselves rusted and sunk into the ground, so many years since they had been closed.

239

The Grand Gates they were called, and the first time Kate Mary had heard it and she had laughed. But she came to realise that once indeed they must have been grand; the creeper-covered ruin to one side a pretty grey stone lodge from which no doubt a woman would have run, curtseying to open the gate; a flock of children at her heels hoping for a thrown penny.

The curving drive would have been weeded and the bushes cut along the sides; the great elms cut back so that they didn't meet as they did now in a green tunnel that kept out the day in a gloomy undersea light.

Old Ulick's grandfather might have kept it like that. Been there standing on the steps of the circular portico to welcome guests as they rounded the last curve in the drive, on to the green space of the lawns before the house itself. A bright-wheeled phaeton might have been standing there and a well-groomed, splendid horse with a groom at his head; dogs bounding round the house at the sound of wheels, and the stable clock just out of sight, chiming sweetly on the hour.

So it might have looked, but now Aunt Margaret knew to drive past the stretch of ragged grass, rampant with thistles, straight round to the stableyard and the kitchen door. The front door itself, its green paint peeling, had not been opened for as long as the Grand Gates had not been shut, except for Aunt Margaret herself, who knew her place.

Kate Mary had once asked, saddened, if Uncle Ulick was very poor.

Aunt Margaret had snorted with derision and a degree of bitterness, thinking of Johnny and his thwarted expectations.

'Poor, is it?' she had said tartly. 'Poor? Isn't he as rich as Croesus, but it's all going to the Church, every penny of it, and the house as well. To be some kind of Convent. Poor! Sure he has it coming out his ears!'

Kate Mary climbed down slowly and reached for some of the parcels. Even from the back, in the cobbled yard with the pretty stable block with the white cupola, the house was sad; dark on this side from the uncared for trees and the rise of the hill. Perhaps when it had known a family, and children calling through the rooms, it had also known happiness. Now it had the forlorn look of a place certain it would never know cheerfulness again.

She had to put the pony away in a stall where the door was falling into slats, and give him a bag of oats; then carry all the sacks and bags herself into the cavenous kitchen with its dark vaulted ceiling covered in smoke-grimed asbestos. No matter what happened to the poor souls roasting in the kitchen in some disastrous fire, long gone owners of the house had made certain nothing would happen to the gentry in the rooms upstairs.

The silent housekeeper, busy at the range, gave her no more than a nod, watching what she laid down on the stone floor.

Aunt Margaret waited silently by the kitchen door.

Then, when Kate Mary was ready, exactly as they had gone to the front door of Caherliss they walked round the weedy path and pulled the old iron bell pull on the peeling front door under the portico of Anfield.

Without a smile the same woman they had left in the kitchen three minutes before opened the door to them and stood aside formally, to let them in. Not for the first time, Kate Mary had to suppress a wild need to laugh, but the cold uninhabited atmosphere of the house quickly quenched it.

A strange house. Big. A gentleman's house in the old sense, but the large square hall with the stairs going up on the left-hand side of it was bare of any furniture at all, only the polished floor thrown with an exquisite rug, from which the light through a stained glass window at the stairs caught the rich gleam of silk.

Aunt Margaret opened the door ahead of them into the drawing-room; a huge room equally bare of furniture, occupying the full width of the house and lit on both sides by large beautifully proportioned windows, square and set with square panes in perfect symmetry; curtainless.

Against one window a table had been covered with a white cloth with foot deep fragile lace. It was set with heavy silver candlesticks and the few small necessary things for serving Mass. A few chairs brought in from the dining-room had kneelers in front of them in old exquisite tapestry, and again in the struggling sun the carpet glowed with the sheen of silk.

241

Kate Mary had long since given up trying to make sense of it all, and Aunt Margaret had never been willing to explain, so she gave all her attention to Cousin Ulick who rose to greet them from the one armchair in the room, carved and gilded and upholstered in crimson velvet as might be the chair for a Cardinal or even of a Pope.

Cousin Ulick himself looked as though the years had long ago dried him, shrivelled from him the last vestiges of the softness of human life, leaving only the parchment skull, whose high cheekbones and wide Irish mouth gave even now some strange troubling hint of Johnny.

But the dark eyes were opaque and dead, and the hand he offered in greeting was cold.

'Are you well?' he asked them, and that's all he seemed to have to say, gesturing them to two of the high-backed chairs before the altar and taking one himself, as though it were the only real business of the day.

The housekeeper came in then and took one of the chairs behind, her apron taken off and a brown respectful hat perched ludicrously on the top of her head. Oh God, thought Kate Mary, if Ned were here! We'd not dare look at each other or we'd split! The odd job man, the last remaining servant, shambled in after her, cap in hand, and the household was complete.

The priest came through the door from the hall, his pale round celibate face showing, even at this holy moment, slavish obsequiousness towards the old man whose relations he proposed to strip of every penny he could lay his hands on.

Through his long boring sermon, unusual in a private Mass, Kate Mary allowed her thoughts to stray: to Ned, as they always did in every quiet moment, with lonely longing; and then, not for the first time, to the curious structure of the house.

The big drawing-room, flooded now with pale sunlight through the beautiful windows, used the same stone-framed fireplace as the dining-room next door. It was set between the two rooms and Kate Mary could see from where she sat, across the swept and empty summer hearth, into the other room, and the lace of the tablecloth laid for lunch.

On each side of the fireplace in each room there was a door, and beside the door vast cupboards, so that the passage from room to room was down a narrow corridor between the length of the great double fireplace and the double cupboards.

Not, she thought, that she had ever seen a fire there, glowing warmly in both rooms. Not even in the winter. And Cousin Ulick, she knew, used these sparse rooms only for occasions, having his own comfortable life in a warm and overfurnished room out near the kitchen, waited on hand and foot by the pug-faced lady in the brown hat.

Dinner was as it always was, a tough old boiling fowl, but even that was better than the mutton they were sometimes given. The fowl was laid down with potatoes in their skins and a head of cabbage cooked whole so that the middle was half raw, but laid down on a cloth of cobweb Carrickmacross lace, with an old silver cruet half the size of Caherliss and embossed cutlery so solid and heavy you could hardly lift it.

The only conversation came from the pallid priest, who kept up a stream of syncophantic comments to old Ulick. He must have had them by heart as well as he had his Mass.

Kate Mary yawned. The dining-room was exactly the same size and proportions as the drawing-room, like two cubes, and now the sun poured through the big windows and the room was stuffy. And she was bored. Only for Aunt Margaret's sake would she ever come here, old Ulick too far out kin of hers to concern her. Her Aunt's cousin.

A bee had somehow got into the warm room and buzzed against the window, looking for the sun and the flowers.

That makes the pair of us, thought Kate Mary, watching him with pity. I want out, too.

Two colours of jelly for the Sunday treat, and then at least the fat priest would go, with is boot-licking talk. And then maybe she and the bee could both get into the garden while Aunt Margaret and her cousin had a chat.

Green jelly. Red jelly. Saying goodbye to the unctuous priest and then sitting down for another cup of tea.

There was a sharp bang like a door thrown back somewhere up behind the wall of the chimney, and Kate Mary didn't realise she was the only one to jump.

'What . . .' she cried, looking to old Ulick who didn't lift

243

his head. On her aunt's face she caught a flash of anger.

With a scuffle and a thump, Johnny landed down out of the chimney into the empty hearth. He ducked his way out, brushing the dust from his hands, smiling as wide and easy as if he had just come back from market.

'Would there be a bit of the dinner left?'

With one glance Kate Mary saw that he was no surprise either to Aunt Margaret or the old man. His mother was furious but not surprised, half risen from her chair as though she would send him straight back where he came from.

And the old man's eyes, she saw, were no longer dead. There was anger in them, as in Aunt Margaret's. Johnny shouldn't have done it. But there was also an uncontrollable blaze of pride and love.

Chapter 10

Aunt Margaret had still been angry on the way home.

'The fool,' she kept saying. 'The eejit, letting the whole world know where he is.'

Kate Mary felt her own anger burn.

'By the whole world, d'you mean me?' she demanded. 'I was the only one there didn't know already.'

Even the silent housekeeper had shown no surprise when she had come in with the fresh tea, and found him at the table.

'And who would I tell?' Kate Mary demanded of her aunt, who didn't answer, but Ned's name hung there between them in the dripping air under their two black umbrellas, and there was no sound in the wet world except the quick clop of the pony's hooves.

Johnny himself had been hilarious and expansive, sprawled there at the table as if he was totally unaware of threat and anger. He was tanned warm brown from the summer in the hills, his eyes dark blue as the cornflowers along the edges of the ripening fields. Alive with a sense of triumph and success, but still wise enough to tell them nothing, except that they had the British bastards on the run. But there was a wildness and fanaticism in his eyes that made Kate Mary uneasy. He had gone over some edge, the killer in him taken over, and he was happy with it.

'No great time longer now, Mam,' he said, 'and we'll all be marching home.'

Only Kate Mary could even begin to understand the pain and raw anxiety behind his mother's tight face; her longing to

245

see the end of it indeed, and her tall son coming back in from the fields for his dinner again, any gun in his hands for no more than scaring off the rooks or getting a rabbit for the pot.

At the top of the table, the old man said little, noisily supping his tea and watching Johnny over the rim of his cup with these bright proud eyes.

Johnny's own eyes were on Kate Mary only, and she felt herself blushing under the intensity of what lay in them. He was restless.

'Can we not even take a walk in the garden?' he said rebelliously, like a sick child kept in, and Kate Mary was glad when the old man shook his head. She knew all Johnny wanted was to get her alone and there was nothing new she could say to him.

'Come on and see my hiding place,' he said then, and shoved back his chair. Kate Mary thought him mad, and it was clear his mother did too. Had he forgotten about Ned? Or, knowing nothing now except his own limited world, had Kate Mary filled his every quiet thought? Did he now feel certain, if he gave it any mind at all, that the policeman was only a passing fancy, soon to be driven off with his tail between his legs? Kate Mary would be one more of the splendid fruits of victory for Johnny.

Nor could he understand how the months away from Ned had done no more than increase her love and longing for him. She felt it an embarrassment to be with Johnny. Even to see him, and be forced to share his secrets seemed a betrayal of the man she loved.

But she followed him obediently into the big fireplace between the rooms. Clear above her she could see the sky, and feel the first drops of rain on her upturned face. But Johnny drew her attention to a ledge some eight feet up in the side of the chimney. Beyond the ledge an open door, and a rope dangling to get up and down.

Kate Mary stared. A priests' hole. She had often heard of them. Priests hid in them in safety in the Penal Days, coming out to say their secret Masses round the countryside.

'It must have a window,' she said, seeing the green overgrown light beyond the door.

'It has.' Johnny was proud as if he had made it himself.

246

'Hidden in the ivy. There's another the other side of the house.'

'It's part of the cupboard!'

'It is. Me Uncle Ulick's family have been hiding men and priests here two hundred years. Since the year of the French itself. Ah, he's a great patriot my Uncle Ulick, and of a great family. Weren't the O'Rourkes the greatest warriors in Ireland. How could they be anything but patriots?'

His eyes were blazing with excitement, and Kate Mary moved away, unwilling to look at him, Patriotism seemed to be only for killing and death. Was there no other way of being a patriot?

Johnny edged her through the fireplace and she realised at once that she was out of sight of the other room. She turned uncomfortably, but he came after her quickly and now his thoughts were not of patriotism.

'Kate Mary.'

He took her by the shoulders, and turned her to him.

'Ah, Kate Mary, I've missed you. B'God, you're more lovely than ever.'

She could hear the hoarseness in his voice, all the months of the hunger and the hills, and knew what was coming.

'Ah, Kate Mary, give us a kiss!'

A kiss, she thought wildly. For God's sake, what was a kiss, and it could be no more than that with the others through in the next room. But she couldn't do it, her sense of betrayal overwhelming her. She struggled to get away from him, and now he held her tighter and the light in his eyes was blazing anger.

''Tis that bloody peeler still,' he shouted at her. 'Well, don't waste your time on him, for before God I'll see to it he never lives to marry you!'

There was violence in his voice, and hatred and jealousy that shook Kate Mary as hard as if he had hit her; bringing tears blinding to her eyes.

'Oh, Johnny . . .'

'Oh, Johnny,' he mimicked her viciously. 'Oh Johnny this, and oh Johnny that, but never the thing I want. There's others'd be proud to have Johnny O'Connor!'

He flung her away from him, and before her astonished

247

eyes, charged across the room. He seemed merely to slam at something in the wall beside a bookcase. About four feet of it opened at the bottom, books and all. Johnny dived through it, and she could hear his boots clattering down stone stairs.

She stared at the dark opening, tears drying on her cheeks, and Aunt Margaret came then, properly, through the two doors, her face expressionless.

Without a word, she closed the bookcase door with a soft click, and turned to Kate Mary as if Johnny had never been there.

'The rain is coming on,' she said. 'We'll go home now and not wait for the tea.'

No hardship not to wait for the tea. Strong tea and stale seedcake; never another thing. Anyway, all Kate Mary wanted was to get out of that house as fast as her feet could take her. Before Aunt Margaret was done speaking she was out in the hall, cramming on her coat and hat to get away.

She hadn't wanted to know. She still didn't want to know, but what could she do now? When Ned had asked before where Johnny was, there had been no lies. She didn't know. She could look him in the eye and say so, and nothing was destroyed between them. Now, if it happened again, she must lie, and Ned who knew her every thought would know that she was lying, and it would never be the same again. He would think she was protecting Johnny; had fallen to his side from the fence where she had sat so carefully and so long.

'I *hate* it,' she cried to Aunt Margaret in the wet silence on the way home. 'I hate it. I hate it all!'

'It's for Ireland,' said Aunt Margaret bluntly, and it was the first word on it Kate Mary had ever heard her say.

'Be damned to Ireland!' she cried, and at that moment meant it. She would go to Honolulu or the Steppes of Russia if she could find peace with Ned there, and no more of this being torn in two.

Her Aunt didn't answer, and the silence fell again, all the way across the sodden bog where curlews cried dismally in the driving rain. They came, still unspeaking, back to Caherliss, and the Lad, who had been watching for them, came down across the pastures with a sack on his head, to open the gate for the owner coming back.

248

It was reported to Ned that they had been to Anfield and he sat and gnawed his nails over a decision to go out to Caherliss and confront them. Ask them had they learnt anything. Threaten them. It was all out around there somewhere that the Volunteers were hiding. He had been twice to the house itself and found no more than a somnolent old man and a woman with a chin like a pug dog, who had watched his search of the big house with barely concealed contempt.

He had found nothing either in the ruined chapel, a little along the hill from the house; only long grass and yellow weeds, and the ancient stones leaning above the graves. But all his instincts told him the place was the perfect strong point; the ridge of hill above it covering all the flat land on both sides. O'Connor would be clever enough to see that. And too clever, too, he told himself carefully, to give anything away to his mother or Kate Mary. So he convinced himself that there was no purpose in going to Caherliss, shrinking from the thought of Kate Mary having to lie to him. If he once forced her to do that, they could never look at each other again.

So, thinking the same thoughts as Kate Mary herself, he shied away, and decided he would go back to Anfield itself and search again. There was something she had said once to him, chattering in the sun above the blue sea and swans and the grey mass of Carrigahowley, about it being an old house full of secret passages and hiding holes. He'd hammer the place to bits, b'God, and see what he could find.

His conscience thrust aside for the first time ever, he convinced himself that if he did this, it would be all that was necessary. It would fulfil his duty.

He shouted for the map of the district around Anfield, and took pencil and paper to plan his raid.

He found nothing, but never knew how close he came to killing Johnny.

The signal had been flashed, as the old Romans used to do on days of sun, by mirror, that the raid was on its way out from Connorstown. Ned and his driver and five Constables in the back of a huge old Humber Tourer.

They had given it to him in answer to pleas that he was

never able to get anywhere with sufficient strength. He knew the way Sinn Fein operated almost as well as they did themselves. His sharp eye caught the flash of the heliograph on the high ground as they crossed the flat stretch of the bog. Once again, he thought to himself that O'Connor knew what he was doing. It was the very devil of an approach, where you couldn't conceal a fairy.

He clicked the bolt on his Lee Enfield.

'Be on your guard, men,' he said. 'We could be ambushed through the woods.'

'And at the house,' he thought. Ringed by trees, it was a place to take anyone by surprise, and little to be done about it. But he argued that were O'Connor actually there, were the place indeed his headquarters, then they wouldn't want to draw attention to it. His men might well come and go, and never a hand lifted against them.

They lurched round the difficult corner where the pony had almost upset Aunt Margaret's trap, rifles and grenades ready for whatever might come rushing through the bracken on the rough stone walls; ready for the warm still afternoon to burst with gunfire; with explosions and blood and death.

Beyond the roaring of the engine as it tackled the hill, there was no sound save the droning of the wood pigeons in the trees around the house. When they stopped, Ned listened carefully to this, looking round him in the green silence.

No one. Had there been a hint of anything, the birds would have flown.

Nor was there anyone extra in the house. Constable Murphy put his heavy shoulder to the green front door, and the rotten wood around the old lock gave easily. They stormed after him across the hall and through the open door into the big drawing-room where a warm turf fire glowed in the strange double fireplace.

Odd, he thought, halted for a moment by the heat on a late August afternoon. But old people feel the cold.

Two Constables went charging along the crumbled loose boxes of what had once been one of the prettiest stable yards in the West. They found nothing but cobwebs and broken walls. Disturbed bats whistled round the cavernous shadows of the coach house, where they could have hidden an army had there been anything to hide them behind, but the four walls stood bare, grey with ancient whitewash, and in place of the glittering splendour of coach and phaeton, or the children's basket trap, a few farm implements fell to rust in the middle of the floor.

Only a horse, looking as old as its owner, regarded them with amazement over a loose box, and an unpolished trap with moth eaten cushions rested in the yard with its shafts in the air.

Another Constable had disturbed the old housekeeper, snoozing in a rocking chair beside the kitchen range. Wet washing strung across it hid the fact that it was almost cold, emptied of turf a quarter of an hour before to kindle the fire between the two rooms.

'It's a raid!' cried the young policeman, thrusting his gun at her.

The old woman opened one of her dog-like eyes.

'Is it that, now?' she said. 'Is it? Well, raid away. There's little you'll find in this house. Mind yer dirty boots.'

Nor did they find anything.

A senile old gentleman that Ned knew to be Johnny's mother's cousin, slept under a rug of coloured crotchet in a small warm room beside the kitchen where the fireplace reeked, smoking with fresh turf. He was as little interested in the whole performance as his housekeeper.

'G'wan,' he said. 'Search for what you like.'

And composed himself to sleep again, plucking at the crotchet squares.

'You're a relation of Johnny O'Connor,' Ned cried at him, trying to save the whole thing from anti-climax, his gun foolish in his hand.

The old man looked at him, slit eyed.

'Amn't I a relation of half of Ireland?' he said, and closed his eyes against the intrusion.

Ned was drawn by the huge cupboards and the double passageway down the side of the fire, but baffled by them. There was something odd about them, and yet he couldn't find them anything but what they seemed.

The deep shelves of the lower ones were crammed with glass and china and tarnished silver, but the upper ones were completely out of reach.

251

'Get me the woman,' he said.

She came, yawning, as indifferent as if a pack of children were playing hide and seek.

'What's in there?' Ned demanded.

'Arrah, nothing.'

'Open it. Get a ladder or something.'

'Can you not look,' she said. 'It has no handles on it. 'Tis only the chimney wall, covered in wood for the look of the thing.'

And when Ned demanded a stick and hammered on it, it did ring like solid wall. Nothing of the hollow sound of the cupboards below it.

Nothing. Nothing anywhere, although they emptied every shelf and cupboard in the house.

They gathered in the hall and looked at Ned, asking with their attitude was this another wasted day?

'Get up the hill and search the chapel,' he said. 'And do it properly or you'll be picked off like sitting ducks on the way up.'

He followed more slowly, with some strange conviction that there would be no shooting yet moving carefully through the trees until he reached the last piece of bare, heather-smelling hillside where the chapel stood.

It stood roofless, the stones of its tiny graveyard leaning in long clinging grass, a tangle of rose briars wreathing the altar and the walls adrift with old man's beard.

No sound but the quiet grumbles of his men as they searched the place; no broken flowers, no trodden grass, only the thin bare sheep path wandering through from one side to the other. All of it desolate and empty under the sultry August sun.

'It hasn't been much of a raid, Sergeant,' Constable Murphy ventured.

'It wasn't a raid,' said Ned sharply. 'It was a search.'

For something he hadn't found. Some secret that the house held that was also the secret of Johnny O'Connor. Some secret that was defeating him.

'Get on down to the car,' he told them. 'And remember you're not safe home yet.'

But they went carelessly through the trees, convinced the

252

Sergeant, who was a clever fellow in the main, was at the moment on some wild goose chase that would get him nowhere.

Ned followed them, and watched their black backs off down the hillside.

'Were I O'Connor,' he thought, 'I could pick off every one with a bullet a piece.'

He would give them hell when he got them back.

He stepped out through the remains of a broken window, away from the sheep path, and stopped with one polished boot in the air. There was something on the ground, blue and square. Carefully, he bent down and picked up an empty Woodbine packet.

'So there you are, my fine boyo,' he said, turning it over in his fingers, feeling the quick surge of excitement. 'So there you are.'

Neither the old man nor the old woman would be coming up here for a fag. No one was here now, but they had been, and they would come again. His instinct had been right.

The net was closing.

He smiled as he slithered down the hill, almost as carelessly as his men, already planning.

Up above, where the bare rock began to push it's way through the scrub and heather, Johnny smiled too, watching him go, his teeth white in his brown face.

He could have taken him then and there, the old Lee Enfield willing in his hands. But there were things to be done yet, before he started that hue and cry.

There would be a time for Ned Brannick, and it was not today.

The Humber started up with a noisy roar, and in the warm back room old Cousin Ulick smiled under his coloured crotchet, not even opening his eyes.

The housekeeper heard it in the kitchen, and took a shovel to get the turf back out of the big hearth into the kitchen range, before it went out entirely.

Clearing the place after the mess they'd made would have to wait until the job man came back. She had sent him up the hill with a sack of the first apples for Johnny and the men, God keep them all.

*   *   *

253

In the early days of September, with the whisper of success sweeping Ireland like a fire, Johnny was wounded.

Their miraculous summer still held. Only the drying grass and the first cold fingers of chill in the nights warned them that their campaign from the hills must soon be over. Thin to emaciation, and sunburnt from the long months of the out-door life, they were telling themselves, overconfident per-haps, that it was the end of it.

By next summer the struggle would be over. Already the English were beginning to talk of Truce and Treaty, and they all felt jubilantly that the victory was in sight.

On a dark night ablaze with stars, they ambushed a train bringing arms and ammunition to the Police and troops of Westport. Ned got wind of it and the ambushers were them-selves ambushed. Joe Lynch and Peter Rohan were left, dead faces turned to the stars, to be brought home on hurdles and laid by stony-faced Police at the doors of their proud, heartbroken families.

Two more the rebels managed to drag away, only to have to bury them in hasty graves at the edge of the bogland, marked so that like so many others they could be brought home for burial when it was all over.

Johnny dug in the pitch darkness with all the rest, blood that he couldn't see running salt into his mouth, determined to give them the honour of helping lay them to rest. He was fretting hazily all the time about the loss, God rest them, of four men in one disastrous night; and as for himself, his head was whirling in spirals of coloured lights, rushing through a darkness far blacker than the night. The bastards! He had felt the bullet go along his scalp as though they had parted his hair with a red hot comb.

Four good men dead, he kept thinking fuzzily, and Joe Lynch like a brother to him. Four good men and not a thing to show for the night's work; four good men; he'd have trouble putting through the raid at Castlebar next week. Four men short. Four . . .

He pitched forward on to the newly dug grave, and they had to drag him off it, his poor handsome face a mess, when they got him to the light of Anfield, of blood caked with the brown soft soil of the bog.

254

They came, of course, by dawn, thundering at the front door of the house and racing through the rooms in their big boots, past the soft warmth of last night's turf rekindled against the cold morning in the double fireplace, and into the kitchen where the housekeeper had the kettle boiling on the red hot range, and the simple-minded job man stacked fresh turf beside it to dry, looking at the racing, frustrated police as incuriously as he would look at the man who came once a year to sweep the jackdaws' nests down out of the chimneys.

They woke the old man from his sleep and shouted at him, and shouted at the woman and learnt nothing and found nothing. But when they were gone, as noisily as when they came, Cousin Ulick came through into the dining-room, in his trousers and the top of his yellowed woollen underwear, his old face anxious. He looked at the fire in the double grate.

'Is he here?'

'He is. He's hurt.'

She didn't tell him about having to scrub the blood off the scullery floor by the light of a candle in the dark just before the dawn; nor of the trouble they all had getting him up into the priest's room, his poor head wrapped in a towel lest he leave tell-tale smears wherever they tried to drag him.

Cousin Ulick's long withered face looked distressed and indecisive, as though he knew there was some action he was past taking. With surprising gentleness, the woman took him by the arm.

'Go on back to your bed now,' she said. 'There's nothing you can do. He'll be all right.'

'Will he?'

'He will. 'Tis only a scalp wound, but it stunned him and he's bled like a pig. He'll be right as rain in a while.'

The old man went, wordless, sadly, knowing that he must now leave the passions of his life to the younger ones. The glory and the wounds, and Ireland always at the end of it.

When Johnny flickered back to consciousness in the late afternoon, the light filtering green through the small window hidden in the ivy leaves, he found himself on the small truckle bed filling most of the space in the priest's room.

'Jesus,' he said, before he even tried to look round, 'my head aches.'

255

Carefully, the lids weighing a ton, he closed his eyes.

The voice that answered him was a girl's, curiously jubilant.

'It will,' it said. 'You have a nasty scalp wound. It's only just stopped bleeding. Keep still, now.'

With immense difficulty he opened his eyes again and swivelled them round to see Bridie Bannion sitting on the floor beside him, her eyes bright with self-importance and the delight of having Johnny to herself, even wounded.

He was ungracious; confused and in pain, and still trying to sort out the fiasco of the rifle fire coming suddenly from behind them, which was about all he could remember.

'What are you doing here?' he demanded irritably. He felt weak and empty, nothing to him but the vast headache, and the last thing he felt up to was Bridie Bannion there, looking at him as if he was her dinner.

'I'm here to look after you,' she said. 'Isn't that what you trained me for? Go back to sleep again now.'

She came and went through the following days, as agile up and down the rope as any man, and he began to be grateful and dependent on her; aware that her hands were clever and gentle and that in her care he was healing, the terrible weakness leaving him gradually, and his head clearing.

Bridie herself had the difficult good sense to be cool and detached with him at the beginning, and as he got better he started to talk to her for who else was there? Being Johnny, he had to talk to someone. All his men knew he was in Anfield but not about the priest's room, for what they didn't know they couldn't tell.

'Weren't we the eejits,' he said to her one day. He was sitting up now, pale-faced and the fine blue eyes a little sunken but himself again. 'Weren't we eejits to be caught like that. And losing four of us. How in God's name did the peelers get wind of it?'

She looked at him carefully, wondering how far she dare go. The time of being closed up with him in the small room, caring for his body as though he was a child, had brought her passion for him to a pitch where she could hardly hold it.

'Somebody,' she said, 'will have told them. Somebody will have informed on you.'

'Ah, who would do that?' he said. 'In Connorstown? Don't they hate everything that walks in a uniform there.'

Her lips tightened with the effort of not answering.

Kate Mary Pearse, she wanted to shout at him. Kate Mary Pearse. Isn't she going with a peeler herself! Wouldn't she tell them anything.

Some prudence held her back; told her that she wouldn't get him that way.

'It must have been someone knew you,' was all she said, trying at least to plant the seed in his mind.

But Johnny was abstracted, and it took no root.

Fine and strong, he healed quickly but would never again be able to hide the furrow ploughed across his scalp. He grew restless and unwilling to stay hidden as his strength came back, and when the watchers above signalled all was clear, he and Bridie would slip out of the back of the house and up through the trees to where they themselves could sit in the drying heather, and see down clear almost to Connorstown.

His lieutenants would come then to talk to him, but he still tired easily and always in the end she was left alone with him. Those blue September days, with the smell of autumn coming up from the woods below them, the first tang of coolness in the air, were some of the happiest she had ever known.

Johnny was easy and agreeable and seemed content to have her there, and she was too obsessed to see there was heavy tiredness in him still, making him too indolent to object to anything. Were it the devil himself who had walked with him at that time, and dressed his sore head every day, he would probably have been just as civil and easy.

He talked to her as if she was one of the men, outlining new plans to her and talking of the victorious future. She listened with poor patience, looking hungrily at his thin face, browner than ever under the white bandage. Now he could get about again, he had retreated sharply from her care, accepting only the dressing of his head. So even that loved, harmless contact with his body was denied her.

The rope was still too much for him, so at night the job man hoisted him up into the priest's room lest anybody take them by surprise. His good night was as cool to her as to any old man, but her craving body blunted her good sense, and she persuaded herself there was a special look for her; a suggestion that he too felt these nights should not be spent alone. In the first darkness she would make her way surefootedly back along the hills to the safe house, hugging her own imaginations to herself like a secret promise; lying awake through the nights, sleepless with desire, waiting for the small square of window to pale into dawn, so that she could go back to him again.

It was inevitable that one day she would go too far.

Johnny was growing restive, irritable, frustrated by the giddiness that still plagued him even though his wound was healing well. Beginning to wonder would it all be over before he was fit to be a leader again, and secretly appalled and frightened at the muzzy confusion that could seize his brain if he attempted to think out and plan even the simplest operation.

In his clear-minded moments, he knew it galled him unbearably to have Liam O'Flyn coming to report to him on all that his, Johnny's, men had done and planned to do. Fearfully, with temper and disapproval, he tried to cover up the fact that he barely understood what he was told, struggling to follow through the haze of his confusion and blinding headache.

Liam O'Flyn! Wasn't it him allowed his fool of a sister make a mess of things in the Post Office, and he had only just got away in time with his own skin. Time was, Johnny wouldn't have even seen him in his path, but they had lost so many good men lately, they were coming now to the scrapings of the barrel.

It was unfortunate for Bridie that she came to Johnny that morning, passed along the hills from lookout to lookout, when Liam had just left him, and Johnny, grim with self-pity, felt certain he had seen contempt and dismissal glittering behind the small man's glasses. There wasn't an O'Flyn, he thought vengefully, could even see the hand before their facves. Blind as bats, all of them. Any thought he had about taking over from Johnny O'Connor could be forgotten.

He was not finished yet. No more than a bit of a blow on the head. Not finished yet. Yet. It seemed to echo and repeat in some hollow place inside his head, and he didn't hear Bridie sliding down quietly through the bushes to drop on the dry grass at his side.

'G'day to you, Johnny. And how is it today?'

In his mood of furious irritability, he suddenly couldn't stand the sight of her. What was she doing with all that paint on her face and she supposed to be a soldier like the rest of them; her tam-o-shanter sideways on the thick red hair and even her uniform dress worn somehow he couldn't put his finger on, but different from all the plain care of the other girls.

He looked into the big green lambent eyes that reminded him now of ripe gooseberries, and had only a muddled recollection of some time long ago being more than half in love with her. A distaste for her overtook him as great as the one he had just conceived of Liam O'Flyn, shot with the unhappy certainty, like a flash of light, that there was little wrong with either of them. It was he, Johnny, that was wrong. But he couldn't hold to the certainty, and glared at her in a way that would have sent a wiser girl flying for cover.

'What brings you?' he said sullenly, knowing well what brought her; wanting it all to stop; wanting to be again the splendid Johnny who had gone whistling over the fields at Caherliss, and raced down from these hills in the nights of the moon to confound the English peelers.

There was a sigh of autumn in the wind through the scrub, mournful as his own feelings, and he laid his sore head on his knees to shut it out.

Obsessed and determined, Bridie saw no warnings. She laid her hand on the dressing on his bent head.

'Well, sure for this, Johnny, but there's other things.'

Her hand crept down, caressing the back of his neck, and all that had filled her mind this last couple of weeks came bursting out.

'Hasn't it been grand, Johnny, really grand, up here, almost alone together? Haven't we got on well, soldiers together? Ah, Johnny, it could always be like that when it's all

259

over. We're the same kind of people, and both for Ireland. Hasn't that Kate Mary Pearse shown herself now for what she is; on the side of the English and probably telling all she knows to that policeman. Do you forget her, Johnny, and stay where you belong. She's no good to anyone, and they say she's no better than she should be with the peeler.'

Johnny's head jerked up, flinging off her hand, and his cursing from the pain was fearful. He looked a long disbelieving moment at the girl's flushed face, her eyes glittering, and her tongue creeping round her full lips in her desperation for his.

'Is it you?' he said then thickly. 'Is it you! Talk like that about Kate Mary! Aren't you the one has crawled out from under a stone, and not fit to speak her name! Get on out of it and don't ever come near me again. I'll look after me own head, and b'God as soon as it's clear enough I'll find some way of getting rid of you!'

Dizzy with the effort, he stood up and flung off down the hill across the open ground, heedless of safety.

Before the woods around the house, he turned.

'Trash!' he bellowed at her, and his voice could be heard at every watcher's post that ringed Anfield. 'Trash!'

Dimly he was aware of having made some terrible mistake, but his poor bruised brain could not imagine what.

Bridie sat a long time before she could gather herself to go away, trembling with the fury of rejection; the sore bitter venom of destroyed pride. And for who, she was thinking bitterly, and for who or what? For that plain Kate Mary Pearse with nothing more than soap and water on her dull face and the drab clothes of an old woman.

In the end she stood up and looked down at the grey chimneys of Anfield among the turning trees, and she spoke aloud, almost inarticulate with rage, still shaking.

'The both of you,' she said. 'The both of you. I'll have the both of you, if I die doing it.'

Putting her head in the air, she went back with proper caution along the hillside, painfully closing her mind to the derisive grins of the lookouts who were only too willing to agree with Johnny's bellowed words, most of them in their day having cut their teeth on Bridie.

She was too coldly furious even to weep, her lovely face like stone.

'The both of you,' she said again out loud, 'I'll have the both of you, so God help me.'

She had to wait almost a week.

All over Ireland the Sinn Fein Volunteers were burning and blowing up the Police Barracks in the country, driving the Police remorselessly into the towns. The country was becoming theirs, reclaimed for Ireland and put under their own well-disciplined rule, even to the Courts from which red-coated Judges and the Resident Magistrates had long fled.

On this black, moonless night, they were off to burn a barracks still holding out behind its sandbags, in a village some long way down the road to Tuam.

A big raid, joining up with another company of Volunteers from the other side of it, and normally Bridie would be tense with excitement and the smell of danger; waiting with the other girls at a safe distance from the raid to do what they could for the casualties and help them home. To have jerricans of hot tea for the raiders themselves, exhausted after their battle. Wasn't it she had wrapped up Johnny's head the night he fell on Joe Lynch's grave there at the edge of the bog.

But tonight, for this raid, she was off duty, and rest times were as carefully organised as the schedule of their raids. A man can fight hungry, Johny used to say, but a tired man can kill his friends.

Johnny! She almost spat on the hillside. In the silence, when the rest were gone, she slipped out herself and got past the first two sentries with the pass word. Then, in the black night, the stars immense in the great arch of the sky above the bog, she slipped like a shadow, running in the wind, along the road to Connorstown. A black shawl covered her uniform, leaving no more than another patch of darkness.

She didn't even turn her eyes as she passed Caherliss, the whole business so fermented in her mind that she now barely understood it would concern real people or what would happen to them. Jealousy and rejection had curdled in her to unreasoning vengeance, and she sped without thought past the house where Kate Mary slept with her lonely dreams of Ned.

261

No one saw her. She saw no one herself until the edges of the town where she had to detour round a patrol of soldiers. Under the shawl she grinned, and now the beautiful green eyes were wolfish.

Born and bred in Connorstown, it would take more than a few English soldiers to stop Bridie Bannion going where she wanted. She vanished into the black night of the village alleys, her mind only on what she had to do.

Before the raiding party returned, she was back herself in the safe house in the hills.

They had been victorious, hoarse and tired and jubilant, the Barracks blazing scarlet in the sky behind them, and not a man hurt or lost.

Only Johnny gnawed his nails down to the knuckles in his narrow bed beside the chimney; mad with frustration that he hadn't been the one to do it.

It was barely dawn when a Constable hammered on Ned's door in the Barracks.

'What is it?'

He was already dragging on his uniform as he opened the door, glancing out to realise there were only the first red strands of day above the grey roofs across the street.

'What is it, Constable?'

'I found this, Sir.' The young man's face was impassive. Whatever it was, let it not for God's sake keep him from going off duty. 'I found this, Sir, skewered to the sandbags outside the door. With this, Sir.'

He handed Ned a letter, no envelope, merely a sheet of folded paper that might come from a child's school copybook. Then he handed him the hatpin.

Ned peered at them both in the grey dimness, then pushed the young man aside and raced downstairs to the noisy hiss of gaslight.

A hatpin with a green bead at the end of it. A letter, printed in capitals. Even so, he realised at once, writing came easily to whoever did it.

'You want Johnny O'Connor,' it began.

Every detail. Not only that he was in Anfield – God

262

dammit, I knew that myself, Ned thought, but I could never find him. He could find him now.

There were details of the room at the side of the chimney. Ned remembered the turf fire scarlet in the dawn and the piled sods blinding out heat in the August afternoon. The strange double fireplace. Wasn't he the eejit not to have suspected so big a fire at that time.

Details of how to open the bookcase in the drawing-room to the underground passage that came out in the Chapel; which stone in the wall to turn to open that end of it.

Priest's hidey holes, all of them, since the Penal Days.

He could fool himself, for several minutes filling his mind with useless details, before he must ask himself who had sent the letter, staring blindly all the while at the green hatpin.

He had never seen Kate Mary with a hatpin at all, nothing but those soft tam-o-shanters that so gently framed her face. Aunt Margaret would have a hatpin. And who would know Anfield better than Kate Mary.

There was no signature, nothing but the tidy nameless printing, and all he could feel was something near to a sense of shame to have Johnny O'Connor put into his hands like this. He'd have preferred to hunt the bastard on equal terms to the four corners of the earth, and devil take the hindmost. A terrible impulse came on him to tear the thing up and pretend he had never had it.

He mustn't pay too much attention to the hatpin.

Anyone could have found a hatpin to stick it up with. Wasn't it the obvious thing to use with a sandbag.

'Will you have a cup of tea, Sir?' The young Constable was back, looking cautiously cheerful. There had been no sudden bellow for no one to leave the Barracks.

'I will.'

Already, with the automatic actions of duty, he was buckling on his belt and revolver.

'And get me the car immediately. I have to go to Westport.'

He had a new car, a dark grey Lancia, and a truck with it for the men. The old Humber had been blown up in an ambush ten days before, the lad of a driver killed at his side in a tangle of blood and bones. But he must nevertheless go off between the grey stone walls capable of hiding death at every bend.

This one was too big to tackle on his own.

A green hatpin. They could send the letter up to Dublin. There were lads there could say at a glance if writing belonged to a man or a woman.

His thoughts were wayward, almost panic-stricken, shying away from the thing he couldn't stand to face: Kate Mary would never do it, not to anyone, least of all to O'Connor. Painfully, Ned still suspected her of loving him. All the weeks he hadn't seen her had left him insecure, picturing her still somehow in touch with Johnny. Wasn't he her family after all?

Inform on him? Kate Mary didn't have it in her. And she wasn't the girl for hatpins and geegaws like that. Wouldn't he have noticed a green lump of that sort sticking out of her head, had she ever worn it.

Carefully he stared straight ahead and steadied himself, realising that had they been ambushed he'd have been a sitting duck, his mind miles away.

Whoever it was, they had Johnny O'Connor in the bag, and that was all he must think of. There'd be a long day's planning with the D.I. His mind began to rove around the possible ways of attack, because before God this one mustn't fail. Kate Mary would hardly have recognised him, sitting there upright in the car, his rifle between his knees and his cold eyes roving the road ahead; his mind plotting her lover's death.

Enough of that, he told himself. Johnny was never her lover, except in Ned's mind. But he couldn't suppress a horrible sick excitement that this would surely be the end of Johnny O'Connor and his brave blue eyes.

He had grown thin since Kate Mary had last seen him, and the sharp waxed points of his moustache were longer, no more the proud efforts of a young man to appear mature but the formal whiskers on a face grown grim with experience, overlaid by an almost frightening immobility of features.

Only Kate Mary could have told them about the sweet sudden smile that could melt his flinty eyes, and the way when he laughed the two spikes of whiskers turned up the sides of his nose.

His men knew none of this. They only knew Sergeant Brannick, who was holy hell if things didn't please him, and it

264

was Sergeant Brannick and not Kate Mary's Ned who ducked out of the car in Westport and strode down the long grey hall of the Barracks.

Before the D.I. could even bid him good morning, he slapped the piece of paperdown on his desk.'

'We have him, Sir,' he said. 'We have him.'

Through these days Kate Mary hardly moved beyond the door at Caherliss lest she should cross some policeman who would question her, burdened by knowledge she never wanted to have, and terrified her lies wouldn't be convincing. Far worse, oh far worse than knowing about the gelignite. Why had he not stayed hidden where he was, and kept his secret instead of filling her with fear and guilt, and the sad sad trial of yet again having to refuse his love?

Oh, Ned. Her anxious mind tried to send a message to him. Ned, my love. Don't come here now with your questions. It would be too much to know everything, and tell nothing.

A small shaven-headed child came padding across the pasture one evening in a pair of broken boots, and stood breathing hard outside the front door.

'What is it?' Aunt Margaret asked him, and behind her Kate Mary stood with a chill certainty of trouble. They always sent children with the messages. They could say the mother had sent them to beg a few turnips, or any other tale. 'What is it?' Aunt Margaret said again to the panting child.

''Tis Mr. O'Connor, ma'am,' he managed to say. ''Tis his head.'

'What's wrong with his head?' they said together.

'A bullet, ma'am,' the child said as though they should have known. And as though bullets were as familiar to him as the potatoes his mother laid on the table. 'Didn't it cut a stream across his head, they said, but to tell ye he's going to be as good as new and Miss Bannion up there looking after him.'

He only lived along the road, the messages having been sent step by step so as not to attract attention. They gave him a bag of turnips and potatoes to make his errand real, and sent him off, the big broken boots slopping across the yellowing grass to the gate.

''Twould have been no harm to give him a pair of Johnny's

265

old boots,' Aunt Margaret said grimly. 'He'll have those worn off his feet delivering all the messages like that these days. And worse,' she added.

It was all she said, and Kate Mary knew better than to offer tenderness or sympathy. Sometimes she wondered did Aunt Margaret do her weeping alone in the dark watches of the night, but put the thought past her. Her aunt would face her griefs taut and dry-eyed, night or day. Setting her an example, who could at any time have given way and sobbed for fear and loneliness for Ned.

No reason now to be anxious for Johnny. He'd be safe out of it for a while, even though he'd probably be going mad with frustration in his small cell beside the chimney. She smiled to think of Bridie Bannion looking after him; with the help of God it would take his mind off herself.

Aunt Margaret looked at her sharply, finding nothing to smile about in Johnny being wounded; remembering that smile later when people said what they did about Kate Mary.

'Get on out,' she said sharply, 'and follow after the Lad.'

Obediently Kate Mary went to the barn for a couple of sacks, and then down to the far fields to follow the old reaper and binder, gathering fallen grain that would help to feed the hens through the winter.

A sore job, and she looked at her roughened hands and her sacking apron and found it hard to believe that she had once been a teacher with a life of her own, nice clothes, and the sweet bliss of looking forward to every Tuesday. Themselves and the swans and the seagulls.

'Get on with it,' said Aunt Margaret, bustling through the gate to help her. 'Can you not see it's a race between us and the rain.'

Kate Mary looked. Sure enough, away towards Croagh Patrick the sky was black, and a heavy sullen light crept over the harvested fields. The end of summer, she thought, and had to shake herself free of a sudden superstitious feeling that it was the end of more than that.

In the still warm sun she shivered, feeling the skin roughen on her arms, and Aunt Margaret looked at her.

'You have a goose,' she said, 'walking over your grave.'

*　　　*　　　*

266

The D.I. had none of Ned's appalled feelings about the identity of the informer. All he cared about was that now at last they had the information to trap O'Connor, and maybe a few of his spawn with him. He didn't give a tinker's damn where it came from.

Vengeance on the informer would surely come from his own friends. No business of his.

'I'd not like to be that fella when they catch him,' was all he said.

Ned felt his spirits rise, steaming away his foolish suspicions. Everyone else thought it was a man. Why should his thoughts fly at once to Kate Mary? Except that she knew Anfield and had been there a month ago.

So had all O'Connor's men, and you could find a rotten apple in every barrel. He shook off the last of his hesitation and felt a fierce elation take its place. Out again after Johnny O'Connor, and this time, by God, he was going to give him to the hangman he had cheated so often.

And Kate Mary would belong to him alone.

'You'll go at night,' the D.I. was saying, standing before the map on the Day Room wall. 'At night. Tonight. And you'll all walk every inch of the way and not so much as strike a match. From those hills you can see the light of even a single bicycle coming out from Connorstown. You can have men from here, and I'll get you some Black and Tans out from Castlebar. We'll have the place surrounded, and whatever those boyos are up to tonight, they'll come home to a warm welcome.'

He looked exhilarated, fine eyes alight.

'I leave it to you, Ned,' he said. 'We'll have them.'

Ned looked at him, tempering his own excitement with a growing, cold deliberation.

He only wanted one of them.

On the table he smoothed out the close plan of Anfield that he already knew by heart.

Johnny's boyos were doing nothing that night, given an evening's rest, and sleeping heavily and gratefully.

Ned couldn't believe his good fortune when he saw them all slipping one by one down the hill in the morning just after dawn; still clumsy and careless, thick with sleep, treading openly across the last stretch above the house where the thistles were spun with the silvered cobwebs of the damp night, and not even the larks had stirred to meet the day.

Five of them. All Johnny's lieutenants; his Council of War as he called them. Sleepless, he had summoned them all at first light to pour out all the plans boiling in his irritable brain through the long restless night.

He had called them to the house. Summer was gone, and the cold and damp of the chapel in these autumn mornings hurt his head.

Everything hurt his head, God damn it, but he wouldn't admit that his judgement had gone cloudy, nagged by his endless headache into lack of caution; driven by frenzied certainty that he and his little handful could end the war.

'God save Ireland,' they all said as greeting as they came up the steps from the tunnel and out through the bookcases.

'God save Ireland.'

Johnny sat in old Ulick's carved gilt chair, the cushions scarlet behind his grey face. The colour of England and of blood. B'God, he had a scheme to offer them today would go far to bring England to her bloodied knees.

'God save Ireland,' he said back to them, and his glittering eyes, still touched with fever, failed to notice the anxiety and doubt in all their faces; their sidelong glances asking each other was Johnny right in the head, and would he ever be again.

'Sit down there,' he said, and they sat where they could on the window seats and the soft silk of the Persian rug, watchful, waiting to know would he come up with anything that made sense, yawning a little. They were all tired and would be glad to have slept longer. There had been no formal taking back of command from Liam O'Flyn, who sat with quiet eyes behind glasses almost as thick as his sister's, wondering was Johnny going to ruin everything for all of them.

Things were going well for Ireland, even talk of Truce and Treaty, and the last thing they wanted now was the lot of them killed in some madcap scheme.

Even as he sat and waited, trying to gauge the look on

Johnny's face, the crack and spatter of rifle fire broke out all round the house.

Carefully, in the damp, dark night, Ned and his men had encircled the sentries. At the first rush of soldiers and police, they did as they had been told, racing for the house as the last place to defend; slithering down the wet hill into the unguarded chapel where the block of stone in the wall stood open to the passage into the house. Careful precaution by the lieutenants, lest it was the house that was surprised and they must get Johnny away quietly.

'You have them there,' shouted Ned, crashing through the broken stones of the Chapel towards the passage, 'like rats in a trap. Just keep them.'

Constable Murphy who had been there before, and two Black and Tans, smashed down the old front door like matchwood. On Ned's instructions they raced through into the drawing-room from where all the men had vanished, and dragged a heavy chest across the bookcase.

'Like rats in a trap,' Constable Doyle echoed Ned, his square face satisfied and belligerent.

He shot over to look up the chimney of the empty fireplace, where the iron door swung open and pale light shone through the small window from the outside. No shadows. No sound.

'Go easy now,' said one of the men behind him. 'He could blow your head off do you try to look in there. He could be waiting this minnit.'

Red-faced, Constable Doyle realised that were Johnny up there, he could have blown his head off already, and no effort to him.

Well, he thought, and felt a little sick, it was one way to find out.

He turned for the back of the house, and the housekeeper and the old man came from the kitchen like a pair of frightened spectres in their white nightclothes, old faces grey as the dawn beyond the windows.

'Where is he?' the policeman demanded. 'Tell us where he is or you'll swing beside him in Mountjoy.'

Old Ulick was shaking too much to speak, but perhaps in the knowledge that it was all over the woman lifted her round

269

face, even more pug-like while crumpled with sleep, but still capable of fierce defiance.

'He's away,' she said, 'out the back. You'll never get him.'

Her defiance faded at another quick spatter of rifle fire, and a despairing shout from the hill.

Behind them there was frenzied hammering on the wall behind the bookcase. The trapped men, coming up in the chapel to the wrong end of half a dozen rifles, doubled back, crashing against each other in the dark passage to get out into the house.

Constable Doyle shoved the old people aside.

'Stay here and watch them,' he said to one of the soldiers. 'Shoot them do they lay a finger on the bookcase.'

They tore along the cold stone passage and he left another soldier at the back door.

'Shoot to kill,' he said.

They dodged from cover to cover through the dilapidated stables and barns, where there was no sound or sign of life. The rifle fire was dying on the hill, only vague shouting telling that anything had happened there at all.

Ned was so sure that Johnny would be in the chimney that he had sent the small party into the house to pin him where he was and block the bookcase. If he tried to escape they only had to pick him off as he dropped into the fireplace.

He himself stayed out on the hill beside the Chapel, seeing that end of the tunnel secure and knowing from the dying rifle fire that knocked chips from the stones around him that his men were overcoming those racing to defend the house.

Now he could go down and complete the actual capture of Johnny. It would be simple. They would light a good fire of wet turf and smoke him out.

Simple. The sun was coming up to a fine bright day and he could see nothing that could be bad in it for him. A day for the fulfilling of dreams and ambitions. For success.

When Johnny came racing from the back of the house, Ned couldn't understand what he was trying to do, where he was hoping to get other than off across the hills for reinforcements. And even then it was the act of a madman. Even if he was mad only for the moment, sick from his wound. The

270

dressing on it stood out white across his head like a marked patch to take a bullet as he burst suddenly from the yard and raced across the high rough ground towards the chapel.

A gamble, thought Ned, and there was plenty of time to think. A gamble, but a mad one. Possibly he had worked out that one lot was in the house, one in the chapel, and the rest guarding the approaches, and thought he could slip through them and away, with his knowledge of the ground.

Ned he never saw, still standing in the dark broken archway of the old chapel, listening to the growing quiet and judging the success of his plans.

He had all the time in the world, watching Johnny slithering and jumping along the rocks that cropped out through the short grass higher on the hill. All the time in the world to feel nothing but wild splendid satisfaction as he lifted his rifle and sighted the classic shot of punishment and revenge of Sinn Fein itself.

He shot Johnny through the kneecap, brought him crashing down into the damp grass and the rough stones, and then went himself, scrambling as fast as he could up the hill, shouting at the men who started from the trees at the shot to stay where they were.

No one but himself could take Johnny O'Connor.

He was crawling and groping on the ground when Ned reached him, blood pouring over the grey stones, dark on the green grass of his Ireland. Somehow he had hit his head as he fell and fresh blood ran from that, a thin line across his eyebrow and down his cheek, on to the front of his white shirt.

He heard the clatter of boots on the stones and when they got close to him he lifted his head.

He grew very still, his face twisted with the agony of the shattered leg, yet he still managed to look up with a glint of challenge and contempt in pain-clouded eyes.

'Ah,' he said, ''tis yourself. Who else could it be!'

Ned groped for the formal words he should say to Johnny O'Connor at this moment, and his tongue failed to bring them out. Triumph died in him and all he could think of was the sorrow of Kate Mary.

With the sun warm over the tip of the hill they stared at each other and Johnny's bloody face twisted with contempt

271

while Ned put everything else from his mind except the fact that he had the biggest Sinn Fein villain in the country by the heels, and there was no cause to bother who he was. Duty was duty.

Johnny looked at the revolver in Ned's hand.

His face was ashen now, and the voice had grown tired.

'Will you do me a favour, Brannick?'

Ned was about to signal the men to close in. He dropped his hand.

'What?'

'Will you shoot me?'

Ned's face was granite, the bones suddenly large beneath his skin.

'Will you shoot me? For the love of Kate Mary, shoot me and don't leave me to hang. You can say I tried to shoot you.'

Ned's eyes flickered to Johnny's gun, thrown yards away when he fell.

'For the love of God and Kate Mary, Brannick, shoot me.'

Only then did the clear euphoria of duty well done tremble to unsteadiness in Ned's mind.

A happier solution that was not in the line of duty? Kill him as he asked, then and there? Why shouldn't he? He could say O'Connor had drawn the gun on him, and no one could see. The men were still all far back.

But Johnny had said, 'For the love of God and Kate Mary.'

Blind fury rose in Ned. No one but he had the right even to mention her name and the word love in the same sentence. He would have a lifetime afterwards to tell himself that the jealous rage engulfing him was nothing more than fury at the bleeding man lying helpless in the heather, pleading for deliverance in her name.

How dare such a traitor even mention her, and the word love?

For a long dreadful moment he glared at Johnny and then lifted his stony face, and raised his arm, and his men came running from the trees.

Duty he told himself. It is no more than my duty.

The inevitable child was sent racing to Caherliss, and Kate Mary and Aunt Margaret were down at the pasture gate as

Johnny went past, both of them white-faced and tearless with shock.

They had taken a farm cart from Anfield, and he was jammed in there with about five police, as many more following behind to keep away the crowds milling along the road behind the cart; shouting and jeering and throwing stones at the uniforms when they dared.

They could see him clearly, and Kate Mary put an arm quickly about her aunt, but the thin staunch shoulders didn't crumple.

He sat on the floor of the cart and seemed to Kate Mary to be masked in blood, the fine blue eyes closed and his head fallen to one side.

Beside him sat Ned, locked to him by a handcuff, and as the cart passed he stared straight ahead into the grey sky that the sun had left, never looking sideways at Caherliss.

Aunt Margaret had begun to pray in a thin voice.

'Hail Mary full of grace,' she said, 'the Lord is with thee,' and in a few moments most of the people following the cart had stopped and a voice lifted to lead the Rosary. In the dirty road and the damp grass they fell to their knees and prayed and wept for Johnny O'Connor.

Kate Mary listened numbly to the prayers rising on the quiet air, and all she could think of was that it was the only time she had seen Ned and Johnny sitting side by side.

When they had passed, she looked away across the bogland. On the first rise of the hills, she could see the lazy column of smoke rising from where they had set fire to Anfield.

Aunt Margaret looked also, and without a word they both turned for the house. It would be as much as their lives were worth to go out there now to help the old people.

Even as it was, Caherliss could be the next.

Chapter 11

By midday, the clouds piling in the west for days were over-head, bringing with them grey, relentless rain that saved Anfield from complete destruction; hanging like a shroud over the countryside. Summer's end and Johnny's end were the one grey day.

Two nights later, with a gap in the rain and a high wind scudding the torn clouds, bottles of paraffin stuffed with burning rags were dropped down the chimneys of the Police Barracks in Connorstown. Two soldiers were killed in the Day Room and others hurled through the unbarred upper windows, the building blazing like a torch.

Nothing was done about the people who gathered in the streets, although it was long after Curfew. They were smiling but silent, triumphant faces lit scarlet by the roaring flames that marked the end of British rule in Connorstown. The next day the gutted Barracks stood empty, Police and soldiers gone, to stand there crumbling for a generation; a gaunt, windowless memorial to Johnny O'Connor.

One by one, the last of his sodden friends came firmly back from the hills, laying claim to the town that was theirs. No one stopped them now from setting up their own small, disciplined Police Force, and their own Court of Law with an Irish Magistrate. As in many Irish towns by now, the Republic reigned triumphant in Connorstown.

With Johnny in the prison hospital in Roscommon, there was no rejoicing: only a steady procession of townspeople out to Caherliss. They talked to Aunt Margaret, ignoring Kate Mary with chilling indifference as though she wasn't there, the hatred in their eyes suppressed only by the presence of her aunt.

'What's wrong with them?' Kate Mary demanded. 'What is it? Why won't they speak to me?'

Her aunt was at the table making barm brack to take to the prison to Johnny. Behind her round glasses, her eyes focussed reluctantly on Kate Mary, cool and hostile.

'Because,' she said bluntly, 'they think you informed on him.'

Kate Mary turned sharply away from her to the window, and stared sightless out into the rain. Impossible. Impossible to bear this, too, on top of the grief tearing her for Johnny. Bright, irrepressible Johnny, no more now than a broken body on a prison bed. She turned back to her aunt.

'And do you?' she asked wearily, in a low voice, knowing they had had this conversation before. But now Johnny was taken and it all meant more. 'Do you think that I did?'

Aunt Margaret poured in a brown and black stream of sultanas and currants before she answered, not looking up.

''Tis sure someone did,' she said. Then she added, 'You'll be all right as long as you're with me.'

Kate Mary could not know that the Sinn Fein Committee had discussed her in the town, sure of her guilt; leaving her alone because they felt her to be all the poor old woman had now, with Johnny gone.

'You'll be all right with me,' her aunt repeated.

'Thanks,' said the girl, looking out again at the rain falling straight as rods on the green sodden fields, and longing to go out into it and run and run and run. God knew where. Just somewhere far away from all that was happening here. Somewhere far away with Ned.

But where was he? And where could they go as long as his duty held him? And how could she leave that indomitable little figure at the table, whose torment showed only in unguarded moments in her tortured, magnified eyes.

Wearily she came back over to the table and began cutting up candied peel.

She was beginning to feel drearily convinced that Ned had never really happened. Just the figment of a foolish dream of long lost happier times.

Two days later, with a lurch of her heart, she saw him come striding up across the pasture, the black car left beyond the gate. The rain was dripping from its sodden hood, and from the shining peak of his cap by the time he reached the door.

Aunt Margaret didn't even move to open it, turning apparently impassive to the kitchen table. Only the knife she lifted to pare a potato slipped in her shaking hands, drawing blood.

Trembling with the terrible combination of pleasure at the sight of him and terror of what news he might be bringing, Kate Mary went out through the porch and opened the front door.

A quick flicker of his eyes warmed her, telling her all she had longed to hear through the lonely weeks, and then he said, over loudly: 'Tis you I have to see, Miss Pearse.'

A raised eyebrow and a jerk of the head asked was the aunt inside, and she nodded. A raindrop hung, ludicrous, on one waxed point of his moustache.

'Come on out to the door, then. Mind now you don't get wet.'

Dear Ned, even now to have care for her. Did he not understand she would stand under Niagra Falls itself, just to be this near to him. But her tongue clung dry to her mouth in the fear that he had come to tell of Johnny's death. It wouldn't be the first time it had happened in prison.

'Kate Mary, my heart, I can't touch you. I have to make this look like an official call.' His voice held the same desperate longing she felt herself. 'That fellow out there in the car is watching us with his eyes out on stalks.'

They could do no more than look hungrily at each other in the rain, and in their silence water sputtered from one of the gutters and drenched Kate Mary's hair. She never noticed and nor did he.

'Listen, my darling,' he said urgently. 'I'm being sent off to Dublin Castle. It could be promotion.'

'A reward?' she said sadly, but he wouldn't look away.

'I suppose so. It was my duty, and I did it.'

'Ah, duty. I wonder if it will make for good memories when we are old, Ned, my love.'

For a moment, he looked disconcerted, and at once she felt ashamed for troubling him in these precious moments. He

276

had had to do as he thought right. If only God had allowed it to be anybody else but Johnny. She glanced at the policeman in the car, but he still had his eyes glued in their direction, making it impossible to reach out a comforting hand. Ned had grown so thin, almost gaunt, the fine skin stretched on the strong bones of his face. God forgive her, it hadn't been easy for him either.

He had recovered himself, moving round to be between her and the watcher in the car.

'Here,' he said, and gave her a small piece of paper. 'Can you get into Westport?'

'Westport, yes. They'd lynch me in Connorstown.'

He didn't question that.

'Well, look. That's the address of a good friend of mine and his wife. I'll write to you there, and do you write to me, alannah. It's precarious times, and Dublin is mortally far away. Will you do that?'

Tears were mixing with the raindrops on her lashes. A few infinitely precious moments, and she had been unkind to him.

'I will, Ned. Oh, I will.'

'Take heart, my small one. It can't go on forever.'

She tried to smile.

'I'm not small. I'm near big as yourself.'

It was unbearable for both of them not to fall into each other's arms, their locked eyes full of anguish and frustration and lonely sorrow.

'I must go now, alannah. God keep you.'

'And you, my love. And you.'

He turned and she took a step out after him, heedless of both the watching man and the drenching rain, never noticing the ink running on the piece of paper in her hand.

After a few paces he turned back.

'I'm sorry,' he said gravely, 'about your cousin.'

He saluted her formally and she could only nod, choked with the loneliness to come: standing to watch until the car drove away between the stone walls dark with wet.

Only when she came back into the kitchen did she realise that the paper in her hand held no more than a smeared mess of ink: all the writing wiped out by the rain.

'Oh, god,' she cried. 'Oh, dear God.'

Then all the careful control went, and she wept, noisily and hopelessly like a child, her wet head down on the kitchen beside the potatoes and the smears of Aunt Margaret's blood.

'Oh, Ned,' she cried. 'Oh, Ned, Ned, Ned.'

And could not care that Aunt Margaret heard her.

Across the table she looked coldly at the weeping girl.

'I'd have thought,' she said, 'that you'd be weeping for Johnny.'

The long drab autumn dragged.

Every two weeks, his mother went laden with food to visit Johnny in the prison: all of them agonisingly aware that he was only there in the hospital until he was fit to be moved. And wherever he went then, he would stay only until he was fit to he hanged.

Kate Mary watched her aunt and pitied her, that she couldn't share her grief. Aunt Margaret wouldn't even admit to its existence, as though grief and sorrow were shameful things, only to be hidden. She came back from every visit a little more grey and drawn, a little smaller.

'He's well enough,' was all she would say tersely when Kate Mary asked after him, until one day in late November when, with obvious difficulty, she opened her small pinched mouth enough to say: 'He's away to Mountjoy in the morning.'

The girl stared at her, appalled. She could feel the blood leaving her face. Mountjoy. He would never leave it.

'To Dublin,' she said stupidly.

'Where else. And there's no visiting him now until his trial.'

She said it with such finality he might have been already dead.

'Will he not write?' Kate Mary cried, flaming into anger at this blind acceptance. 'Will they not let him write?'

'What would he have to write about?'

He didn't write until the end of October, when it was to tell them they thought him well enough now to stand his trial on November 14th.

'Just in time,' he wrote, 'to have me hanged for Christmas,' and Kate Mary's heart withered away at the baldness of the words. Had Johnny been there to say them, there would have

278

been a derisive sparkle in his eye, a wry twist to his mouth, helping to take away bitterness.

'Will you go, Aunt Margaret?'

'Doesn't he tell me in the letter not to?'

He did indeed urge both of them to do no more than go to Mass for him that morning. But where would Kate Mary go to Mass, with Anfield a smelly ruin and only hatred for her in Connorstown.

'I'll ask that tame Father they have in Anfield would he come over here and say Mass in the house,' her aunt said with surprising sensitivity, then she looked over at the girl who flinched away from the expression in her eyes.

'I'd have thought,' she said, 'you'd want to go to the trial. Won't your man be there, giving evidence against Johnny. Won't he be proud and pleased with himself, and you proud of him into the bargain.'

The flatness of her voice was more terrible than if it had held all the hatred and venom that inflamed her eyes. Instinctively Kate Mary half stood, as though someone had raised a fist to hit her.

'I never lifted hand or voice against Johnny,' she said sadly.

'Nor for him either,' said her aunt, and she knew she would never get past that. There was no comfort for either of them.

Of course, she had thought immediately of going to the trial in the hope of contacting Ned, but grieving for both him and Johnny, she knew she could never do it.

The story of violence and blood on the hill behind Anfield was something she must learn to live with. To have them facing each other across the cool official atmosphere of a Law Court, with Johnny already defeated before he opened his mouth, was something different, and she knew that no sight of Ned would make up for the impossible anguish that would cause her.

She didn't want to see him again until everything was over, and they could set it all behind them. If she could find him. nowhere was there light or hope.

Johnny, may God love him, had known when he forbade it that it would be too much, and was probably thinking even more of her than of his mother. Or was it that he could not stand to see her in the same room as Ned Brannick?

Once again the whole bitter business brought her to tears, and her aunt watched her dispassionately, not realising that this time they were all for Johnny.

Carefully they put the days past them, one by one, and then on the dull cold morning of November 1st, a young lad called Kevin Barry was taken out and hanged at Mountjoy Jail, on the flimsiest evidence of treason. So great was the outcry and the fierce reaction of violence all over Ireland, that the authorities for a while dared not even mount the trials of other rebels. Johnny wrote, much of his letter blacked out, to say that his had been postponed.

Neither of them could find anything to say, faced with the prolonged misery of waiting. A week, a fortnight, a month could bring no more hope, and there was nothing to do but get through the extra time: painful, senseless time filled with nothing but the inevitability of grief, morning the same as night, and both of them no different from the sadness of noon.

Kate Mary could only tell herself how much worse it must be for him, alone in his cell in the grey prison, equally aware of the inevitable end.

The poor Lad lumbered between them, watching them without words of help, mutely bringing them the very best of the vegetables and potatoes, and trying to get them to laugh with him at the capers of his new puppy.

They waited through the wet month of December, during which, in the last fury of the dying struggle, most of the city of Cork flared to the night skies, with it the Police Barracks, and the Barracks of the Essex Regiment in Kinsale, and all the big mansions of the Ascendancy along the south coast, ending with the blaze of the town of Skibbereen.

Victory was in sight, but it was all too late for Johnny.

He was tried finally on January 1st. 'They are planning the best New Year God can give me,' he wrote, 'and the sooner the better. It is for Ireland and without regret.'

All through his mockery of a trial, a tall white-faced Head Constable with light red hair scanned the crowded angry courtroom for a face.

From the dock, Johnny watched him with a sardonic smile.

'The last card is mine, Brannick,' he thought to himself. 'I told her not to come. I wouldn't give you the pleasure of resting your eyes on her, you treacherous bastard.'

He was sentenced to be hanged on January 8th, 1921, to be allowed one visitor on the evening before his death.

Aunt Margaret sat before the fire, erect and still scorning to yield to grief. Her hands lay on her white apron and the turf light in her glasses hid the blind anguish of her eyes that was all ever to betray her.

'Do you go to see him, Kate Mary,' she said, and it was an instruction not any wish made out of kindness.

'Not you? It's your place, Aunt Margaret.'

'No. You go.'

She would give no reason, refusing even to admit that it would be more than she could bear.

'Could we not both go,' the girl said gently, longing to say to her that if she could accept grief and pity, it could all be easier for her. 'I'd wait for you outside.'

Her aunt shook her head and only said abruptly, 'Will we say a Rosary for him.'

They knelt down on the hard kitchen floor and the Lad came in from the yard and joined them, the puppy running from one to the other, wondering what it was all about. They prayed there in the dying firelight for their brave, bright Johnny, but it was only Kate Mary and the Lad who came down in tears.

When they were done, Aunt Margaret, dry-eyed and aloof, went to the press beside the hearth and took out the pen and the bottle of Stephen's ink, and sat down at the kitchen table writing someone a long letter in her thin, upright hand, going back crosswise between the lines when she had filled the page.

Kate Mary went to bed, drifting sadly along the vestibule with her candle, touching this and that for comfort, as though it was she, and not Johnny, who was leaving Caherliss for ever.

At the end, she looked out at the dark rise of the High Garden, shapeless in the black night, and thought of the start of it all: the bullets and the gelignite. And wondered now would Johnny still think it had all been worth it.

*   *   *

Two days later, Aunt Margaret said to her curtly, not looking at her: 'Take all you have with you when you go to Dublin. You'll not be coming back.'

Kate Mary stared, knowing her mouth was open.

'Not coming back?'

'Not here.' She was in the rocking chair beside the window, and fiercely she rocked it, backwards and forwards, as though driven by the intensity of what she said. 'I don't think it right you should be living in Johnny's home after it's all over. After it all,' she added, and meant the whole sorry story and her own doubts about Kate Mary that she had never openly expressed.

'After what, Aunt Margaret?'

Sadness gripped her. The old woman went on rocking, staring blindly and fiercely out the window.

'You think I informed on him – you really do?' Kate Mary could only whisper.

'I can't think otherwise.' The answer was implacable.

The girl couldn't even be angry, so terrible the charge, thinking only of the poor grief-twisted old woman who made it.

'But you can't manage here alone,' she said.

'I've written to the girls, in the Convent,' she said. 'They'll take me there to stay with them.'

The girls. Kate Mary thought of the whey-faced nuns between thirty and fifty, long lost, every one of them, to any of the light and life that girls might know.

'And the farm?' she asked. 'What of the farm?'

'The Lad will have the farm.'

And that was it. Aunt Margaret turned her back on all that had been her life as furiously as she turned it on Kate Mary. There was no son of Johnny's to go on holding it together for, so there was nothing left. Torn with sorrow for her, the girl realised that no matter what else had seemed to be in her world, nothing had mattered except Johnny. But the tight old face that had shrunk to the size of a withered apple would admit no sympathy.

'Why did you protect me then?' she couldn't help asking. 'It's been only you between me and the people of Connorstown.'

'Aren't you me own flesh and blood,' was the sharp answer, and then the thin mouth shut like a trap, making it clear there was a limit even to such a tie.

Did she insist on staying, Kate Mary realised, she would be thrown to the pack the moment Johnny was dead.

Aunt Margaret had been doing what she thought to be her cousin's duty to her child, but no more.

Duty. Duty again, Kate Mary thought. Duty. She wondered if she would hate the world until she died.

The Lad came to her in the cold dark yard as she was closing in the hens, the last flares of scarlet and yellow away to the west holding already some stormy promise of the spring to come.

'Miss Pearse. Miss Kate Mary,' he said awkwardly, a big shadow in the dusk, the soft new puppy gambolling around his boots. She could sense the terrible anguish that held him.

'Kate Mary, I would never want it this way.' The words came in a rush lest he never manage to get them out. 'This is your home and where you belong. I have no right to it. 'Tis you should be here, not me.'

He found it all very hard, words never coming to him easy.

Kate Mary touched him gently on his rough sleeve.

'Do you think I informed on Johnny?' she asked him.

'Ah, for God's sake,' said the Lad. 'As well think the Blessed Virgin herself did it. You have to pity the creature,' he added then. 'She's near demented.'

They stood in silence for a moment, wrapped in sorrow, as though Johnny were already dead. The Lad had used more words than Kate Mary had ever heard him use before, and he had none left. He made one more effort.

'Maybe,' he said hesitantly, 'maybe after some time you could come back.'

She shook her head. Too much had happened. Wherever she went she would never come back to Caherliss.

'Do you marry,' she said to him, 'and have a son to give it to.'

He didn't answer that.

'I'll drive you to Westport in the morning,' was all he said, and turned away, calling the puppy. Then he looked back.

'Give him the good word for me,' he said, and she could no more than nod. Tears choked her, but she daren't give way to them, fearing if she did she would never stop again.

Later, she refused firmly to think of the future as she packed a large portmanteau with everything she owned, tugging at the straps to make it close.

''Tis well,' she said to herself grimly, 'that I have little.'

Aunt Margaret had said no goodbye the night before, taking her candle and going silently to bed: behaving as though Kate Mary were already gone. She was still in her room in the morning, the kettle cold on the hearth and the fire covered with ash. It was the Lad who came in and kindled it, and made Kate Mary a cup of scalding tea. She shook her head against anything to eat, and when it was time to go, stood a long moment outside her aunt's door. Then she turned abruptly and went out to where the Lad waited and the trap in the pitch dark yard.

As they drove out the gate, the first birds were singing, and the clouds split to a primrose dawn above the grass of the High Garden.

She didn't allow herself to look back.

At Westland Row, she had no idea where to go, walking out bewildered towards the street, where even the drab city was soft in one of those sudden days that come to Ireland after Christmas: the sky clear and innocent as if it had never looked down on anything but happiness.

The violets, she thought stupidly, will soon be out along the roadside at Caherliss. And slammed her heart shut against the pain.

Pulling herself together, she thought there must always be hotels around the city station, but how would she know which one would be suitable for a woman alone?

In the station entrance, an elderly porter leaned on a barrow and watched her. There was never much business off the trains from the west, where people never had two half pennies to rub together from one day to the next.

Carefully he approached her. The poor young creature looked frightened to death and in need of help.

'Can I take the bag anywheres for you, Miss?'

Startled, she looked at him, and could find nothing to alarm her, nothing but kindness in the faded eyes and the lined old face. His drooping white moustaches were stained along the edges by the dark brown of porter.

Still, she said, 'No – no,' then took courage. Who else could she ask?

'I'm in need of a hotel,' she said, and he looked away from the naked distress in her eyes. What trouble was on her, before God? 'One,' she said, 'that – one that – '

'Now God keep you, Miss. Haven't I daughters of my own, and I'd not like to see them alone in a city. I know the very place for you, and it no distance. Give me your bag now.'

'It – it won't cost much?'

Everything she owned in her purse, and God alone knew how long it would have to last.

'No more,' he said, 'than would keep a canary bird.'

Numb with relief, trusting him at once, she followed him across the wide busy street outside the station as he threaded his way nimbly with his barrow between the clutter of cabs and drays and the occasional noisy splutter of a motor car.

Above the peeling and dilapidated door, there was a fading sign that held the name of the hotel, almost directly opposite the station.

The Mountjoy Hotel.

The very sight of the name drained the strength from her, as though she stood already at the prison doors, knowing Johnny to be inside, in the last evening of his life.

'Where?' she whispered to the old man. 'Where is the prison. Is it far?'

He stopped abruptly as he lifted her bag off the hand cart, and his lively old face grew quiet. So that was it. God help her, so that was it. The Lord have mercy on her. Almost he offered to go with her, but even in her distress there was a quiet dignity that stopped him from intruding.

He told her, without comment, and it would be about ten minutes' walk, and inside the shabby hall of the hotel gave her over to a homely woman in a soiled apron and a pair of carpet slippers, lank strings of her hair escaping round a plump, red face.

But her eyes were kind and shrewd, and she nodded as the

285

porter put down the portmanteau, and said to her, 'Willya look after her a bit, Gracie. She's new to the city.' Then he looked straight at her and added, 'Maybe you'll remind her the way to Mountjoy this evening.'

'Ah, God,' she said, and blessed herself rapidly and made no comment, taking Kate Mary's arm.

'Come on, acushla,' she said, 'I have a nice room back here and it'll save you climbing those stairs. And I'm near at hand do you want anything.'

Do you find, she was saying in other words, that you can't bear it on your own.

But like the old man, she didn't try to intrude.

Kate Mary tried to give him tuppence.

'Do you keep it yourself, child,' he said. 'The city is a hard place.'

As though he was her father, he reached out wordlessly and made the sign of the cross on her forehead with his thumb. Leaving her a blessing, then turning back to weave his way over to the station with the handcart, his old eyes full of pity.

'Twould have to be Johnny O'Connor, he thought. Three of them tomorrow, but the only one from the west there would be Johnny O'Connor. God and his blessed Mother help them both. 'Twas a terrible thing to put over you, this last visit.

Six o'clock, the letter had said, and they had told her it would be no more than ten minutes to walk it. Not even to waste one moment she left at twenty to six, washed with a loneliness so fearful it seemed to take even thought and understanding from her; putting her feet carefully one before the other down the shabby street below the flawless sky. Even here, well away from the city centre, there were gutted buildings and wrecked and boarded shops; streets ripped by the weight of armoured cars. A lorry passed her with a wire cage over it, and the prisoners, guarded by two Black and Tans, were defiantly singing. She saw none of it, intent only on the terrible effort to understand that after all this time, she was going to see Johnny. And that tomorrow he would be dead.

Before she ever reached the prison she reached the crowds, and they grew progressively thicker as she went on, pressing right up to the dark gates of the prison itself. Priests were

286

among them, and there were candles lit and statues and holy pictures held up in desperate plea to the saints, the cadence of vesper and response, and of the Rosary going from wall to wall in all the grey space outside the walls. Sorrowful vigil for yet more of their country's youth.

It was difficult to press her way through them but when they realised where she was going, the prayers faltered and they cried out blessings and pity and even messages for Johnny and the others, as though it were their own sons going to die. She felt her cool, false composure cracking and could have shrieked at them to leave her be, that she must not go to Johnny grieving and weeping like one of them. Johnny's head would be up, and so must hers be.

With almost panic-stricken relief she saw the wicket gate open in answer to her ring, and when she had shown the letter through a grille, they let her in. She had been prepared to hate the cold hard men who had taken Johnny to this place but they seemed diffident and distressed themselves by what they were doing, their eyes compassionate under their flat caps. She spared a moment of involuntary pity for them, for weren't they Irishmen themselves and only doing what they saw as their duty.

Like Ned.

She dared not think of Ned.

The man who would hang Johnny in the morning would not be an Irishman. An Englishman with a French name.

In the middle of her disjointed thoughts, they searched her purse and her pockets.

'You have no need,' she said sharply. 'Even did I bring him a gun, he'd be too proud to use it.'

The warder looked at her.

'I've no doubt, Miss,' he said. 'We have respect for him. But we have to do our duty.'

Duty, duty. Who had broken Ireland? The wild ones like Johnny who had begun it all, or the ones who had kept the long dreary battle going because they had to do their duty?

There was a dead, sad silence in the long corridors of cells, but faces she failed to notice looked out through every grille and the very air was thick with restless tension that held every prison before an execution.

Kate Mary was only aware that these last yards down the galleries of drab brown oilcloth and up the bare echoing stone stairways, seemed the longest of all her journey.

His cell was high in the building. She hadn't counted the stairs, but it was high enough to be filled with the last soft evening light through the bars of the window.

It made it worse.

Had he been in shadow then the terrible change in him would not have been so inescapable; the bones not so prominent in his pale and sunken face; the lankness not so obvious in his once thick and shining hair. When he stood up to kiss her, he moved like an old man.

Only the eyes were no different, sunk into his wasted face but still the blazing and undefeated blue of her beloved Johnny.

Were it not for them, she thought, appalled, I might never have known him.

The door stood open and there were two warders outside, listening to every word that was said. Even though they turned their backs compassionately, there was constraint between her and Johnny and at first they couldn't speak.

Then suddenly he grinned, lighting his drawn face with all the old devilment.

'You'll not have to mind those lads, Kate Mary,' he said. 'They have to be here to see I don't make a run for it, or go out in your dress or something. They wouldn't even let me see you in a visiting room, lest the fairies take me on the way downstairs.'

Kate Mary managed then to smile with him, and they talked a while of all the simple things, of Caherliss and the crops and the Lad's new puppy, as though in time Johnny would walk out home and see them all.

When he asked after his mother, she told him that she was well and bearing up as they would expect her to and listened to his pity for her without any word, not telling him that Aunt Margaret had thrown her out of Caherliss, or why.

They fell silent then, and when Johnny spoke again it was of himself, but she couldn't know if he really meant it, his blue eyes were so bright and teasing.

'Kate Mary, alannah, you're more beautiful than ever. You know, don't you, that if you'd loved me, I'd have stayed at

288

Caherliss and never put a foot into all this trouble.'

She stared at him, shocked and sad, with a overwhelmed burden she knew was not hers to carry.

'You wouldn't put the responsibility on me, Johnny, surely. It was never true.'

He shrugged his narrowed shoulders.

'Who knows.' he said.

Even in this sad and final moment, she felt angry with him.

'Ah, Johnny,' she said sharply. 'You were always telling me you loved me, but you loved Ireland more.'

She looked at him, gravely and direct. Now his own eyes had changed, the bantering gone: dark with sorrow, and yet proud.

'Were I married to you, Johnny, you'd have gone off just the same, for Ireland, wouldn't you? You'd have left me any time, for Ireland.'

Sitting on the bench that became his bed at night, Johnny didn't move his head but his eyes lifted to the high barred window as though he could see through it, and look reflectively at all the length and breadth of the green, loved land.

When he turned back his face was more than she could bear, ravaged by naked honesty.

'True for you, Kate Mary,' he said slowly. 'Today above all days we have to stop the laughing, and give the heart where it belongs. I have loved no one, man or woman, as I have loved Ireland, and that can be written on my grave for the day of victory.'

Her throat thickened, tears rushing hot to her eyes. He had forgotten there would be no flower-laden grave for him, with loving words raised on a stone above his head. Only a plain name above a pit of quicklime in the prison yard.

'Well then, Johnny, my dearest Johnny,' she said thickly, 'can't you let me have my love for Ned in happiness? Can't you leave me that?'

In her love for Ned, please God there would be life. Johnny's love for Ireland had held the mark of death on it from the very start.

She thought his eyes more blue and brilliant than she ever remembered them as he looked at her. Suddenly he lifted her hands and kissed them.

'I'm a sod, my darling girl. A black-hearted sod. You

289

deserve better.' Croookedly, he grinned. 'They'd never let me into Heaven in the morning, would they, full of dark unwilling thoughts about your man?'

His face grew deeply tender.

'Go with your man, alannah,' he said. 'With my blessing. And God go with you both. To a long life and a respectable grave. Just sometimes remember ould Johnny O'Connor who had neither and thought it all worth it for a dream for Ireland. Tell them all that. It was worth it.'

Helplessly she cried then, almost suffocating in the rush of her hopeless tears, standing up blindly and obediently when the warder touched her on the shoulder and told her gently it was time to go.

Johnny stood up too.

'Kate Mary, my life's love, don't leave me with tears. I have no sorrow for myself. My death is for Ireland, and it's no more than a reward.'

He paused and smiled at her, clear-eyed and contented and without fear; the old unquenchable smile, his eyes like blue jewels in his head.

'For us,' he said, 'my Kate Mary, remember what the poet said. Sure we knew the two days.'

Miraculously, with those sweet nostaligic words, she managed to stop crying and smile back at him, seeing no more the wasted pallied man but the young, splendid Johnny with eyes as blue as flowers and the flush of the country on his skin. Singing as the cart rattled between the grey stone walls, all the rich colours of his Ireland, blue and green and gold around them.

Worth his dying for, in his own mind, and who was she to cause him grief.

'Ah, we did, Johnny. We knew the two days.'

He lifted a hand in salute as they led her out, and still smiled.

All the way out through the sombre prison, with the barred gates clanging shut behind her, she could think only of what he had said.

We knew the two days.

She knew the poem well. Like so many in Ireland, a tale of sorrow and lost love and perfection; a blaze so brief as to be

290

hard to remember. But the poet said he and his love had had the two days, and that was more than many ever knew at all.

So must she remember Johnny: a bright gift from life that couldn't last.

When she stepped through the wicket gate into the street, she would have been glad to turn at once and run straight back into the prison, confronted by the packed multitude of grieving faces, all turned towards her like a sea of sorrow. They were jammed into the grey streets as far as she could see: voices lifted in anguished point and counterpoint of Litany and Rosary which she had been able to hear before they ever opened the gates. They were praying for the souls of Johnny and the others who would go with him in the morning, praying for Ireland.

They blocked her way with their weeping, extravagant sympathy, compassion in their faces and the same exalted resignation that she had seen in Johnny's.

If these lads were the sacrifice that Ireland needed, they seemed to say, then Ireland must be given them with a fine heart.

Suddenly she hated them all, as if they had reached out in their grey sacrificial mass and taken Johnny. Were they not all so willing to die for Ireland, she thought blindly, they might have tried harder to find some way of living for her. She remembered telling Johnny, and he had laughed at her, that their grandchildren would be fighting the same battle.

Johnny would have no grandchildren.

She began to feel frantic, besieged, struggling to push through them. She resented the pitying hands that reached out to her, tried not to scream at them that she was not one of them. She was not resigned for Johnny. There must be other ways than death.

Panic was rising in her desperate need to get away, and her clear distress brought only more clinging compassion, drowning her in resentment.

Suddenly firm hands closed on her shoulders and brought a halt to her stampede.

'Go easy, Kate Mary. Easy, my love. Let me take you home.'

She simply took it for granted that he was there, not questioning.

'They're in love with death, Ned,' she cried wildly. 'In love with it! And they expect everyone to be the same.'

Her weeping shook her from head to foot. Her own grief she could have coped with were she left alone, but the great collective sorrow of the crowd had broken her. Ned took her in his arms and hushed her as he would a child, the sad tide of hymns washing round them.

In the end she steadied and looked up at him, ready to be aware of the miracle that had brought him.

'Ned! How – ?'

He was barely to be recognised in an old grey suit with a brown muffler wrapped around his neck, a grubby bahneen cap pulled down to his eyes. He had even taken the wax from his moustache and brushed it down soft over his mouth.

Foolishly, the moustache seemed to be all she could focus on, the tears of her grief and anger still on her cheeks.

'I liked the little spikes,' she said, and found herself laughing weakly, knowing it stupid but unable to think of anything else to say.

Firmly, trying to assume his own tragic face to melt with the crowd, his arm tight around her, he was getting her away.

'Come on, girl,' he said urgently. 'They'll kill me if they realise who I am.'

She paused shocked, the danger in his being there not yet clear to her.

'Who will?'

'For God's sake, Kate Mary, either side. Whoever gets there first. This lot would string me to the nearest lamp post, and d'you think Dublin Castle would give me a medal for being at a wake for Johnny? Come on while we can still go!'

They spoke no more, Kate Mary seized by frightened urgency until they were well clear of the keening crowd.

'Oh, Ned,' she said then. 'I never thought of it being wrong for you to come here, dangerous. You're quite right. But oh, dear Heaven, was I ever more glad to see anyone. I should have known you'd find me. I was praying – '

In the empty street he tenderly kissed away the tears threatening her again.

'My poor girl. Poor little love. Come, I'll take you home.'

Only then did the full truth of her circumstances strike her: concealed even from herself. She had already all she could face in Johnny's death.

All her world and home was in the brown portmanteau left in the hotel at Westland Row. All this she had thrust to the back of her mind in the monstrous effort of emotion it had taken to go and see Johnny.

She drew away and looked at him, her lovely face pinched and small with all her different griefs.

'And where would home be?' she said sadly. 'Where will home be for me now?'

The plump landlady was called Mrs. Conroy.

Kate Mary introduced Ned to her as a friend from down west, and after one look at her shocked face the woman led them to her own parlour at the back of the house.

'Sit down there now,' she said, pulling a large and shabby armchair close up to the fire. 'Sit down there and I'll get a good decent pot of tea to put the heart into you. Ah, the poor creature,' she said audibly as she went out the door. 'The raging black-hearted devils. May they roast in hell.'

Ned looked at Kate Mary.

'D'you see?' he said. 'She'd put a carving knife through me did she have an inkling who I was.'

Shivering, the girl held out her hands to the glowing turf.

'Like me and Connorstown,' she said sadly.

'What about Connorstown?'

He longed to touch her, comfort her, hold her in his arms and coax away the dreadful sorrow from her face. But he felt the tolerance of the landlady might not go that far.

'What happened in Connorstown?'

She told him then that all Connorstown believed she had informed on Johnny, even her aunt who had thrown her from the house.

Grimness settled on Ned's face above the stringy brown muffler.

'Kate Mary, I above all people know that's not true!'

'Tell that to my aunt.'

He was silent a while, staring into the fire.

293

'Does Johnny think that?' he asked her then.

Kate Mary thought of Johnny as she had left him: the love and tenderness in the wasted face.

'We never spoke of it,' she said wearily. 'But no. No, I'm sure he didn't.'

Ned reached out and gripped her hand so hard it hurt her.

'You'd have done better,' he said, 'to have been a good Sinn Feiner and married Johnny.'

The turf light sought the high strong bones of his face, the lines of sorrow and anger etched upon it. Kate Mary lifted a finger and smoothed them as though to ease their pain. She managed to smile at him.

'That, Ned Brannick, is for me to decide.'

Mrs. Conroy came in with a tray and they battled their way through the thick strong tea in heavy white cups, and solid slices of country bread and dry seed cake, knowing they would give offence if they didn't eat it all.

Ned threw the last piece in the fire, watching it crumble to ash.

'You'll go to my mother,' he said then.

'Your mother!'

'Who else?'

But, Ned, maybe she won't want me!'

He smiled at her then, his full tender smile that held both his love for his mother and for her.

'The Mam will want you,' he said. 'You're mine and she'll want you.' He smiled again. ''Tis my father could turn you from the door, or put you out with the cattle.'

'But Ned – '

'No anxiety,' he reassured her. 'No anxiety. My father may do all the crowing, but 'tis the Mam that rules the roost.'

'She may not like me.'

His smile was gentle again in the rosy light.

'She'll like you, alannah. And you'll like her. Now I have to go. I'm near enough to all kinds of trouble today, without being late back. I'll be with you at Westland Row half an hour before the Mail goes, and I'll tell you what to do. Half an hour.'

And he was gone, leaving her lost in a storm of love for him. Big Ned with his hard-boned, severe-looking face, and yet he

294

knew enough to leave her quickly without one word about tomorrow: knowing that if she spoke of it she might never manage it as Johnny would have wished.

'Don't leave me with tears,' he had said.

And with God's help, she wouldn't. But, oh Ned, my love, my love, why did it all have to happen? Why couldn't we have had it easier, you and I?

In the morning, she crept out, unable to face the sweaty, enveloping compassion of Mrs. Conroy, and took her careful unbelieving footsteps to a church she had noticed the previous evening, not far from the prison.

Even at that distance she could hear the tide of prayers outside the gates, murmuring like surf on some unseen shore. Blindly, as though only the familiar gestures would carry her along, she blessed herself at the holy water font, and moved up the church to a seat close to the altar. Kneeling, saying carefully the prayers before Mass that she had learnt as a child, blessing herself again and sitting up to wait for Mass to begin, unable to admit even one prayer for Johnny lest she break apart. Weren't they saying enough prayers for him out there in the street.

The priest came from the vestry and up on to the altar, and she realised, still remote and disbelieving, that he was vested in black. Lifting his hands the Priest began the Mass for the Dead.

'*Introibo ad Altare Dei.*
Ad Deum qui laetificat juventutum meam.'

'I will go unto the altar of God.
To God who giveth joy to my youth.'

The bell tolled suddenly from the nearby prison, and the priest paused as though with everybody else he listened for the fearful collective sigh from the praying thousands as the black flag fluttered up from the prison roof.

Behind Kate Mary a woman gave a great gulping sob and a man hushed her. She herself could feel no more than a faint surprise at someone else's grief: all feeling drained from her, a numb shell of a body as empty as if they had opened her veins and let the blood seep out until there was nothing left to feel or live with.

On the altar, the black-robed priest seemed far, far away and no concern of hers, the words of the Mass a ritual of habit.

The churches round had taken the note from the cold short prison bell, and now the solemn passing bells were ringing out of step, multiplying the years of Johnny's life.

'To God,' she thought, 'who giveth joy to my youth,

John Patrick O'Connor. January 8th. 1921. Aged 26 years.'

At Caherliss on the night of the execution there was a wake for Johnny, even though there was no corpse to lie in state in the shadows of the wall bed under black crosses stitched on hoarded linen sheets.

They came through the quiet night from Connorstown and all the country round, men and women and even the older children, in their asscarts and in their working carts and on their bicycles, the very poorest plodding long Irish miles on foot. They crowded in terrible silence into the big kitchen of Caherliss, lit only by four tall wax candles burning on the table in Aunt Margaret's fine brass candlesticks. When they came in, through the open front door or through the scullery from the yard, one and all they dropped to their knees and blessed themselves as though Johnny indeed lay waxen in the candlelight below the fine sheets with the mourning crosses.

'I'm sorry for your trouble, ma'am,' they murmured to Aunt Margaret, who sat immobile in her rocking chair, the candlelight in her glasses, making no response to anyone who spoke.

When they left her, they went and sat or stood where they could find a space and, growing weary of the silence, whispered amonst themselves.

'Wouldn't you think she'd even have a bottle of whiskey?'

'The poor creature. Sure it's no ordinary wake.'

'I do mind when old Eddie Fitzsimmons died, they had barrels of porter and even a bit of dancing.'

'Well, wasn't that proper for one who died at a great age. Johnny, God ha'mercy on him, was no age at all.'

And they all fell silent again, looking nervously at Johnny's mother lest they had offended by the mention of his name.

The woman didn't even have a tear in her eye, never mind talk about him.

When they felt proper time had been given for respect to the corpse that wasn't there they left, and in minutes others had taken their places: sidling in, raw-faced from the cold, to fall on their knees in the shifting shadows of the candles and take their turn listening to the awestruck whispers of the Lad, who swore hoarsely that the night before, as God made him, he had heard the banshee crying above the roof of Caherliss.

'And it wouldn't need much of a banshee,' whispered back a cynical listener, 'to know that Johnny was going to die. Didn't we all know it, and the newspapers as well.'

Into the middle of the whispers and the silences and the candlelight, Bridie Bannion burst in, coming so suddenly that she brought with her the cold air of the night through the flung open door, raw as her own intrusion.

Her hair was wild and her clothes untidy, as though she had run all the way from Connorstown, and the green gooseberry eyes were desperate with fear and guilt, ranging the crowded room from face to face with the door still open behind her as if she might even yet turn and run.

In the end, she thrust herself towards Aunt Margaret, who regarded her with the same blind indifference as she had welcomed everybody else. This seemed to drive Bridie to some brink of despair, hoping perhaps to tell what she had to tell in gentle words that might come easier.

She wheeled from the old woman's chair and faced into the packed room, where the silent mourners seemed to have drawn closer together.

'Twas I did it,' she shouted hoarsely, and the noise of her voice was an offence to the whispers and the candles and the ghost of Johnny in the wall bed.

''Twas I did it, never Kate Mary Pearse. 'Twas I informed on Johnny. When I couldn't have him for myself, I'd not give him to her. Ah, God forgive me, Mrs. O'Connor, I did it. And now he's gone and the whole of it my doing.'

She was too frightened now even to cry, the confession over, knowing well what would happen to her but unable to hold it back. The big green eyes roamed the terrible silence now totally different from the respectful silence of sorrow. No one spoke but a few of the men looked at each other slowly and nodded. Judge and jury and sentence passed.

When they got up and moved towards her, she only whimpered but no more, accepting that sentence like the soldier she had been but trembling, trembling like the candle flames in the draught from the open door as six men moved forward and surrounded her without a word, thrusting her out and closing the door behind them.

No other word was spoken out of respect for the dead, but it was clear on all their faces that their children's children would still be telling the story of the goings on at Johnny O'Connor's wake. Respect alone held them from bursting into talk, and kept them there the length of decency that their visit demanded.

All they could do was watch Aunt Margaret from the sides of their eyes, so that they might add to their tales some impression of fury for hadn't the whole world been saying it was Kate Mary Pearse, and thinking it, too.

But the old woman gave them nothing other than that she seemed suddenly to grow smaller in her chair, and for a moment the eyes behind the round glasses had grown large with shock.

Unable to keep quiet with such a scandalous piece of news, the visitors went out group by group as soon as decency allowed them, and the old woman and the Lad were left alone beside the dying fire.

The Lad fondled his puppy, searching for the familiar in the face of an upset almost too great for his simple mind.

Suddenly, across the hearth, Aunt Margaret blazed at him.

'I know what you want to say,' she said harshly. 'Never mind the informing. If she'd been willing to marry him, he'd be here today. And all she wanted was some lig of a policeman.'

Even in his simplicity, the Lad knew this was the nub of it. The informing was nothing. There would be no forgiveness for Kate Mary, who hadn't wanted her Johnny.

Chapter 12

Kate Mary spent a quiet, almost secret year in Ned's home at Clumbane. He had been right that his mother would accept her.

He came to Westland Row as he had promised to see her on to the Mail for Galway, still in the old grey suit and the brushed down moustache. He looked tired, she thought, and immensely old and stern, marked like so many of them by the strain of a life they no longer believed in.

He apologised for not being able to get away to her that morning, and she brushed it aside, not wanting to remember.

He would have been doing his duty. Duty, she wanted to cry at him. Duty! What has it ever brought us but sorrow? Give it all up and let us settle down and rear our children.

But she knew her Ned and could only look with love and passionate longing at his drawn face, and listen carefully to his instructions as to how to get to Clumbane.

There was a letter for his mother.

'But, sure,' he said. 'She knows all about you long ago.'

'Does she, Ned. Does she now? Really?'

Her own sad face brightened as though that in itself were some hopeful promise for the future.

'She does indeed. Did you think I'd not tell her something so important.'

He was smiling at her, gentle, trying to keep her from crying again, her poor face already blanched and red-eyed from the morning's tears.

'Look now,' he said, 'there's your man and his whistle. Get in now, my heart. And you'll see, you'll be a lot closer to me when you're with my Mam.'

Dumbly, she nodded and did her best to smile at him.

'Your father won't turn me out?'

But the train was moving, sliding away along the platform, and he ran with her as long as he could, waving the old cap when he could no longer keep up.

She remembered reading about a torture of years gone by where they had tied the four limbs of a man to four horses, and then whipped the animals until they pulled him apart. The train felt to be doing the same to her: tearing her body away from her heart, that must lie forever with the tall diminishing figure in the worn grey suit.

Another train passed them, clanking into the station, and he was gone.

The train was late into Galway, stopping several times to the rattle of rifle fire somewhere off in the fields.

Nowhere, she thought to herself in the dim January afternoon, could there be a city as grey as Galway. Grey as her own loneliness and grief.

She didn't want to reach Clumbane and all its explanations after dark, so she decided to stay the night in the city. At least she knew this time where to go, turning into a narrow street out of Eyre Square to a small hotel where she had stayed several times with her aunt. As she looked out through the lace curtains of her window, on to a darkening street, she wondered was Aunt Margaret already little more than a stone's throw away: taking her grief and her bitterness to God, in the Convent of the Presentation across the Corrib Bridge.

Firmly, striving to think of nothing but the future, she put it from her mind.

In the morning she got a lift in a tinker's cart out from the ravaged city of Tuam to Clumbane. The house was closer to the road than Caherliss, only a few yards over it to the still blue water of a lake. As Kate Mary climbed down from the cart her thanks to the tinker were perfunctory, all her thoughts claimed by a tall, white-haired old woman who had opened the door and come a few steps along the short pathway to the gate.

The girl could have smiled. So like Ned, she would have

known her anywhere. So like Ned it was ridiculous.

But she kept her pleasure to herself, remembering that Mrs. Brannick didn't know her, putting her portmanteau down at the gate lest she seem to be presuming a welcome. She realised the tinker was watching it all with high, delighted curiosity, and knew it would be all over Tuam that night, but she advanced gravely to the old woman who stood waiting with her hands folded on a spotless apron. She realised that Ned had not acquired all his bearing and his dignity from being a policeman.

'I'm Kate Mary Pearse,' she said bluntly, unable now the moment had come to think of anything else to say. 'I have a letter from Ned.'

Ned's splendid smile touched his mother's face.

'Who else would you be?' she said, a slight sardonic humour in her eyes. 'Haven't we known about you long enough. Ah, put that away.' She gestured at the letter the girl was pulling out, and went on firmly to forestall the tears of relief and near collapse gathering in Kate Mary's eyes, 'Go on down there, and get that bag. What made you leave it at the gate?'

'I thought – I wasn't sure – '

'Ah, get along with you,' answered Ned's Mam firmly. 'And tell that tinker gawping down there I want a new frying pan on his way back.'

Between the bag and the tinker, she forgot to be distressed, exactly as Mam had intended, and in a few minutes was being ushered into the house with the same practical good nature that forbade grief: into a big kitchen where, much as Ned had left him when he went off years back to be a policeman, a bent old man sat with an ancient paper spread before him on the table.

'This is Ned's girl, Kate Mary,' Mam said, and the girl caught the faint tremor of nervousness in her voice. Maybe the old man was more of a power than Ned said. 'She's to stay awhile.'

Faded rheumy eyes lifted to Kate Mary from the paper, and she knew it was important to meet them straight and steady.

'Hrm,' said Ned's father, and that was to be about all he ever said in her presence.

After that it was like living in Caherliss, but without the bright enlivening presence of Johnny. The hens, the pigs, turning the hay in the fields along the lake shore when the summer came: all in the company of Ned's brother Patrick, who was almost as taciturn as his father, and also did not know what to make of her. He was furiously antagonistic to anyone connected with his policeman brother, but the whispers that crept across the country from Connorstown told another story of her altogether. He was civil to her and little more, not sure if her friendship would damage him as one of the local Sinn Fein leaders, with victory in their grasp.

The first weeks of that last year saw unparalled violence, the administration, in the form of the Auxiliaries and the Black and Tans, grasping desperately at sliding authority. Houses were burned indescriminately for every ambush; viscious killing became the answer to the smallest crime. Even children were not spared. Fear stalked the country before the wild vengeance of the defeated, and with it went homelessness and starvation, helped only by the relief from America distributed by the White Cross. In these last months, the resistance of Sinn Fein grew desperate, so many of the young men executed or wounded or dead, and the loyal supplies of food fading away in a land that was starving itself.

But they fought on and on, and by the time summer lay silver over the lake, and the purple flags stood like soldiers around its edges, there were the first whispers of peace, although with the violent objections of Northern Ireland it was not until July 11th that a truce was signed.

Sinn Fein laid a chilling hand on the rejoicing country. A truce, they pointed out, was not an agreement, and unless terms were right there could be further war.

Nevertheless the green, white and yellow flag flew bravely in the streets. Around blazing bonfires at the crossroads people danced with happiness they had long forgotten, ignoring now their hunger and their homelessness. Enough that they could walk their own streets without fear of a random bullet, or of the torch being put to what was left of their homes.

Only the North would not agree, and as Kate Mary read that in the week-old paper, with Ned's Mama humming in tuneless happiness above the range, she felt yet again the cold and dreadful memory of what had once said long ago to Johnny, and what she still feared and believed.

Our grandchildren, she had said, will be fighting the same battle.

Now he was dead. Please God, not for nothing.

But for the old lady's sake, and increasingly for her own, for Ned was more precious to her than any grandchildren they might never have, she smiled with everyone else and let happiness grow through her; even venturing with Mam into the shattered remains of the once prosperous small city of Tuam, where the people were reopening their wrecked shops and getting business back together.

Gradually, as the rowans grew red along the edges of the road and the bracken dried in the ditches, she came to the understanding that there should be nothing left now but happiness: living only for the rare letters from Ned, sent through the parish priest, whose mail no one would dare tamper with.

He thought he was safe, he said. They wouldn't kill any policeman now, though what his future would be he didn't know. As soon as he did he would tell her.

As best she could, she lived in patience, watching the fattening of the Christmas goose through the shortening days, happy in the clear pleasure Mam took in having her in the house, and slowly regaining the beauty she had lost in the last terrible days in Caherliss.

Waiting for Ned and the future.

He came one evening before Christmas, without warning, the two old people looking at each other in fear they hadn't yet lost when the knock came at the door.

Kate Mary looked at them and went herself to answer it.

There was kissing then in that house that had never known it before, and he was pressed into the chair before the fire, the night chill still about his clothes, with his Mam bustling to get the whiskey bottle while the old man sat staring, not uttering a word of welcome any more than he had said one of goodbye.

The pan had to be put on then, and thick slices of bacon cut from the sides hanging from the rafters. Kate Mary was sent

303

scurrying to the freezing dairy for eggs, and the fresh brown loaf laid out for breakfast.

Mam whispered urgently to the old man, who with great reluctance put on his jacket and went out into the yard.

All the time Ned's eyes never left Kate Mary, and in the end he must have found the response he sought for he reached out and caught her skirt and brought her to a halt beside him.

'I'm here for something special,' he said, and she could see from his eyes that it was something good and splendid.

'Are you out?' she said breathlessly.

'Not yet.' The mother listened carefully from above the sizzling bacon. Ned was not in uniform, neither was he in the old grey suit but spruce and tidy in navy blue, his stiff white collar gleaming. 'Not yet,' he said again, and then suddenly, 'Are you any good at getting up early in the morning.'

'Amn't I up early every morning!'

She saw the grin curling the corners of his long mouth. Sharper than Kate Mary, Mam had straightened up and left the bacon to take care of itself, all her attention on her son.

'Could you be in to Tuam at six o'clock in the morning?'

'Why, Ned? Why?'

Carefully he took a sheet of paper from his pocket and unfolded it. Kate Mary caught a glimpse of her own name.

'Well,' he said, 'I have here a document that says Kate Mary Pearse can get married when she wants to. It's called a special licence. And I arranged with the P.P. on my way up here that six o'clock tomorrow would probably be as good a time as any.'

'If you want to,' he added politely, and now the great grin was all over his face.

Kate Mary couldn't speak, nor could she stop the tears of delirious happiness from creeping down her cheeks. In spite of his father's disgusted stare, Ned kissed them away.

'No more tears,' he said. 'No more tears for us.'

'At least,' she gulped, 'they're happy ones.'

By the range, Mam blessed herself.

'Isn't God good,' she said, her old face as radiant as the girl's. 'Isn't God good, James.'

James didn't answer, scowling over at the pan from which a smell of burning, wasted bacon filled the room.

When he had managed to please even his mother with the amount he ate, Ned turned to Kate Mary at his side.

'Will we take a turn down to the lake,' he said. 'Tis a grand night.'

Once again she could barely speak. To be alone with him, after all this time, without fear or danger.

'We will,' she whispered, and already her fingers were twitching to run all over the loved bones of his face.

Mam fussed about them being well wrapped up against the cold and they bore it as patiently as they could, going out then into the black night drenched with stars, the lake a pale gleam across the road.

After living only in their minds for so long, the reality, the actual flesh and blood, was almost confusing. Outside the door, they walked a little way awkwardly apart, and then at the roadside were compelled to wait while some farmer late from market, and none too sure of himself, ambled past at the slow pace of his tired little donkey, peering at them in the darkness.

That small separation thrust upon them broke the barrier. By the time they were on the lake shore they were in each other's arms, but still talking polite and foolish rubbish about the stars and the light on the water and the fine night, still not quite believing in each other.

Until Ned drew her abruptly to him and kissed her.

It was like the breaking of a dam. No asking. No pointing out that they would be married anyway in the morning. Tender first, breathless, speechless with a tenderness so long held back; so long submerged in formality and pretence.

Even tenderness fled then, driven by the gale of passion, and when Kate Mary felt him pulling at her clothes she did no more than help him blindly, urgent as he was himself, until wordlessly they crashed together down on to the stony shore, their feet unheeded in the edges of the water, never knowing it any different from the feather bed in the Good Room where they would sleep tomorrow night.

Conscience rumbled in Ned. Even as he sought her, he gasped words of apology which she stilled with her kisses. They lay in the end, inert, spent, Ned, still on top of her as though he would cover her forever from all harm, did not move.

'Ned,' she whispered in the end.

'What is it, girl of my heart?' His voice was muffled in her hair.

'I've a big stone in me back.'

She felt the laughter rumble all the way down his long frame, and then he rolled away.

'My God, Kate Mary Pearse,' he said. 'You'd spoil anything!'

There was no laughter from her. She reached over and took his face between her hands: the loved face she had waited for so long. Gravely she kissed him.

'I couldn't,' she said. 'Nothing could ever spoil that. Oh, Ned, I didn't know. I just didn't know.'

She kissed him again.

'Get on away out of that,' he said hoarsely, 'before we start all over again and the Mam comes looking for us. Get yourself covered now before you catch cold.'

She hadn't realised that it was cold. As she groped for buttons that had gone missing, sorting the tangle that hadn't waited to come off properly, she marvelled that she felt no guilt, no panic about the priest and confession. Not one moment of regret. Only the sense of absolute rightness and perfection, and the foolish feeling that she had never before actually seen the moonlight on the lake, or truly felt the touch of the night wind. Never before known even of the full existence of her own body, that had been hers alone for so long.

Never before known anything about anything.

Tranquilly she smiled up at him, doing up her blouse as best she could without the missing buttons.

'D'you know, Kate Mary,' he said. 'You have the stars in your eyes.'

'Where else,' she asked him, 'would they be.'

Back in the house, the old lady was at the kitchen table, sewing a lace collar and cuffs on to Kate Mary's best dress.

'My grandmother wore them at her own wedding,' she said, smoothing the thick heavy lace. Pleasure as clear as their own happiness shone in her lined face. There was goose down like fur all over her hair and her dress, and a few feathers, and Kate Mary thought of the day Ned had come to search Caher-

306

iss and come out of the henhouse with his own hair full of eathers. She glanced at him, but all his gentle attention was on his mother.

'You plucked the goose?' he asked her.

'I did. I'll put it in the oven before we go to Mass in the morning.'

'And giblet soup?' Kate Mary joined in all her plans.

'I have that on now!'

'But, Mam,' said Ned. 'It isn't Christmas for another fortnight.'

She snapped her thread and looked up at them both with the faded eyes that had yet no need for glasses.

'Isn't it Christmas for us all tomorrow.'

Then she glanced shrewdly from one glowing face to the other, and back to Kate Mary.

'I'd think it about the right time,' she said, 'to start calling me Mam.'

There was no discussion as to what she should call old James. He had long gone to bed.

It was a chill bright day of January, just over a year after Johnny's death, when Ned strode one day over O'Connells Bridge in Dublin, heading back towards the Castle, groomed and smart in his dark uniform, the badge of Head Constable bright on his sleeve.

Not even the ruined and burnt out buildings or the sandbags or the armoured cars that still crawled the street, could dim either the sun or his own feeling of content. Only time now, and he would be with Kate Mary for the rest of his life. Only time.

He was off duty, brooding contentedly on the future and wondering where they might settle, watching a few swans idling on the green river, bringing to his mind the sharp blue sea below Croagh Patrick.

Then he saw Bridie Bannion coming towards him over the bridge.

He knew her at once, the too short skirts and the luscious legs just as they had always been but the arrogance was gone from her; the flamboyance of her body submerged in sad untidiness.

307

And there was something odd about the hair straggling from under her green cap.

He realised she had seen him, and would have passed her; part of all he wanted to forget. She stopped in front of him. The green eyes looked a little wild. Her pale face, with the freckles standing out on it, held an expression as if the sight of him was more than she could bear.

'There ye are,' she shouted at him, and people passing turned to look at her. 'There ye are and yer badge on yer sleeve and in there in the Castle. But 'twas I gave you him. 'Twas I got him for you.'

Her careful speech was forgotten, the words pouring out in the thickest accent of the west.

Ned was embarrassed and tried to go on.

'Got who?' he said.

Tears were in her throat now and her voice no more than an urgent and distraught whisper.

'Johnny O'Connor. 'Twas I informed on him. Put the paper outside your door. He was mine, and no Kate Mary Pearse was going to have him from me, bad cess to her.'

Dear God in Heaven! Ned's face was as full of sad pain as her own. This war had been meant to be about politics. About pride and freedom and a new life for Ireland. All their small part of it had finished up no more than a sorry hand of love and jealousy and hate, and death coming in to hold the fourth card.

'Did they find out?' he asked her, and she nodded and now the tears brimmed from the exquisite green eyes and rolled unheeded down her cheeks.

Of course. That's what had happened to her hair. They would have shaved her head and tied her half naked to a gatepost out in the country until someone came by who was willing to release her.

'I told them,' she said miserably. 'I couldn't live with it. I can't now.'

For a moment Ned stared at her, startled by the echo of thoughts and doubts already gnawing round the edges of his own mind.

There was a long silence and she never lifted a hand to wipe away the tears of guilt and sorrow. A cloud of seagulls wheeled and screamed around the shell of the burnt out Customs house along the river, and a string of barges went past beneath the bridge, disturbing the swans, moving down towards the docks and the sea.

Formally, Ned touched the peak of his cap.

'We have all of us, Miss Bannion,' he said sombrely, 'to live with what we have done. It is often no more than our duty.'

Swinging away from her and round her, he went on over the bridge and turned right along the Quays, wanting painfully for a few moments the solace of the bright river. But the brightness was gone, although the sun still sparkled on the water, and when he tried to think of Kate Mary he couldn't bring to mind her beloved face.

Little more than a fortnight after that, bonfires blazed again at the crossroads and there was dancing in the streets to celebrate the disbanding of the R.I.C. Gratefully, almost as ready to celebrate as the people they had fought so bitterly for six years, the Police took off their uniforms and returned to their lands and homes and families.

But not Ned.

The letter had come from him in London.

'Glory be to God,' said Mam. 'Isn't that a terrible place. What will he do in London?'

Be safe, thought Kate Mary. Be safe somewhere we can start our life at last. Her heart was singing a *Te Deum* and she was ready to be wild with happiness, having to make an effort to be gentle with Mam's anxieties.

'London?' she said, smiling. 'Isn't that the place where you can go digging for gold in the street?'

'Only eeejits think that,' Mam answered sharply, and they went on to the rest of the letter.

For his part in the capture of Johnny O'Connor, he had been told that he couldn't stay in Ireland. Had indeed been put out with a gun in his back and twenty-four hours to go taking little more than he stood up in.

Kate Mary knew her man. Behind the plain words, she could sense the anguish of sudden exile, the loneliness tearing him in a strange city, far from the green country he had loved in his own way as much as Johnny ever did.

'I must go to him,' she cried. 'At once.'

But the end of the letter told her to be patient, and wait until he had somewhere ready for her to come to. Be patient, girl, he wrote. It's all coming to us.

Except Ireland.

The last letter came in March, all about a small town in Hertfordshire that called itself a Garden City, with a garden for every man to grow a few vegetables and the streets lined with trees, and some of them with flowers like it was a Botanical Garden. He seemed bewildered but, in his cool way, charmed by the place, and to Kate Mary it sounded like Heaven.

'I have a house rented for you, pet, and a big garden where we can keep a few hens. Water flowing from taps,' he wrote. 'No pumping any more, and even a bathroom.'

Kate Mary felt faint with delight.

Flowers. She'd grow flowers in the garden and put down a bit of green for the child to run on. Maybe they wouldn't miss the green fields so much if there was somewhere for the child.

She hadn't told him, but she was sure by now that she was not going to Ned alone, smiling faintly at Mam's compassion for her wan face at breakfast in the mornings.

When could she go?

Come as soon as you can, the letter said. You are all I want here. I have enclosed two five pound notes, they have given me a good pension.

She looked from the neat copperplate to the money in her other hand that she had barely glanced at.

'Mam,' she whispered, 'I'm going.'

The old woman struggled to keep from her face the raw sorrow of coming loneliness.

''Tis where you belong, child,' she said.

Belief in it all did not really come until she was on the Mail Boat, drawing away from Kingstown in a blue windy evening, smoke torn from the chimneys along the shore and the waves rough the moment they left the shelter of the curved walls.

It seemed a thousand years since she had left Clumbane this

morning, Robert with unaccustomed kindness driving her to Tuam to catch the connection for the Mail. She couldn't bear to remember the tears Mam failed to hold back.

'But you'll come over to see us, Mam.'

The old woman shook her head.

''Twill not be for me, child.'

There was a sudden gentle blessing from the old man, reminding her of the porter at Westland Row on the evening before Johnny's death. Fresh pain she hadn't wanted at this time, but she bent her head gratefully as, at the door, he made the sign of the Cross on her forehead as if he had been her own father and she a loved child going on a journey.

The spires of Kingstown were already growing dark, merging into the mountains, lights springing like a necklace along the edge of the land, and the Hill of Howth a vast shadowy bulk over to her right. Only the pointed peak of the Sugarloaf, behind the town, held the last touch of gold from the western sun. Even as she watched it faded and Ireland began to slip into the night.

Firmly she turned and made her way forward along the deck. The boat was crowded. Many were fleeing Ireland at this time, but she managed to get herself a seat on the upper deck in the very prow of the steamer.

The wind flayed her face and the cold bit through her thin coat, but she was determined to stay there until she could see the lights of Holyhead rising from the sea.

England.

Their new life. And Ned.

Their first three sons were born and scrambling round them in the garden Kate Mary had so lovingly planted, when she had an official-looking letter from Westport.

Nervously she wondered should she leave it for Ned, and then she opened it.

'Ned,' she said, when he came home for his dinner. He had found work as a clerk to an accountant in the rapidly expanding town: still meticulously punctual and predictable, swinging off his high black bicycle at exactly ten past one and twenty to six every day.

'Ned, would you like to go back to live in Ireland?'

He halted in his tracks as he was hanging his bicycle clips on the hallstand.

'No,' he said at once, and didn't look at her. 'Why ask?'

'I had a letter from a solicitor this morning. Old Cousin Ulick had died and left me Anfield. Some money, too, but I doubt I'd get that out of Ireland. I thought he was leaving it all to the Church.'

Ned stood absolutely still, his back to her.

'Sell it,' he said, and went abruptly out through the kitchen into the garden.

She went to the window and watched him, standing rigid with his fists clenching and unclenching at his sides, pretending to stare at the green spears of his onions pushing up through the good dark soil.

Even when he was an old man, and Kate Mary grey-haired, walking with her grown children among roses in the garden of their bigger house – even then he would sit for long periods, jangling his money in his pocket and staring seemingly at nothing. Never able to tell himself before God, honestly, that he had denied Johnny his easy death out of duty, and not because he hated him for daring to have even a small share of Kate Mary's love. Out of jealousy for even that small part that was so much less than he had.

Growing, as he got older, ever more nailed to routine and time and punctuality, as though any hint of casualness might admit a self-knowledge he couldn't bring himself to face.